A Season In Purgatory

A Season
In Purgatory

Dominick Dunne

CROWN PUBLISHERS, INC.
New York

Published by Crown Publishers, Inc.,
201 East 50th Street, New York, New York 10022.
Member of the Crown Publishing Group.

Random House, Inc. New York, Toronto, London, Sydney, Auckland

CROWN is a trademark of Crown Publishers, Inc.

Manufactured in the United States of America

ISBN 0-517-58386-0

To Hannah
with love

PART ONE

1972

———————

Harrison Burns

THE JURY is in its third day of deliberation. Early in the day, the jury foreman requested that Judge Edda Consalvi have the testimony of Bridey Gafferty, the Bradleys' cook, read back to them, and in the afternoon the foreman asked to see the weapon—half of a baseball bat —and the autopsy pictures of Winifred Utley's bludgeoned body, the pictures that had caused so much distress to Winifred's mother, Luanne Utley, when they were presented as exhibits by the prosecutor during the trial. After both requests by the jury, there was much comment in the press corps as to the interpretation and, as always in this case, considerable diversity of opinion. The air is charged with tension. Judge Consalvi has proved herself a martinet. Yesterday she ordered the bailiff to oust from her courtroom the reporter from *Newsweek* after he grinned broadly and snickered when the court reporter reread Billy Wadsworth's statement that the defendant, Constant Bradley, after cutting in on him at the country club dance, said to Winifred Utley, "Do you mind dancing with a man with an erection?"

They, the Bradleys, have a special room where they all sit together during recesses and breaks, so as not to be on view to the media or the merely curious, but occasionally one of them emerges to use the telephone or the bathroom facilities. Today I saw Kitt in the corridor of the courthouse. We passed so closely that the skirt of her blue-and-white silk dress brushed my trouser leg, but she walked past me, eyes straight ahead, without speaking. It was not so much that she cut me. She simply did not, by choice, see me. I have become nonexistent to her. By now I am used to that, both from Kitt, who once meant so much to me, and from the whole Bradley family. I won't even mention what happened yesterday in the men's room, when I encountered Constant at the adjoining urinal. Oh, hell, perhaps I will mention it. What difference does it make? Constant was standing there next to me when, suddenly, without speaking a word, he turned and aimed the strong

1

steady stream of his urine in my direction, soaking my blazer and trousers. Once before, in my youth, I had seen him do such a thing, to a boy no one liked called Fruity Suarez, when we were in school at Milford. His face then was filled with impish levity, a spoiled boy playing a mischievous prank. Yesterday, there was no trace of mischievousness in his look. Only hate. But it was Kitt's disdain, not Constant's piss, that was the more wounding.

Of course I know that, in telling the story that I am about to tell, I run the risk of losing everything that I have achieved and acquired in my life, including my reputation. I know also that I will be earning the eternal enmity of the family, and I have witnessed over the years, sometimes at very close range, the meaning of their eternal enmity, when it was the lot of others to experience it. They, the family—who are referred to, among themselves and even sometimes in the press, as the Family—are not my own family, but the family that I was accepted into twenty years ago.

I first came as a school chum of Constant's, a month-long visitor at the Bradley estate. We were then at Milford, a school in Connecticut for privileged boys from rich Catholic families, which had been founded seventy-five years before by a Catholic millionaire, whose wealth came from copper mines, and whose son had been turned down for admission to Groton, because, the millionaire felt, he was an Irish Catholic. Constant's four older brothers had preceded him at Milford, all having excelled there, and all were still affectionately remembered by the headmaster and faculty.

We were not taught by priests but by lay teachers, who were called masters. Priests would have made it a religious school, which it was not, although there was chapel every day, with prayers, and Mass twice a week, on Sundays and Thursdays, at seven in the morning. We went unquestioningly through the motions of Mass, Communion, morning and evening prayers, First Fridays, and Lent without a thought about the existence of God.

After Constant's early disgrace and expulsion, which coincided with the somewhat sensational death of my parents, I, bookish by nature, was thought by his family to be a good influence on Constant. In time, I was pleasantly but remotely tolerated by his famous father, Gerald Bradley, who had little time for anyone not of his own flesh and blood or connected importantly to the worlds of politics, high finance, or, occasionally, I was to learn, the criminal element.

On the day of Constant's expulsion, he leaned out the dormitory

2

window looking for the family chauffeur, Charlie, who was being sent to take him home.

"Oh, my God," he said, pulling himself back into the room when he saw the long black Cadillac drive slowly down the hill from the entrance to Hayes Hall, where our rooms were.

"What?" I asked.

"My father's come, too," he answered. For a moment his calm left him. From the dormitory window we watched Charlie open the door for Mr. Bradley to get out of the car. He was dressed in a chesterfield coat with a velvet collar and a gray homburg. Even from afar, it was easy to see that he was a man to be reckoned with. His face had the peculiar characteristic of being composed of features that were at odds with one another, mismatched pieces, out of scale, each more properly belonging to someone else. His nose was too large. His lips were too tight. His eyes were too dark, both in hue and intensity. Yet, in time I would learn that women, for whatever reason, found him attractive, although his fortune may have accounted for some of his attractiveness. His manner was aggressive; he lacked gentleness. Even in moments of affection with his daughters, whom he adored, there was a roughness about him. It was said that he inspired fear in those who worked for him. I never doubted that. I believe his sons feared him, too, although they also loved him and would have done, did do, anything he asked of them, right up to the time that his malady affected his requests.

He made his way to the headmaster's office. When he emerged forty minutes later, we were summoned to the car. Charlie, nodding a hello, loaded Constant's bags and my small suitcase into the trunk. We were aware that boys were watching the awkward family scene from all the windows of Hayes Hall.

I might as well not have been there, for all the attention Gerald Bradley paid me. The chauffeur drove. Gerald and Constant sat far apart on the backseat, each in a corner. I sat on a jump seat. We drove in silence most of the way. Finally, nearly two hours later, as we arrived at the long drive that led up to the Bradley house, Gerald spoke. "You're not like your brothers," he said. "You'll always get caught." Unmistakably, there was contempt in his voice. I turned slightly. Constant looked at his father, beseechingly. I assumed this look was to implore his father not to proceed with his contempt in front of me, but it wasn't. He wanted only to please him.

"What could I have done?" he asked.

3

"You could have lied, you damn fool. You could—should—have lied, said those pictures weren't yours."

In time, I became a great favorite of Constant's mother, Grace, which was a lesser honor in that household, as she was sometimes a figure of fun to her own children, particularly her sons, because of her religious fervor, which was excessive, and her obsession with fashion, which was equally excessive. She was consumed with what she always referred to as "the latest style," although often she was overwhelmed by the splendid clothes she wore, so that the impression left was of the color or cut of her garment rather than of her. There was a chapel in the house where a private Mass was said for Grace Bradley every afternoon. Her greatest friend was Cardinal Sullivan, who often came to tea and talked of family and religious matters with her. "Cardinal is coming to tea," she would say excitedly on the day of his visit. She never said "*the* cardinal," when speaking of Cardinal Sullivan. She said only "Cardinal," as if Cardinal were his first name. She enjoyed kissing the cardinal's ring, which she accompanied with a deep curtsy, like that of a lady-in-waiting to a monarch. For an instant there would be a look of ecstasy on her face, as if the contact between her lips and the emerald of the cardinal's ring—an emerald believed to have once belonged to Cardinal Richelieu, which Grace had bought at auction in Paris, and given to Cardinal Sullivan on his elevation—brought her closer to a communion with God.

"We'll put him in Agnes's room," said Grace, about me, figuring out the logistics of the bedrooms of her house on her fingers. "Tell Bridey to make up Agnes's room for Constant's friend." I had never heard of Agnes, and no one explained who she was. I felt I shouldn't ask, and didn't.

Later, I became a friend of some of Constant's brothers and sisters, but not all. Gerald Junior, who was called Jerry, never liked me much, nor did Maureen; but Sandro did, and Desmond, when he appeared, and Mary Pat, and Kitt, the youngest of the girls, although, until it happened—the thing that happened with Winifred Utley—most of the older ones remained shadow figures to me.

"He writes," said Constant, by way of explaining me to his siblings at dinner on my first night in the house.

"I hope to," I corrected Constant.

Gerald Junior snorted, a sneering sort of snort, as if the admission of such a future vocation suggested a maimed masculinity. He was maimed himself, a cripple, the result of an early car accident that had

4

left him partially paralyzed from the waist down, the cause of which being one of the many things that went undiscussed in the family.

Then, surprisingly, the old man, who had more or less ignored me, came to my rescue. "Books? Are you going to write books?" he asked me in a loud voice from the head of the table.

I, scarlet with embarrassment at being the focus of attention, replied, somewhat incoherently, "I hope to. Yes, sir. In time."

"Hmmm. Interesting," he said, as if filing away some information for future use. Then he turned to Gerald Junior. "People respect people who write books."

"I just love to read," said Kitt, then only fourteen, looking over at me with approval.

Actually, I had been to the Bradley house once before, six months prior to Constant's expulsion, on an unannounced visit, accompanying Constant, while his parents were away, his mother in Paris ordering clothes, and his father in California on business. Or so he thought. We had slipped away from Milford School on a holiday afternoon, when we were presumed to be hiking, and hitchhiked the sixty-eight miles from the school to his family's home. He said that it was something important, but it turned out to be the sort of thing that was important to Constant, though hardly worth the risk that was involved with the adventure, especially as it was, months later, the cause of his expulsion.

The purpose of the trip was to retrieve some magazines he had ordered, of naked women, which were sent to the recipient in plain brown wrappers. He had not dared to have them sent to the school, where, under the prying eye of Miss Feeley, the headmaster's secretary, who sorted the mail and had an instinct for the prurient, he risked detection and expulsion. Instead, he had had them sent to his home, alerting Bridey, the Bradleys' housekeeper, who doted on him, to keep an eye out for the envelope and put it away for him. It never occurred to poor Bridey, a daily communicant, that she was secreting pictures of naked ladies, in sexual frolic with each other, beneath her darning basket in the sewing room on the second floor of the Bradley house. It was Bridey's secret hope, never voiced, that Constant might one day become a priest.

We were picked up by a nice woman in a blue Buick who spotted us for the prep school boys we were by our tweed jackets and gray flannel trousers. She was going in the direction of the city where the Bradleys lived and offered to drop us off at a junction where it would be easy to get another ride into the city. Constant, of course, charmed her during the drive, as he always charmed ladies of all ages, and she ended up taking us directly to the gates of the Bradley house, twenty miles and twenty-five minutes out of her way, where she gaped openly at the huge Tudor edifice beyond. She had a daughter, she told him, whom she hoped he could meet one day. Her daughter's name was Winifred Utley, and she went to Miss Porter's in Farmington, she said. If he had asked her to come in, she would have.

Constant had an uncanny ability to readjust the features of his face for an instant and assume the expression of another person. This minor talent, combined with the further ability to assume another's voice and gestures, sent people into gales of laughter, which was not always kind laughter. While waving farewell to her, he became our just-departed driver. We laughed all the way up the driveway to the house, as he enacted an imaginary scene in which he begged Mrs. Utley to let him marry her daughter.

"This is some house," I said, as the Tudor mansion loomed in front of us. "My God!"

"They're all away," he replied. "Ma's in Paris with Maureen. My father's somewhere on business. I never know where. Kitt and Mary Pat are at Sacred Heart. Jerry's usually with Pa. Sandro's in graduate school at Yale. Desmond is a doctor, practicing at St. Monica's Hospital downtown. That about sums it up."

"No slaves?"

"Yeah. Lots of Irish girls, but I don't think any are here. Probably only Bridey. She runs the place."

At the front door, he took out a key and inserted it. We walked into the hallway. Ahead was an impressive winding stairway with a wrought-iron railing. To the left was a large living room, extravagantly decorated in dark-red velvet damask and Chippendale-looking furniture. I stared.

"Ma's always having the place done up," said Constant. "I never know what to expect. That room was green last time I was here."

It was not a room in which they sat much. It was, according to Constant, "for show," used only for parties, or when Cardinal Sullivan came to dine, or on the magnificent occasion when the Pope was received. Was there anyone who did not know that the Pope had visited the Bradley house in Scarborough Hill on his last trip to the United States? Oh, of course there was, but there weren't many Catholics who did not know, and all of us, every single one, at Milford knew. It

6

set Constant apart from the rest of us. "The Pope visited his family," the masters always said when they talked about him, and they said it with awe.

Alone, as family, they used the room they called the family room until Sally Steers, their decorator, convinced Grace to begin calling it the library. In the place of honor over the fireplace was a large color photograph of His Holiness. Elsewhere, on every table, were family photographs, including the annual Bradford Bacharach Christmas-card portrait of Gerald and Grace and all the children, except Agnes, posed in great formality in front of the fireplace in the living room, which was sent to an ever-increasing list of more than a thousand people. There were pictures of Gerald with political figures: Lyndon Johnson, Hubert Humphrey, and Eugene McCarthy, all of whom had dined at Scarborough Hill. There were pictures of the girls in riding habits and velvet hats, and of the boys in various athletic uniforms, including Jerry, before the accident, erect and handsome, in ski clothes on the slopes of Aspen. There were cups and trophies on the mantelpiece and on the shelves of the bookcases, and red and blue ribbons from horse shows framed on the walls. Here also was the piano that Grace liked to play after dinner, when she gathered her children around her to sing Irish songs.

On a bench in the curve of the stairway Constant noticed two coats, tossed there casually, as if the owners were in a hurry. One was a man's coat and the other a fur coat, either mink or sable. I did not know the difference then. Constant picked up the fur coat and looked at the satin lining. There was a label from Revillon Frères, and the initials *STS* intertwined. A strange, distant look came into his face as he dropped it back on the bench.

"Did your parents come back?" I asked.

He signaled me first not to talk and then to follow him. We went through a doorway into a back hallway. He peered into the kitchen to check on Bridey, but she wasn't there. I followed him up a back stairway. Opening a door to the second-floor hallway, he peered out and then walked down to the sewing room, where he found the envelope beneath Bridey's darning basket. Then we retraced our steps to the first floor.

"I don't think we should leave by the front door," he said. He spoke quietly, as if he were afraid of being overheard upstairs. "We'll go out through the kitchen."

"I actually was never in a house this large before. I would be keen

7

to see something more than the back halls and the maids' stairway," I said.

"Some other time," he replied. While the older siblings were still a bit in awe of the enormous house in which they lived, Constant and Kitt, the youngest two, accepted it completely. It was a casual thing for them, all they had ever known.

Later, back at school, when I asked him what had happened at his house, he said, "That mink coat wasn't my mother's."

"Was the other coat your father's?"

"Yes," he answered.

"But—?" I wanted it to be spelled out to me, what I thought he meant.

A slight scowl appeared on his face, clouding the clearness of his forehead. I had seen that look before. It appeared whenever there was what he perceived to be a criticism of anyone in his family. It meant, I knew, not to pursue the subject at hand. I didn't.

The next morning on the tennis court, Constant and I waited for Kitt and Mary Pat to finish their match with the tennis teacher before we played. "Hi, kid," said Kitt, when she walked off the court. Kitt called everyone kid. They all called everyone kid, but mostly Kitt. When she said it to you, you knew that you had been accepted, that you were not exactly one of them, but one of the people who orbited around their magnificence.

Constant was everyone's favorite in the family. He was flattered out of his senses from earliest childhood. Kitt was Constant's favorite. She had the puzzling kind of good looks that are unconnected with beauty yet are more arresting, and a flippant outspoken manner that delighted her siblings but disturbed her mother.

"Where is she?" asked Kitt, walking past a new maid with a frightened expression who opened the door of her mother's house. Kitt often referred to her mother as she and her.

"In the pantry."

"*Mother* in the *pantry?* Doing what? Firing the cook?"

"Doing the flowers."

"Oh, yes, the flowers."

She was then, when I first met her, a student at the Sacred Heart Convent in another small Connecticut town. No Farmington, no Foxcroft, for the Bradley ladies. They went to the Madams, as the Sacred

8

Heart sisters were called. The Madams were the aristocrats of nuns, from good families themselves, and rich ones. Agnes Bradley, the eldest sister in the family, I later discovered, was said to have longed for the veil, longed to have become a Madam herself, but madness intervened. Her madness. The thing the family never talked about. She might have been dead, as dead as the dead brother whose plane went down in Vietnam. She was away, in an institution in Maine, tended by hardworking nuns, not Madams, who might have been nurses or social workers had they not received a vocation. No one ever spoke about Agnes, except Kitt, who went to visit her before Christmas each year and on her birthday. Once she took me with her. Agnes thought that I was Constant, whom she had never seen other than as a baby, and Kitt nodded for me to pretend I was. It would have been too complicated, she said later, to explain who I was and what my relationship was to her. Agnes, except for her vacant look, had the appearance and voice of her father. But her mind was that of a ten-year-old. Kitt brought her silver rosary beads, blessed by the Holy Father in Rome, because Agnes claimed someone always stole her beads. Kitt was infinitely patient with her. Agnes, with her unpainted lips, talked incessantly of the Virgin Mary and the power of prayer. "I'll call you on Sunday," Kitt said to Agnes on leaving. "Oh, goody, goody, Trinity Sunday," replied Agnes, clapping her hands.

Dear sweet Kitt. I believe that she loved me, as I certainly loved her, but that all happened later and is no more than a subplot to the story that I have to tell. Only my own participation in that emotional turmoil brings me to mention it so early in this account. My knowledge of the events that follow is mostly firsthand, the rest comes from conversations with Constant and Kitt, and, occasionally, their far less well off cousins, Fatty and Sis Malloy. "I'm the one who talks too much," Kitt once said. "They're all down on me. Even Pa, and let's face it, I'm the apple of Pa's eye."

For reasons pertaining to their moment in time, Gerald and Grace Bradley were neither accepted nor received by the society of their city, for the Irish—even the rich Irish, and the Bradleys were very rich— were considered in those days to be not altogether correct. "They're not the kind of people you invite to dinner," said Leverett Somerset, in his snubbing way of speaking. He loathed the Irish, particularly the Bradleys. The Bradley money had not been fashionably come by. It was not from insurance, or banking, or stocks and bonds. Gerald's father, Malachy, who amassed the nucleus that Gerald later turned into the Bradley fortune, had been a butcher who prospered in the grocery business and, before he died, became the president of a small bank in the Irish section of the city. In later years, Gerald always referred to his father as a banker, but those who remembered, especially people like the Somersets, always referred to him as a butcher. Gerald attended the Catholic schools of the city, Catholic University in Washington, and law school at Harvard. His early financial circumstances were further enhanced by his marriage to Grace Malloy, the daughter of a plumber who had prospered in the plumbing supply business. By the standards of the day, the combined incomes of the two newlyweds made them well-to-do. In a relatively short time, Gerald was thought to be the finest Catholic lawyer in the city and was personally responsible for the legal affairs of the bishop and the Church. Already a genius in money matters, particularly in the acquisition of real estate, Gerald doubled, trebled, quadrupled, et cetera, into the stratospheric level, the original butcher and plumber money, at the same time that Grace was giving birth to Bradley child after Bradley child.

The Bradleys were inordinately admired by the Irish community from which they sprang but were shunned by the Protestant community who controlled the business, politics, and society of the city. In those days, the Irish, the Poles, the Italians, and the Jews resided on the east side of the city, while the Protestants lived more graciously on the west side. It was a surprise to all when Gerald Bradley bought the old Scarborough house, once lived in by Governor Scarborough, in the fashionable section known as Scarborough Hill. It was doubly surprising when Gerald Bradley then tore down the venerable house and built in its place an even larger mansion of gray and brown stone in the Tudor style. If it was not the handsomest house in the city, it was certainly the largest, and its construction caused much comment at the time, not all of it favorable, as well as a steady stream of cars filled with sightseers hanging out the windows to stare at the vast structure. By then the Bradley name was on every tongue.

"Who do these people think they are?" asked Piggy French, one of their new neighbors.

"I now live next door to the butcher's son," said Leverett Somerset, a remark that was repeated over and over again at the country club, a club so exclusive that it had no other name than The Country Club.

"There's a capital *T* on the *The*," Leverett Somerset always said when he discussed the club.

Understanding the restrictions of the day, the Bradleys made no attempt at social intercourse with their polished neighbors. Nor did they mingle much with their own kind, having become separated from them by their immense wealth. But they found great pleasure in one another's company. Loud screams of laughter and playful rivalry emanating from the Bradley swimming pool and the Bradley tennis court could be heard ringing through the air of the sedate neighborhood. "My word, don't they make a lot of noise, those Bradleys," Louise Somerset, Leverett's wife, said on more than one occasion. The two families were never to understand each other. Louise Somerset was not sure whether it was an impertinence or an act of kindness when she received a Mass card from Grace Bradley following the death of her mother.

Gerald was a stern disciplinarian to his children, demanding of them that they always be a credit to their Catholic background even while he prepared them for their infiltration into the Protestant world of private schools, dancing classes, seaside summers, country clubs, and Ivy League colleges. Grace, doing her part in the infiltration, contributed importantly to the symphony orchestra and attended every winter concert with one or more of her daughters, wearing a mink coat that Mrs. Somerset, her neighbor, told everyone was much, much too long. "She's perfectly nice, Mrs. Bradley," said Mrs. Somerset, after a symphony board meeting, "but I wish she wouldn't wear gloves when she pours tea."

There was amazement in all quarters when Gerald Bradley was proposed for membership in The Country Club, the only Irish Catholic until then ever to be proposed. The Prindevilles, longtime members, were Catholic, too, but Helen Prindeville would be the first to tell you that they were French Catholic, which was, in her eyes, quite a different matter altogether. Piggy French, Buzzy Thrall, and Neddie Pawson, speaking for the majority of the membership, were prepared to blackball the proposal of Gerald Bradley. None of them took notice of Corky, the bartender, who overheard the contretemps while serving them drinks in the men's locker room, and later repeated it word by word to the other employees, most of whom had grown up in Bog Meadow. Piggy French went so far as to call Gerald Bradley unclubbable.

"He lacks the social graces," agreed Buzzy Thrall.

"Where do you suppose all that money comes from?" asked Neddie Pawson. "Are we sure it's aboveboard? I mean, how can you make that much money in that short a time and have it all be legal? I mean, there won't be fraud stories at some time in the future, will there, Leverett?"

"No, no, no," said Leverett Somerset impatiently. "Like him or not, and I don't, thank you very much, the man is a financial genius. He should be in government. He should be dealing with the deficit, not trying to get into society."

"The only society he's ever going to be in is the Holy Name Society," said Buzzy Thrall, and they all laughed.

"He keeps a mistress, I hear. Sally Steers, their interior decorator," said Piggy French.

"How do you know that?" demanded Leverett Somerset.

"She went to Farmington with Eve Soby," replied Piggy French. "He gave her a mink coat."

"So do you," said Leverett.

"So do I what?"

"Keep a mistress."

"But I don't have priests to dinner and popes to tea. And, besides, I don't *keep* her. I *see* her. It's quite a different thing altogether."

The behind-closed-doors session became stormy. Bitter things were said. Finally, however, all acquiesced, reluctantly. It was, people said, a payoff, a silent deal arrived at by Gerald Bradley and his neighbor, Leverett Somerset, having to do with a business venture in which Somerset, in financial distress, allowed himself to be bailed out by the butcher's son. Gerald Bradley also agreed to undertake the costs of damages, not covered by insurance, caused by a recent hurricane to the clubhouse porte cochere.

One of the most outraged members of the club was old Bishop Fiddle, the Episcopal prelate lately returned from a long and fashionable ecclesiastical tenure in Paris to spend his retirement years in Scarborough Hill. His mother was a Scarborough by birth, the sister of the late governor, and he was the uncle of Louise Somerset. He found the Bradley membership in the club appalling and voiced his opinion to anyone who would listen, despite the objections of his wife.

One Thursday night, as the Bradleys entered the dining room en masse, the bishop signaled Gerald to his table with a wave of his spoon. He was eating vanilla ice cream. His patient and long-suffering wife had tied a large napkin around his neck so that the ice cream would not spill on the purplish red rabat beneath his black suit. On a gold chain around his neck he wore a cross which he tucked into his left breast pocket. When he spoke, the stentorian tones of his clipped tight Yankee voice carried throughout the large dining room.

"I find it fascinating that the club has liberalized its bylaws to allow such a notorious person as yourself to join," said the bishop. Vanilla ice cream dripped down his chin.

Gerald, who despised the tone of that sort of voice, leaned low toward the bishop. "Fuck you, Bishop," he said in the prelate's ear.

The old man turned red with rage. "What did he say?" he asked his wife.

"He said, 'Fuck you, Bishop,' " replied his wife.

That night there was much laughter and gaiety at the Bradley table. Only Grace, who longed to be accepted, did not join in the fun. After all, she complained, she was the one who would have to meet Mrs. Fiddle at the next meeting of the symphony board.

"I always thought the Somersets were so damn rich," I said to Constant when he told me the story of how his family came to be members of The Country Club.

"Well, they are, or were, but they just let their money sit, in that WASP way of theirs, while the smart people, like my father, who understand that money has to move, has to be invested, pull out at the right time, reinvest in something else, whether it's real estate or the market or whatever, get richer and richer. And, after seven or ten years, the once-rich Somersets look poor by comparison."

Every Thursday, which was known in the community as cook's night out, most of the members and their families dined at the club, and the Bradleys took up the habit, arriving promptly at seven-thirty with their great brood of growing children. They occupied a long table with Gerald at one end and Grace at the other, and for the seventeen years of their membership, until they moved away from the city, after Winifred Utley's death, they did not take it amiss that they were never more than nodded to by the Protestant membership, or ever addressed, even once, by their first names. They felt they were special, the most successful of their own kind.

My family, too, were of that persuasion and heritage. We, too, were children and grandchildren of immigrants who had prospered in New England; but our prosperity, although heralded in our city, was mild

compared to the prosperity of the Bradleys, who, even then, fifty or
sixty years ago, according to my grandfather, who admired them ex-
cessively, were known as having accumulated wealth comparable to
the Rockefellers'. My father, however, was less admiring, specifically
of Gerald Bradley. He said the Bradley money was tainted. He said
Gerald Bradley consorted with undesirable people for financial gain.
He said Gerald Bradley had a reputation in the business community
for shady dealings. More and more, the older I get, I think of things
my father told me, although, when he was alive, I did everything I
could to avoid his presence after becoming aware, at a very early age,
that I was a disappointment to him, not at all the sort of person he
would have picked for an only son, had such an option been open to
him. Had he lived, I would have disappointed him more, probably. I
was a frequent source of displeasure, unlike all the Bradley children,
who, for the most part, delighted their parents. But then, we were very
different from the Bradleys. Not so rich. Not nearly so rich. We were
merely well-to-do. Although highly thought of, successful even, my
father had never risen above the vice-presidential level in the Derby
branch of a great insurance company in Hartford. We had Olds-
mobiles, not Cadillacs. We had a maid who doubled as a cook. I was
sent to good schools, but on partial scholarships. Even our sort of
Catholicism was different. Our sort was underplayed. Never denied,
but underplayed. Theirs was flamboyant, flaunted even. They attended
Mass at St. Martin of Tours Cathedral, to which Gerald had given the
rose window and the carillon, and they sat in two pews, one behind
the other, always the same two front pews, as if they were reserved
for the family, like opera seats on Monday nights. Grace, ostenta-
tiously pious, regularly checked her brood and whispered instructions.
"Look at the altar, Constant," or, "Sing louder, Mary Pat." Everyone
carried rosary beads, always silver, always blessed by the Holy Father
in Rome, and missals. Everyone received Communion, father, mother,
and all eight children. They knew they were watched. They enjoyed
being watched. "What a wonderful family," the other parishioners
said, as they stared at the ladies with their necks arched in devotion
beneath their black lace mantillas, and listened to the resonant voices
of the men loudly calling out the responses. Afterwards, on the church
steps, they mingled a bit, speaking affably to the people they knew, or
to the people they were introduced to, or to the priest who had just
said the Mass. Grace, who even then shopped in Paris, always took
great pains to dress in a manner that brought admiring glances from

the women of the parish. Then they returned home for their Sunday breakfast, heaping platters of bacon and eggs, served by Irish maids in black uniforms and cooked by Bridey Gafferty, a large pudding of a woman who had been with the family for years and years and knew without being told how each person liked his eggs. There were cousins they rarely saw who lived in the part of the city known as Bog Meadow, where both Grace's and Gerald's families had themselves once lived. The cousins, who were called Fatty and Sis Malloy, were the children of Grace's brother, Vinny, who had never done well. Fatty, with his red brick of an Irish face, might have become a cop or a fireman if his father's sister had not married a man who prospered so magnificently and who didn't want a nephew in a dark-blue uniform who might one day prove to be an embarrassment to his Bradley sons. The Malloys didn't fit in, but sometimes they were asked to breakfast on Sunday after Mass. It was a great treat for Fatty and Sis, but a chore for the rest of them, even Grace, whose niece and nephew they were. Afterwards, Constant, who could imitate Fatty to perfection, even the way he held his fork and drooled his soft-boiled eggs on his double chin, would bring the family to tears of laughter as he reenacted something his cousin had done at the breakfast table. Only Grace did not laugh.

Meals at the Bradleys' were lively events. Conversation and arguments were encouraged on all topics: religion, politics, the arts. "Opinions. Have opinions," I heard Gerald say over and over again. Wine was always served at dinner, and sometimes at lunch, even if there were no guests. Gerald believed in teaching his children how to drink at home. "I've always gone on the theory that a young man or woman is less likely to make a fool of himself later on in college if he learns to drink under his own roof in the presence of his father and mother. Am I right, Grace?"

"Yes, dear," replied Grace, who did not really approve of the practice but who never disagreed with her husband. "But not when Cardinal's here," she added, shaking her head.

"Sip it. Don't gulp it, Constant," said Gerald.

"Not you, Kitt. You're too young," said Grace.

"Oh, Mother," moaned Kitt.

"One glass only, Miss Kitt," said Gerald.

With such a large family, there were frequent birthdays, and graduations, and anniversaries, and all were observed with toasts, each family member rising in turn to toast the honored person. It was conceded that Constant gave the best toasts in the family. "He's so good on his feet," Grace said every time.

Constant Bradley, my friend, was a spectacular young man in every way. He seemed almost too good to be true. His name, his looks, his trim six-foot-two athletic frame, strained reality. He possessed a refinement of face that his parents did not have, and his vocal pattern was less strident than that of his parents and older siblings. His bearing, wit, and style caused much comment, especially among the young ladies at the various boarding schools in Connecticut and Massachusetts who had heard of the handsome young heir to the Bradley fortune. He had a facility for sports, especially the kind thought of as gentlemen's sports: tennis, golf, squash, lacrosse, and sailing. In spite of the fact that his family's wealth was of only two generations' standing, he had acquired all the outward manifestations of privilege and bore them with the not-unattractive arrogance of a patrician. Perhaps, behind his splendid looks, there was a hint of menace, but I would not have seen it then or, if I did, I would have thought it an enhancement. All the daughters of the same Protestant families who abhorred the Bradleys were mad about Constant. His blond good looks left debutantes across the ballrooms of every country club where he danced gasping with desire, especially young Louise Somerset, Leverett Somerset's daughter, who was called Weegie. Any one of them would have defied her family if Constant had been inclined toward them, but Constant, even then, was attracted to the forbidden fruit, and the forbidden fruit was Weegie Somerset, who was to be, in two years' time, the prettiest debutante of her season and the social catch of the city.

They fascinated each other from the time they met in Mrs. Winship's dancing classes, when they were thirteen. He went to her school for her dances, and she went to his school for his. He was asked to her parties at her house, where his family had never been asked, and where the only things Irish or Catholic were the maids, in their black silk uniforms and white starched caps and aprons, who beamed at him in approval, knowing that he was the son of Gerald and Grace Bradley.

My friendship with Constant was a surprise to me. I was one of the unspectacular members of our class at Milford, one of the quiet ones, even though I was the possessor of an unusual sort of celebrity. I remained aloof from the rest of the boys, although, in truth, my aloofness was merely an act of self-defense; I longed to be one of them. Constant played bridge very well, which made him a great favorite of Mr. Fanning, the French teacher, who wore beautiful tweed jackets and entertained the bridge-playing group in his rooms each night after dinner and before study hall. I was not part of that set. I disliked Mr. Fanning, who seemed to cater to all the rich boys.

It was Mr. Fanning who came to me one night in study hall.

"Harrison," he said. "The headmaster wants to see you in his office. Immediately."

My heart quickened. I wondered what I had done wrong. Mr. Fanning, usually dismissive of me, was looking at me with concern.

"Is something the matter?" I asked.

"You must get to the headmaster's office," he said firmly.

There, in Dr. Shugrue's office, where I had only been once before, when my father entered me in Milford, I was told that my mother and father had been murdered. I did not cry, although I sank into a chair in front of his desk while he told me the facts of the horrible event.

"Mrs. Shugrue is making up our guest room for you to stay the night. It will be better than going back to the dorm," he said.

By the time I returned to study hall to pick up my books and papers, word had gone round of my shocking news. Everyone stared at me. In the silence, Constant Bradley, solicitous, helped me gather up my things. The next morning Aunt Gert came to take me home. Leaving the school, aware that boys were watching out the window, I wished that she had brought my father's Oldsmobile, black with whitewall tires, rather than her Chevrolet, four years old and badly in need of a wash.

After Detective Stein, who was investigating the case, visited me at school one day, to report only that there were no leads in the double murder, Constant sought me out. The celebrity of the case never really exceeded the limits of the city in which it occurred, but everyone at Milford knew, and Dr. Shugrue, the headmaster, had exhorted the boys not to question me on my return, an exhortation ignored by Constant. At first, his interest in me was no more than blunt curiosity. He asked me the kind of questions no one else, for propriety's sake, dared to ask. If they had come from anyone other than Constant, I would have ignored the questions, or walked away, but I was entranced with his attention, and replied, discovering that I was eager to have a friend in whom to confide. When he asked me to sneak into the village one afternoon, which was forbidden, to see a film he particularly wanted to see, I was thrilled to be his accomplice, although I was the type who never broke the rules. Soon we became inseparable. He had the most elaborate and expensive stereo equipment of any boy in the school, and each week all the latest cassettes arrived from a record store in New York. He knew the lyrics to every James Taylor song. We smoked pot and drank beer, risking expulsion. For me, it was thrilling. I didn't mind telling him the answers to test questions; I even took it as an honor. Sometimes, between confession on Saturday afternoon and Communion on Sunday morning, he succumbed to powerful sexual urges and masturbated. "I beat my meat," he said to me. In those days he beat his meat a great deal, especially after the new issue of *Playboy* came out each month. Occasionally, not always, I accompanied him in the masturbation experience, such acts were certainly not uncommon to boys in boarding school, but my eyes were on him, not on *Playboy*. The next morning, fearing the headmaster's wrath if he did not go to Communion, he more than once paraded up the center aisle to the Communion rail, where, fearing also God's wrath, with its attendant promises of eternal damnation and the pains of hell if he received the Blessed Sacrament while in a state of mortal sin, he became lost in the crowd of communicants, and then returned to his pew, head bowed in pious post-Communion prayer, without having received the Sacrament, although no one but I was aware of his ruse.

There was someone called Diego Suarez in our class. A rich South American boy, the son of a fashionable diplomat in Washington, whom everyone, for obvious reasons, called Fruity. He pretended not to mind the name. A louse, a gossip, an unpopular fellow, he was the single exotic in our youthful Catholic midst. When autumn began to turn cold, he wore his top coat over his shoulders, in a flamboyant manner, the sleeves dangling by his side or swirling around him when he turned abruptly to address somebody. It was a style made famous by the Duke of Windsor, he told us, who had been a great great friend of his grandfather's in Palm Beach, although few of us knew then who the Duke of Windsor was. Fruity had spent a summer in Beverly Hills and told lesbian stories about movie stars with great authority, which shocked, disappointed, or titillated his teenage audience. "Oh, yes, it's absolutely true," he told us. "Everyone in Hollywood knows about the two of them. It's a notorious affair."

It was Fruity who started the rumor that I was transfixed by Constant Bradley. "I can see the famous Bradley charisma has transfixed you, Harrison," he said one day on our way to study hall in his loud, affected voice, for all to hear. "You cannot keep your eyes off him." I blushed. For a while, everyone in the school talked about it. Constant, untroubled, roared with laughter at the story, while I suffered in silence. Denials were issued. The story died down. Eventually, in time, Fruity Suarez was kicked out of school for making an unwanted advance toward Jerome O'Hagen, the captain of the football team, who reported him to the headmaster. Secretly, I was delighted to see Fruity go, although I remained silent, my glee unexpressed. Years later, on the Concorde, on my way to Paris to cover Marlene Dietrich's funeral, I ran into a classmate from that period, and we reminisced about those days at Milford. "Whatever happened to Fruity Suarez, do you suppose?" he asked. "Just sort of vanished, didn't he?" I thought for a moment, wondering to myself whether to tell him what I knew. "Yes, vanished," I answered finally. "Perhaps dead, for all I know."

Transfixed. What an odd word. Was I transfixed by Constant Bradley? Yes, I was. I was completely transfixed by Constant Bradley.

2

IN CONTRAST to the Bradleys, I often described my family as being merely well-to-do, but when my parents' estate was settled, and our house sold, it developed that we were not that well-to-do at all. My father, it seemed, had made some bad investments. There was insurance, but I had very few assets and no relations to speak of, except Aunt Gert, a maiden lady, the older sister of my father, who would have taken me in, adopted me even, but it was not a prospect that I found enticing. Her life was drab. She raised money for the Maryknoll Fathers, who were missionaries in far-off places. And, by then, I had had a taste of the Bradley kind of life.

"Are there things you want saved?" asked Aunt Gert. She was wrapping glasses and china in newspapers.

"Why?"

"For when you marry?"

"Like what?"

"The dining room table was your grandmother's. And the sideboard."

"All right, I guess."

Later, going out, she said, "Where did you get that tie? It looks very expensive."

"It *is* very expensive. Turnbull and Asser. London. It belongs to Constant. He lets me wear his ties."

"Aren't you seeing too much of those people?"

"I don't think so. I like them. I like their kind of life. They're exciting."

"Your father wouldn't have approved."

"But my father is dead."

She turned away. "Do you keep in touch with Detective Stein?" she asked.

"No."

20

"Why?"

"If he had something to tell me, I'm sure he would have gotten in touch," I replied. I did not like to talk about my parents' murder.

"Tomorrow is the anniversary of your father's death."

"My father and mother's deaths."

"Yes, of course. I am having a Mass said. You'll be there, won't you?"

"All right."

"Is that beer you're drinking? I think you're too young to drink, Harrison."

"Mr. Bradley thinks young people should learn to drink at home. They serve wine at meals. Even Kitt, the youngest, is allowed a glass. That way, he says, young people will know how to drink when they go out in the world."

"Mr. Bradley, Mr. Bradley! That's all I hear anymore. You are bewitched by those people, Harrison."

"I like them. I like their life."

I returned to Milford to finish the fifth-form year and then in June went to visit with Constant again, after receiving a letter from his mother inviting me. Kitt and Mary Pat were home from their convent school. The Bradley life seemed to be an endless summer of tennis and swimming and golf at the club. There were always tennis pros and golf pros to give the children lessons, and often they stayed to lunch. There were spring dances at The Country Club. The family liked having me around because I could be counted on to dance with Constant's sisters, whom no one else danced with, while Constant was off dancing with Weegie Somerset. Constant was invited to parties that his sisters weren't invited to.

"Why do they all have such wonderful names, like Polly and Jiggsie and Gussie and Weegie, when we're all Mary Pat and Maureen and Agnes?" asked Kitt, looking out at the popular girls on the dance floor.

"Well, the Minskoff girls don't get invited either, and they're driven to school by a chauffeur," said Grace.

"Is that supposed to be a comfort, Mother?" asked Kitt.

Although Constant was still in disgrace because of his expulsion from school, the opulence of his life was in no way diminished. For his seventeenth birthday, his father gave him a new car, a Porsche convertible, and we went for long drives. One day we drove to New

Haven to have sport coats made at J. Press. I had no money for such extravagances, but Constant, with his patrician disregard of money, insisted on paying.

His brothers and sisters treated the expulsion as a joke. Gerald minded only that he had been caught with the dirty pictures, not that he possessed them. He would have minded only if they had been pictures of men, not women, he said, and the family, except Grace, roared with laughter. His anger was directed at the headmaster who had expelled his son. "After all, I have done quite a few things for that school," he said over and over. Grace was more troubled. She insisted that Constant confess to Cardinal during one of his visits, and he did.

"What kind of pictures were they?" Gerald asked Constant.

Constant, embarrassed, reddened and did not answer.

"Beaver shots, showing pink," interjected Jerry.

Gerald chuckled.

Much of the dinner-table conversation in the Bradley family that summer had to do with the reinstatement of Constant into Milford. If Constant had had more than one year to go before graduation, Gerald would have applied to any number of other schools for his son, but he felt that Constant would not be able to distinguish himself in a single year with boys who had already been together for three years. At Milford Constant had managed to become a popular figure, captain of the tennis team, and a reasonably good student, and Gerald was loath to toss all that aside, because it would figure in getting him into Yale the following year. The problem was that the headmaster of Milford, Dr. Shugrue, showed no inclination to have Constant return. He had been particularly offended by the nature of the dirty pictures that had been discovered on the top shelf of Constant's closet, and he looked upon him as a poor moral guide to the younger students, all of whom knew the reason for his expulsion.

One night at dinner Grace suggested giving a building to the school.

"What do you mean, give a building? I already gave the goddamn chapel, and the carillon in the steeple," replied Gerald from his end of the table. "And they still kicked my kid out."

"Don't take the name of the Lord thy God in vain, Gerald," replied Grace. "They must need something. Maybe a science building, Gerald. Or a new library. They always need libraries, don't they?"

"What about your friend, the cardinal?" asked Gerald. "Couldn't he go over and talk to Shugrue, Grace? Couldn't you talk him into that?"

22

"He would do that, yes. Although I think Dr. Shugrue should go to see Cardinal. Not the other way around. After all, a cardinal is the next thing to the Pope. And a headmaster is only a headmaster."

"However you work that out. Let's call him tonight," said Gerald.

"He's coming to tea tomorrow. I'll take it up with him then," replied Grace.

"Fine. Fine," said Gerald.

"And he can offer the school a science building from you?" asked Grace. "Or a new library?"

I wondered if I would be so fascinated by the relationship between Gerald and Grace if I did not remember so vividly the mink coat tossed casually on a hallway bench that was not Grace Bradley's mink coat. At Milford, when boys talked about Constant after his expulsion, they said that his father had mistresses. There was talk of a Mrs. Steers, who was the former stepmother of a boy in our class, and a New York decorator in the fashionable firm of Cora Mandell, the most esteemed of all the decorators. I realized then that when we were in the house, Gerald was upstairs with a woman who was not his wife. I was still young enough to be shocked. Not only that Gerald Bradley had a mistress. But that he brought a mistress into his wife's home.

"What is Mrs. Steers's first name?" I asked her former stepson.

"Sally. Why?"

"No reason." I remembered the initials on the lining of the fur coat.

Still, Gerald and Grace were very much a married couple and would stay that way. They agreed on things. Their religion was important to them. They had a mutual interest in their children and in the achievements that they foresaw for their family. But there was very little overt affection between them. They talked at dinner in the presence of their children, but afterwards Grace and her daughters sat together in one room and chatted, while Gerald and his sons usually sat in another room and watched television or talked about sports.

Wandering from one room to the other one evening, after I had been staying there for several weeks, I heard Grace say, "Yes, he's very sweet. I just wish he was taller. I want tall men for my girls." I supposed she was talking about me. Kitt and Mary Pat were seated with her.

"No, you want tall *Catholic* men for your girls," said Kitt, and they all laughed.

When Grace saw me, she motioned for me to sit beside her.

"Where are you from, Harry?" Grace asked.

23

Kitt whistled softly as she read a fashion magazine.

"Ansonia," I replied quietly. It was not a town where they were likely to have been.

"You probably know the Rooneys, the Martin Rooneys?" she asked.

"No."

"They live on—what is it called? Woodside Circle?"

"I don't know Woodside Circle, and I don't know the Rooneys."

"Ruth was one of the Cudahy triplets?"

"No."

"One of them married Teddy Aherne?"

"No."

"They all made wonderful marriages, those girls."

"Mother, he doesn't know the Rooneys, and the Rooneys live in Greenwich," said Kitt, looking up from her magazine. "What's that town of yours, Harry?"

"Ansonia," I said again.

"Never heard of it," said Kitt.

"It's near Derby."

"Believe me, Ma doesn't know anyone there. No offense, Harry," said Kitt.

"No, no, of course not," I said.

Kitt resumed whistling.

"So rare when all the girls in a large Catholic family make good marriages," said Grace.

"Whatever are you going to do about all of us, Mother?" asked Kitt. "You'll never approve of anyone we bring home."

"The Blessed Virgin cries when you whistle, Kitt," said Grace.

"Oh, Mother," replied Kitt.

"Yes, Kitt, it's true. I know. Ask Cardinal. Don't whistle."

"Yes, Mother."

Grace turned back to me. "Harry. That doesn't seem like a saint's name," she said.

"It's short for Harrison."

"Certainly there is no Saint Harrison."

"No. It was my mother's maiden name."

"My, that's very Protestant. Our neighbor Leverett Somerset's mother was a Leverett."

"But we aren't Protestant," I said.

"Constant said that your parents are dead?" asked Grace.

"Yes."

"Was it an automobile accident?"

"No."

"A plane crash then?"

"No. They were shot by an intruder."

"Good heavens! You mean murdered?"

"Yes."

"How ghastly! Do you mind talking about it?"

"Yes."

"Then I won't ask you anything about it. But just tell me this: did they catch the person who did it?"

"No."

"You mean the murderer is wandering around loose?"

"Yes."

"One of these days, they will catch him, you know. He'll be arrested for speeding, or something, and it will all come out, and then you'll have to deal with the whole thing."

"Mother!" said Kitt.

"Well, it's true," insisted Grace.

"Even so," Kitt replied. "It's Harry's private business. Mother doesn't mean to pry, Harry. She just can't help it."

"I shan't repeat what he said, but his words were very strong," said Dr. Shugrue to Cardinal Sullivan, about his conversation with Gerald Bradley on the day of Constant's dismissal.

"Yes, yes, Gerald is quite terrifying when he is angry," agreed Cardinal Sullivan. The cardinal went to see Dr. Shugrue at Milford, and then Dr. Shugrue went to see Cardinal Sullivan at the cardinal's mansion. There were several meetings.

"Gerald kept coming up with the name of someone in the class called Fruity Suarez. He said what Constant did is nothing compared to what the boy Fruity Suarez does. Who is Fruity Suarez, Dr. Shugrue?" asked Cardinal Sullivan.

"Oh, Cardinal, don't ask. The headmaster's nightmare."

"Oh, you mean—?"

"Yes."

"Oh, dear," said the cardinal. "We have that problem in the clergy, too, from time to time."

Cardinal Sullivan came away with the distinct impression that Dr.

Shugrue did not care for Constant Bradley. There was more to his dislike than the discovery of dirty pictures, but what that was the cardinal did not know, or did not choose to disclose to the Bradley family. The offer of a science building or a library had been made and accepted, but there was a stipulation. A paper had to be written by Constant, five thousand words on morality, before he could be reinstated. While the family went to a seaside cottage in Rhode Island, Constant was to stay behind in the house and write his paper. I returned to Ansonia. A friend of my father's got me a summer job on the *Hartford Courant*. In the event that there might not be enough money for me to go back to Milford for my sixth-form year, I registered at a public high school. In late July I received a telephone call at my aunt's apartment from Gerald Bradley.

"Hello, Harrison."

"Hello, Mr. Bradley." I had never talked to him on the telephone before. As always, he made me nervous.

"My son needs to write a paper before the headmaster will reinstate him into Milford. Are you aware of that?"

"Yes, sir. I thought he wrote it."

"Have you read it?"

"Yes, sir. He sent it to me."

"Not good, is it?"

"I don't know."

"Not good enough, that's for sure. Constant doesn't have a way with words the way you do. I have a plan."

"Yes?"

"I'd like you to write the paper for Constant."

"Me?"

"You want to be a writer, right?"

"Yes."

"Here's a chance to see how good you are."

"But, uh, if Dr. Shugrue should find out?"

"He won't. It'll be our little secret."

There was a moment of silence.

"You might wonder what you get out of this?"

"Oh, no, sir. I'll be happy to do it."

"You must never say that, Harry. You must always put a price on everything. That's what business is all about."

"I couldn't take money, sir."

"A supporter must be rewarded for his support. You must learn that lesson early on, Harrison," said Gerald. "Are you aware that your father's estate is considerably less than what people imagined it was going to be?"

"Yes, sir." I wondered how *he* knew such a thing. It was information I had not even told Constant.

"Are you aware that there might not be enough money to send you back to Milford for your senior year?"

"Yes, sir."

"And you would like to go back, would you not?"

"Yes, sir."

"Consider it done. Your tuition paid for, that is. Providing, of course, that your report meets with Dr. Shugrue's approval and Constant is reinstated."

"Yes."

"This is what's known as a business deal."

"Yes, sir."

"No one must know, of course. None of the others in the family."

"Yes, sir."

"Just you and me. And Constant, of course. The tuition money will be paid to your aunt. And she will in turn pay the school. That way, there will be no connection in the headmaster's mind."

"I understand. But my aunt. What will my aunt think? My aunt has different ideas."

"Your aunt is apparently very fond of the Maryknoll Fathers. Missionaries. Good works. In foreign places. I am prepared to make a large donation through her to the worthy fathers. Believe me, Harry, I have been around longer than you. It will be an irresistible offer."

"Why?" I asked.

"Because I have great hopes for my son, Harry. I believe he has the makings of greatness in him. When he has outgrown his boyish pranks, that is."

I had heard from Constant that Gerald had had great hopes and political plans for Constant's older brother Desmond, but Desmond had disappointed his father by becoming a doctor and disappointed him again by marrying inappropriately. Gerald thought it was a waste that his son's aspirations were conventional. "There's no real money in becoming a doctor," he had pleaded with his son, but Desmond was not to be dissuaded from his calling. Gerald found some consolation, but not much, in the fact that Desmond went to Harvard Medical School. He enjoyed saying that his son was at Harvard.

But then Desmond eloped with a maid in the house.

"You married *who?*" cried Grace, when Desmond came to tell her his news.

"Rosleen."

"*Rosleen?* The maid? Who opens the doors? Who passes the peas? You can't be serious."

"I am serious, Mother."

"Well, we'll see to that. Have you given a thought to what your father's reaction is going to be? Bridey, get me Cardinal on the telephone. We're going to have this marriage annulled."

From that moment on, Rosleen was referred to by Grace as Miss Whatever-her-name-is. Bridey, whose distant relation Rosleen was, collapsed in tears. "She's not a bad girl, Mrs. Bradley. She comes of decent parents. She's never gone astray." But her tears were not for Rosleen. They were tears of embarrassment at the impertinence of Rosleen for reaching so high above herself. She sorrowed, but she did not want to be part of Rosleen's disgrace.

"I can't call Cardinal, Mrs. Bradley. I just can't. She is my own flesh and blood," pleaded Bridey.

"How long have you been with me, Bridey?" asked Grace.

"Seventeen years, madam," replied Bridey.

"Don't I send you back to Ireland every year for two weeks and pay all expenses so that you can visit your family?"

"Yes, madam."

"And were you not allowed to meet His Holiness the Pope and kiss his ring? And receive his blessing? Right here in this very house?"

"Yes, madam."

"How many people do you know who can say that?"

"No one, madam."

"And didn't I hire all your little cousins and nieces from Ireland to work as maids in our house here, and at the seashore, even that slow one with the learning disability who ruined all my Porthault towels because she couldn't figure out the new washing machine?"

"Yes, madam."

"And arrange for a scholarship for your nephew at Holy Cross Dental School?"

"Loyola."

28

"What?"

"Loyola Dental School. Not Holy Cross."

"Whatever. Didn't I arrange for the scholarship?"

"Yes, madam."

"Shall I go on listing things, or have I made my point?"

"You've made your point, madam."

"Thank you, Bridey. Get me Cardinal on the telephone."

Gerald, in crisis, took over. He was a bad husband in that he kept mistresses, but he was his wife's most devoted ally in the raising of their children and in their ever-more-important status in public life. He cheated on her, but he denied her nothing, always encouraging her to entertain and never complaining about her extravagant gifts to the Church or questioning her enormous bills from the Paris couture. Her handling of Desmond's transgression, calling Cardinal Sullivan the first thing, met with his utmost approval. He had been off with Sally Steers at the time. "Marvelously handled, Grace," he said warmly, and she basked in his praise.

"I make no secret of my distaste for Rosleen," he said to Desmond in the presence of the whole family at dinner. "This must be a lesson to all of you in the family. You are marks for adventurous people trying to better themselves through you. When the time comes for marriage, your mother will find the right person for each of you." In a week's time, Cardinal Sullivan assured Gerald and Grace that there would be no trouble obtaining an annulment, but that such a thing would take time. Desmond was sent to Europe until matters were straightened out. A Mr. Fuselli, an acquaintance of Gerald Bradley's, was dispatched to remove all records of the marriage from the registrar's office. Rosleen, the maid, was sent away. Money was paid to her. Not a lump sum, but a generous monthly allowance, an assurance that nothing untoward in the way of publicity would ever be done, or the money would stop. Rosleen resisted the suggestion that she return to Ireland. Instead she traveled west. She had friends in Arizona. Desmond then returned to medical school.

Early on, he distinguished himself in his chosen field, and, at thirty-three, became the president of St. Monica's Hospital, the youngest president ever, although there were those, among them Dr. Francis X. Gerrity, who said that the Grace Bradley Wing, built by Desmond's mother, had hastened his ascendance to the presidency, over Dr. Gerrity, who at fifty-eight had had reason to expect that the presidency would be his.

Then Desmond performed an emergency operation, while wearing a dinner jacket, having been called to the hospital from a dancing party at The Country Club, on a young black boy named Walter Potts, who had been shot in the heart during a gang fight in the Bog Meadow section of the city. In a daring medical feat that astonished the interns and nurses in the operating room, he held the wounded heart in the palm of his hand while he removed the bullet, and then sewed it up and replaced it in the chest of the young man, who, to the amazement of all, lived. The operation was reported on the front pages of the morning and afternoon newspapers of the city and then, with a little help from Gerald, who had a gift for promotion, in the national weekly magazines and, of course, all the medical journals. He told his son's story over and over, referring always to Walter Potts as "a little black kid this high, about as tall as a trash can."

Even at The Country Club, members who did not ordinarily speak to Gerald stopped to congratulate him on his son's medical celebrity, and Gerald began to see the advantages of having a son in the business of what he called "good works." There were other sons to carry on his dynastic dreams, Sandro, of course, but particularly Constant. And the club members, who did not go to Desmond themselves for their medical problems, or to St. Monica's Hospital, began to send their Irish maids to him, as an acknowledgment of his abilities.

For two weeks I worked nights on Constant's paper, while keeping my daytime job on the *Hartford Courant*. I had never worked so hard on anything. I wanted to do it for Constant, whose friendship I treasured, so that he would be reinstated at Milford for our senior year, and I wanted to do it for Gerald Bradley, who had shown me the possibilities that he foresaw for Constant's future. I saw my own future being in Gerald Bradley's hands, as if he might do for me, when the time came, what my own father could never have done.

I found that, in writing in another person's name, as if I *were* Constant Bradley, I possessed a courage that I did not ordinarily possess when writing in my own name. All my timidity vanished. My dead father had found me flawed and imperfect, and I had accepted his judgment; but writing as Constant I became sure of myself and experienced true joy in the writing process. I wrote about Constant's grandfather, as if he were mine. And his father and mother. I wrote about being a member of a large Catholic family. I stressed the importance

30

of family, something I had never felt in my own life. I wrote about the obligation of the wealthy to help others who were less fortunate. I wrote about the significance of early education, particularly an education at Milford, in preparing Catholic boys to enter the Ivy League colleges and to carry with them the Catholic values learned at school. I wrote about leadership. I wrote about a future public life that would embody the values that I had learned at Milford. All these things would have sounded preposterous coming from my lips, but not from the lips of Constant Bradley.

I mailed the twenty double-spaced typed pages to Gerald Bradley at an office he kept in New York. As per his instructions, there was no covering letter. I waited but heard nothing in reply. A week went by. Then two. Finally a telephone call came to me at my aunt's house. It was from Gerald. He invited me to come to spend the Labor Day weekend at the seashore in Rhode Island. He said the whole family would be there. There was to be a celebratory dinner in honor of Constant. I waited for him to say something about the paper that I had written, but he said nothing.

"What is the reason for Constant's celebration?" I asked.

"He is returning to Milford," replied Gerald. "The cardinal has arranged everything."

That night Aunt Gert told me that she had received the tuition money for me to return to Milford for my sixth-form year. She told me that she had also received a donation of five thousand dollars for the Maryknoll Fathers. She was alternately joyful and perplexed.

"Why would Mr. Bradley do that?" she asked.

"I don't know," I replied.

"Your father didn't like him," she said. "He said he mixed with disreputable people."

"I don't believe you're going to turn down the five thousand dollars for the Maryknoll Fathers, are you, Aunt Gert?"

"No, I'm not," she said. "They need the money so badly. Bishop McGurkin will be so pleased."

"So Gerald Bradley can't be all bad, can he?"

"There are people who think that money buys everything. I think Mr. Bradley is one of those."

"But you're not going to turn down his money?"

"Be careful, Harrison. That's all I ask. Their kind of life, it's very

31

dangerous to be around those people when you don't have their kind of money.''

Their cottage at Watch Hill was a huge shingled structure with fourteen bedrooms and verandas across the front and sides looking out to the ocean and the golf course. Even though it was only rented for the season, Mrs. Steers, the decorator, had come from New York to pull it together for them. It was Mrs. Steers who knew of the house and told Gerald about it. She had summered in Watch Hill as a child and knew everyone there. It was Mrs. Steers, forty, handsome, twice divorced, who told Gerald all the things he wanted to know so that his children would grow up familiar with things he had never heard of when he was their age. From her he learned about sheets and towels that came from Paris, which people who knew about such things recognized at once without being told they came from Paris, and nothing would do for his house from that moment but sheets and towels from Paris with scalloped edges and floral terry cloth.

"Do you have any idea how expensive they are?" gasped Grace, on the telephone from Paris, where she was ordering her new clothes.

"I can afford them," replied Gerald. He spoke such lines authoritatively, even to Grace. What he wanted was to be done, no further questioning, no further comments.

Chintz slipcovers were made for the sofas and chairs. Green-and-white-striped awnings shaded the verandas, and the wicker furniture was painted white. Pink geraniums were planted in white painted boxes all along the verandas, and an entire summer garden was planted. Everything was under the supervision of Sally Steers. It was in Watch Hill that the usually compliant Grace began to complain. She thought all the decorating was too much of an extravagance for so short a time, but Gerald insisted. Next year he might buy it, he said.

"But don't you like your garden?" asked Gerald.

"Blue, blue, blue, blue, and I hate blue flowers," said Grace. "I wanted roses, not forget-me-nots and delphiniums.''

Gerald understood that her complaints had nothing to do with forget-me-nots and delphiniums.

At the entrance to the house, Gerald's new maroon Rolls-Royce was parked. Like the house in Scarborough Hill, the seashore cottage became a house to be stared at and pointed out by drivers-by, but, like the house at home, only the golf pros and tennis instructors hired by Gerald to teach his children came to lunch. Even with Mrs. Steers's introductions, the Bradleys remained outsiders.

Gerald was not a weekend father, up from the city on Friday nights and returning to the city on Monday mornings. He was there for long periods, doing his business on the telephone. While watching his children swimming in the pool, he called Dom Belcanto, the singer, in Hollywood, who was thought to have underworld connections. And Senator Zwick, and Charles Arbelli, the editor of the *World,* and Terrence Noonan, the editor of the *Sentinel.* Sometimes men came to see him. Some were introduced to his wife and children. Some weren't. A man named Johnny Fuselli came and went from time to time, meeting behind a closed door in a downstairs room that Gerald used as an office. He drove a bright red car. He was never introduced. He was never asked to lunch, but he always took a swim in the ocean, and we were impressed with his powerful strokes.

"He's quite a swimmer, isn't he? I believe he had Olympic aspirations once, but something went wrong. He probably flunked a urine test at one of the trials," said Gerald to Jerry. "Moe Dailitz told me the story, but I can't quite remember."

"A little cocaine in the bloodstream perhaps?" suggested Jerry.

"Something like that. So he went to Vegas and Atlantic City instead," said Gerald, chuckling over his joke. "The Olympics' loss is our gain."

I supposed Mr. Fuselli was one of the disreputable people Aunt Gert had mentioned to me. Maureen, the elder sister, said he was handsome in a cheap sort of way. She told her mother that all the maids had crushes on him.

"Who's Mr. Fuselli?" I asked Constant.

"One of Pa's lieutenants, I suppose," he replied. He elaborated no further. I did not persist in questioning. It was Kitt who enjoyed chatting about the people who came and went in her father's life. Mr. Crotty, she said, was in cement. Mr. McSweeney in tugboats. Mr. O'Malley in taxicabs. And Johnny Fuselli in crime, she said, breaking out into gales of laughter. "He used to have something to do with slot machines in New Jersey."

"Shut up, Kitt," said Constant. "You talk too much."

Gerald wanted his children to excel. He sat by the court and watched them play or stood on the green and watched them tee off, barking out instructions. "You should have used your backhand on that shot,

Constant," he called out. "And returned it to the other side of the court, where Des couldn't reach it."

"You're right," said Constant. He pulled up the front of his Lacoste shirt to wipe the sweat off his face. Weegie Somerset, who loved him then, watched from the sidelines, looking longingly at his exposed stomach and chest.

Gerald always wore a large straw hat to protect his white skin from the strong rays of the sun. Even with protection, his skin turned red with the minimum of exposure, and lotions were always being applied. He sat under an umbrella and removed his terry cloth robe only to go into the pool to swim his forty laps, dropping it at the edge of the pool so that he could put it on again instantly as he was walking up the steps to leave the pool. Grace came to the pool only after the sun had gone down. On my first day there, the afternoon of the celebration in honor of Constant, I was lying on a lounge chair by the pool, reading *Gatsby*, and I heard the following conversation between Gerald and Mrs. Steers, who seemed unaware of my presence.

"You're not a popular man, Gerald," said Mrs. Steers. "You have no close friends. Haven't you noticed that? There are many people who are afraid of you, who will invite you to their house for dinner for that reason, but they don't like you. You're always on the telephone, but no one calls you up just to chat. No one invites you to play tennis. Do you think your children notice those things?"

"I have plenty of people to play tennis with," replied Gerald.

"Yes. People you pay. Why keep bucking your head against the wall, Gerald? The old guard, what Cora Mandell calls the good families, are never going to accept you, no matter how much money you have, no matter how big your house is, no matter how many sets of Porthault sheets are on your beds."

"Give me time."

"It won't happen, Gerald, believe me. You're an outsider. You always will be. Oh, sure, they'll take your contributions for the symphony. They'll let you pay for the repairs to The Country Club after the hurricane damage. They'll even have you to dinner once a year. But when your son wants to marry one of their daughters, you'll see what they really think about you. To them, you're a mick. You're the butcher's son who still smells of raw meat, and nothing you ever do is going to change that."

Gerald winced. His face turned scarlet.

"I know, Gerald. That's the world I grew up in," she said.

"So what do I do?" he asked.

"Get out of there. You are simply in a wrong location."

"I can't."

"For part of the year you can. There's Florida. There's California. You can buy a big house in Palm Beach, or a big house in Beverly Hills, and make a splash there. Less provincial. Your kids will be assimilated in a way that they'll never be here."

"What about home?"

"Use it for your country seat. Keep it up. Keep the gardeners. Keep the butler. Visit it a few times a year. It will be a reminder of who you are and what they're missing. Because, by that time, they'll be reading about you and your kids."

"The butler couldn't take care of that place."

"That is a tidbit problem. What's that cousin of yours? Sis Malloy? The one who knows where all the furniture goes. Move her in. Put her in charge of the house."

"Grace will never want to leave."

"Buy the new house first. Then tell her about it."

"She won't want to leave Cardinal."

"Cardinals are a dime a dozen."

"No, they aren't."

"Then Cardinal will come to visit."

Mrs. Steers flew back to New York that afternoon. Cora Mandell, in whose firm she worked, was doing up a house in Southampton and said she needed her help. *Immediately.* Cora knew what was going on and didn't like it. It was she who had first been called in to do up the Bradleys' brand-new Tudor house, and then, because she was so busy, she had turned it over to Sally Steers to do the follow-up work. "Actually," Cora said, "they're my favorite upstarts. One step beyond antimacassars, but Grace is really quite nice, when you get used to all that talk about novenas and stations of the cross and holy days of obligation. She's avid, terribly well meaning, very religious, not very bright, but I like her immensely. But be careful of him, Sally. Gerald Bradley has wandering hands. You'll feel his hand on your knee, and higher, under the tablecloth, at the same time he's talking with Cardinal Sullivan on the other side about Church matters."

"I know how to handle that," said Sally.

"I hope so. He is irresistibly common, not unattractive in an Irish sort of way, and wildly rich. He is, you will discover, a giver of mink coats from Revillon Frères."

In the beginning, the Bradleys were so unused to the splendors of furniture and decoration with which Cora Mandell had surrounded them that when pieces or objects were moved about in the course of family life, their correct positions in the rooms could never be found exactly. Only Sis Malloy, the cousin, could remember, but no one wanted to ask Sis. Twice Mrs. Mandell returned to the house to re-arrange things and restore her perfect balance. "Symmetry, Mrs. Bradley," she said. "Always remember symmetry." On her second visit, she brought Sally Steers with her to photograph each room, as well as each tabletop, and the photographs were used for reference should things be moved out of place again. Mrs. Steers placed discreet pieces of tape on console tables and mantelpieces to show exactly where the export china plates were to be placed on stands. Often she stayed to lunch.

"Let me see, let me see, how should I do this?" said Grace. "You here, Des, next to me, and you, Constant, sit by Maureen, and Father Daly, on my right, and Mrs. Steers, next to Father, and Gerald on the other side of Mrs. Steers. And Mary Pat next to Daddy."

"You do that so well, Mrs. Bradley," said Sally Steers. "It takes me forever, and I always end up with a husband and wife sitting next to each other, or two people who hate each other."

"Do your miracle with the lobster, Bridey. You know how Mr. Brad-ley adores your thermidor. Or is it your Newburg? I never can remem-ber, but you know, Bridey," said Grace. That night the family gathered for a festive evening with toasts and speeches to Constant. Nice old Irish maids in summer pink uniforms passed cheese puffs before din-ner. There were eighteen in the group. The men dressed in blazers and white trousers, and the women in linen dresses. The tennis pro was there. The golf pro was there. Some business friends of Gerald's from Boston. A convent friend of Maureen's who was being looked over as a possible wife for one of the older brothers. And Weegie Somerset, who was staying with the Utleys down the beach.

"Oh, take off your jackets. Do. Do. It's frightfully hot, and the air conditioners are not really working well," said Grace, who enjoyed her role as hostess. "No, no, don't you talk, you two. I've seated you next to each other at dinner." After a whispered conversation with

36

Bridey, who appeared on the veranda, Grace moved from group to group and with a timorous wave of her hand toward the dining room gave the signal that dinner would be served.

After dinner, Gerald suggested to Constant that he read to the family the paper he had written that had so impressed Dr. Shugrue. Constant hopped to his feet and stood in front of the fireplace as his parents, brothers and sisters, and guests settled in chairs and sofas around the room to listen to him. From the inside pocket of his blazer, he removed the twenty typewritten pages that I had mailed his father weeks ago. When he started to read, I forgot that it was I who had written the words. They became his. He talked about his grandfather arriving poor from Ireland, working hard in a butcher shop to make a life for his family. He talked about his parents. "I once said to my mother, 'When you were young and first married, and the future was still uncertain, not yet defined, did you have any idea that Pa was one day going to be so successful?' And my mother said, 'Oh, yes, I always knew. Your father exuded power.' " He talked about his brothers and sisters. He talked about family, the importance of family. Like an orator, he held his family spellbound. When he finished, they broke into applause.

"You're going to be a politician," said Gerald. "You are a great speaker, Constant."

His sisters crowded around him. His brothers patted him on the back. His mother kissed him. His father hugged him. Weegie Somerset, so quiet in the noisy crowd, smiled proudly. I had no way of knowing then that Gerald saw in me the possibility of becoming the resident hagiographer for the Bradley family, particularly for Constant. Neither Gerald nor Constant looked in my direction. Only Kitt met my eye. She knew. Later, when everyone was preparing to go to the Labor Day dance at the beach club, we walked outside to one of the connecting verandas that encircled the house and sat down side by side on wicker rockers painted white.

"I like this house, don't you?" she said. "It's so old money. People in Scarborough Hill call us *nouveau*. Did you know that? Constant probably wouldn't tell you that. Those people at the club think our house is *nouveau*, too."

She reached over and pulled the cigarette I was smoking out of my hand and took several puffs. Everyone still smoked then. There was no talk of fatalities, or very little.

"If the Blessed Virgin cries when I whistle, imagine what she must be doing when I smoke," she said.

37

I laughed.

"You don't laugh very much, Harry. It looks nice on you. You should do it more often."

"You sound older than fourteen," I replied.

She handed me back the cigarette. "You're going to discover something about yourself one day, Harry," she said.

"What's that?"

"You have a real talent for fiction."

"What does that mean?"

"You wrote that paper for Constant, didn't you?"

I flicked the cigarette out over the railing. It landed in a shrub. I walked down the stairway to the lawn and retrieved it from the shrub and stamped it out on the ground. I didn't reply. I remembered Gerald's warning.

Kitt remained on the veranda watching me. She understood. "But it was Constant's delivery, though, that was the whole thing, wasn't it?" she said, retreating from, rather than pressing forward with, her assertion of my authorship. "I mean, he was marvelous."

"Yes, yes, it was the delivery," I replied, anxious to disassociate myself from my own work. "He speaks wonderfully."

"He's always given the best toasts of anyone in the family. Especially after a few glasses of wine."

Inside the house, Constant, bored now that he was no longer the center of attention, yawned audibly and got unsteadily to his feet. "Let's go to the club," he said. "The music's already started."

That night at the beach club dance, Constant became seriously intoxicated. I had noticed before, while drinking beer with him surreptitiously at school, that his natural charm and wit gave way to a morose side of his character with the first signs of intoxication. I have not often been drunk in my life, but that night I was, too. My purpose was to keep up with Constant, to do what he did. On my own I would not have had so many drinks. Other than my duty dances with the Bradley sisters, I avoided the dance floor, preferring to watch rather than participate. I wandered about staring at people I didn't know and probably never would. There was not an angry or worried face among them, or so it seemed to me then.

Finally I went toward the bar and stood there, ordering another drink I didn't really want. It was the only place a single man could linger without being asked to whirl some young lady around the dance floor. When I went outside to smoke, through the French doors that led to the beach, I heard voices and saw in the darkness two figures pressed up against the back wall of the cabanas. Because of my condition, my memories of the conversation I overheard between Constant and Weegie Somerset are somewhat fragmented. I was torn by guilt at snooping on my friend but troubled by the unpleasantness of the intimate scene I overheard. It was not the whispering of lovers. His voice was harsh, like Jerry's, devoid of its usual refinement.

As I turned to walk in the opposite direction, I heard Weegie Somerset say, "Hey, hey, hey. That's it. That's enough, Constant. Tongue in the mouth is very advanced for me."

"Don't give me that," said Constant.

"Don't give you what? I'm serious. That's it, Constant. A little kiss. A little tongue. Period."

"I know you want it. Here, touch this. It's hard as a rock."

"If I wanted it, Constant, which I don't, it wouldn't be out here in the sand leaning against the back of the cabanas, believe me. Now, let go of me. I'm going back inside."

"No, you're not."

"You've torn my dress strap."

He slapped her very hard. I didn't see him, but I heard the sound of the slap and then Weegie's surprised cry.

"You're mean when you're drunk," she said between sobs.

"I'm not drunk," he said.

She pulled away from him and started for the club.

"It wasn't hard," pleaded Constant. "It was just a tap."

I hurriedly returned to my place at the Bradleys' table in the club. Shortly thereafter, Weegie came in through the same French doors. She turned back to speak to Constant outside. "I can't take this. I just want you to know I can't take this." She left the club in tears. No one knew that night that she would never speak to Constant again.

"What happened?" I asked Constant the next morning when he awoke.

"Nothing," he replied.

"Don't say nothing. She cried at the beach club. We all saw her."

"Nothing," he repeated.

"I was outside, Constant. I went out to smoke. I heard."

Constant turned his head to the wall and didn't answer. Whenever Weegie Somerset's name came up after that, he remained silent.

*　　*　　*

Two weeks later we went back to school for the sixth form. Things were more serious that year. Even though the architectural drawings for the new Bradley Library at Milford were framed in the entranceway to the dining hall, Constant knew that one more infraction on his part would mean permanent expulsion and eliminate his chances of getting into college. He played on the lacrosse team in the fall, skied on the ski team in the winter, and was captain of the tennis team in the spring. He never sneaked into the village to see a film. He no longer hitchhiked places on free afternoons. He went to Communion on Sundays, and he maintained a B average.

All thoughts were on college. Constant knew that his father expected him to go to Yale or Harvard. No Holy Cross, no Villanova, no Fordham for the Bradley boy. It had to be the Ivy League to please Gerald.

That Christmas, the Somersets gave Weegie a dance in their house next to the Bradleys' house in Scarborough Hill. Her photograph appeared in the newspaper, and she was called the most popular debutante of the season. Although Constant exhibited indifference, I knew he felt a pang of disappointment when he heard that invitations to Weegie's party were in the mail and he had not received one. None of the Bradleys was invited. The snub infuriated Gerald Bradley.

"I saved Leverett Somerset's ass when he was in financial trouble," he said to Grace.

Grace cringed as she always cringed when Gerald used profanity. "I think it must have something to do with Constant and Weegie," said Grace. "They don't see each other anymore. It's just as well, really. He's too young to get serious. And she's not a Catholic."

"My children should be at that party, and I'm going to find out why they weren't asked," said Gerald.

"How?"

"I'm going to call Leverett."

"No, Gerald. Don't," said Grace. "I think something must have happened, don't you? With Constant and Weegie?"

"What do you mean?"

"I don't know what I mean, but Mary Pat said that night last summer at the beach club dance, Weegie ran out crying."

"Hmmm. So they had a fight. So what? That's no excuse for us to be humiliated by being the only people at the club not invited to the debut."

"Why don't we take the children to Florida for Christmas, Gerald. We'll stay at the Breakers. Let's not be here when the party happens."

Constant, to everyone's surprise, chose not to go to Florida. He was concentrating on his studies. Getting into Yale meant everything to him. I was summoned to come and keep him company over the holidays. On the train going up to the country, I spotted a familiar figure. There, in her mink coat, was Mrs. Steers, Sally Steers, looking too glamorous by far for the local train, reading a house magazine.

"Mrs. Steers?"

"Yes?" She looked up.

"I'm Harrison Burns."

"Yes?" She did not recognize me. I blushed in embarrassment. I had in those days the kind of looks that people tended to forget.

"I met you in Watch Hill. At the Gerald Bradleys'."

"Oh, yes, of course. I do remember. You're the friend of Constant."

"Yes."

"Who writes?"

"Hopes to."

"Yes. Sit down, for heaven's sake. You never know who's going to plop down next to you. I'd rather it be you."

"You're not the sort of person I expected to see on the morning local out of Grand Central."

"I'm doing a house in Fairfield—the Hardwicks, do you know them? —and my driver's sick, and I can't drive. Such a nuisance. How are the Bradleys? Have you seen them? I don't see them so much now that the house is finished. I finally weeded out all that reproduction Chippendale and got them to buy the real thing. Next Gerald will be into art. You mark my words. Rich people always atone for their sins with art."

"But he already has art," I said defensively.

"A very bad Renoir, too sappy for words, but Grace likes it, naturally, and that head of Christ by Zurbarán with the crown of thorns and the blood coming down the face. Puhleeze. I had to beg him on bended knee not to hang it in the living room."

I had heard she was not so much in evidence anymore. I assumed the ardor had cooled. "I'm on my way there now. But they're in Florida for the holidays. Except Constant. I'm going over to keep him company for a few days."

41

She looked at me. "You're very fond of Constant, aren't you?"

"We are friends, yes."

"I felt it was somewhat more."

"More?"

"It happens in England, that sort of thing, in those public schools they have. You know, Eton, Harrow, those schools. Mad crushes, that sort of thing."

There was nothing accusatory or mocking in her voice or attitude, but what she was suggesting was a matter about which I was extremely sensitive. I was not then adept at deflecting conversation from one subject to another, so I remained silent, only looking at her quizzically, as if I did not understand her. She, unperturbed, seemed not to demand an answer.

"When is Fairfield?" she called out to the conductor.

"Next stop," he said.

She took a compact out of her bag, opened it, and looked at herself in the mirror. "Do I need lipstick?"

"No."

She began to brush her hair. "Poor Grace," she said.

"Why do you say 'poor Grace'?" I asked.

"It's that Catholic thing. Their wives are for children, not for pleasure. Keep them preggers, and play. I'm surprised she stopped when she did. Of course, there were those miscarriages. Three, I think. Or maybe four. Her little saints in heaven, she calls them. She tries so hard to please Gerald. All that ghastly singing of Irish songs around the piano after dinner. I thought if I had to listen to 'I'll Take You Home Again, Kathleen' one more time, I'd go mad. That quivering contralto. She buys all her clothes in Paris, spends an absolute fortune, and still looks wrong. She didn't even know how to lay the table properly, and all that sort of thing, when I started doing the house for them."

I was stunned to hear a mistress discuss a wife in such a manner.

"You were there that day, weren't you, by the pool, when Gerald and I were talking? I saw you, reading your book, but I knew you were listening. Gerald didn't see you. I suppose someday you will write a book about them all. I mean, they are fascinating, in their Irish way. Oh, so keen to belong. But watch them. Twenty years from now. Or less. Fifteen. Ten even. Everyone in the country will know who they are. Mark my words. Tell me your name once more. I'm hopeless with names."

"Harrison. Harrison Burns."

"Oh, of course. Harrison."

"I won't," I said.

"You won't what?"

"Write about them. They are my friends."

"You're a damn fool if you don't. What is writing but putting down what you see, what you know? You are having a bird's-eye view of a dynasty in formation. Remember it all. Keep a journal. It will all come in handy. I wish I could write. Give me a call when the time comes. I could fill you in on a thing or two."

I looked at her, stunned by what I thought of as her disloyalty to the family that was paying my tuition at Milford and had taken me into their bosom, but I also did not want her to stop talking. I was caught between wanting to know everything there was to know about the Bradleys and hesitating to learn it from a discarded mistress. She seemed not to notice either my shock or my disapproval as she continued.

"They discuss only their triumphs. You must have noticed that by now. Poor Agnes. The retarded one. Hidden away. Unmentioned. As if she had done something wrong. And Gerald Junior, or Jerry, as they call him. Do you know about the accident?"

"I know he was in an accident."

"He was driving eighty miles an hour. And being blown at the same time. You didn't know that? Your precious Constant didn't tell you that? See what I mean?"

"I didn't know that. What happened to the girl?"

"Broke her neck."

"Where is she?"

"In a wheelchair somewhere. She's all taken care of, of course. Financially, I mean. Gerald's awfully good about that. Paying off for their carelessnesses."

I wanted to ask her questions, about Agnes, about Jerry, but I didn't want to interrupt her.

"Constant is the one, of course, in whom all hopes are centered. Gerald adores him. Grace, too."

"Why do you think all hopes are centered on Constant?" I asked.

"Jerry had that frightful accident and is a cripple. Smart, of course, but no public career now. Desmond married a maid for ten minutes and then became a doctor. Sandro might run for something, governor or state senate. Maureen could amount to something. She's the smart-

43

est, but she's also a girl, and Gerald is not that advanced in his think-ing. The other girls will all marry well—they'd better, if they know what's good for them—but it's Constant who's going to be president of this country if Gerald has his way."

"Good God," I said. I had no idea that Gerald Bradley's aspirations were that high.

"But your friend drinks too much."

"Oh, that. You mean that night at the club? You heard about that? With Weegie?"

"Yes, I heard about that. But more. I have been married to two alcoholics. I recognize the signs. It's the way he drinks. Notice it. He never sips. He gulps. One night at the club, he was always tapping his glass for the waiter to bring him another. Couldn't wait. Couldn't keep focused on the conversation until he had another full glass in front of him."

"He was just having a good time."

She took no notice of my defense of him. "One day he will be a drunk. You mark my words. Too much is expected of him. And all Gerald's careful planning will go up in smoke."

The train came into the Fairfield station. Her mind reverted to the career part of her life. She gathered her things. She put on her dark glasses. She waved out the window to a chauffeur standing on the platform. "That's the Hardwicks' chauffeur," she said. We said good-bye. She got off.

Kitt was at the station to meet me, not Constant. I almost didn't recog-nize her. The braces on her teeth had been replaced by a retainer. She no longer dressed like a child. She was becoming pretty. I noticed for the first time how much she resembled Constant. As always, she talked nonstop.

"I hope you're not disappointed it's me here to meet you and not Constant. He's in one of his moods," explained Kitt. She took off her glasses and placed them on top of her head. It was a gesture she had copied from Maureen. "Friday night's Weegie Somerset's coming-out party, and he wasn't invited. None of us were. Not that I would have been anyway, I'm too young. If you could have heard my father on the subject! That's why they went to Florida, to get out of town. They're at the Breakers. You've probably heard that. I'm so glad you could come. Constant couldn't bear to be alone. There was only

Fatty and Sis Malloy for company, and that wouldn't do at all for Constant. At least he can bring you to the club. He brought Fatty to the club once, and he knew all the bartenders and waitresses from Bog Meadow, and shook hands with them. You can imagine how that went over."

"What about you?"

"I'm off to Florida tomorrow. I've been to a sweet sixteen party in Spring Lake. One of the girls at the convent had it."

We walked outside. Constant's Porsche was double-parked. There was a ticket on the window.

"Oh, hell," she said. She took the ticket off the windshield and tore it in half.

"You shouldn't do that," I said.

"My father has a man, Mr. Fuselli, Johnny Fuselli—you met him in Watch Hill, the one Maureen thought was handsome in a cheap sort of way? He takes care of tickets and things like that for us."

"A gangster type in a red car?"

"The very one."

"Won't he need the pieces?"

"Not Johnny. That's what he gets paid for. Hop in."

"Are you old enough to drive?"

"No, but I will be soon."

"Shouldn't I drive?"

"Not on your life. This is Constant's new Porsche, and it's my only chance to drive it. Now, where the hell are my glasses?" She looked in her bag.

"They're on top of your head," I said.

She roared with laughter. "I'd love a cigarette," she said.

For a novice Kitt handled the car very well. "Look at that creep, will you?" she said, honking the horn at a slow driver. She cleared the busy section by the railroad station and we headed west out Asylum Avenue for the drive toward Scarborough Hill. Kitt never stopped talking.

"Doesn't your family ever want you?" she asked.

"My family is one maiden aunt who talks about missionaries all the time," I replied.

"Are you Constant's ott?" asked Kitt.

"I don't know what an ott is," I answered.

"Someone who's always available."

I blushed. I was always available.

45

"My mother has otts. They're people who are useful and do convenient things. Mother has otts who write the place cards for her but who aren't asked to the party and pretend they don't mind. She's a godmother to their children but she wouldn't dream of having them be godmother to any of hers. It's an unequal friendship."

"Are you asking me if that's what I am?"

"Yes."

"I hope not."

"Don't let him boss you around. He has the tendency to boss."

"Don't go too fast."

"I will if I want to."

She increased her speed as we got closer to the tree-lined streets of the west side of the city.

"Great excitement. Sandro's running for Congress. I bet you didn't know that."

"I didn't."

"Congressman Lopez died in office, and Sandro's going to run for the rest of his term."

"Isn't he awfully young?"

"He's almost twenty-six. Pa doesn't think he's too young. Pa says he has charisma."

"Is he qualified?"

"The Catholics will all vote for him. Pa will see to that."

"That's not an answer."

"Winning is all that matters. Family motto. We all used to think my brother Desmond would be the first to run for office. After Jerry's accident. But he wanted to be a doctor, and then he married a maid. Did you know that?"

"I think I may have heard something about it."

"Oh, the to-do over that. Ma's tears. Pa's rage. The cardinal placating. Poor Rosleen. She didn't know what hit her. She was quite pretty, but there was no way she would do at all. My father said to Desmond, 'You sleep with girls like that. You don't marry them.' Poor Bridey, the cook, I felt so sorry for Bridey. She was Bridey's second cousin, or in-law, or something, I can never keep all Bridey's relations straight. We're all meant to marry well, you know. Constant is always supposed to bring home boys from Milford for Mary Pat and me to meet, but you're the only one he's ever brought."

I couldn't help but feel that I was somewhat of a disappointment in that department.

"Of course, all my friends at the convent are mad about Constant. But whenever I bring any of them home, he doesn't even look at them. He just likes girls like Weegie Somerset. You wait and see. He'll marry a Protestant when the time comes. Oh, and the to-do about that when it happens, if he doesn't marry a Catholic."

"I've never heard a family talk about being Catholic as much as your family does."

"But you're Catholic."

"But we didn't talk about it all the time. I think you're driving too fast."

"I can't imagine what happened between Constant and Weegie. Something. I mean, they didn't invite any of us to the party, and Mr. Somerset owes my father a lot of money. My father will get even with Mr. Somerset. My father always gets even. They say that's Irish, getting even."

"Slow down, Kitt."

"Oh. You're right. There's a policeman behind us. Red light flashing."

"You'd better pull over. What about the license?"

"Just keep quiet and let me do the talking."

It was an un-Christmas Christmas in the Bradley mansion. There were wreaths on the doors and electrified candles in the windows, but there was no Christmas tree. The house, usually bustling with noise from so many occupants, seemed eerily quiet. Constant's presents had been left on the bench in the hall beneath the stairway, as well as two for me, one from Grace and one from Kitt, but he exhibited no curiosity about them in the days before Christmas. By then I was used to his spoiledness, his sullenness, his occasional bad temper, especially when he drank, but I was still in his thrall, and overlooked such deficiencies, as they were rarely directed toward me. When he wasn't the absolute center of attention, he was restless. He whistled little tunes under his breath, or paced, or tapped his foot incessantly, or snapped his fingers, or cracked his knuckles, or beat time to a song on the radio.

"You're not relaxing to be around," Kitt said to him before she left for Florida.

Constant looked up, surprised, as if she had discovered something secret in him.

Fearing she had upset him, she mocked herself. "You lack my inner peace," she said, crossing her arms in front of her and assuming an expression of nunlike humility.

"Fuck you," he replied, good-naturedly. They both roared with laughter.

Bridey, the cook, wanted to serve us our meals in the dining room, with candles and flowers, but Constant said he preferred to eat on tables in front of the television set. A few times Fatty and Sis Malloy came by for lunch or dinner. Their lives were pointedly different from the Bradley kind of life, and they seemed pathetically grateful to be included in anything at the grand house in Scarborough Hill. Fatty worshiped Constant and seemed not to mind when Constant teased him unmercifully.

"I ran for the car as soon as I got your call," said Fatty.

"The last time Fatty ran was when he missed the ice cream truck," Constant said to me.

"I think you hurt his feelings," I said later to Constant.

"Fatty's used to having his feelings hurt. He knows we all love him," said Constant.

On the day of the night of Weegie Somerset's dance, catering and florist trucks began arriving early in the morning at the great gray stone house next door to the Bradleys'. Delivery men carrying armloads of pink roses scurried into the house. Several hundred gold ballroom chairs were stacked in the driveway in front of the house while the trucks were being unloaded. Constant stood in the window of his parents' bedroom and watched the activity. In the late morning he had a long talk on the telephone with his father in Florida. When he came back into the room, he said, "Come on. You've got work to do."

"What?"

"Every year at Christmas my father gives turkeys and food packages and oranges to the poor of the city, and shoes to the little children. They traipse us down there every year, my brothers and sisters and me, all dressed up in our best clothes, and we hand out the stuff, and my father makes a speech, and my mother sits there in her mink coat like the queen, and the priests thank everybody. This year, my father says, I have to do it, and he says that you have to write me something to say."

"Like what? I wouldn't know what to write," I said.

"Yes, you do. Christmas and peace and giving and loving and family, and all that shit. My father said anything about family always gets them. Work up a tear. Nothing long. Just a few paragraphs. You know how to do it. Oh, and get something in about Sandro running for Congress.''

"Shouldn't he be here, preparing for his campaign?''

"He will be. After Florida. Then full steam ahead. Pa will call in the heavy artillery. They all owe him favors, all those politicians.''

Fatty and Sis went with us to the auditorium of the Malachy Bradley School, named for Gerald's father, in the section of the city called Bog Meadow. There were hundreds of bags of groceries, and turkeys, and crates of oranges, and boxes of children's shoes. Fatty and Sis and the priests and nuns lined up the people and passed out the goods, but most of them wanted to receive their packages and their turkeys directly from the handsome young Bradley boy, so smartly dressed in his blue blazer and gray flannels from J. Press. A photographer appeared, and a cameraman from the local television station.

"I see a resemblance in you to your grandfather,'' an old woman said to him. "I'm Agnes O'Toole. Your grandfather Malloy, God rest his soul, lived right near us over on Front Street when they came over from the old country. God bless you, Constant. We're grateful to your wonderful family.''

"Thank you, Mrs. O'Toole,'' said Constant, smiling and friendly. At times like that, he was condescendingly good-natured to his inferiors, and they, in turn, were enchanted. "Certainly, I've heard my mother speak of you and your family.''

"My late husband, Francis X. Moriarity, worked for your grandfather Bradley in the butcher shop over on Sisson Avenue,'' said another old woman. "A fine man he was.''

"Thank you, Mrs. Moriarity. My grandfather always had a great affection for that shop on Sisson Avenue,'' said Constant.

"God bless you, Constant,'' said person after person, receiving his packages.

Constant basked in their praise and admiration. He became, if anything, handsomer, and more loquacious than he had been since the Labor Day dance at the beach club in Watch Hill. His spoiledness, his sullenness, vanished. All morose thoughts of Weegie Somerset evaporated, at least for then. He found a personal thing to say to each person to whom he spoke.

"What's your name?'' he asked a little girl.

"Maureen,'' she answered.

"Why, I have a sister called Maureen,'' he said, picking her up and talking to her for several minutes. He faced her around so that the cameraman and photographer could get her picture. "Fatty, give me one of those Hershey bars for young Miss Maureen here."

When he stepped to the microphone, he was in full possession of himself. "I am so sorry my father and mother could not be here this year to greet each of you personally, but they have had to forgo a Connecticut Christmas this year. Business has taken my father to Florida. I talked to him this morning, and he said to tell everybody he will be back here handing out the turkeys himself next Christmas. My mother, too, sends her love and best wishes to all. Our parents are bringing us up to play some part, to get involved in politics and public service. My brother Sandro, as you probably know, is running for the rest of the late Congressman Lopez's term. And we expect you all at the polls."

The crowd, all clutching their bags, listened raptly as Constant spoke. He spoke with an easy familiarity, as if he were standing at the dinner table in the Bradley dining room, giving a toast. "I remember once my mother went to confession to Cardinal Sullivan. She couldn't think of any sins that she had committed since her last confession, so she made some up. My father asked her later what sins she had made up. She said she was too embarrassed to tell him, they were so awful. 'I want to know,' insisted my father. She said she'd whisper them to him. He listened. 'You call those sins?' he said." The crowd roared. Then he became serious.

"We are a close family. My grandfathers, Malachy Bradley and Kevin Malloy, both lived here in the Bog Meadow section of the city and it remains close to all of us in our family. My father will be setting up scholarships here at the Malachy Bradley School for outstanding students to get college educations. In closing, I wish you a happy Christmas and a gift of loyal family relationships."

Later, driving west to Scarborough Hill in his Porsche, he was exhilarated with his performance. "Did you see the way they kept coming up to me?" he asked. "All those old ladies who said they knew my grandfathers?"

"It was masterful with the little girl, little Maureen, Constant," said Fatty Malloy. "It was like you were running for office."

Even Sis Malloy, or Prim Sis, as Mary Pat and Kitt called their cousin behind her back, was excited by the afternoon. She knew who all the people were, and tried to explain to Constant their place in the early lives of his grandparents, but Constant's interest was in their reaction to him rather than in who they were. "Mrs. O'Toole was thrilled you said your mother talked about her family," said Sis Malloy.

"I just made that up," said Constant. "I never even heard of the O'Tooles before."

"Oh, Constant, you're such a tease," said Sis.

"You're the one who should be running for office, Constant."

"I will be one of these days."

"When you run for whatever you're going to run for, Constant, I want to be your campaign manager," said Fatty.

"And this guy's going to be my speech writer," said Constant, pointing his thumb in my direction. "It was a great touch to work in the cardinal, Harry. They ate that up. How did you know that story?"

"You told me once at school."

"Do you remember everything I say?"

I did remember everything he said, but I didn't answer. "How did the photographer and cameraman know to come?" I asked.

"Oh, Pa, I'm sure," answered Constant. "He's a friend of Tom O'Gorman at the paper."

"From Florida he arranged it?"

"Oh, sure."

That evening we watched Constant on the local news at six, holding Miss Maureen, and the newscaster gave a glowing description of the bounty of the Bradley family every Christmas to the poor of the city.

"I wonder if they're watching next door," I said.

By eight o'clock, cars were beginning to line both sides of the street in front of the Bradley and Somerset houses. The shouts of parking boys could be heard. Constant's elation of the afternoon vanished. It had been snowing for several hours; the trees outside the windows were shining white. We had dinner in the library, looked at television, and never mentioned the lavish affair that was going on in the next house. We drank two bottles of Mr. Bradley's best red wine.

I examined one of the bottles. I read the label. I saw the words *Mouton Rothschild* and the year *1955*. I knew nothing about wine, but I knew enough to be impressed.

"Life is too short to drink cheap wine," said Constant, watching my reaction. He disappeared into the kitchen and returned with a third bottle and a corkscrew. Coming into the room, he tripped on a rug.

"Don't you think maybe you've had enough, Constant," I said.

"Mind your own goddamn business," he said sharply. His sapphirelike eyes flashed dangerously. "Don't forget you're only a guest in this house. I'll drink what I want."

I blushed at the brush-off. It was true. I was only a guest, the kind of guest who could not reciprocate the generosity of the host. I had never asked him to Ansonia, or to meet Aunt Gert, and I never would. We sat for a few minutes in silence. Then I went upstairs to my room. I knew I would leave in the morning.

Several minutes later the door opened and Constant stood there. "I didn't mean that, Harry," he said. "Don't get hurt, or start feeling inferior. I've already got enough to deal with. Friends?"

I nodded. "Friends," I said.

"We look on you as practically a member of the family," he said. "That's what Ma says anyway, and Kitt and I concur."

"You can be so nice, Constant, and then again, you can be so awful."

He nodded in agreement. "I'm going out for a little air," he said around midnight.

"Pretty cold out there," I said.

"Need to clear the head," he replied.

"Want company?"

"No."

Outside, he walked down the long driveway to the street. Some older people were leaving the party early and stood in a cluster under the portico in front of the Somerset house while the parking boys ran to get their cars. Constant retraced his steps before they saw him and came back up the drive. He walked past the front door and went around to the rear of the house, trudging across the deep lawn through the snow to the tennis court at the back of the property. A half hour later, when he had not returned, I walked through the snow across the lawn to the tennis court. He was sitting on a bench by the side of the court, listening to the dance music coming from the house next door. His head was in his hands.

3

THE SITUATION in Scarborough Hill between the Bradley house and the Somerset house did not improve. Just as Kitt predicted at Christmas, Gerald Bradley got even with Leverett Somerset, in the way that he knew how to get even best. Financially. He invited him to lunch at The Country Club. He never mentioned the dance from which his family had been excluded, as if it were a matter of no consequence to him. Instead, in the most businesslike manner, he told him of a surefire deal in Texas real estate, in which a great deal of money could be made quickly, the kind of rapid turnover by means of which Gerald had built his own fortune and at which he was known to be so skilled. The prospect of quick money was irresistible to Leverett, as Gerald knew it would be. The once-solid Somerset fortune had dwindled and disappeared over the years.

Each man put up an equal amount. Gerald could afford to lose on the deal. Leverett could not; he borrowed to raise his share. Then Gerald, who knew the Texans, quietly pulled out of the deal, his money intact, without telling his neighbor, and Leverett Somerset, several months later, suffered a total loss of his investment. Kitt, the chatterbox, told me this at Easter. Things that appalled me later did not appall me then. So fascinated was I with that family that even what Gerald did to Leverett Somerset did not seem wrong to me. I took it as a sign of Gerald's financial superiority.

One day Maureen Bradley and a young man named Freddy Tierney, whom Constant had heard about from Kitt, came by the school in Maureen's green Jaguar to see the plans for the new library that Gerald was building. Dr. Shugrue, the recipient of the Bradley largess, interrupted his overcrowded schedule to show Maureen the hilltop site where the groundbreaking had already taken place and then took her

53

into the entranceway of the dining hall to go over the drawings of the new building. It was to be of red brick, surrounded by maples and hemlocks. "Lovely," she said over and over, as she made suggestions for changes. She thought the windows on either side of the front doors should be larger. The architect, Louis I. Kahn, who had also designed a much heralded library at Phillips Exeter Academy several years before, happened to be there at Milford that day. He did not agree with her suggestions, but Maureen insisted. There was a bossy side to her. "My father thought so, too," she said, and she smiled sweetly, implying, without stating, that her father was paying the bills, and it had better be done her way. After a look from Dr. Shugrue, the architect, courtly, courteous, complied. He knew there weren't many Mr. Gerald Bradleys around to foot such enormous bills.

"You see?" said Maureen. Her point had been proven. She looked to Freddy Tierney, as if wanting him to be proud of her for her expertise, and he was.

With the headmaster's permission, she took Constant and me to lunch at an inn in the village. She and Freddy sat very close together and giggled and laughed through lunch. When Freddy excused himself to use the facilities, as he called it, Constant immediately said, "All right. Give."

They had met in Florida at the Breakers over Christmas. He was from Lake Forest. His family was in the meat-packing business in Chicago. He had graduated from Princeton and was working in the family business.

"Isn't he divine?" asked Maureen.

"Bucks?" asked Constant.

"Big bucks," said Maureen.

"Catholic?"

"His sister was in my class at Sacred Heart. His father's a Knight of Malta."

"All the right credentials."

Maureen whispered to Constant, "You promise you won't tell?"

"Promise," said Constant. He crossed his heart.

"We're engaged."

"Well, well, well, this calls for champagne," said Constant.

"It certainly does not. You're not out of trouble yet, although Shugrue says you're trying hard. But Freddy wanted to meet you before we told the family, as you were the only one not at the Breakers over Christmas."

54

* * *

I believed myself to be as happy in those days as I had ever been. But then, suddenly, it came to an end. Constant and I had taken our college boards, and we were anxiously waiting to hear if we had been accepted at Yale. I had applied for a scholarship.

I went back to Ansonia for Easter vacation. Aunt Gert wanted me to go with her on a driving trip to Halifax—there were priests there she had raised money for—but I didn't really want to. Then a letter came from Constant.

Dear Harry. Tried to call. No answer. Leave Aunt Gert to her missionaries, for God's sake, and get your butt over here to keep me company. I need someone to talk to. You can tell me the plots of all those books you read, and whether they're good or not, and I'll pretend I've read them too. Like The Great Gatsby *you're always talking about. Shugrue will be impressed. I'm tired of being a cheap success at bad parties. "Oh, isn't Constant marvelous?" "Isn't he the funniest thing ever?" "Isn't he handsome?" You know it's all crap. I don't have to pretend in front of you. Let me know what train you'll be on. Sandro won the runoff. He's off to Washington. Pa's ecstatic.*

Constant

P.S. Maureen's engaged to Freddy. Did you see the announcement in the New York Times *Sunday? Summer wedding. Ma's over the moon.*

Of course I went. Halifax could wait. They were all home that Easter. The curve of the staircase in the hall was filled with dozens of lily plants. Maureen and Mary Pat and Kitt did a great deal of shopping for new suits and Easter hats, although they wore black lace mantillas to church. The papers were full of Sandro's victory in the congressional runoff and Maureen's engagement to Frederick Tierney of the Chicago meat-packing family.

At The Country Club, Gerald walked with a new swagger as he herded his family and their guests in to dinner. We went through the religious rituals of Holy Week. Holy Thursday. Good Friday. Holy Saturday. Easter Sunday. Cardinal Sullivan came to Scarborough Hill for Easter lunch. All the family was there, with the new additions of Freddy and me. The lunch was Bridey Gafferty's Easter specialty. Roast lamb. Browned potatoes. Mint jelly. And chocolate soufflé.

That day during lunch, Leverett Somerset came to the door of the Bradley house. One of the maids answered the door. The gentleman, as the maid referred to him later, said that he wished to speak to Mr. Bradley.

"The Bradleys are at Easter dinner," she said.

"I would like to speak to Mr. Bradley. *Now,*" said Mr. Somerset. There was a commanding tone reinforced by several drinks that sent the maid, Colleen, scurrying on her mission, leaving the distinguished neighbor outside the front door, like a tradesperson.

Colleen came into the dining room. Constant was on his feet, holding a wineglass, in the middle of a toast to Freddy Tierney. Grace with a lifted hand cautioned for the maid not to interrupt. "We've checked him out, of course, using all of Pa's Chicago connections, and you all know about Pa's Chicago connections," said Constant. The family laughed. "And he passes muster. He is very midwestern, from good people, substantial, which means money, and he is conscious of all the amenities. Ma likes him because he reads his missal at Mass. Pa likes him because he reads the financial pages first. And Maureen likes him because, well—"

"Now, wait a minute, before you get too graphic, Constant, about what Maureen likes about Freddy. Remember, we have a cardinal here," called down Desmond from his end of the table.

Cardinal Sullivan roared with laughter, and the family chimed in.

"Ignore my sons, Cardinal," said Grace. "What is it, Colleen?"

The maid murmured something into Gerald Bradley's ear, but he ignored her secrecy. "Speak up, speak up," he said.

"There's a gentleman called Mr. Somerset at the front door," said Colleen.

"Tell him we're at lunch."

"I did, sir. He insisted on seeing you."

"Ask him to wait," said Gerald.

"I think he's been drinking, sir," said Colleen.

Gerald threw his napkin on the table, pushed back his chair, and went to the dining room doors. There was an indication of a strut in his walk. He liked confrontations. He was good at them.

"Gerald," called Grace after him.

Gerald glanced back at his wife. With her eyes she indicated to him

56

the cardinal, seated to her right. "Perhaps Mr. Somerset would like to have coffee with us in the library after lunch," she said. "I'm sure Cardinal would like to meet Leverett Somerset." She proceeded to fill in Cardinal Sullivan on the stately background of Leverett Somerset.

"Give him hell, Pa," called out Kitt.

"Kitt!" cried Grace in an astonished voice. "You simply cannot speak like that, especially in front of Cardinal. You must forgive her, Cardinal."

"Mr. Somerset owes Pa money, so naturally he hates Pa, but Pa says that always happens in business when you bail someone out," said Kitt.

"*Shhh*," said Jerry. "I want to hear this."

In the front hall, Gerald walked to the door that Colleen had left ajar. He did not ask his neighbor into the house. "You've come at an inconvenient time, Leverett. I happen to be entertaining Cardinal Sullivan," said Gerald.

Leverett Somerset, in financial distress, was in no mood to pay deference to a cardinal.

"What have you done to me, Gerald?"

"Done?"

"Oh, please. No games. You pulled your money out of the deal. You did not tell me. It is indefensible," cried Leverett Somerset. His voice, with its classic old-family Yankee accent, traveled through the rooms.

"Why did you humiliate my son by not inviting him to Weegie's party?" demanded Gerald.

Somerset looked at him, stunned. "Because of a party invitation, you did this? To get even? Is that it?"

"Getting even is a code of behavior I live by," replied Gerald.

"That would be your sort of code of behavior, yes," said Somerset. The contempt in his voice was unmistakable.

"Do I detect a superior tone in your patrician voice?" asked Gerald, unperturbed, in charge of the scene. Inside, the Bradley offspring enjoyed hearing the exchange. There was muffled laughter in the room. Leverett Somerset was no friend of their family, and their father was putting the Yankee snob in his place. Only Constant seemed uncomfortable, but his distress was unvoiced and went unnoticed.

"Are you aware of what your son did to my daughter?"

Gerald shrugged. "A spat. A boyfriend-girlfriend spat. It happens. What is the big deal? They're only kids."

"Do you want to know why my daughter would not have your son to her party? Or want to ever see him again in her life?"

"That is what I want to know."

"Because your son assaulted my daughter."

"Assaulted?"

"You heard me. Assaulted."

Gerald stepped outside under the porte cochere and closed the front door behind him. At the same moment, following a signal from his mother, Desmond got up from the table and closed the dining room doors. The rest of the conversation was not heard inside. Constant, appalled by the charge, told me later. Words were exchanged. Hate words.

"He grabbed her. He twisted her arm. He tried to force himself on her. He would have raped her if she had not started to scream. He put his hand over her mouth. He frightened her."

"I do not believe that."

"Believe it. And when you stand at your Communion rail next time to take Communion from your precious cardinal, thank your God I didn't bring charges against your son. Weegie wanted to go to the police that night in Watch Hill. Her mother said to her, and I concurred, that people like us do not go to the police in such a circumstance. Nothing comes of it but bad publicity and a ruined reputation. The problem with that kind of thinking is that people like your son get away with assault and are only punished by not being invited to a dance."

"Get out of my house, Leverett."

"I'm not in your house, Gerald. I'm outside your front door."

"Get off my property."

Later, Constant related to me this conversation he had with his father after Leverett Somerset departed.

"Is this true, Constant?"

"Not true, Pa."

"You swear?"

"I swear."

"What happened?"

"She led me on."

"And then backed off?"

"Yes."

"That trick."

"Yes."

"Did you hurt her?"

"Only by some things I said. Nothing physical. I swear to you, Pa."

"Thank you, Constant. I believe you."

He began to go.

"You know, Constant, girls like the Somerset girl, and girls like the girls your sisters bring home from the convent, they're for kissing, nothing more, especially at your age. Do you understand what I'm saying?"

"Yes, Pa."

"And stay away from the maids. At least maids in this house. We've already had that experience with Desmond and that tramp Rosleen, trying to nuzzle her way into the family."

"Yes, Pa."

"I'll get Johnny Fuselli to put you in touch with some of the other kind of girls. It'll be good experience for you. That way, there's no problems. No misunderstandings. That's all this is with Weegie Somerset. A misunderstanding. Aren't I right?"

"Exactly, Pa."

Jerry suggested a game of softball. Before his accident, he had been the best athlete in the family, and he still enjoyed games, even though he could no longer play. In the family, there was never any hesitation when games were suggested. They all loved to play, both the boys and the girls. Sides were chosen.

"I'll ump," said Jerry.

"Be careful of my daffodils," called out Grace.

"Who has the bat?"

"Everything's in the mud room. Bat, balls, gloves," said Fatty Malloy. The Malloys always knew where everything was in the Bradleys' house. The mud room was stocked for all sporting occasions, enough for family and guests. There were tennis rackets, and dozens of cans of tennis balls, and golf clubs, and dozens of packages of golf balls, and riding hats, and riding crops, and croquet sets, and swimming pool gear, and gloves and softballs and bats.

"I'll get very angry if my daffodils are trampled," said Grace.

"Oh, Mother," said Kitt and Mary Pat.

I hated to play with them. They were all too good. And they were all too merciless if you missed a ball, or made a mistake of any kind, or, God forbid, struck out.

"That was your fault, Harrison," called out Jerry. "You let that ball go right through your legs."

"Sorry," I called back.

"Hit it to Harrison," yelled out Sandro when Kitt was at bat, meaning that I would be sure to miss it.

She did. She hit it hard, straight out to second base. I caught it. I threw it to Constant on first. She was out. Cheers from Constant and Mary Pat.

"You would have to catch it the one time I'm up," said Kitt.

"Sorry," I said.

"You can't be sorry about everything," she said.

Constant was the star of the afternoon, of course. He hit a homer with Fatty and Mary Pat on base. He loped around the bases, joyously, savoring his moment. At home plate, he picked up the bat and swung it over his head. "And I did it with a cracked bat," he said. Then, with both hands, he sent the bat flying high into the trees over onto the wooded area of the Somerset property. Kitt and I ran to retrieve it. "It has to be here somewhere," she said. We couldn't find it. The wooded growth between the two estates was heavy and dark.

"What's the big deal? There's about ten more bats in the mud room. Get another one, Fatty," said Jerry.

Then Gerald called down from the terrace, "The Wadsworths are complaining that you're making too much noise and spoiling their Easter egg hunt."

"Screw the Wadsworths," said Jerry.

There were cheers and roars of laughter.

"How are my daffodils?" called out Grace.

"Trampled," yelled back Kitt. "Every one dead or maimed."

The family made their way back across the lawn, past the tennis court and the pool, up to the terrace of the house. It was time for Sandro to leave for Washington. Already the family referred to him as the Congressman. Charlie, the chauffeur, was standing by to drive him to the airport. Maureen and Freddy Tierney were flying to Chicago to spend time with Freddy's family. Desmond was on duty at the hospital. Farewells were being said.

Through the woods a young girl appeared.

"Hi," she called out. Only Constant and I were still near the softball area, collecting gloves.

"Hi, yourself," said Constant.

"Now, don't blame me for this, I'm only the messenger, but the Wadsworths sent me over to ask you to quiet down a little," she said.

"We're spoiling their Easter egg hunt. We already got the message by telephone. Look, we even stopped playing," said Constant.

"Well, that's my chore, completed." She turned to go.

"What's your name?" asked Constant.

"Winifred Utley."

"Winifred Utley." He repeated her name. "I've never met a Winifred before."

"Indirectly you have."

"How?"

"My name means nothing to you?"

"You have a very pretty face, Miss Winifred, but your name means nothing to me."

"I know who you are. All the girls at my school know who you are. You're famous. My mother once picked you up when you were hitchhiking and drove you home from Milford," said Winifred.

"Oh, my God, of course," said Constant. "Do you remember, Harry? Mrs. Utley? In a blue Buick. She went twenty miles out of her way for us. Brought us right here to the house."

"I remember Mrs. Utley," I said. I remembered Constant imitating her speaking voice as soon as we were out of the car.

"My friend Harrison Burns here was in the car that day. Rather ill-fated, that jaunt, as a matter of fact," said Constant.

"How?"

"I got kicked out of Milford after that."

"But I thought you were graduating from there in June."

"I am. My father is giving a new library, and I got back in. It's how bad rich kids get through life."

"I think you're a big tease, Constant."

"I think you're adorable, Winifred." He looked into her fresh lively face, the face of a fifteen-year-old, a face that depended for its prettiness on her youth. It would probably never be so pretty as right then. "What are you doing here?"

"I just told you that. The Wadsworths sent me over."

"I meant, what are you doing here in the city?"

"We've moved here. My father is the new president of Veblen Aircraft."

"Where do you live?"

"Right near you. We're on Varden Lane, behind the Somersets' house."

"I know that house. The Prindevilles used to live there."

"That's it."

"There's a shortcut behind our tennis court."

"I know."

"Perhaps a midnight rendezvous is in order."

"On the shortcut, you mean?"

"Yes."

She giggled. "Not likely. I've heard of your reputation."

"From whom?"

"All the girls at school talk about Constant Bradley."

"Good or bad?"

"Depends on who's doing the talking." She giggled again and ran off through the woods the way she had come.

Two nights later Constant, Mary Pat, Kitt, and I had dinner at The Country Club. It was the girls' last night before they returned to the convent. Grace and Jerry attended a political fund-raiser in the downtown part of the city. Gerald had gone to New York "on business," as Constant always said with a wink when he thought his father was with one of his lady friends.

"He's got a new one. Eloise Brazen," he said.

"Certainly your father didn't tell you that," I said.

"No. Fuselli did."

"Who is she?"

"Career girl. My father likes career girls. Less problems extricating himself when it's over."

"No more Sally Steers?"

"Sally bit the dust."

Most of the talk at dinner was about Maureen's wedding. It was to be the first time that Mary Pat and Kitt would be bridesmaids.

Constant was in a good mood, entertaining his sisters, even teasing the waitress, who refused to serve him wine because he was underage.

"My father lets me have wine at home, Ursula," he said to the waitress. Constant always remembered the names of the help.

"Then you better go home to your father," she replied.

"Oh, these provincial places," said Constant.

"He's only teasing you," Kitt said to the waitress. "He's a big tease. He knows perfectly he can't have wine at the club."

There was an elaborate clearing of the throat from Mary Pat. "Uh, oh," she said, ominously.

"What?" asked Constant.

"Check out the door to the dining room."

The Somersets were arriving with their daughter. Mr. Carmody, who seated the members, led them to a table next to ours, but midway across the dining room Leverett Somerset, without halting Mr. Carmody, changed his direction and guided his wife and Weegie toward an empty table at the opposite end of the room.

"Sit here, Weegie," he said. He seated his daughter with her back to our table.

"Well, at least we're almost finished," said Kitt.

Constant excused himself from the table. "Be right back," he said. He walked out of the dining room and turned right toward the men's locker room. Beyond the locker room was a men's bar for drinks after tennis and golf. The bartender, Corky, was just closing up.

"Hi, Corky," said Constant.

"Mr. Bradley," he replied.

"Can you give me a drink, Corky?"

"You know I can't serve anybody under eighteen."

"Yeah, I know. But there's nobody around."

"Club rules. State law."

"Yeah, I know." He placed a ten-dollar bill on the bar. "Have you seen my cousin, Fatty Malloy?"

"I saw him at Father Curry's wake last week."

Constant placed a second ten-dollar bill on the bar and pushed the money toward the bartender. "Come on, Corky. Scotch."

"Vodka. It looks like water," said Corky.

"Pour in a little more."

"Take it in the locker room. Don't drink it in here. I need this job."

When Constant returned to the table ten minutes later, I could tell he had been drinking. He did not look in the direction of the Somersets' table. From another room came the sound of dance music.

"What's the music?" Constant asked the waitress.

"There's a junior club dance in the lounge," answered Ursula.

"How come you aren't there, girls?" he asked his sisters.

"No dates, and besides I'd rather be having dinner with you sixth-formers," said Kitt. "Much better than dancing cheek to cheek with

those pimply faces, like Billy Wadsworth. You have to promise on the
way out we pass through the lounge so that everybody can see we're
with you, even though you'll probably be mobbed on the dance floor
by all the preppy girls wanting to dance with you. Promise?"

"Okay."

We made an elaborate exit, led by Constant and Kitt, walking
through the lounge straight across the dance floor to the hallway. Several girls stared at Constant. One girl stopped in the middle of a dance
with Billy Wadsworth and said, "Hi, Constant."

"Oh, here we go," said Kitt.

"Oh, hi, Winifred," said Constant. "Do you know my sisters, Mary
Pat and Kitt? You know Harry. This is Winifred Utley. She's new in
town."

"I saw you in the dining room. I was hoping you'd come in, even
though this group is too young for you," said Winifred, walking away
from Billy.

"We're just passing through on our way out," said Constant.
"We're not dressed for the occasion."

"You wouldn't stay for just one dance? Imagine how popular I'll be
back at school if I can say I've danced with Constant Bradley," said
Winifred.

"That's entirely up to my sisters," said Constant.

"Oh, please tell him it's all right," said Winifred. "Just one dance.
Everyone says he's such a wonderful dancer. The dance is over at
ten, and I have to be home by ten-thirty. I have the strictest mother
ever."

"We'll stay here with Harry," said Kitt.

He led Winifred off to the dance floor. "Do you mind dancing with
a man with an erection?" he asked.

"You're a naughty boy, Constant Bradley. Cute, but naughty," said
Winifred.

"Did Bradley say what I thought he said?" asked Billy Wadsworth,
scowling.

We watched the dancers for a while. Constant, older than the other
boys by a year or two, was the only one on the floor not in black tie,
but it was he and Winifred who dominated the young group, causing
others to stare at them. Then he disappeared in the direction of the
men's locker room again. After several numbers, he came over to
where I was standing. "Why don't you take the car and drive the girls
home. I'm going to stay and dance with Winifred for a bit."

"Billy Wadsworth doesn't appreciate you, Constant," said Kitt. "He's the one who brought her."

"He'll get over it," replied Constant.

"How will you get home?" I asked.

"I'll get a ride."

"Do you want me to come back for you?"

"If you want."

"Good old Constant. He always dumps us," said Kitt.

The telephone rang in the Bradley house. Grace Bradley was a light sleeper. She switched on the reading light inside the canopy of her bed and looked at her bedside clock. It was two o'clock in the morning. Late-night calls always alarmed her. She thought of Gerald in New York on business. She thought of Sandro in Washington. She thought of Maureen in Chicago with Freddy.

"Hello?" said Grace Bradley, at the same time making the sign of the cross.

"Mrs. Bradley? This is Luanne Utley. I'm terribly sorry to bother you at this hour. I'm looking for my daughter, Winifred Utley. She was supposed to be home at ten-thirty, and she hasn't come home. I'm out of my mind. My husband is out of town."

"Who is this?" asked Grace, confused.

"Luanne Utley. Mrs. Raymond Utley. My husband is the new president of Veblen Aircraft. We bought the Prindeville house on Varden Lane."

"Yes? Isn't it awfully late to be calling?"

"I'm looking for my daughter, Winifred."

"Why would you think she'd be here? It's two o'clock in the morning. Do my children even know her?"

"Your son Constant danced with her at the club junior dance tonight."

"I don't think my son was at a dance, Mrs. Utley. I think he had dinner with his sisters."

"Please. Would you look, Mrs. Bradley? I'm sorry to bother you. I know it's a terrible hour to call anyone. Winifred said she'd be home at ten-thirty. She's never late. Ever. I am worried about her. Could you put your son on the phone? Please."

"Hold on," said Grace. She got out of bed and put on her robe and slippers.

The room that I usually used in that house, the room that had once been Agnes's room, before she was put away, had lately been used by Freddy Tierney, and I was sharing a room with Constant. I was in that room asleep when Grace opened the door and turned on the light. Immediately I awoke and sat up in bed.

"What's the matter?" I asked, startled to see Grace Bradley standing in the doorway.

"Where's Constant?" she asked.

I looked over to his bed. It was empty. It had not been slept in. "I don't know," I said.

"There is a woman on the telephone. Mrs. Utley. She is looking for her daughter. She said that Constant was dancing with her at the club. Do you know if that's right?"

"Yes, he did dance with her."

"Are Kitt and Mary Pat here?"

"Yes, I brought them home. Constant stayed. I went back to pick him up when the dance was over at ten."

"And the Utley girl. I can't remember her name. Was she there?"

"Winifred. I assumed she went home with Billy Wadsworth. He was her date."

Grace went to an extension phone in the upstairs hall and picked it up. I got out of bed and followed. "No, Mrs. Utley. Your daughter is not here. . . . Yes, he is, but he is asleep."

Grace looked at me for an instant, as she told her lie.

"He said your daughter went home with Billy Wadsworth. . . . Oh, I see. You've talked to Mrs. Wadsworth, and to Billy. . . . I wish I could help you, Mrs. Utley. . . . Oh, no, I wouldn't call the police," said Grace, quickly. "You can't be in a safer neighborhood than this. It's patrolled hourly. Maybe she slept over with a girlfriend from school. I'm sure it will be all right."

She said a few more comforting things. Then she hung up. She looked at me again. There was an expression of enormous sadness on her face, a look I had never seen before. "Girls, girls, girls," she said. "Constant's just like his father. And his brothers. Look where it got Jerry, this sort of thing. A cripple. And that girl in a wheelchair for the rest of her life."

I didn't reply. I didn't know what to say.

"How old is this Utley girl?"

"Fifteen, I would think."

"Fifteen. Imagine her being out at this hour. I may not have any control over the men in my life, but I most certainly do over my daughters. Will you go downstairs? If Constant is there with her, drive her home, will you? Varden Lane. Tell the silly girl her poor mother is frantic. Good night, Harrison.''

I watched her walk down the long hall to her own bedroom. I, like Sally Steers, always thought she didn't know of her husband's infidelities. I realized then that she chose to ignore them. At her bedroom door, she turned back to me and saw me watching her. "Don't tell Mary Pat and Kitt about this. I don't want my daughters to know such things go on in this house.'' She went into her bedroom.

I looked out the window. Constant's Porsche was in front of the garage, where I had parked. I quickly pulled on my trousers and a sweater and a pair of loafers. I went down the hallway as quietly as possible and down the stairway. At the entrance to the living room, I cleared my throat as loudly as possible to warn them if they were in the act of making love. There was no reply. The room was quite dark and silent, except for the loud ticking of an antique clock on the mantel. I switched on the lights. The room was empty. I turned and walked over to the library. The door was shut. I knocked. I loudly cleared my throat again. There was no reply. I opened the door and walked in. "Constant?'' I whispered. I turned on the lights. There was no one there. I turned on the lights in the dining room. It was empty. And in the lavatory under the curved stairs in the main hall. Empty. Turning quickly, I knocked over one of the dozens of Easter lily plants, and the blue-and-white cachepot in which it sat broke on the marble floor. I waited for a moment to see if anyone upstairs had been awakened by the noise. There was silence. Then I turned on the lights in the small room off the main hallway which Gerald used as an office. It, too, was empty.

Suddenly, there was a tap on the window. Someone was standing outside. I froze in fear. My parents, whom I rarely thought of, flashed through my mind, how it must have been for them at that moment when their attacker was upon them. The window was of a Tudor design with small diamond-shaped panes. With the lights on in the room, it was difficult to see out. There was another tap, more urgent.

"Harry, Harry,'' the person said in a loud whisper. Standing outside the window was Constant.

I ran over to the window. It opened out. "Jesus Christ, you scared me," I said.

"Shhh," he whispered.

He looked slovenly, dirty, his shirt unfresh, torn, darkly stained, his trousers unpressed. His skin was pale. His hair was sweat-wet and slicked back. There was a sore on his lip.

"What the hell is the matter with you?" I whispered.

"Oh, Harry," he said. He was crying. "I need help."

I put my leg through the window, but it was too small to get out of. "Shit," I said.

"Be quiet. Don't wake up anybody," he whispered.

"I'll go out the kitchen door," I said.

I tiptoed through the hall to the kitchen. Bridey's room was next to the maids' dining room off the kitchen, and Bridey was known to be a light sleeper. The other maids, Colleen and Kate, slept up on the third floor. I continued to tiptoe until I got to the door. As quietly as I could, I unfastened the lock, the double bolt, and then the chain. Outside, Constant was standing by the door, breathing heavily.

"Why are all the lights on?" he asked.

"I turned them on. I was looking for you. Your mother sent me downstairs."

"Ma? Why?"

"Mrs. Utley called. Winifred's not home. She called the Wadsworths. Your mother thought you were with her downstairs in one of the rooms, but she didn't want Mrs. Utley to know that. Where is she? Is she with you?"

"You better go back in and turn out the lights. They'll attract attention if someone drives by. Like a police car."

"I think Mrs. Utley is going to call the police."

"Oh, my God. Shut out all the lights, Harry. Quick!"

Alarmed by the urgency in his voice, I went through the downstairs, turning out the lights in the living room, library, dining room, lavatory, and office. When I went back out the kitchen door, Constant was standing in the same place, as if he were in a trance.

"What's the matter?" I asked.

He turned and walked away toward the tennis court. I followed.

"You've got to help me, Harry. I need you. I need you like I've never needed anybody in my life. Are you my friend?"

"Sure I'm your friend. You're the best friend I ever had."

"No matter what?"

"No matter what."

"Follow me."

We went across the lawn, past the tennis court and pool, to the area at the bottom of the property where we had played softball on Easter Sunday. He continued walking into the woods. It was pitch dark.

"Here," he said finally, stopping. "We have to move her deeper into the woods."

"Who?"

"Winifred. We have to move Winifred."

"Is she hurt?"

"She's dead."

I couldn't see his face in the dark.

"Dead?"

He dropped to his knees. There in front of him on the ground was Winifred Utley. She was wearing the same pink dress she had on at the dance at the club, but it was pushed up on her so that part of the skirt covered her face. Her panties were pulled down to her knees. I reached out to touch her, but her face and head were covered with blood. I recoiled. I realized that the stains on Constant's shirt were blood.

"Constant, what happened? Who did this to her?" I spoke in a whisper. My heart was thumping in my chest. I knew that a time of my life had come to an end. A door had shut. Nothing would ever be the same.

"Help me move her deeper into the woods, closer to her own house."

"Why move her? We have to go for help."

He ignored me. "I'll get her head. You get her feet."

"But why?"

"I have to get her off our property. If I drag her through the woods, they'll be able to tell. Get her feet."

As we started to lift her, she let out a faint moan.

"Constant, she's not dead." I was joyous. We placed her down on the ground again. "I'll go for help."

"No, you won't. She's beyond help. She's more dead than alive."

Then he picked up a baseball bat, the bat from the softball game on Easter Sunday, the bat that he had flung into the woods because it was cracked, the bat that neither Kitt nor I had been able to find. It was broken in two. The head of the bat was covered with blood.

I heard another sound from Winifred. Still staring at him, I knelt down to look at her. I could hear the gurgling sound of saliva in her mouth as she expired. I covered my own mouth to stifle the scream that was forming there. "She just died," I gasped. My voice was barely above a whisper, but, unmistakably, there was the beginning of panic in it.

When he spoke, his voice was harsh as he enunciated each word carefully. "You cannot panic, Harry. You cannot lose your head. Do you understand? We have to stay very very calm. We have to do everything right. Tomorrow, when all this is over, we can fall apart, or mourn, or whatever has to be done, but not now. Do you hear me, Harry?"

I stared at him.

"Do you hear me, Harry?"

I nodded my head.

"Say the words, Harry. Say, 'I hear you, Constant.' Say, 'I will stay calm. I will not fall apart.' Say it."

"I hear you. I'll stay calm. I won't fall apart."

"Good. This has happened. We can't undo it. We have to deal with the situation as it is. Do you understand?"

"Yes."

"Take her feet."

Numbly, I followed his orders. I performed my assignments in mute stupefaction, distancing myself mentally from what my hands were doing. We lifted her up again, but this time I did not look at her. We moved deeper into the woods. Then, at a head signal from Constant, we moved in the direction of Varden Lane, which backed onto the Bradley and Somerset estates. When we were within sight of the three-story red-brick Utley house, we saw that there were lights on on several floors. There, at a second signal from him, we laid her down behind a clump of bushes. He began covering her with leaves. Calmly, he wiped his fingerprints off the head of the bat with the tail of his white Brooks Brothers shirt.

"We better get back to the house. Don't talk on the way. I don't want to wake up Charlie in the chauffeur's apartment over the garage."

"What about Winifred? Do we just leave her?"

"Winifred? What about me? It's too late for her. I'm the one we have to think about. It was her fault. The whole thing was her fault."

*　　*　　*

We reentered the house through the kitchen door. We stood in the dark for a moment to see if the house was quiet. He placed the head of the bat down on the counter.

"Get a garbage bag from under the sink," said Constant. He began to take his clothes off—shirt, trousers, undershorts—and piled them into the garbage bag. Then he placed the bat in the same bag. Standing naked, he said, "You better take your clothes off too. Stuff everything in here. Shoes too."

I did what he said. He tied up the bag and took it outside. I followed him. "I'll put this in the trunk of Bridey's car in the garage. We can get it out tomorrow. They might search my car. They won't search hers."

I was amazed at his calmness. He came back into the kitchen. Suddenly a light went on. "Who's there?" came a voice. "Who's out there?"

"It's me, Bridey. It's Constant. No need for you to come out. I was just getting a glass of water. Go back to bed. It's late. Sorry to disturb you."

"What are you doing up at this hour, Constant?"

"Go back to sleep, Bridey."

When the light went off, he signaled for me to follow him up the back stairs. He opened the door and looked out into the upstairs hall to see if his mother was up before making his way down to the room that we were sharing.

Inside, he said, "Take a shower. Quick. Use a brush on your fingernails in case there's dirt from the woods. Then get back in bed and try to sleep until morning."

He picked up the telephone and dialed. "Long distance? I'd like the number of Eloise Brazen. B-R-A-Z-E-N. It's on Park Avenue in Manhattan. I'm not sure of the exact address. Somewhere in the Eighties." He waited. "Thank you." He dialed again.

"Hello?" I could hear the sound of a woman's voice awakened from sleep.

"I would like to speak to Gerald Bradley. . . . I don't have a wrong number, Miss Brazen. Please put my father on the telephone. *Now*. . . . I know it's three o'clock in the morning. I am sorry to awaken you. Put my father on the telephone. . . . Pa, it's Constant. Get home. Get home as quickly as you can. Get a car and driver. . . . Yes, I am. I'm in some trouble. Trouble like you never knew. . . . Not on the phone. There's been an accident, a terrible accident. They're going to say things about me that aren't true. But it was an accident. I swear to you, Pa. It was an accident. . . . What? Yes, good idea. Phone Fuselli. Leave now, Pa. Hurry.''

Constant stepped into the shower. He washed his hair. He washed his body. He washed his hands. He scrubbed his nails with a brush. He went to a bureau and took out a white Brooks Brothers shirt identical to the bloody shirt that he had just placed in the garbage bag. He put it on and got into bed. I stared at him.

"If they ask me for my clothes, I'll give them this shirt. It'll be used by morning. There's another pair of gray flannels in the closet.''

"I don't have an extra pair of shoes, or another pair of trousers.''

"I have everything. Don't worry.''

"Where's your blazer?''

"It must be in the Porsche.''

He looked out the window. "Jesus,'' he said. He recoiled from the window in order not to be seen.

"What?''

"There's police cars on the street.''

"What are they doing?''

"Driving slowly. Flashing the searchlights on the lawns.''

I stared at the man who had been my friend, as if he were another person whom I did not know. Turning from the window, he looked at me.

"Why are you staring at me?'' he asked.

"You have a cut on your lip,'' I replied.

He put his hand on the spot and walked to the bathroom mirror. He turned his head slowly from side to side, studying the blemish, as if it were an assault on his good looks rather than a possible clue to a murder.

"Constant,'' I said.

"What?''

"Why? Just tell me why? So I can understand.''

He turned from the mirror and looked at me. "She screamed,'' he said without emotion. Horrified by what he said, I covered my mouth with my hand. He walked toward me, taking off his shirt as he did. It dropped on the floor. He stood naked in front of me, his hands on his hips. His body slowly undulated, as if in time to music. Then he put his hand on his penis and started to rub it back and forth. "Here. Take it,'' he said. "It's all yours.''

"No.''

72

"It's what you always wanted, isn't it?"

"No."

"Don't tell me no. I know you always wanted it. Here it is at last. Go ahead. Go ahead."

When I awoke, unrefreshed, from a troubled and fitful sleep, the other bed in the room was empty. Gerald had returned to Scarborough Hill at six in the morning and was locked in the library with his son. Jerry appeared at seven from his apartment. There were telephone calls to Sandro in Washington. At eight the family gathered for breakfast. They were a family who normally abounded in good cheer at the breakfast table, vying with one another to tell their familial or social adventures of the night before. Grace was keen to tell of the political dinner she had attended, at which she had been placed next to a young priest, Father Murphy, who had been passionately devoted to Sandro's recent campaign in Bog Meadow. She tried several times to tell her story but Gerald's attention was elsewhere than on his wife's latest favorite priest. It was obvious that Grace and the girls knew nothing of the drama that was unfolding around them.

"Constant dumped us last night, Pa," said Kitt.

"What do you mean?" asked Gerald.

"Our brother Constant's a ladies' man," said Mary Pat.

"We were having the most wonderful evening at the club, Mary Pat, and Harrison, and Constant, but first he got moody when Weegie and her parents came into the dining room and then, as soon as he saw that new girl in town, what's her name, Winifred Utley, whose father is the new president of Veblen Aircraft, and she said, 'Hi, Constant,' she couldn't take her eyes off him, and he said he hoped she didn't mind dancing with a man with an erection, and he just dumped us and went off and danced with her, leaving us stranded, and poor Harrison here had to bring us home."

"Kitt!" screamed Mary Pat.

"I can't believe what I'm listening to," said Grace. She looked at her husband. "She couldn't know what she's talking about."

Gerald and Jerry looked at each other.

"Didn't Harrison ask you to dance?" asked Grace, trying to change the subject. She looked at me as if it were little enough I could have done for all the time I had spent in their house.

"No, but that was all right. The music sucked," said Kitt.

"I hate that expression, Kitt," said Grace.

Constant, late, arrived in the dining room. His hair was wet. He was dressed with his usual flair, his blazer retrieved from the Porsche, a clean shirt open at the neck, gray trousers, loafers. Only the dark circles under his eyes belied the freshness of his appearance.

"Morning, Ma," he said, bending to kiss her on the cheek.

"You're late," she said.

"I've been swimming laps in the pool," he answered.

"Isn't it still a bit chilly for that?"

"Swimming laps in a cold pool is supposed to be great for a hangover," said Kitt.

"And how would you know?" asked Grace.

"My roommate's father's an alcoholic," she said.

Grace turned to look at her son. "A Mrs. Utley called me at two in the morning looking for her daughter," she said.

"You see, Pa?" said Kitt. "A ladies' man."

"Did you cut your mouth, Constant?" asked Grace.

"Shaving," said Constant.

Bridey walked into the dining room from the kitchen with Gerald's eggs.

"Tell Bridey what you want for breakfast," said Grace.

"Just coffee, Bridey."

"You must have more than coffee. Bring him some juice and a boiled egg, Bridey."

"No, Ma, really."

"An English muffin then."

"You certainly were up late," said Bridey. "He woke me up at three o'clock in the morning. I couldn't imagine what in the world he was doing in my kitchen at that hour."

"Not three, no, no, no, Bridey," said Gerald. "The dance was over at ten. He was back from the club long before eleven. Wasn't he, Harrison? Harrison drove him."

They looked at me. Before I could answer, the sound of a car coming up the long pebbled driveway caught the attention of everyone. "Gracious, who could be arriving here at this hour of the morning?" asked Grace.

Gerald and Jerry went to the window and looked out. "It's Fuselli," said Gerald. He nodded to Jerry.

For a severely crippled man, Jerry Bradley moved very quickly. He left the dining room and walked across the hall to answer the front door before Colleen could get to it. Johnny Fuselli was standing there.

"Move your car around to the back by the garage," said Jerry. "My father doesn't want to have too many cars in the driveway. Here's the keys to the cook's car in the garage. It's a Pontiac. Drive it out of town somewhere and dump the garbage bag in the trunk. Then Pa wants you to come back here."

"What's the big mystery?"

Jerry ignored his question. "Make sure that garbage bag doesn't get found."

"I wanted to take a quick swim in the pool first," said Johnny. "Okay?"

"We've got other things to do now than swim in the pool. Ask Bridey in the kitchen for a cup of coffee, but don't tell her you're taking her car."

"Mary Pat, tell Charlie I want to see him, and tell him to have the Cadillac gassed up," said Gerald in the dining room. "I want him to take you girls back to the convent this morning," he said.

"No, Pa," said Kitt. "Not till this afternoon. We don't have to be back until five."

"Now. You have to leave now. I'm going to need Charlie this afternoon to drive me."

"We could take the train," insisted Kitt.

"Pack your bags, girls. You're going now. Your mother and I will be over for Parents Day. Grace, why don't you help the girls." He signaled to his wife to get the girls out of the room.

Kitt stopped at the dining room doors. "I sense a mystery in this room this morning," she said. "What do you think, silent Harrison? You're the writer in our midst."

I did not reply.

"Mother Vincent will think we've done something wrong and you're punishing us, Pa," said Kitt.

"Give your old man a kiss, girls," said Gerald. While he was hugging his daughters, he turned to his wife. "Why don't you drive back with the girls, Grace? You always enjoy seeing Mother Vincent. I'm sure she'll want to hear all about Maureen's wedding." He looked at her with a steely gaze that demanded compliance.

Grace, silent, nodded. She understood the look.

"This Father Murphy you met last night, the one who worked so hard for Sandro's election. Why don't you ask him to dinner this evening, Grace? I'd like to meet him."

"Such short notice, Gerald," said Grace. "He's certain to be busy."

"Doing what? Attending a Sodality of Mary meeting? Or the Knights of Columbus potluck dinner? Or the Wednesday-night bingo game in the parish hall? Believe me, Grace, he'd rather come here to Scarborough Hill. You can bet your bottom dollar on that."

After the girls and Grace left the room, Jerry said to his father, "What's with the priest? What are you inviting him to dinner tonight for?"

"It might be good to have a priest in the house this evening, just in case," said Gerald.

Bridey reentered with a fresh pot of coffee.

"Just leave the coffee on the table, Bridey. Don't bother passing it around," said Gerald.

"That Italian guy drove out of here with my car," she said.

"I told Mr. Fuselli he could borrow it," said Jerry. "He was having trouble with his."

"But I have the marketing to do this morning, and Mrs. Bradley's clothes to be picked up at the cleaners, and—"

"He'll be back, Bridey," said Gerald, waving her away.

After she returned to the kitchen, there was a moment of silence, except for Gerald tapping his fingernails on the mahogany dining table. Then he spoke.

"About last night. You didn't hear or see anything last night, did you, Harry?" He stared at me. As did Jerry. Constant looked down at his plate. Throughout, he remained quiet as things were done for him by his father and brother. There was no censure. That would come later, in privacy. Here, in the turmoil whirling around them, there was only calm and order.

For a moment I did not speak. I stared back at Gerald Bradley's fierce unblinking eyes beneath his graying bushy eyebrows. He looked aged by the strong morning sun coming in the dining room windows.

"I didn't hear you reply," he said. "Did you answer me?"

"What?" I whispered.

"I said, you didn't hear or see anything last night, did you, Harry?" repeated Gerald Bradley.

"Yes, I did. I, uh, I saw Winifred Utley," I said, my voice scarcely above a whisper.

"Oh, no," he said, brushing away the incontrovertible facts as if they were annoying bugs at a summer picnic. "No, no, no."

"I did." I began to cry.

"You're going to be all right, kid," said Jerry. What he said was meant to be comforting, but there was a slight tone of impatience in his voice.

"I'm not crying for me," I said, sobbing now. "I'm crying for her."

"Let me be alone with Harrison," said Gerald to his sons.

Jerry and Constant rose from their places. For an instant my eyes connected with Constant's. There was in them a look I did not recognize, as if another person's eyes had taken possession of his sockets. Then he walked slowly to the door, opened it, and went out. Jerry remained behind.

"I'd like to stay, Pa," he said.

"Then close the dining room door."

Jerry closed the door and then returned to the table, moving his seat up next to his father's.

"This family has been a good friend to you, Harry," said Gerald.

"Yes, sir."

"We have made a home for you since the tragic deaths of your parents, have we not?"

"Yes, sir."

"I assume you are grateful for that."

"Yes, sir."

"And Constant has been your special friend, has he not?"

"Yes, he has."

"Ever since your tragedy?"

"Yes."

"Do they know yet who killed your parents?"

"Probably a transient. A drifter, they think. Someone off Interstate Ninety-five."

He snapped his fingers, trying to recall something. "What's her name? Your missionary lady?"

"Aunt Gert."

"Yes, Aunt Gert. I sent her a rather large check for her Maryknoll Fathers."

"Yes, you did."

77

He breathed in and exhaled noisily. The preliminaries had been established. The heart of the matter was at hand. "A terrible thing has happened here, Harry."

"Yes."

"It was, of course, an accident. A terribly tragic accident. You know that, don't you?"

I looked at him.

"It is possible that others might misinterpret the sad facts, once they are known. People like us, we are targets for criticism. Should, at some point, you be questioned, you must say that you knew nothing, saw nothing, heard nothing. Do you understand me, Harry?"

I nodded.

"I need your word of honor, Harry."

I looked away from him.

"Have you heard from Yale, Harry?"

"No."

"You applied for a scholarship, didn't you?"

"Yes."

"What are your chances?"

"Dr. Shugrue has great hopes."

"And if the scholarship doesn't come through? Where will you go then?"

"The state university, I suppose."

"Is that the University of Connecticut?"

"Yes."

"U-Conn, isn't that what they call it?"

"Yes."

"It doesn't have quite the ring in the ear that Yale does, does it?"

"No."

"That's not really what you want, is it, U-Conn?"

"No."

"You're a smart boy, Harrison. A very smart boy. I know that. Shugrue knows that. I'm sure Yale knows that. You'll probably even get your scholarship. But do you really want to go through college as a scholarship student? Waiting on tables for your classmates? Wiping up after them? That's what it's going to be like for you. Having your sport jackets paid for by Constant. Oh, yes, I know all about that. Wearing his shirts, his ties. Don't you get tired of that? Don't you want your own things? You're even wearing Constant's shoes; I noticed when you came in to breakfast. Where are your own shoes?"

"In the garbage bag in the back of Bridey's Pontiac that Johnny Fuselli drove out of here in," I replied. "Along with half of the bat and all Constant's clothes with the bloodstains on them."

Both Gerald and Jerry looked at me, aghast.

"Look, Harrison," continued Gerald. "I am prepared to pay your full tuition for all four years of college. I am prepared to put you on an allowance that will enable you to have the sort of things that people like Constant have. In fact, my New York lawyer, Sims Lord, will be contacting you shortly in this regard. To hand you a contract, signed by me. A guarantee in writing for a very privileged education. Witnessed. Notarized. Able to stand up in any court, in your favor. But there is a price for all this, Harry. A very modest price on your part. Silence."

"Mr. Bradley. I saw what happened. I saw Winifred dead. I saw the bat that killed her. It was the bat we lost at the softball game on Easter Sunday when Constant threw it into the woods. He had already hit her with the bat, many times. I helped him move her."

Suddenly Jerry, silent until then, spoke. His voice was not pleasant. "You realize, of course, that makes you an accessory to the crime, don't you?"

"Yes."

"That is a very serious charge."

I nodded.

"Do you know what the consequences of this could be for you?" asked Jerry.

I looked at him. I realized at that moment that I had never liked him. Nor he me, from my first night at dinner in that same dining room when he belittled my aspirations to become a writer. His father intimidated me. He did not.

"Do you?" he repeated.

"Less, I would think, than the consequences for the person who actually killed Winifred," I said. "Mercifully, I missed that part."

"That's enough, Jerry," said Gerald, waving his hand at his son to back off. "Let me handle this. More coffee, Harry?"

"No, thanks."

"Constant is a good boy. You know that."

I felt his statement did not demand an answer, and I gave none.

"He is a young man with a great future."

I nodded my head but did not reply. We sat in silence.

"These things pass," he said. "People forget. Life just goes on."

"Oh, I won't forget."

"Yes, you will."

"No. I am to blame, too. I lifted her up. I helped him carry her off your property back to the edge of the Utleys' place."

"I want you to tell me exactly what happened. After you brought my daughters home, did you then return to the club to bring him back here?"

"Yes."

"Did you drive the Utley girl home, too?"

"No."

"Did you see the Utley girl?"

"Her name is—was—Winifred."

"Of course. Did you see Winifred when you went back to the club to pick up Constant?"

"Yes."

"Did you speak to her?"

"Constant did."

"What did he say?"

"He said, 'Why don't you dump Pimple Face and drive home with me?' "

"Did she reply?"

"She said, 'I came with Billy Wadsworth, and I'm going home with Billy Wadsworth.' "

"How did Constant act?"

"He was drunk."

"Drunk? How could he be drunk?"

"He slipped the bartender in the men's locker room twenty dollars."

"How do you know that?"

"I asked him the same question you just asked me."

"What happened to you when you got home?"

"I went to bed."

"What did Constant do?"

"He stayed downstairs. He said he wanted another drink."

"Then what?"

"I was awakened by Mrs. Bradley. About two."

"Go on."

"She had received a call from Mrs. Utley saying that Winifred had not come home. She came into the room to see if Constant was in bed."

"And he wasn't?"

80

"No."

"Was that the first time you knew he hadn't gone to bed?"

"Yes."

"Do you know if there was a plan for him to meet the Utley girl—I mean, Winifred?"

"If there was, he didn't tell me."

"Go on."

"Mrs. Bradley thought Constant was downstairs in one of the rooms with Winifred. She asked me to go look. She told me to drive Winifred home."

"Yes?"

"I did as she told me to. I turned on the lights. I went through all the rooms. He wasn't there. Then there was a tap on the window. He was standing outside. He asked me to go with him."

"And you went?"

"Yes. That was when I saw her. She was almost dead."

"That was when you say you carried her?"

"That was when I helped Constant carry her."

Gerald and Jerry looked at each other. Again no one spoke.

"I would like to go to my room," I said.

"Yes, of course. Go to your room. Rest. We'll talk later," said Gerald. Then another idea came to him. "Perhaps it would be better if Johnny Fuselli drove you over to your aunt's house in Ansonia. Stay there until you go back to school. It's best you are not here. How do you feel about that?"

"All right."

"No, Pa," said Jerry. "That's not a good idea. He drove the girls home from the club and then went back and picked up Constant and brought him home. It's going to look funny if all of a sudden he's not here."

"We don't know what he's going to say."

"He's not going to say anything. He's Constant's friend. You're not going to say anything, are you, kid?" he asked.

"Stop calling me kid," I said. "It doesn't fit the bill anymore. I've become old overnight."

I rose and walked to the dining room doors. Just as I was about to open them, Gerald spoke again.

"Didn't you have a little sneaker for my son? A little fairy feeling?"

I turned back to look at him. The discovery of that feeling by Constant's family had been a great fear for me, but, once it had been verbalized, I looked Gerald in the eye as I gave my answer so he would understand that it was not a hold he had over me. "I would not put it that way, but if I ever did, sir, I don't now," I replied. The feeling had ended, I realized, with the look I saw on Constant's face as he calmly used the tail of his Brooks Brothers shirt to wipe his fingerprints off the baseball bat with which he had killed Winifred Utley.

4

THREE HOURS LATER, at twelve-thirty, the body of Winifred Utley was discovered by Belinda Beckwith, a fourteen-year-old friend of Winifred's, as she cut through the wooded area that separated the estates of Leverett Somerset and Gerald Bradley. Belinda, already aware that Winifred was missing, first saw a foot, shoeless, sticking up from a cluster of leaves. She approached what she knew would be her friend's body and saw a vestige of the pink dress Winifred had worn at the club dance the night before. Fearful of fainting, reluctant to scream, she retraced her steps to her own house, where she hysterically told her mother of her frightful discovery. Mrs. Beckwith first called the police and then went immediately to the home of Luanne Utley.

The word spread through the neighborhood. Maids and butlers and gardeners and chauffeurs were seen in little clusters talking from house to house, passing on the latest information. Blood. Bat. Body bag. Her dress up. Her pants down. By late afternoon, the gruesome story was the talk of The Country Club. I had been sent there by Gerald to retrieve Constant's tennis racket from his locker. He had two more rackets at home and another two at Milford, but Gerald insisted that he would need the racket in his locker for the spring term at Milford. I knew that I was actually being sent to listen to what was being said at the club.

Leverett Somerset heard the news on the ninth hole of the golf course from Piggy French.

"They found her on my property?" he asked, shocked.

"Between your place and the Bradleys'," said Piggy.

"I don't know that I remember Winifred Utley," said Leverett. "Was she at Weegie's dance last Christmas?"

"Yes. They'd just moved here. Ray and Luanne Utley's daughter. Veblen Aircraft," said Piggy. "Chip Wadsworth drove Billy and Winifred home from the dance. They went to the Wadsworths' house for a Coke with a few other kids, and Winifred walked home from there.''

"Oh, for God's sake. Ray Utley's daughter. What a terrible thing to happen in a place like Scarborough Hill.'' Leverett immediately hopped in his golf cart and returned to the club.

Corky, the bartender in the men's locker room, kept the members informed of the latest reports. He had played high school basketball at Our Lady of Sorrows High in Bog Meadow with one of the detectives assigned to the case and was up on everything. "She was beaten so brutally in the attack the baseball bat broke in half, but they only could find half of the bat,'' said Corky, excited by his sudden prominence. "The other half's missing.''

Ursula, the waitress, who was serving drinks in the ladies' locker room, told Louise Somerset, Eve Soby, and Felicia French that she had seen the Utley girl only the night before at the junior dance. "She was wearing the prettiest pink dress,'' she said. "Corky says it was pulled up to her waist when they found her. Winifred just loved to dance. You should have seen her and Constant Bradley dance together. Everyone in the place stopped to watch them. Of course, he's the best dancer ever, if you ask me.''

At the mention of Constant Bradley's name, Louise Somerset's face darkened. When Ursula moved on to take orders at another table, Louise leaned forward and whispered something to Felicia French and Eve Soby.

"You never told me that before, Louise,'' said Felicia.

"We decided not to talk about it at the time,'' said Louise Somerset.

"Was Weegie hurt?'' asked Eve.

"Scared mostly. You promise not to talk about that?'' asked Louise. "Leverett would kill me if he knew I told.''

"Oh, darling, of course not,'' said Felicia.

"My lips are sealed,'' said Eve.

Reporters and television news people filled the area, ringing the doorbells of the great houses in Scarborough Hill, wanting to interview anyone who knew Winifred Utley. Buzzy Thrall's gardener made the mistake of telling one reporter that "everyone'' was at The Country Club, playing golf, and within a quarter of an hour the club veranda was crawling with reporters and photographers, trying to get inside.

"Don't let any members of the press into this club,'' ordered Leverett Somerset, acting in his capacity as club president. "You know how they make places like this sound when they write about them in the

papers. They'll say we don't have any black members. They'll say we
don't have any Jews—which we do, by the way, the Minskoffs—when
what they should be writing about is who killed Winifred Utley."

"How about the police?" asked Corky.

"What about the police?" replied Leverett.

"Can we let them in?"

"Of course. We welcome the police."

At the Bradley house, Bridey Gafferty answered the door over and
over and said each time to the reporter or newscaster that none of the
family was at home. Johnny Fuselli, who had returned from dumping
the garbage bag, across the border in a nearby state, offered to stand
guard at the gates at the end of the driveway and keep out the reporters, but Gerald declined the offer, saying it might be misinterpreted by
members of the media. My clothes were moved from Constant's room.
I was back in the room that I had come to think of as my own, next to
Constant's, the one that Grace Bradley once referred to as Agnes's
room, although Agnes had not rested her head on those pillows for
many years. Constant remained in his room throughout the day, visited
from time to time by his father and brothers. Jerry, when he wasn't in
the dining room with his father, sat most of the time in the upstairs
sewing room with a pair of field glasses watching the police at work on
the far side of the tennis court. What would come to be known as the
Bradley family machine began to move into action. Sandro arrived
from Washington. Desmond appeared and told his father that the autopsy was being performed at St. Monica's Hospital by Dr. Liu, the
state's chief medical examiner. Johnny Fuselli moved all the cars to
the back of the house so that they could not be seen from the street.
Then he changed into trunks and hopped into the pool and began
swimming laps furiously. In no time, Jerry appeared at the side of the
pool.

"Pa wants you out of the pool. It doesn't look right, you swimming
in the pool when they're looking for a body out there," said Jerry.

"They found the body," replied Fuselli.

"Pa wants you out of the pool. *Now*."

When Jerry told his father that Johnny Fuselli was out of the pool,
Gerald said, "Get Fuselli out of the way completely. I don't want him
around the house or on the grounds if the cops should come to call."

"Where did he dump that garbage bag, Pa?" asked Jerry.

"I don't know. I don't want to know. And you don't want to know either," said Gerald.

Twice I was asked to go into the dining room and talk with Gerald and his sons, the first time to go over detail by detail the conversation we had had after breakfast, and the second time to report on what was being said at the club. I listened to them as they directed my beliefs and future actions. The atmosphere was tense, at times disagreeable, in the room.

After being dismissed the second time, I was told by Jerry to wait in my room. I stood in the guestroom looking out the windows. An endless phalanx of police and photographers and cameramen and newspaper reporters roamed the area from estate to estate, like posses. Should an identical crime have occurred in a less affluent place, it would have attracted far less media attention. But the houses in Scarborough Hill were big, the grounds sprawling, and the residents rich. The rich residents remained indoors, by choice, peering out at the unwelcome intruders. The Wadsworths' split rail fence collapsed under the weight of reporters' behinds leaning against it. The Somersets' prized boxwood hedges were uprooted by a television crew from Hartford. Grace Bradley's daffodils were trampled, irretrievably lifeless now, and the gate to the Bradley tennis court was pulled off its hinges when a fallen branch from a tree was momentarily mistaken by a reporter for the missing part of the baseball bat. Everyone in every house called the intruders vultures. Only at the Utley house was proper respect shown.

I longed to talk to Constant, but I knew the family wanted me to stay away from him until all the stories were in sync. I wandered into the kitchen to look for a Coke in the refrigerator. The maids were having an early supper in their dining room off the kitchen before setting up the family dining room for the evening meal where Father Murphy was expected. I could hear their conversation.

"I thought I heard something, Bridey," said Colleen.

"No, you didn't," replied Bridey.

"I did. They were standing outside, under my window. Two o'clock in the morning. I looked at my clock. The voices traveled right up. I could hear, clear as a bell."

"Who?"

"Constant, and the friend. What's his name? Harrison? The quiet one. 'Go inside. Turn off the lights,' I heard Constant say. Something like that. And Corinne tells me—"

"Who's Corinne?"

"Mrs. Somerset's maid next door. She says Constant hit Weegie Somerset last summer."

"No."

"I swear."

"Do you want my advice, Colleen?"

"Sure."

"Do you have your green card yet?"

"No."

"Then keep your damn mouth shut. Or the first thing you know, you'll be on Aer Lingus, right back to Roscommon where you come from. The Bradleys are the finest family in this city. And don't you ever forget it."

"Yes, Bridey."

"And I'd keep away from that Corinne, if I was you. Too many people here got too much to say about things they don't know nothing about."

When I was walking back up the stairs, the doorbell rang again. Bridey rushed in from the kitchen, wiping her mouth with the back of her hand, and answered the door. The conversation at the front door was different from the usual conversations of that day, with Bridey telling reporters no one in the family was at home. I heard her say, "Oh, yes, sir. Come in, sir. Mr. B. told me you was coming." In a moment, a tall, distinguished-looking man wearing a gray chalk-stripe suit entered the hall. He headed toward the dining room.

"I wouldn't go in there if I were you," I said from halfway up the stairs.

"Oh, why not?" he answered, looking up at me.

"It's the family. They're locked in together. There will be a lot of Bradley bad temper to deal with if you walk in when there is a family conference going on. I know. I have just had the experience."

"Oh."

The door of the dining room opened, and Jerry came out. For an instant, before he closed the door behind him, the faces of the family members could be seen, their attention focused on Sandro, the congressman, at the head of the table.

"Harrison, I need you," said Jerry.

I knew when Jerry called me Harrison rather than Harry that I was going to be asked to do something that I did not want to do.

"We've been talking," said Jerry. "The family, that is. We have something else for you to do. We thought that you would be the perfect one to do it for us in this terrible time.''

With a motion of my head, I indicated that there was another person present.

Jerry turned and looked at the stranger in the hallway.

"Can I help you?" he asked.

"I wanted to see Gerald," said the man.

"And who are you?"

"Sims Lord."

"Oh, Mr. Lord, excuse me for not recognizing you. I know we've never met, but I have certainly heard a great deal about you from my father. I am Jerry Bradley, the oldest son."

The two men shook hands. "Actually, we have met," said Sims Lord.

"Oh? When?" asked Jerry.

"You were slipping in and out of consciousness at the time. It was in St. Monica's Hospital after your accident. Your father brought me in to handle the settlement for young Miss McBride."

"Oh, right," said Jerry, looking over at me. It was a story he did not want me to know. He turned back to Sims Lord. "I know that my father will want to see you immediately. May I take you into the library? He is having a meeting at present, but I know he will want me to disturb him to let him know that you are here. Wait here, Harrison. I need to talk to you. Come this way, Mr. Lord."

When Jerry returned a moment later, he said to me, "Look, what we want you to do is go over to the Utley house and pay a call. People are apparently dropping in, leaving food or cakes. It's better that you go, rather than a member of the family. Bridey has prepared a ham and a casserole. Take those with you. See what the attitude is. Listen to what is being discussed, that sort of thing."

"They won't know who I am. How should I identify myself?" I asked.

"A houseguest. Say you saw Winifred last night at the dance. Say how sorry you are. Say Mrs. Bradley is out of town for the day, bringing her daughters back to the convent. Say the family will be coming to call later. We're counting on your charm, Harrison." There was a slight tone of sarcasm in his voice. We looked at each other with dislike. "Do it the way you eeled your way into this family. Oh, I beg your pardon, charmed your way into this family is what I meant."

* * *

The ham and casserole were taken from me at the door by a maid. She said that the Utley family were seeing no one, except the police.

"This is from the Bradleys," I said.

"Oh, yes, the Bradleys," repeated the maid. "I'd better write it down. I'm getting confused with all these names and who's bringing what. Mrs. Utley wants me to keep track. Now let me see here. You've got the casserole. Tuna, isn't it, and the ham?"

"Yes. From the Bradleys. They will be by to call later."

"Yes."

As she started to close the door, I could hear voices behind her in the hall. "Thank you, Captain. Thank you, Officer," a woman's voice said. "We'll be in constant touch, Mrs. Utley," said a man's voice. "Call us at any time, night or day, if you have any questions or you think of anything."

The door opened all the way, and two police officers came out.

"I was just delivering some food to the Utleys," I said in explanation of my presence on the doorstep, although they had asked me for no explanation. They continued on their way toward the street, where their police car was parked.

"May I help you?" asked a woman. She was dressed in black. I had not remembered what Mrs. Utley looked like from our car ride with her, when she picked up Constant and me hitchhiking to Scarborough Hill the first time I went there, but I recognized her immediately. Although her face was mostly hidden by dark glasses, I could see that in other circumstances than these she would be pretty, but there was an indication of utmost despair in the slope of her shoulders.

"I'm a houseguest of the Bradleys, Mrs. Utley," I said. "Mrs. Bradley has taken the girls back to the Sacred Heart Convent, and I was delivering some food from the family. They'll be by to call when Mrs. Bradley returns."

"Thank you," she said. She removed her dark glasses. Her features were slack in her face.

"I'm so sorry, Mrs. Utley. I'm so terribly sorry," I said.

"It's out of order. It's out of order," she said. Her voice was barely above a whisper. "It shouldn't be this way."

"I know. I won't keep you, Mrs. Utley."

"My husband's at the funeral home, picking out the casket. I couldn't go. I couldn't deal with it."

89

"Yes."

"I remember you," she said, looking at me.

"You gave us a ride, Constant Bradley and me, when we were hitchhiking home from Milford."

"Yes. I remember you that day in the car. I don't think you said a word the whole ride, except thank you when we arrived," she said. "What's your name?"

"Harrison Burns. I'm so sorry, Mrs. Utley," I said.

Our eyes met.

Returning from Mrs. Utley's house, I held myself together as I walked past the reporters at the end of the Bradleys' drive. Once inside the front door, however, I collapsed on the bench in the curve of the winding stairway and began to cry. The memory of Mrs. Utley's tragic face would haunt me for years to come.

The doorway to the dining room opened, and Jerry came out. "Someone get him upstairs," he said. "Get him out of the way. We don't want the maids to see him."

I rose and walked up the stairway as fast as I could and went into my room and closed the door. I lay on the bed and buried my face in a pillow, trying to blot out my memory of Mrs. Utley's face. After a few minutes, there was a knock on the door.

"Please, please, let me alone," I called out. "Please."

The door opened. Des came in and closed the door behind him. He sat on the bed.

"This is a terrible thing that has happened, Harrison," he said. He spoke in a gentle voice. "You mustn't mind Jerry, you know. He means well. Sometimes he is abrasive in his manner, I know. He did not mean it when he said that you had eeled your way into this family. Believe me. We, his brothers, have all had to deal with his manner through the years. But his heart is in the right place. You see, he has missed out on his life. It is what makes him the way he is. Pa, though, cannot do without him, and no one can doubt that he loves his family."

I was in no mood to listen to excuses for Jerry. I had never liked Jerry, from the first day I met him. Nor had he liked me. Des must have sensed that, for he proceeded in a different direction.

"Listen to me, Harrison," he said. "It is important that you pull yourself together. At some point, the police will come here. As they will come to every house in the neighborhood. As they will come to talk with everyone who was at the club last night at the dance. It is simply procedure. There is nothing to worry about. But it would not do at all for you to be hysterical. It will present a wrong picture.

"Let me get you a glass of water." He rose from the bed and went into the bathroom. When he returned, he was holding out a glass.

I took it from him. "Thanks," I said.

"I have here some Valium, Harrison. It is a tranquilizer. Very mild. It is important that you be calm. I suggest that you take two now."

"No. I don't need a Valium. My mother took Valium," I said.

"Let me explain to you about us, Harrison. Our family, I mean. We are the disappointments, you see. Kevin, who was killed in Vietnam. There were great hopes for him. Jerry, who got maimed in a car accident. He is the most like our father. There were great hopes for him. And then me, who married a maid and became a doctor. I flunked in my father's eyes. Sandro has done all the right things. He will do well in Congress. He will go on to the Senate. He will hold the seat for years to come. But Sandro is not a leader. Sandro is a second-in-command. And very good at that. The best, probably. But a second. He lacks that thing that it takes to go all the way, like my father has. Constant has it. You know that better than anyone. You are his friend, his very best friend. Constant is the hope.

"Two. Take two now. That's a good fella. Now, why don't you go in the bathroom and wash your face and comb your hair and straighten your tie? Ma ought to be home soon from the convent. And Father Murphy is coming to dinner. And Pa would like you to be at the table."

Late in the afternoon, the Bradley limousine turned in at the gates of the house. Grace was returning from the Sacred Heart Convent, filled with news about Mother Vincent, but her car, driven by Charlie, the chauffeur, was surrounded by reporters and cameramen.

"What in the world is going on out there, Gerald?" cried Grace, entering the house. "There's more press outside than when the Pope came to tea. Poor Charlie. He was so afraid he'd hit someone."

Gerald did not reply. His brow was furrowed. His scowl was deep. His expression was pessimistic.

Grace looked from one to another of her sons. "I've never seen such gloom. Has someone died, Gerald?"

"Yes."

"Oh, dear God in heaven. Not Cardinal?"

"No, Grace. Not Cardinal."

"Who?"

"Winifred Utley."

"Who in the world is Winifred Utley? Oh, you mean the girl whose mother called me last night?"

"Yes."

"Oh, heavens. The poor thing. What happened? An automobile accident?"

"She was apparently murdered."

"Murdered? I must sit down." She sat on the bench in the hallway beneath the winding stairway. "Do they know who did it?"

"No."

"It's terribly sad and all that, but what does it have to do with us? We didn't even know her, did we?"

"Constant danced with her last night at the club. He will most certainly be questioned."

"Even so."

"You're right, Grace. It has nothing to do with us. It's just that it's such a tragic thing, happening right here in the neighborhood."

"Thank God the girls are back in the convent, in case there's a dangerous man running about. That poor woman. Mrs. Utley. She was so frantic last night. Do you suppose the girl was already dead when she called? I'll send flowers, and a note. What do you think of a Mass card, Gerald? They probably aren't Catholic, with a name like Utley. Will they mind, do you think?"

"No. How could they mind? That would be lovely, Grace. Oh, by the way. Your priest called. Father Murphy. He'd like very much to come to dinner tonight."

"Have you told Bridey?"

The *Scarborough Hill Times* carried the story on the front page.

SCARBOROUGH HILL GIRL, 15, BLUDGEONED TO DEATH

by Gus Bailey

The 15-year-old daughter of a Veblen Aircraft executive was found bludgeoned to death this afternoon in a clump of bushes 600 feet from her home in the exclusive Scarborough Hill estate section.

The body of the girl, Winifred Utley, clad in the pink dress she had worn the evening before to a junior club dance at The Country Club, was found shortly after noon by Belinda Beckwith, a 14-year-old neighbor and friend of the dead girl.

Thomas Riordan, detective captain of the Scarborough Hill police, said Miss Utley had apparently been killed by several blows to the head in an attack that took place not far from the Utley home on Varden Lane.

The body of Miss Utley, who was 5 feet 5 inches tall, weighed 120 pounds, and had long blond hair, was then apparently dragged to a nearby wooded area where it remained undiscovered for hours despite an intensive search of the surrounding neighborhood by policemen who were alerted by the victim's mother, Luanne Utley, at 3:45 A.M.

The family's home is in the virtual center of a well-guarded private community that occupies an area of stately homes south of the Connecticut Turnpike.

Miss Utley's father, Raymond Utley, the recently appointed president of Veblen Aircraft, was reported flying back to the city from Atlanta tonight. He had been on a business trip.

The police said that Miss Utley was last seen at about 10:30 last evening, leaving The Country Club, an exclusive private membership golf and tennis club in the Scarborough Hill area, after a junior club dance. She was in the company of William Wadsworth III, 15, the son of William Wadsworth, Jr., the vice president of Ross and Redmond, a New York–based accounting firm. Mr. Wadsworth picked up his son and Miss Utley and drove them back to the Wadsworth home. From there Miss Utley, after visiting briefly, walked back to her own home on Varden Lane, three houses away.

Police declined any comment on whether Miss

Utley had been sexually assaulted, pending an autopsy tomorrow.

Detectives continued to comb the wooded area tonight by floodlight for clues in the slaying, which has shocked this community of wealthy and well-known families since word of the murder began to spread this afternoon.

The state police mobile crime laboratory was called to the scene and representatives of the county prosecutor's office were on hand to supervise the collection of evidence.

Both the Beckwith girl, who found the body, and her mother, Pauline, refused to discuss the discovery of the body or describe the Utleys, who are not well known in the community. The Utleys moved here only six months ago.

We were at dinner when the police arrived: Gerald and Grace, Jerry, Sandro, Desmond (who was on a break from the hospital), Constant, Sims Lord (who was Gerald's New York lawyer), Father Murphy, and me. Father Murphy was from a slum parish, and the grandeur of the Bradley mansion, after the poor working-class houses he was used to visiting in the course of his duties to the sick and dying, was almost overwhelming for him. He had never thought of Catholics in terms of such wealth. He sat to the right of Grace, as an honored guest, and Sandro, the new congressman, sat on his other side. All the Bradleys had a charm that could make even the shiest guest feel at ease, and the conversation at dinner, before the arrival of the police, dealt mostly with the recent election. If Father Murphy was aware of the slaying that had occurred the night before so close to the house in which he was dining, he did not mention it.

"We are a very close family, Father Murphy, and our father has brought us up to understand the obligations that people like us have toward those who are less fortunate than we," said Sandro. "We have been brought up to play some part, to get involved in politics and public service. It is what we aspire to. Hopefully, people are interested in what we have to say."

"Oh, they are, they are, Congressman," said Father Murphy enthusiastically. "This is a grand family, the Bradleys, an example of good Catholic family life. You will be a credit in public life."

94

"Both my grandfathers were immigrants who moved to this city, lived in what is now your parish, attended Mass in what is now your church, and prospered. In fact, both my parents were baptized at Our Lady of Sorrows. But they never forgot their origins, and it is my hope in Congress to introduce a bill that will provide increased welfare payments—"

A police car drove up the drive, signaled by the crunching sound of the white pebbles beneath the tires. It stopped in front of the porte cochere. The doorbell rang. No one in the dining room acted as if anything out of the ordinary was happening.

"Colleen, would you answer that?" said Gerald. She was passing a large silver tray on which were enough lamb chops for each person at the table to take two.

"Just put that on the sideboard, Colleen," said Grace. "Bridey will pass it. Or Nora, is that her name? The new girl? Why don't you send her in. Let her pass. It will be good training for her." She turned to Father Murphy. "It's such a problem, training some of these girls, Father, when they first come over from Ireland. They hate wearing the maid's uniform. 'What day am I going to have off?' is the first question they always ask. Thank God for Bridey. Seventeen years she's been with me. I don't know what I'd do without her."

Father Murphy, baffled by such a problem, had no answer for Grace. Nora, the new maid, nervously picked up the tray of lamb chops and passed it to Grace.

"No, Nora, the other side. You serve from the left, and you remove from the right. Pass it to Father. On the left, Nora. Serve from the left. Now serve the congressman. Thank you, Nora." She turned back to Father Murphy. "Now, of course, they're all frightened that there's a murderer in the neighborhood, and they say they won't wait on the corner for the bus, they want to be driven by Charlie the chauffeur when they have their day off. Can you imagine?"

Colleen came into the room. "There's a Captain Riordan and a Detective Potts in the hall. Shall I ask them to wait in the kitchen until you're finished?"

"Oh, good heavens, no," said Gerald. "Have Captain Riordan and the detective come in."

When the officers entered the dining room, Gerald and his sons stood. They were the same two officers I had seen at the Utleys' house that afternoon. "Good evening. I'm Gerald Bradley and this is my wife, Grace Bradley."

"How do you do? I'm Captain Riordan, and this is my associate, Detective Potts."

"Potts. Potts. Any relation to Walter Potts?" asked Gerald.

"Brother."

"Really? There on the other side of the table is my son, Dr. Desmond Bradley, who took the bullet out of your brother's heart at St. Monica's Hospital."

"Oh, for heaven's sake," said Grace. "Imagine. Did you know about that, Father Murphy? Desmond actually held the heart of that young man right in the palm of his hand and removed a bullet. It was in all the papers at the time."

Desmond walked around the table and shook hands with the officer. "How is Walter? He used to come and see me in my office, but I haven't heard from him lately."

"He's okay," said Detective Potts. "He's in trade school over on the east side."

"Isn't this an amazing coincidence?" asked Gerald. "These are my sons. Desmond you've met. Congressman Sandro Bradley, up from Washington. Gerald Junior, whom we call Jerry. And Constant. You have come to see us on a mostly male evening, Captain. My two younger daughters have just gone back to the Sacred Heart Convent this morning, and my older daughter is in Chicago visiting the family of her fiancé. There is Sims Lord, my business associate from New York, Harrison Burns, a school friend of one of my sons, and Father Murphy from Our Lady of Sorrows Church in Bog Meadow."

"Evening, Murf," said Captain Riordan.

"Hello, Tom," said Father Murphy.

"You know each other?" asked Gerald.

"From the parish," said Father Murphy.

"Murf? He called you Murf, Father Murphy?" asked Grace, in a surprised tone.

"We were in high school together," replied Father Murphy.

"Even so, you are an ordained priest," said Grace.

"I'll speak to Detective Riordan about showing me a little more respect, Mrs. Bradley," said Father Murphy with a smile.

"And I, Mrs. Bradley, regret my impudence," said Detective Riordan, smiling at Father Murphy. He turned back to Gerald.

"Now, gentlemen," said Gerald, "would you care to pull up some chairs? After they clear, Bridey and Colleen will bring in the dessert and coffee, and we would be delighted for you to join us."

Gerald Bradley was the richest man in the city, but he never forgot his roots. He understood the value of not distancing himself too far from his simple origins. "Those people," he once told Constant, after Constant had neglected to speak to an aged friend of his grandfather at a funeral, "are best to have on your side."

"It's profiteroles, Detective. Bridey, my cook, prides herself on her profiteroles," said Grace. "With chocolate sauce."

"No, thank you, I'm afraid we're here on business, Mrs. Bradley."

"Oh, yes, this terrible neighborhood tragedy. Mrs. Bradley has just sent flowers and a Mass card round to Mrs. Utley," said Gerald.

"Yes, I did, the poor woman. Imagine having that happen. She called me last night, simply frantic, looking for her daughter. What kind of a girl was she?"

"We actually don't know the Utleys," said Gerald, interrupting his wife. "They're new here. Do you have any leads?"

"We've found a bat," said Captain Riordan.

"A bat?"

"A baseball bat."

"Was that the murder weapon?"

"We'd like to ask your son some questions."

"Which of my sons?"

"Constant."

Constant raised his hand. "Here," he said pleasantly. "I'm Constant."

"Is there a room where we can talk in private?" asked Captain Riordan. "In a house this size, there must be."

"Oh, that's not necessary," said Gerald. "We are a very close family, and we are all concerned with what has happened."

"It would be better in private," said Captain Riordan. "There are some intimate details we would like to discuss."

"No, no, no. Father Murphy and Mr. Lord are both family friends. Go right ahead. We are all so terribly concerned about this tragedy," said Gerald. "I find it very difficult to believe that someone from this community could be responsible for a murder."

Captain Riordan, dissatisfied, nodded. "It has been my experience that most criminal cases come down to liquor, lust, or loot," he said. He removed a notebook from his back pocket and addressed himself to Constant. "My colleague, Detective Potts, is going to tape-record your answers."

"Fine," replied Constant.

"We understand you were at a dance with Winifred Utley last night at The Country Club."

When Constant spoke, he was completely at ease. No sense of guilt hung over him. "I was not actually at the dance. The dance was for the younger set, the fourteen-, fifteen-year-old crowd. I'm seventeen, about to be eighteen. I was having dinner at the club with my sisters and my friend."

"But you danced with Winifred Utley, did you not?" asked Captain Riordan.

"Oh, yes, that's true," said Constant. "I did dance with her, but then I went home."

"How well did you know her?"

"I didn't know her. I met her once before. I was leaving the club after dinner with my sisters and my friend, and she asked me to dance."

"She asked you?"

"Yes."

"And your sisters? Your friend?"

"They went home in my car."

"How did you get home?"

"My friend Harrison Burns here came back to drive me home."

"Which one is Harrison Burns?" asked the captain.

"I am," I replied, raising my hand as Constant had done.

He looked at me, recognizing me from that afternoon. "Oh, yes. You were at the Utley house this afternoon, weren't you?"

"Yes. I was delivering some food from the Bradleys to the Utleys' maid," I replied. I had not told the family of my conversation with Mrs. Utley.

"Is that right, what Constant said? Did you return to the club to drive Constant home?"

"Yes," I replied. I was as at ease as Constant. "I first brought Mary Pat and Kitt home. Then I returned after a bit to pick up Constant."

"Did you go out again after you came home?"

"No."

"Did you, Constant?"

"No."

"Is there any way you can prove that, Harrison?"

"No. Only my word." I was prepared for the test. My answers were the correct ones.

"I see." Captain Riordan made a note on his pad.

"Mrs. Bradley can prove it, Captain," said Gerald, suddenly. "She went to their room when Mrs. Utley called her at two in the morning looking for Winifred, and both the boys were sleeping like babies. Isn't that so, Grace?"

Grace stared at her husband down the length of the table. "Uh, yes," she answered. "Yes. I didn't have the heart to wake them up."

"I see," said Captain Riordan.

I did not look in Grace's direction.

"I have a very personal question to ask you, Constant. It would really be better to speak in private," said the captain.

"There are no secrets in this family," said Gerald. "Go right ahead with whatever you have to say, Captain."

"Did you, uh . . ." Captain Riordan looked over at Grace Bradley and then at Father Murphy. He drew in his breath and then went on with his questioning. "Did you, uh, did you tell Winifred Utley that you had an erection when you danced with her?"

"Good heavens," cried Grace, bringing both hands up to her mouth. She beckoned to Bridey and whispered in her ear, "Get Nora and Colleen out of this room."

"Of course my brother would never say any such thing as that," said Jerry.

"Wait a minute, Jerry," said Constant. "I did say that, yes. I'm embarrassed, Father Murphy. Excuse me. But it was only a joke."

"A joke?" asked Captain Riordan.

"A bad-taste joke, to be sure, but a joke. And Winifred took it as a joke. She was not insulted. In fact, her very words were, 'You're a naughty boy, Constant Bradley. Cute, but naughty.' Isn't that right, Harry? Harry heard her."

"Yes. That's exactly what she said."

"May I see the clothes you wore last night?" He looked down at some notes on his pad. "Let me see. A blazer. A white shirt with button-down collar. A striped tie. Gray flannels. Loafers."

"Good Lord, who gave you such an accurate description of my son's attire?" said Gerald, laughing.

"Corky."

"Corky? Who is Corky?" asked Gerald.

"Vincent Corcoran. The bartender in the men's locker room at the club who served your underage son drinks," said Captain Riordan.

There was a moment's silence in the room.

"Yes, I'll get my clothes," said Constant. "That is, if Bridey hasn't put everything in the laundry by now. In this house, you no sooner take something off than Bridey has it in the washing machine.''

''I'd like your undershorts as well.''

''If Bridey hasn't put them in the laundry.''

''Why undershorts, for God's sake?'' asked Sandro.

''Ejaculation stains, Congressman,'' replied Captain Riordan.

''Oh, Father, how terrible for you to have to hear such a thing,'' said Grace. ''The profiterole is melting, Gerald. Can Bridey pass it?''

''It was my understanding that the girl wasn't raped,'' said Desmond.

''How could you know that?'' asked Captain Riordan.

''Dr. Liu, the state's chief medical examiner, did more than six hours of forensic examination on the body and said that she had not been sexually molested.''

''May I ask how you would know such a thing?''

''I am the chief of staff at St. Monica's Hospital, where the autopsy was performed.''

''And Dr. Liu reported his findings to you?''

''I am also the president of the hospital.''

''I see.'' He exchanged a glance with Detective Potts.

When Constant left the room, Gerald said, ''I assume you are questioning more people than just my son?''

''Oh, yes. Everyone who was at the dance. And the group who went back to the Wadsworths' house after the dance.''

''Do you know what I think, Captain?'' asked Gerald.

''What?''

''Kids like this, in a neighborhood like this, wouldn't be responsible for such a terrible crime. These kids at the club are not druggies. Oh, they may drink an occasional beer or two, or even three, from time to time, but they're good kids. They're all from good homes. It was probably a transient. A drifter. Someone off Interstate Ninety-five. Have you thought of that?''

''Your son was drinking vodka, not beer,'' said Captain Riordan.

''Are you sure you won't have dessert and coffee, Captain?'' asked Grace.

''No, thank you, Mrs. Bradley. We're on duty.''

''Anyway, the profiterole is ruined. Look, Gerald, it's all melted,'' said Grace. ''Bridey will be furious.''

''Perhaps then you'd do us the honor of closing the meal with grace, Father Murphy,'' said Gerald.

Father Murphy bowed his head. All at the table except Sims Lord, who was not a Catholic, bowed their heads. "In the name of the Father, and of the Son, and of the Holy Ghost. We give Thee thanks, O Lord, for these Thy gifts, which we have just received through Thy bounty. Amen."

As the group walked into the hall from the dining room, Constant came down the winding stair carrying an armful of clothes. "Bridey's slipping, Ma," he said. "She didn't pick up the laundry today. Let me get a garbage bag from the kitchen to put all this in, Captain."

"Never mind that. Detective Potts has a bag. Let me see. Shirt. Tie. Jacket. Loafers. Socks. Undershorts." He looked at the soles of the shoes. "These loafers are black. I thought they were brown."

"No. Black. I didn't bring my brown ones home from school for the vacation," said Constant.

"I see," said Captain Riordan. Then he lifted the undershorts in the air.

"Oh, Father Murphy, come into the library," said Grace quickly. "I want to show you some of the family pictures. Did you know that the Pope came to this house on his last visit to the United States?"

"Is it possible that we could search the house while we are here, Mr. Bradley?" asked Captain Riordan.

"Search my house?" asked Gerald.

"Do you have a search warrant?" asked Sims Lord, speaking for the first time since the arrival of the police.

"No."

"Certainly you know you cannot search a house without a search warrant," said Sims Lord.

"I am aware of that. But I thought as long as we were here, you would not object."

"I can guarantee that my client does not object in principle, but I think this must all be done according to Hoyle," said Sims Lord.

"Fine. No objection," said Captain Riordan. "Would you tell me your name once more?"

"Lord. Sims Lord."

"Sims Lord." He wrote down the name on his pad. "You are a lawyer?"

"Yes."

"You said your client would not object. Who here is your client?"

"I am," said Gerald. "Mr. Lord handles all my acquisitions and business transactions, but he is also a great family friend."

"I see."

"May I ask what is it you would have been searching the house for?" asked Jerry.

"The bat."

"I thought you said you had the bat."

"We have part of the bat only. It broke in two during the assault. There is an indentation on the side where it came in contact with the victim's head."

"Where was the bat found?"

"In the wooded area beyond the far side of your tennis court near two large pools of blood," said the captain.

"Look. I see no reason why the captain and the detective can't search the house, Sims," said Gerald. "Certainly we have nothing to hide."

"It is just the procedure I was thinking of," replied Sims Lord.

"You could sign a consent to search premises without a search warrant," said Captain Riordan.

"Fine, fine," said Gerald.

Riordan indicated to Detective Potts to go ahead with the search while he prepared the paper for Gerald to sign.

From the library could be heard the sound of the piano. There were several melodious chords and then came Grace's contralto voice. *"I'll take you home again, Kathleen, Across the ocean wild and wide, To where your heart has ever been, Since first you were my bonnie bride."*

The group stood around in the hall. Gerald signed. The brothers talked among themselves. Presently Detective Potts returned with a baseball bat.

"Found this in what the maids in the kitchen call the mud room," said the detective. "There's a whole bunch of bats there, all the same make."

"We keep all our athletic equipment in the mud room," said Gerald. "My sons excel at sports."

Captain Riordan examined the bat.

Constant, watching, snapped his fingers. "Of course," he said. "We were all playing softball, the whole family and our guests on Easter Sunday. I hit the ball and the bat cracked, and I flung it into the woods, and nobody could find it. Do you remember, guys?"

"That's so," said Jerry. "My God, and that's the bat whoever killed Winifred used."

There was a silence.

"We'd like you to come down to the station with us, Constant," said Captain Riordan.

"For what?" asked Gerald.

"Fingerprints."

"Yes, of course," said Constant pleasantly. "I understand totally. No problem, Pa."

"We will also need a hair and blood sample."

"Fine."

"I am a lawyer, too, Captain," said Jerry. "If you don't object, I'll go along with my brother."

"And Harrison Burns, too. We'll want your fingerprints," said Captain Riordan.

The following day Constant and I were due to return to Milford, but Gerald felt that it would be inappropriate for Constant not to attend the funeral of Winifred Utley, and I, as a guest who had been at the club the night before her death, was included. Gerald called Dr. Shugrue and said that we would be one day late in returning.

We arrived at the funeral in the Bradley limousine driven by Charlie. There were television and news cameras positioned outside the church. I spotted Detective Potts, the brother of Walter Potts, standing across from St. John's Episcopal Church, behind a car. He was holding a camera with a telephoto lens, photographing mourners. Constant and I had barely spoken to each other since the night Winifred died, but I nudged him to make him aware, simply indicating with a nod of my head in the direction of Detective Potts. He looked.

"That's standard procedure," he said calmly, returning his gaze to me. "They always do that."

Constant walked tall and handsome, his face serious. To a stranger he would have appeared to be just a concerned friend of the deceased. He took his mother's arm as they ascended the steps outside the church. Standing at the top of the steps was Captain Riordan, who was watching the crowd. All the people that I had come to recognize as belonging to the club seemed to be entering the church at the same time. Piggy and Felicia French. Buzzy Thrall. Eve Soby. "The club crowd," as Gerald always referred to them. Constant spoke to several younger people he knew, but I sensed that they withdrew from him as quickly as possible. Gerald, walking side by side with me and Jerry, followed Constant and Grace up the steps.

On the altar were various floral arrangements. Ushers handed a printed program to each person entering the church. On the top was printed IN LOVING MEMORY OF WINIFRED UTLEY. JANUARY 22, 1958– APRIL 30, 1973. The pastor's name, it said, was Timothy Farquhar, Jr. The organist's name, it said, was Emil Toland.

The church was filled to overflowing. Both the sadness of a young girl's death, years before her time, and the notoriety of her killing brought forth a crowd that was unusual for funerals at St. John's. We, the Bradleys and I, sat midway up the center aisle of the church. Late arrivals had difficulty finding seats, and the ushers asked people to move in farther in their pews to make room. Some people, wanting to see everything, stood so that the latecomers could pass in front of them to the interior parts of the pew, keeping the aisle seats for themselves.

The coffin was already in place. On top of it was a simple spray of yellow roses. Luanne Utley quietly entered from a side door, followed by Mr. Utley. Mrs. Utley touched the coffin. "It's out of order. It's out of order," she said. Ray Utley put his arm around his wife's waist and led her to their seat in the front pew. They then leaned forward and lowered their heads in prayer.

Leverett and Louise Somerset arrived late, with Weegie behind them. As they walked up the aisle to the front of the church, Constant turned and looked at Weegie. At the same time Weegie turned her head and looked at him. They continued up the aisle and were seated in the pew directly behind the Utleys. Mr. Utley looked around to greet Leverett, and Leverett, in turn, gently patted Mr. Utley's shoulder.

The service was simple and brief, marred only by one minor altercation when two of the ushers threw out a television cameraman who tried to film the service for the evening news, after sneaking into the organ loft. At the completion of the final prayer, the Reverend Mr. Farquhar announced that the interment would be private but that the Utleys would greet friends in their home following the service.

"So stark, wasn't it? I find those Protestant services terribly cold and impersonal," said Grace, looking out the window of the Bradley limousine. We were sitting in the car in front of St. John's after the service, waiting for the other cars to start. "No kneeling. Just leaning forward and bowing their heads to pray. Not a tear, did you notice? Just, 'Hymn number one sixty-nine, first and third verses.' Or Psalm number whatever. Or Scripture this or that. I think there's nothing like a eulogy at a time like this. People need it. Oh, that minister! What was his name? Timothy Farquhar, wasn't it? Such a cold fish. So Protestant, wasn't he? Personally, I like to cry at a funeral. Do you remember Cardinal's eulogy when the Ryan girl was run over by that bus, Gerald? So moving. Not a dry eye in the cathedral.''

No one replied.

"And so short, the whole thing. I don't think we were there twenty minutes. I like a Mass myself. And a choir. I sent a Mass card to Mrs. Utley, by the way. She probably won't even know what it is, but I think it's important. Look, Gerald, there's a photographer trying to take our picture. He's running along right next to the car.''

"Everyone look straight ahead," said Gerald. "Pretend you don't notice.''

"Why would he want to be photographing us?" asked Grace. "I've never seen photographers at a funeral before.''

No one replied.

"Gerald, do you really think we have to go to the Utleys' house? I mean, we didn't know any of them. I never knew what the woman even looked like until I saw her in the church today. Pretty little thing, in that sort of Waspy way, do you know what I mean? Like half the women in the club. They all look alike, don't they? Those gold barrettes they wear. And the pageboy. They all dress alike, too. Peck and Peck. Odd to wear dark blue, instead of black, to a funeral, I thought. What in the world did she mean when she said, 'It's out of order. It's out of order'?''

"I don't know," replied Gerald.

"Do you know, Jerry?" asked Grace.

"No.''

"Constant, what did she mean?''

"I don't know, Ma.''

"She meant it was out of order, the natural order of things, for a child to die before her parents," I said.

"Oh.''

There was silence in the car.

"What do you say, Gerald? Do we have to go? I sent flowers. I sent a note. I sent a Mass card. We went to the funeral. We signed the book in the church so they'll know we were there. Why should we go to the house?''

"We're going, Grace," said Gerald. "We'll go through the line. We'll all say, 'Sorry for your trouble,' and we'll leave. No one take a drink if drinks are offered. Does everyone understand? No drinks. Nor a sandwich. We'll just go through the line and then we'll leave.''

"But why?" insisted Grace.

"Because our son was one of the last people to see her alive, that's why. It's a courtesy.''

"I suppose you're right.''

"Don't go too fast, Charlie," said Gerald to the chauffeur. "We don't want to arrive at their house before the Utleys do.''

"Did you notice our flowers, Gerald? The cross of white orchids? With the purple centers? I thought ours was the prettiest wreath there.''

The atmosphere in the Utley house was subdued. In the sunroom a bar had been set up. A maid in a black uniform passed cheese puffs. Most people stood in line quietly, waiting to offer their condolences to Mr. and Mrs. Utley. Gerald and Grace stopped to speak to friends. I stood behind Constant in the line.

"I'm Constant Bradley, Mrs. Utley," he said. He held out his hand.

Luanne Utley looked at Constant and nodded. She did not offer him her hand in return.

He returned his hand to his side. "I am so terribly sorry about Winifred.''

Luanne continued to look at Constant. Then she turned to look at her husband, who followed her gaze back to Constant.

"I saw her on the night it happened. At the club dance. I am so sorry.''

She nodded.

"I don't know if you remember, but you once gave me a ride home from Milford right to the door of my house when I was hitchhiking with my friend, Harrison Burns. You were so nice and went out of your way. Do you remember?''

"I remember," replied Mrs. Utley. "I think there are people behind you waiting to say hello.''

He turned to me behind him. Grace and Gerald had caught up. "This is my mother and father, and Harrison Burns, whom you have met. He was at the club the other night, too.''

Grace and Gerald held out their hands. "I'm sorry for your trouble," said Gerald. "I am so terribly sorry, Mrs. Utley," said Grace.

"It makes you question if there is a loving God," said Luanne Utley.

"I believe there is, I suppose, but I don't understand His plan. I don't know why this had to happen to a girl as innocent as Winifred was, with so much to live for."

Then Mrs. Utley looked beyond Constant to the next person standing in line to speak to her. "Hello, Felicia," she said, holding out her hand. "Thank you for coming."

If Constant was aware that he had been snubbed, he gave no indication of it. Leaving, someone—Buzzy Thrall we later heard it was, from the Utleys' maid who told Colleen—said, "He roughed up Weegie Somerset last summer in Watch Hill." We walked on as if we had not heard.

5

AS THE WEEKS went by, there was an outcry by the residents of Scarborough Hill, fueled by a reporter named Gus Bailey, who seemed to have an obsession with the case, that no arrest had been made in the Winifred Utley murder. Back at Milford for the spring term prior to graduation, we read the accounts of the police work in the newspapers. Constant discussed them with a curious detachment, as if they had to do with other people than ourselves. Finally, in response to the ever increasing criticism, the police chief answered his critics in a press conference that was televised in part on the local news.

"I believe I know who killed Winifred Utley," said Police Chief Dennis Quish in an opening statement.

I watched the television set, scarcely daring to breathe. I could feel the more rapid pace of my heart. We were in the Common Room of Hayes Hall, in the free period between dinner and study hall. It was crowded with boys. I looked over at Constant. He watched the set, surrounded by the coterie that always gathered around him during this period, the bridge-playing group. He seemed unperturbed by Quish's statement. There on the screen behind the police chief was Captain Riordan, who had quizzed us, separately and together, for hours, who had taken our fingerprints, who had taken hair and blood samples from us.

"It is my theory that there were two assaults, the first in the wooded area that separates the Somerset and Bradley estates, where a struggle occurred, and the second where the actual killing took place, nearer to the Utley house," said Chief Quish.

"Are you willing to share your thoughts on who it is?" asked Gus Bailey. Bailey had followed the case from the beginning.

"No, I am unwilling. I cannot prove it, so I cannot reveal it," replied the chief.

"Has this person been questioned?" asked Bailey again.

"Yes."

"Has this person taken a lie detector test?"

"No."

"Why?"

"Legal reasons."

"Do you feel you have been impeded in your investigation?" asked Gus Bailey.

"Impeded?"

"Intimidated then?"

"By whom?"

"Wealthy people. Powerful people. Someone who could be protecting someone."

"I think the police have done a good job. Had there been a cover-up of any kind, I think it would have come to light by now. You cannot keep secrets in America."

"That has not been my experience, Chief Quish," said Gus Bailey.

"I have read your accounts of this case, Mr. Bailey," replied Chief Quish.

"Why has the medical examiner's office refused to release a copy of the autopsy report?" asked Bailey.

"I do not know that. That is not under my jurisdiction."

"Is it not customary for the autopsy in a homicide to be performed in Farmington?" asked Gus Bailey.

"Usually, yes."

"Why was it done at St. Monica's Hospital?"

"I do not know."

"So what happens?"

"We wait. People have a way of tripping themselves up in time," said the police chief.

"Have you discussed your theory on who you think killed Winifred Utley with anyone?" asked Bailey.

"I have told Mrs. Utley, Winifred's mother, the name of the person."

"Do you believe she will reveal the killer's name?"

"I believe she will not reveal the name."

"Why?"

"There is no proof. Only a feeling. But I have a written statement from Mrs. Utley."

"Will you read it?"

"Of course. This is from Mrs. Raymond Utley, Luanne Utley, the mother of Winifred Utley." From his inside pocket Captain Quish took a folded piece of blue writing paper and opened it. The message was handwritten. "I quote: 'Please, please, if you know anything, come forward. There must be someone who knows something who has remained silent. Somebody knows.' "

I looked across the Common Room to Constant. For an instant our eyes met. Then quickly we both turned back to the television set.

"Captain Riordan? May I ask you the same question I asked Chief Quish?" asked Gus Bailey.

"What question was that?" asked the captain. He moved up from behind to take his place beside Chief Quish.

"Has your investigation of this murder been impeded by wealthy and powerful people?"

"I think Chief Quish has already answered that question, Mr. Bailey," said Captain Riordan.

Years later, at the trial, in the corridor of the courthouse, Captain Riordan, by then retired from the force, recalled that period for me. It was on the day that Kitt cut me in the hallway and Constant pissed on my trousers in the men's room. Riordan, watching the Bradley family move as a group to the elevator for the lunch break, said to me, "Maybe it was the Bradley money. Maybe it was their position. But I believe I was subconsciously intimidated by them. I always thought you knew more than you were saying. I didn't suspect you. I didn't think you were responsible, but I thought you could be protecting Constant Bradley. But also, I didn't want to believe it, about anyone in that family. Look at the good they'd done for the poor of the city. I mean, I grew up in Bog Meadow. I grew up on stories of the Bradleys. Do you remember Ben Potts, the detective who was with me, the black guy? He said that night after we left the house, 'Listen, that guy Desmond saved my brother's life. He operated on my brother wearing a tux. He held my brother's heart in the palm of his hand while he took the bullet out. My brother'd be dead if it weren't for him.' And Congressman Sandro. Senator Sandro now. I voted for him then. I vote for him still. And the crippled one. What was his name?"

"Jerry. Gerald Junior."

"Jerry. He almost had me convinced it was a transient off I-Ninety-five. And then there was Father Murphy. He was a straight-shooter all the way. I didn't know until I saw him sitting at that table having dinner that he was an old friend of the family.''

"But he wasn't. That was his first time there. He was a dress extra, but he didn't know it.''

"I found that out later. It was a performance they put on for us, everyone participating, everyone playing a part. In all my years of police work I never had a suspect as willing to have his prints taken as Constant Bradley, or to be helpful in every way. In contrast, Billy Wadsworth, the other suspect, was snotty and difficult. And so was his old man. His old man told me Constant had roughed up the Somerset girl the summer before in Watch Hill, but she denied it and so did her family.''

The program ended. Someone switched off the television set. That Constant had been near such a drama, that he was the last person to have danced with the ill-fated Winifred Utley on the night of her death, that he had been questioned by the police, fingerprinted, and released, enhanced his glamorous image at Milford. It was of far greater significance to his classmates than the visit of the Pope to his family's home. For them, Winifred Utley had achieved the sort of mythic quality accorded to film stars who die tragically and too young, and Constant had become part of her legend.

"What was she like?'' the boys asked him over and over. "Tell us about Winifred.''

He never balked at the questions. He seemed never to mind talking about her. "I hardly knew her,'' he replied. "I'd only met her once before the night we danced together. She came through the woods at Easter, onto our property. We were playing softball, and she'd been sent over from Billy Wadsworth's house to tell us we were making too much noise and were ruining the Easter egg hunt at the Wadsworths'. Ask Harry. He was there. She was a pretty little thing, wasn't she, Harry? So fresh. So lovely. And a wonderful dancer.''

But I went unquestioned by the boys. That I was there, too, that I had an acquaintance with Winifred Utley, meant very little to them, much as Constant tried to include me. I had never amounted to much in the eyes of the boys at Milford, even though I was about to be the valedictorian of our graduating class.

The weeks went by. Nothing happened. The story ceased to appear in the newspapers and on the television news. Only Gus Bailey relentlessly pursued it. People talked of other things. I was tortured by the knowledge I possessed, but Constant seemed untroubled by thoughts of Winifred Utley.

"Does it ever haunt you, about Winifred?" I asked.

He looked away from me. He looked to the right, then to the left, as if in search of an answer. But then he said, quite simply, "I never give her a thought. It happened. It's over. It was her fault. There's nothing that can be done about it. We have to go on with our own lives. Why do you keep brooding, Harry, for Christ's sake?"

There was irritation in his voice as he said the last sentence. He walked away from me. He wanted not to see me anymore. At the door of his room, he turned back. "Besides, murder's not the big deal it used to be."

We heard from Yale. We were in. Constant was elated. He ran to the hall telephone to call his father. Their conversation was loud and joyous, with whoops of Bradley delight emanating from Constant. I did not experience the elation I had expected to feel when I became the recipient of such glad tidings. We prepared for graduation. Constant, ever popular, was to be class speaker. I was to write his speech. And I did.

The entire Bradley family arrived in two limousines. I was standing with Aunt Gert as we watched the cars come slowly down the hill to Hayes Hall. Charlie drove the first with Gerald and Grace, Congressman Sandro, Dr. Desmond, and Jerry. Charlie's brother, Conor, who was called in on special occasions when the entire family went places together, drove the second with Maureen and her fiancé, Freddy Tierney, Mary Pat, and Kitt. Kitt looked adorable, even with the retainer on her teeth.

Grace carried a garden parasol that matched the silk print of her Paris dress. "It's the latest thing," she said to Mrs. Shugrue, the wife of the headmaster, who had remarked on its usefulness on such a sunny day. "All the ladies at the races at Longchamps had them this year." When she saw me, Grace kissed me on both cheeks. "Hello, Harrison, dear. My, how smart you look in your white trousers and blazer. Gerald, have you seen Harrison?"

Gerald greeted me in a jovial manner, much the friendliest he had ever shown me. I introduced them to Aunt Gert. She, dressed primly, acknowledged the introduction primly. She was no fan of the Bradleys, thinking they had somehow bedazzled me with their excessive lives, but Gerald greeted her warmly, called her Gert, and introduced her in turn to all of his children. "This is Harry's aunt, who does so much good for the missionary fathers," he said. "We are all so fond of your nephew, Gert." Even Gert, by the end of the day, was not impervious to the Bradley charm.

The family moved like royalty through the crowd of parents, students, and faculty, smiling and affable, waving to those they knew, kissing the cheeks of some, chatting, introducing. They walked differently at Milford than they did at Scarborough Hill, as certain of themselves in those surroundings, where they had given the chapel, the carillon, and the new library, as if they were in horse-drawn carriages waving to their subjects at Ascot. Congressman Sandro, Dr. Desmond, and Jerry had all preceded their graduating brother at Milford, and their return for the ceremonies was the occasion for fond greetings with favorite masters. The faculty all addressed Sandro as Congressman. He was the only Milford alumnus sitting in Washington, and over and over that day they spoke about his future as a senator and then, "with God's will," as they always intoned, they predicted that he would one day be in the Oval Office.

"This is my fiancé," Maureen kept saying over and over to everyone she met, introducing Freddy Tierney, who had not gone to Milford. Later in the day I heard from Kitt, the family chatterbox, that harsh words had passed between Maureen and her father in the wake of Winifred Utley's death. Maureen said that her upcoming wedding would be ruined by all the negative attention on her brother. She told her father that Freddy did not want Constant to be an usher. Gerald would brook no criticism of any of his children, especially not from his daughter's fiancé, who was not yet even a member of the family. When he spoke, according to Kitt, his voice was like ice. "Constant is going to be an usher in your wedding, whether Freddy Tierney likes it or not, and your sisters and you are going to dance with him for all to see, just as you and Freddy are going to sit in the front row at his graduation from Milford and cheer for him. Or there is going to be no wedding. Do I make myself clear?"

On the long walk up the hill from Hayes Hall to the chapel, where Mass was to begin the graduation ceremony, students and parents lined the walk as the graduating class, in caps and gowns, and the faculty marched through. Then, following Mass, the ceremony took place in the gymnasium. The Bradleys had the whole front row of seats that had been set up for the parents and friends of the graduating class.

Dr. Shugrue had revised his unfavorable opinion of Constant since the dirty-picture episode. When he introduced him to speak, he said, "Constant Bradley is what everyone has in mind when they think of a son. At Milford, he has been an honor student, vice president of the student body, house president of Hayes Hall, and captain of the tennis and lacrosse teams. Oh, lest you think he is too perfect, there have been the occasional lapses of a disciplinary nature—" Here the student body roared with laughter, everyone remembering his near expulsion of the year before. Dr. Shugrue, in good humor, held up his hand to quell the laughter and continued. "But these we must blame on an overabundance of youthful vitality. If there were such a thing at Milford as a vote on the student most likely to succeed, there is no doubt that Constant Bradley would win that vote hands down."

When our names were called and we went forward to receive our diplomas, no one received more applause than Constant Bradley. His family accompanied their applause by cheers and shouts, and a stamping of feet by his brothers, and Constant acknowledged his ovation with a wave and charming smile. I realized that in spite of what had happened life would continue almost unchanged for Constant and his family. His mother and sisters, ignorant of the facts, would remain steadfast in their adoration of him. His father and brothers, who knew of his culpability, would overlook it, as if it were nothing more than a youthful prank that had gotten out of hand, the memory of which would be dimmed in time by his subsequent maturity and success. They believed in him. He was their hope.

When I went forward to receive my diploma, the applause for me was courteous, nothing more, despite the honors I had received, until a voice from the front row, Kitt's, yelled out, "Yay, Harrison," and her enthusiasm drew laughter from the crowd and an increase in the volume of applause. I wonder now, looking back, remembering, if I could have known then that one day we would meet in another place, married to other people, and fall in love. For that moment at Milford, all that I had witnessed such a short time before in the woods between the Bradley and Somerset estates seemed like nothing more than a nightmare from which I had awakened.

Later, lunch was served under a yellow-and-white-striped tent set up in front of the Bradley Library, which was still under construction.

Gerald pushed back his plate of lobster salad, gulped down his iced tea, and asked me if I would accompany him on a tour of the new building.

"Be careful of that scaffolding," he said. "You see, those windows on either side of the front door were Maureen's idea. She told the architect that they would brighten up the entrance. Of course, she was right. Even the architect agrees now. Maureen's a bright girl."

I did not reply, merely nodded. I knew he was making conversation until he got around to the subject at hand.

"You seem quiet."

"I have always been quiet, Mr. Bradley. I have simply become quieter."

"Why?"

"Because I am a participant in a cover-up. Because of what Mrs. Utley said on television—you must have heard Chief Quish speak for her when Gus Bailey questioned him. She said, 'Somebody knows.' I am that somebody."

"Who is this reporter, Gus Bailey? He persists in keeping alive a story that has run its natural course. He has suggested things about us, without calling us by name, because he knows I will sue if he does. He has made it appear that we have impeded the progress of the police. But he will stop. That much I know. Fuselli is doing a check on him. Where he's from. What he's about. Everyone has something to hide."

"Not Winifred Utley. She had nothing to hide," I said.

"Have you ever been to Europe, Harrison?" asked Gerald, shifting gears. He did not want to pursue my statement.

"No."

"Never been to London or Paris?"

"No."

"That should be part of every young man's education, such a trip as that. A great learning experience. Wouldn't you think so?"

"I suppose."

He reached into his inside suit pocket and pulled out two envelopes. "You will see that Sims Lord has drawn up the contract I spoke about some months ago. Any dealings through the years of your education you should take up directly with Sims. The tickets to Europe are a little graduation gift from Mrs. Bradley and me. You have been a wonderful friend to our son and to our family. You know that you will always be a part of us."

"You are sending me out of the country?"

"I am sending you on the trip of a lifetime."

"For how long?"

"Until university begins in September."

"Will Constant come, too?"

"No."

"I suppose that would make it convenient for you," I said.

He paused before he spoke. "You're a curious boy, Harrison," he said. "Why in the world would my sending you on a trip to Europe, all expenses paid, the experience of a lifetime for a young man your age, make it convenient for me? Explain that one."

"You would then have only one thing to worry about: Constant. Instead of Constant and me. I am the wild card, am I not?"

"Wild card?"

"I suppose my proximity is a little unnerving during this period."

I expected his wrath, but that day Gerald held his temper in check. There was not an inkling of it.

"It is terrible that this suspicion has fallen on Constant. Terrible. The boy is innocent. His own mother saw him in bed at the time it happened."

"No, she didn't," I said.

He ignored me.

"There are terrible stories being spread about Constant. Buzzy Thrall, Piggy French, Eve Soby—that whole club crowd. They say that he roughed up Weegie Somerset last summer in Watch Hill. A lie. A terrible lie. Vicious. You know that. You were there." He plowed on with his diatribe, not allowing me time either to agree or disagree with his statement. "Constant is a good boy. We all know that. Careless occasionally, yes. Bad, never."

"Careless," I repeated, nodding at the word. "What an odd word for you to use."

He looked confused. "That's all Constant is. Good, but careless."

"Have you ever heard of Gatsby, Mr. Bradley?"

"Who?"

"His friend Nick said, about the Buchanans, but he might have been talking about the Bradleys, *'They were careless people. . . . They smashed up things and creatures and then retreated back into their money or their vast carelessness or whatever it was that kept them together, and let other people clean up the mess they had made.'* I feel that I have been entrapped by Constant's carelessness."

116

Gerald appeared displeased. "It seems to me that this family is doing quite a lot for you," he said. With a sweeping gesture he indicated the contract for my education and support and the airline tickets for a summer abroad.

"It seems to me I am doing quite a lot for this family," I replied. I felt braver than I had ever felt in Gerald Bradley's presence. "I do not think you are getting the short end of the stick in this bargain, Mr. Bradley."

He ignored me. "I myself called on Mr. and Mrs. Utley. They, naturally, are distraught over their loss. I know what that is like. I remember all too well the night of Jerry's accident, when we didn't know if he would live or die. I think they are convinced that Constant did not see Winifred again once they left the club that night."

"I don't equate the two things," I said.

"What things?"

"Jerry's accident and Winifred's death."

"Of course, you're right, in principle. One died. One didn't. But each is a tragedy."

"It's more than that. One innocent girl was beaten on the head with a baseball bat until she was dead. Jerry's dick was in some girl's mouth while he was driving eighty miles an hour with a half dozen beers in him and he crashed into a tree."

I think if I had been one of his own children, he would have struck me. The look on his face was frightening.

"Where did you hear such a vile story as that?"

"Not from Constant. He plays by the family rules. You have no worries there."

"From whom then?" he insisted.

I shook my head. Sally Steers's name was not to come from my lips. "May I ask a question?"

"What?"

"Have the police questioned Weegie Somerset?"

"Yes. And she denied that Constant had roughed her up. She said they had an argument and that was all. She said that nothing physical happened. I was able to tell that to Mr. and Mrs. Utley."

Then, from outside, came Kitt's voice. "Harrison, are you in there? Harrison?"

"I'll be right out, Kitt," I called back.

"Stay away from Kitt," he said, pointing his finger at me. "She knows nothing."

"Who does know?" I asked. "It would be helpful for me to know that. Does Mrs. Bradley know?"

"Good God, no."

"Maureen?"

"No."

"Who knows?"

"Jerry. Sandro. Desmond. Myself. No one else."

"Not Johnny Fuselli?"

"Yes, Johnny Fuselli. He would never talk. He works for me. I trust him totally."

"And Sims Lord?"

"Yes, Sims. He knows. He is my lawyer."

"That's quite a lot of people to keep a secret, Mr. Bradley."

"That's my worry, not yours."

We did not look through the rest of the Bradley Library. It had merely been a place to be alone. We rose to go back to the tent.

"I want to stop in here a minute," he said, indicating the men's room. "Shugrue said the urinals are working."

He stood in front of one of the urinals while I waited. Not wanting to part on an unfriendly note, he spoke in a confidential tone. "I'm getting older, Harry," he said. "When I was a young man and sat on the toilet, my cock used to touch the water. Now my balls do."

It was meant to be a joke, to smooth possibly troubled waters between us. I was meant to laugh. Before Easter I would have. That day I didn't.

"Sometimes you look like a defrocked priest, Harry," he said.

I had things to say. "Liquor does not elate your son, Mr. Bradley. It brings out the dark side in him. You should know that."

"You're making too much of this. Getting drunk is a thing all young men do when they're seventeen, or eighteen, or nineteen," said Gerald.

"Not Constant. There is no exuberance in Constant's drinking. No sense of wild oats. No fun. It goes straight to the dark part of him."

"Oh, please," said Gerald impatiently.

"A former mistress of yours pointed it out to me first. I said 'Oh, please,' too, at least I said it to myself. But she was right."

"What dark part?"

"He killed a woman when he was drunk, Mr. Bradley. What's darker than that? What happened could happen again."

"Never. It was an accident."

"That's the party line, I know. 'It was an accident.' But don't use it on me. I was there, remember. I saw. And listen to what I'm telling you about Constant. It could happen again."

"I thought you were his friend."

"I am. Or I was. That's why I'm telling it to you."

He zipped his fly and moved away from the urinal. He brushed some sawdust from the elbow of his blue linen suit. He moved toward the main doors of the library. Then he stopped and returned to where I was standing. He reached into his pocket and brought out two envelopes. In one were airline tickets. In the other was my contract from Sims Lord. He dropped the two envelopes on a board that connected two ladders and then moved outside to rejoin his family. He did not ask me to come along. I did not want to. I felt that I had become another version of the girl in the wheelchair, whoever she was, wherever she was, the one in the car with Jerry. Silenced by big money. My soul was lost, but my future was bought and paid for.

On the day I was to leave for Europe, business class, I was informed by Sims Lord that the Bradleys' chauffeur, Charlie, would drive me to JFK and accompany me to the Admirals Club to wait for my flight. It seemed to me an unnecessary inconvenience to have Charlie come from Scarborough Hill to Ansonia, but Sims said that Gerald had insisted. To offset the disapproval of Aunt Gert, who was embarrassed by the luxurious limousine parked in front of her apartment house, another example to her of the Bradleys' bedazzlement of me, I offered to sit in the front seat next to Charlie, as if I were a friend of the chauffeur, but he would have none of it. "Oh, no, Harrison. Mr. B. wouldn't approve of that," said Charlie. "You get right there in back, and I'll open the door for you."

Along the way, we talked. Or, rather, Charlie talked, all the time looking at me in the rearview mirror. Like everyone around the Bradleys, his conversation was totally about the doings of the family. Maureen's wedding was the big family news. The wedding dress was being made in Paris by Mr. Givenchy, which he pronounced *Jivinchy*. The swimming pool was to be covered over with a dance floor, and the tent, which was going to be almost as long as a football field, was being decorated by Cora Mandell, the great decorator, and lined in French toile. There were to be ten bridesmaids. Mary Pat and Kitt were to be maids of honor. Congressman Sandro, Dr. Desmond, and Constant were to be ushers. Jerry was to be Freddy Tierney's best man, but he wouldn't be taking part in the procession up and down the aisle, "because, you know, of his limping like that." Cardinal was going to say the nuptial Mass in the cathedral, and Cardinal was going to read the papal blessing from His Holiness in Rome.

We sped on toward the airport. I wanted not to hear any more talk about the Bradley family, from which I was being separated, but at the same time I wanted to know everything about them. I knew in my heart I would never again see Scarborough Hill, which had been more of a home to me than my own home had ever been. I wanted to be far, far away from it, and at the same time I already missed it. Charlie talked on. The Washington crowd was coming, he said. Congressman Sandro was becoming a popular figure down there, and he was bringing a large contingent from the capital. The governor had accepted, with the missus. And the mayor, with the missus. The cardinal's sister was coming, and a great many of the clergy. The Leverett Somersets were going to be out of town, as were the Thralls, the Frenches, Eve Soby, and Mr. and Mrs. Utley.

"How are the Utleys?" I asked.

"I wouldn't be surprised if they moved away in time," answered Charlie. "A terrible reminder every time they look out the window of their house. It must have happened while she was making all those phone calls to Mrs. Wadsworth and Mrs. B. and the other mothers that night."

"Let me ask you something, Charlie," I said.

"Shoot."

"Were you in your apartment over the garage that night?"

"I was."

"One of your windows looks out toward the tennis court, doesn't it?"

"It does."

"Did you hear or see anything?"

"No, no. Not a thing. I could sleep through an earthquake. That's what I told Captain Riordan."

We rode on for a bit.

"The story seems to have dropped out of the papers," I said.

"And a good thing."

"That reporter, Gus Bailey. You don't hear anything of him."

"Terrible, what that man was reportin'," said Charlie. "Insinuatin' all kinds of lies."

"It was always a surprise to me that nothing ever happened to him," I said. "That his legs weren't broken. That he wasn't beaten up." I was thinking of Johnny Fuselli. I always imagined that that sort of thing, broken kneecaps, would have been in his line of work.

"There's all kinds of ways of taking care of people," said Charlie.

"What do you mean?"

"You don't hear of Gus Bailey anymore, do you?"

"No, you don't, now that I think of it," I said. "Are you saying—?"

"All I'm sayin' is, if you make your livin' that way, something eventually is going to happen to you. Why should people accept having their lives ruined by a person like that."

I stared at him in the mirror.

"When you do what Gus Bailey was doin', you put yourself at risk, and I'm sure he knew that," said Charlie.

"But certainly Mr. Bradley wouldn't be party to anything like that," I said.

"Good God, no. No possible way."

"Who then?"

"There are people out there only too glad to carry out your wishes for you. For a price, of course. People you never have to meet. People whose names you don't know, nor do they know yours."

"Who puts the deal together?"

"Brokers, I suppose you call them."

"Like Johnny Fuselli?" I asked.

Then the car pulled up to the front of the airline building, and his attention was diverted. Skycaps, seeing the limousine, gathered around the car. "Here we are," said Charlie. "I'll see to your luggage. Don't worry, I'll handle all the tipping. That's the way Mr. B. wants it. You go over there by the counter, and I'll meet you as soon as I park the car. Have your tickets ready and your passport. And then we'll go up to the club and wait for your flight. You got plenty of time."

"Fine."

"Oh, by the way. I almost forgot."

"What?"

"Mr. Constant said to tell you good-bye."

I turned away from Charlie and walked inside. An hour later I was on the plane for London. I did not see Constant Bradley again for sixteen years. By then his family had moved away from Scarborough Hill.

PART TWO

1989

———

New York

6

IT WAS happenstance, nothing more, that drew the exceedingly private Harrison Burns to public attention. Although he was well known by reputation, he was, by his own choice, unpublicized and only rarely appeared in the sort of social world to which his celebrity entitled him. In the course of his adult life, Harrison Burns had become used to solitude. He lived alone since his estrangement from his wife and often dined without companionship, usually at a corner table of a neighborhood restaurant, Borsalino's, always with a magazine or book. "It's not particularly fashionable," someone had told him about the restaurant. "Literary people and artists go there. But the food is sublime. Northern Italian. No frills."

His looks were not at their best in repose. A deep scowl between his eyebrows gave him the appearance of being older than he was, and a faintly pessimistic turn of his lips gave the impression that, when alone, he dwelt on disagreeable thoughts. This impression often deterred people from approaching him. But in conversation, or on encountering a friend, his face came to life, readjusted itself, and became actually inviting. Never handsome, he seemed pleasant enough looking then, and it was this unexpected warmth that made him appear so. Often people would say to him, "I thought you looked familiar, but I was afraid to approach you." Or, "You're different from what I thought you were going to be."

So Harrison Burns was not surprised when a well-dressed lady, past middle age, who had been staring at him throughout his meal with a questioning look, suddenly approached him and asked, "Are you who I think you are?"

There was a time, in the beginning of his celebrity, when he would have answered, "Who do you think I am?" But now, ten years later, he had learned to reply to such a question by simply offering his name. "My name is Harrison Burns," he said quietly.

125

"Yes, of course. I knew I recognized you. It was driving me mad. I've read all your books."

He nodded in an agreeable manner. It was not an unpleasant sensation, being acknowledged, but then came the awkward moment that Harrison had come to know when strangers approached him. The silence. The slight embarrassment. How to continue, or how to withdraw. Sometimes there was a book to sign. He liked that better than forced conversation. There was a finality to the ceremony. "Tell me your name once more," he would say, before writing. "Catherine? Do you spell Catherine with a *K* or a *C*?" Then a brief message. Then the signature, with the oversized *S* at the end of Burns. And then it was over. Thanks and farewell. But this woman did not move on. An instinct told him her interest in him was something other than literary.

"There's no reason you should recognize me," she said. "It's been so many years."

He looked at her more closely. "Actually, I don't," he said, even while he realized there was a remote familiarity to her face. Women at his lectures sometimes came up to speak to him and told him intimate things in conversation and then were disappointed two years later on a subsequent visit to their city when he did not remember either their faces or where their conversation had left off. "Help me," he said.

"I'm Luanne Utley," she said.

"Good heavens, Mrs. Utley." He jumped to his feet. "Please forgive me for not recognizing you. It was inexcusable of me."

"Well, our acquaintance was brief, and traumatic, and sixteen years ago. I've had the advantage of seeing you on television or your picture in the papers. Please don't stand."

"Are you alone? Is Mr. Utley with you?"

"No. Ray died three years after Winifred's death."

"I didn't know that. I hadn't heard. I'm very sorry. That's all I ever seem to have said to you: 'I'm very sorry.' "

She nodded. "I moved away from Scarborough Hill. Too many memories."

"Of course. Have you married again?"

"No. I saw someone for a while a few years back, but I ended it. It wouldn't have been fair to him. There is still unfinished business in my life."

"Please sit down. Please join me."

"Just for a minute. I'm on my way out. I asked my friend to wait for me outside."

"Would you like some coffee?"

"No, no, nothing," she said. "How are the Bradleys? One never stops reading about them. There are so many of them, one or the other is always being written about. Now, of course, they're everywhere, but in those Scarborough Hill days they were never really accepted."

"I suppose."

"They were certainly the toast of Paris when Gerald was the ambassador there. Mary Pat marrying the count, and all that. It was the talk of Scarborough Hill. I suppose you were in Paris during all that."

"No, I wasn't. Actually, I haven't seen any of the Bradleys in years."

"Really?" She seemed surprised. "Not even Constant?"

"No."

"But you were such good friends. You were at Yale together, weren't you?"

"I didn't go to Yale, after all. I stayed in Europe for a year after Milford, and when I came back I went to Brown."

"I see. Have you married?"

"I have. I am separated at the moment."

"I'm sorry."

"We are trying to work it out. Marriage counselors, that sort of thing."

"Are there children?"

"Twin boys. Age two."

"I hope you do."

"Thank you."

"You've done awfully well in life."

"Lucky, I guess."

"So law-abiding in everything you write. That fascinating thirst-for-justice theme of yours running through everything." Their eyes met. "If you weren't a writer, I bet you would be in law enforcement. I think that's why so many people like reading you."

"Well, I am the child of murdered parents, after all. Did you ever know that?"

"Good heavens, no. We have something in common."

"Yes."

"Did they catch the person who killed your parents?"

"Persons. There were two of them. Dropouts. Druggies. It was apparently a random thing, looking for money, being surprised, panicking, shooting, killing."

"Did you go to the trial?"

"No. That was the year I stayed in Europe. That was why I stayed in Europe. I didn't come back until it was over."

She looked at him for a moment before she spoke. "I can't imagine staying away from the trial. I would want to be there. Every day. I would want to look the killer right in the face. I would want to make him meet my eye." She had begun to become impassioned. Then she caught herself and shook her head. "Well, at least they caught your killers. There is a finality to that. They're away, I assume."

Harrison nodded. "Twenty years."

She rose. "I should go. I hope I haven't ruined your dinner with this morbid talk."

"Oh, no. I'm delighted to have seen you, Mrs. Utley. I have thought of you often."

"And I you. Do you remember Captain Riordan?"

"Of course."

"I keep in touch with him. He's a nice man."

"I'm sure."

"He's about to retire. I'll miss him. He never gave up hope that he would solve it. I never did, either."

"You didn't?"

"No. Somebody knows. One day somebody will come forward."

"But it's been years."

"Whoever it was had to have had help carrying her. She wasn't dragged, you see. She was carried. Someone at her head. Someone at her feet."

Harrison stared at her, without replying.

She met his gaze. "It was in the police report," she said.

"Oh," said Harrison, surprised. "You have seen the police report?"

"Yes. It's curious, though. Parts of the police report are blacked out. I never could understand that, who had that power."

Harrison said nothing.

"I've offered a reward. Did you know that?" asked Mrs. Utley.

"No."

"Yes, just last month. For information that would lead to an arrest. Quite a lot of money, really. Fifty thousand dollars. I figured whoever it was who helped him was a teenager then. Now that person would be in his young thirties. Married, probably. Having children. Buying a house. I thought whoever it was who knew who had done it could use fifty thousand dollars. I thought he would have outgrown that blind loyalty teenagers have to each other.''

Harrison swallowed. "Any takers?" he asked.

"No. Not yet. Captain Riordan always thought you knew something you weren't telling."

"Me?"

"I mean, he didn't suspect you. He thought *you* might be covering for someone."

"No. I wasn't, Mrs. Utley. I wasn't covering. I was in bed that night. Mrs. Bradley came in my room when you called her, and Mrs. Bradley never told a lie in her life."

"Good. I always liked you, Harrison. From that car ride. Do you remember?"

"Oh, yes, I remember. In your blue Buick. But Constant did all the talking. I'm surprised you even remembered me. I hardly opened my mouth."

"That's what I liked about you. Boys like Constant Bradley are too smooth for me. And then you came by our house on the day it happened, with the ham and the casserole."

"Yes. From the Bradleys. I was only delivering."

"I know. I'd like to give you my card."

"I'd like that."

"I have an apartment at Park and Sixty-second. The telephone number's on it."

"Thank you."

"Good-bye, Harrison."

"Good-bye, Mrs. Utley."

By then the Bradleys had settled into their money. People now called them wealthy rather than rich, sometimes even "fabulously" wealthy, when they were written about in columns. No one ever called them *nouveau* anymore. They kept but rarely used the house in Scarborough Hill, as if following the suggestion of Sally Steers to Gerald Bradley many years before, when she was his mistress. Instead, since returning from the ambassadorship in France, they maintained establishments in New York and California, as well as a large summer cottage at the end of Long Island, with several smaller cottages on the property for the married members of the family and their children. They had moved into the small world of people who followed one another's lives in newspaper columns and saw pictures of one another's houses in *Architectural Digest*. They were on terms of friendship with the sort of people who were written about—film stars, socialites, and politicians —and their own names and pictures frequently appeared in the press as having been at this fashionable event or that. The trained eye of the media watcher could detect the assistance of public relations in their recurring mentions. The people from Scarborough Hill watched from afar. They were still not impressed with Gerald Bradley and his brood, although Kitt, the youngest daughter, had made her debut there, not at a grand private dance in her own home like Weegie Somerset's four years earlier, but with a group of debutantes at a cotillion at The Country Club. The following year she had been asked to join the Junior League, the first Catholic girl to be so honored in Scarborough Hill. She had been a bridesmaid in more weddings than she could count. Still, however, the Bradleys remained outsiders.

In Scarborough Hill, Mrs. Utley's tragedy was largely forgotten. Whenever the story surfaced, as it sometimes did, people had begun to say, "What was that girl's name who was killed with the baseball bat?" The Utleys had been new there when it happened. They had no history in the community and had moved away afterwards. The part of the story that everyone remembered was that the Bradley boy, the handsome one, Constant, was briefly suspected but never indicted. Some even began to say he got a bum rap, that he was suspected only because people at The Country Club hated his father and spread the word that he had roughed up Weegie Somerset one summer in Watch Hill, a story that Weegie herself denied. Except for cheating in an ethics examination, for which he had been suspended for a term, and for an altercation with a state trooper who once stopped him for speeding—"Do you know who I am?" he was alleged to have shouted at the trooper—his record at Yale had been admirable. Most agreed, however, that when the time came for Constant Bradley to marry, he would have to look for a wife elsewhere than Scarborough Hill. And he did.

In the meantime he took up polo. He had his own string of ponies. He played in Palm Springs and Palm Beach and Colorado Springs, and one of the columns reported that the Prince of Wales had been heard to say, "Good play, Constant," during a chukker. Adoring women followed his every match. In time it stopped. He ceased to play. His ponies were sold. It was Jerry who pointed out that it made him look unserious, like a playboy rather than the politician his father wanted him to be. "People on food stamps might have a hard time relating to a candidate in jodhpurs with a string of polo ponies," said Jerry.

There had been another incident, as the men in the family had begun to call Constant's transgressions. This one had been without notoriety, known only to the participants and the family. The girl, Maud Firth, a Chicago debutante, whom the family firmly believed was lying, said she had become frightened of him and, in trying to leave the hotel room where she had gone with him, had been tackled from behind and knocked down. In the process she hit her head on a bedside table and received a cut on her scalp that required seventeen stitches. Constant claimed that she was drunk, which she was.

"What the hell's the matter with you? You're young. You're handsome. You're rich. Every girl is crazy about you. You can get anyone you want. Why did you have to hurt her?" asked Jerry.

"I didn't hurt her. She hurt herself," replied Constant. "She tripped and fell."

"It's me, Constant. Jerry, your brother. I'm on your side. I'm not Detective Riordan back in Scarborough Hill. I want to know why."

Constant looked at his brother. "I couldn't get a hard-on," he said matter-of-factly.

"Until you got rough with her, isn't that it?"

Constant looked away. "Something like that."

Jerry reported the exchange to his father and Des and Sandro.

"Well, as we all know, there's no anger like the anger of a soft dick," said Gerald. Gerald's enthusiasm for his favorite son never wavered. In Constant, Gerald saw the aspirations for national prominence, even a place in the country's history, that he himself had been denied because of his unpopularity and the size of his fortune, which the jealous would always believe had been come by illicitly.

"Pa, you're not taking this seriously enough," said Jerry.

"I admire a man with a healthy appetite for pussy," said Gerald.

"I'm not sure how healthy his appetite is, Pa. We just might have a sicko on our hands here," said Jerry.

"Constant is no sicko," said Gerald firmly. "Let me talk to him."

They met in the Grill Room of the Four Seasons in New York. Gerald lit a cigar, much to the annoyance of the group in the booth to his left, book publishers, and the group in the booth to his right, a former secretary of state and a former senator.

"They don't like that you're smoking a cigar, Pa," said Constant.

"Fuck 'em," replied Gerald, puffing, inhaling, exhaling. "They're out of office. Now, tell me exactly what happened."

"I did not commit an offense of any kind, Pa. They know who we are. They know there's money," said Constant, in explanation of the incident.

"I hardly think the Firths of Lake Forest are after our money," said Jerry. "You know who her father is, Pa, don't you?"

"Seventeen stitches is a lot of stitches, Constant," said Gerald, ignoring Jerry. "Were you drunk?"

"No, Pa. I had a few drinks, but I wasn't drunk. She was shitfaced, however. She tripped. That's what happened."

"This guy's got a drinking problem, Pa," said Jerry.

"No, he doesn't," said Gerald emphatically.

"He needs help," insisted Jerry.

"No son of mine is going to go to one of those public meetings in a church hall and raise his hand and say he's a drunk. Listen to me: that is not going to happen."

"Pa, he won't have to go to those public meetings and raise his hand. There's a place in Minnesota, and another one in Palm Springs. They work miracles there. Do you remember how Pierce O'Donnell used to drink? He threw up in the tent at Maureen's wedding, do you remember? Well, he stopped. Completely."

Gerald, displeased, puffed his cigar. "If there's one thing that drives me up the wall, it's these holier-than-thou people who are always off to their stupid meetings for their public confessions," he said.

"Pierce didn't even drink when Alice ran off with Andy Mahoney and left him with the kids," continued Jerry.

"Now, everyone listen to me," said Gerald, laying down the Bradley law. "What is going to happen is that you are going to stop drinking for a month, Constant. Completely. Pretend it's Lent. That means beer as well as liquor. And that means wine, even with meals. Starting right now. Here, waiter. Take this glass away. You can do that, can't you?"

"Yes, Pa, of course."

"Then we'll discuss whether he has a drinking problem or not. One other thing. If you need to get rough, tell Fuselli. There's girls you pay for that. There's girls who enjoy it. I've told you this before. I'm not going to tell you again. Stay away from the nice girls. Is everything understood?"

"Yes, Pa."

For several minutes they ate their grilled swordfish in silence.

"Who did you say Alice O'Donnell ran off with, Jerry?" asked Gerald.

A distinguished elderly man, a former senator and cabinet minister, passed the table on his way out of the restaurant and waved the cigar smoke away from his face.

"Hello, Abe," called out Gerald. "Say hello to my sons here, Constant and Jerry."

The next day, Johnny Fuselli was called in. Money was paid to Maud Firth. Police records were removed. Constant was grounded. No Aspen that Christmas. The incident was forgotten.

"We have to think about getting him married. Then he'll settle down," said Gerald. "But it has to be someone absolutely right. A Weegie Somerset type, but Catholic."

The search was on for a wife for Constant, someone who would fit in with Gerald's dream.

The night Harrison Burns dined at Borsalino's was to have been a quiet evening for him, an early solo dinner, at the same table Arrigo always gave him toward the back of the room, where he wouldn't be disturbed. He liked to be finished with his meal and gone before the arrival of the crowds who filled the place to capacity every night. Then he had intended to go back to his apartment on Lexington Avenue and write an article on a madwoman in a mental institution in Maine, incarcerated for shooting her father's lover, who carried within her a secret that he hoped to discover. Secrets meant to be carried to the grave had become somewhat of an obsession with him in his writing.

But the encounter with Luanne Utley had upset him. He briefly allowed his mind to wander into an area of thought that he had banished from his sensibilities sixteen years earlier, on a 747 flying to London. Scraps of conversation came back to him. "Somebody knows," Luanne Utley had said then. "I am that someone," he had told Gerald Bradley. And Gerald, on the day before Harrison left for

Europe, had said over the telephone, "These things don't last long, you know, this media concentration on a single story. Something else will happen. You mark my words. A plane crash with someone famous on board. Or an embezzlement involving a society figure. Or a bank scandal. Or the suicide of a film star. And then the spotlight will be off this story. Off us. The focus will shift. By the time you come back home, people will have forgotten."

"Yes, sir," he had replied, wanting to be off the telephone, already regretting the deal he had made.

But Gerald was not to be hung up on. Gerald was not finished with his lecture. "Attitude has a great deal to do with it, Harrison. Constant understands that. He doesn't look guilty. He doesn't act guilty. He doesn't think guilty. People who might have suspected him finally say to themselves, 'No, it can't be him. He couldn't have done it. It's a bum rap.' Learn a lesson from that, Harrison."

He traveled that summer from London to Paris to Rome to Madrid. It was, as Gerald Bradley had stated more than once, a dream trip for a young man. Each day he was dutiful in his visits to museums and churches and architectural wonders. Nights he attended plays and operas and concerts. Nearly always he was alone. The trip lacked only the elation that such an adventure should have inspired. Never once did his spirits soar with the joy of good fortune.

There was a letter from Grace, poor Grace, who was never told anything, who didn't know that he had been expensively dismissed from the family circle. She sent it to Ansonia, and Aunt Gert forwarded it to a pensione where he was staying in Florence.

"My dear Harrison," she wrote:

We all miss you so much. We couldn't understand how you could go off like that without saying good-bye to any of us, even Constant. We all liked you so much and thought of you as almost a member of the family. Kitt talks of you often. She says you'll be famous one day. She was the most popular bridesmaid in Maureen's wedding. All the ushers wanted to dance with her. Mary Pat caught the bouquet. I was so proud of my girls. You've never seen a prettier tent. Lined in French toile. Cardinal read the papal blessing. There wasn't a dry eye.

He knew he would never answer her letter. He had made a bargain. It had rained the night before, and the Florentine morning was dark and chilly. There was a fire in the fireplace. He rose from the breakfast table and dropped Grace's letter into the flames. She did not write again.

One day in the Uffizi Gallery, he ran into Mr. Fanning, the French teacher from Milford, who was spending the summer abroad. Although they had never been close at Milford, they greeted each other warmly and dined together one evening at Harrison's pensione.

"Quite nice, your pensione here," said Mr. Fanning, looking about the dining room. At a corner table, an old countess entertaining teen-age grandchildren gave an unmistakable air of well-being to the surroundings. "You seem to be doing all right for yourself. I take it that your parents left you well off to be able to enjoy this sort of holiday."

Harrison blushed and did not reply. He hoped that Mr. Fanning mistook his reddened cheeks for modesty over the good fortune of his inheritance from his slain parents rather than shame over the hush money on which he was living.

"What do you hear from Constant?" asked Mr. Fanning.

"I just had a letter from Mrs. Bradley," replied Harrison, and he began to fill Mr. Fanning in on the news of Maureen's wedding, not wanting it to appear that the Bradley friendship was severed.

"Yes, I was there," said Mr. Fanning. "When the cardinal said, 'I now pronounce you man and wife,' there were cheers and whoops and yells and stamping of feet from all the brothers and sisters. I'd never heard anything like it in church before. It was more like a political convention than a Mass."

"It's the family way. They do those things," said Harrison.

While in a taxicab in Rome, he pulled up in front of the Grand Hotel during a torrential rainstorm. Standing there, desperate for a cab, waving frantically, were the newlyweds Maureen and Freddy Tierney. Maureen, holding an umbrella, was dressed in black to the ground, her hair covered by a black lace mantilla. Harrison did not need to be told they were on their way to the Vatican for an audience with the Pope. For an instant his eyes connected with Freddy's before he told his driver that he had meant the Hassler Hotel, not the Grand, and the cab drove on.

"I could have sworn I just saw that friend of Constant's who never says a word," said Freddy. "What's his name?"

"Harrison. Harrison Burns. Ungrateful little creep. Ma said he didn't even send us a wedding present, after all my family did for him," replied Maureen. "We're going to be late, Freddy. I told you to hire a car and driver. Oh, no, you said. There's always plenty of cabs. Ha ha ha. My shoes are soaked. Look, there's someone getting out of a cab. Run, Freddy.''

When the summer ended, he was preparing to return to begin Yale. He dreaded his reunion with Constant. The secret they shared had driven a wedge between them. Then, mercifully, came the call from Detective Stein to tell him that the slayers of his parents had been arrested. It was not sleuthing that had solved the case. Two youths had been caught in a holdup at a 7-Eleven store, and the story of the Burns murders in Ansonia had come out.

"When will you be coming back?" asked Detective Stein.

"I wasn't planning to come back," replied Harrison. The sentence came out of his mouth, unbidden. No such thought had crossed his mind until that moment.

"Oh?" Stein was surprised.

"I am taking courses at the Uffizi."

"I heard from your aunt Gert that you were going to Yale in September."

"No. There has been a change of plans."

"How long will you stay over there?"

"Until after the trial."

"That could be the better part of a year."

"That's how long I am going to stay."

"Don't you want to see these guys?"

"No."

"Your aunt Gert worries about you."

"Tell her I'm fine."

Like everyone else, Harrison Burns had read of the social and business triumphs of the family that had mesmerized him for so long, but he never discussed them. Their name rarely passed his lips. Claire, his wife, had an aversion to the family, too. He had been married to her for over a year before he discovered, quite by chance, that she had been one of the ten bridesmaids in Maureen Bradley's wedding. She was reading aloud to him at breakfast the obituary in the *Times* of Cora Mandell, the famous decorator.

" 'She was legendary for her taste and for a client list that over the years featured such names as Phipps, Vanderbilt, Guest, Rockefeller, Niarchos, Onassis, and Bradley,' " read Claire. " 'It was at the wedding of Maureen Bradley in 1973 that she took her terrible fall from the top of a ladder while pinning a French toile lining to the tent, breaking both her legs.' ''

Claire put down the paper.

"Is that the end of the obituary?" asked Harrison.

"No, there's more," said Claire. "I remember that, when old Cora Mandell fell off the ladder. It was the night before the wedding. I was a bridesmaid in that wedding."

"You were?" asked Harrison. There was astonishment in his voice. "You were a bridesmaid in Maureen Bradley's wedding?"

"Yes."

"You never told me that."

"It didn't occur to me to tell you. It was not a major event of my life. Besides, I never mention the Bradleys."

"Why?"

"A bad memory."

"What? Tell me."

"The old man, Gerald, wandered the halls on the night before the wedding and came into my room and got into bed with me. Put his hands all over me. It was revolting. Practically raped me. Thank God he came before he got it in me. I threatened to scream if he didn't get out. He was terrified of Grace hearing me and left. I stayed through the wedding itself, not to cause a ruckus. There he was in the cathedral with his silver rosary beads and his eyes closed while the papal blessing was being read by their in-house cardinal. I wanted to puke at the hypocrisy."

Harrison nodded.

"I snuck out before the reception. I left my bridesmaid's dress in a wastebasket in the room where I slept. Seven hundred bucks it cost. Quite a lot for a bridesmaid's dress. Especially back then. It was very pretty. I could have worn it again as an evening dress, but I didn't want to. I've never seen Maureen again. Not even a Christmas card. But the old man sent me a mink coat. Hush money, I suppose."

"From Revillon Frères?"

"How in the world did you know that, Harrison?"

"Did you keep it?" he asked.

"Of course I kept it, but I never wrote a thank-you note."

"How did you even know Maureen?"

"I met her in Florida one winter. I was really a friend of the guy she married," said Claire. "Freddy Tierney."

"Did you send her an announcement when you married me?" Harrison asked.

"No. I wasn't the first friend of the Bradley sisters that their father tried to poke. I always thought the girls knew and closed their eyes to it. Why?"

"I knew them, too."

"You never told me that, Harrison," said Claire. "But there's so much about you you don't talk about."

"That's what you get for taking up with a younger man," said Harrison.

"Yes. A glum, somber younger man. Where did you know the Bradleys?"

"I knew Constant at Milford. I sometimes went to Scarborough Hill for weekends."

"Do you keep in touch?"

"No."

"Why not?"

"Schoolboy friendship. No more. Outgrew it, I suppose. I went to Europe after graduation and never saw him again."

"He's so good-looking. I'll say that for him. In the family they all said he was going to be president one day. Maybe he will. Who knows? I remember all the bridesmaids were mad about him. They all wanted to dance with him. He was a wonderful dancer. And he gave the funniest toast the night before at the bridal dinner at that club they belong to."

"The Country Club. Capital *T* on the *The*. They made a big deal out of that," said Harrison.

"Yes. But there was something odd about him. The local people avoided him, the Scarborough Hill people. At the club, there was a bartender, I can't remember his name. Corky, something like that. He told me about a murder that had taken place there some months before. A girl who was new to the city. And Constant had been dancing with her on the night of the murder. Did you know about that?"

"No. Listen, what time is it? I can't be late."

"Yes, yes, run off, Harrison. You always seem to be running off when there is the slightest thing to discuss that might help us to get to know each other better. Imagine that we are only now discovering that we both know the Bradleys, and know them rather well. What does that say about us?"

Harrison laughed. "Listen, you married an orphan. I don't have a past story. Only Aunt Gert. And she's in St. Mary's Home, and gaga.''

They had then been married for over a year. She had come along with an editor from his publishing house to the launch party of his first book, an indictment of the Wall Street financier Elias Renthal, who was serving six years in Danbury for his part in an insider trading scandal.

"I'm so glad you nailed Renthal," said Claire, when she was introduced. "Awful what those awful men are doing."

She was tall, grave, intelligent looking, and, finally, pretty. "But I must say I felt sorry for poor Mrs. Renthal," she added. "She seemed quite decent."

"I liked her, although she wouldn't be interviewed," replied Harrison. Someone else was waiting to speak to him, but Claire was in no hurry to move on.

"I saw on your book jacket you went to Brown," she said.

"Yes."

"I went to Brown, too."

"Really?"

"Ahead of you by several years."

A photographer hired by the publisher asked them to turn and face him, and took their picture. "Be talking," he instructed them. He thought they were together. The next night they dined together. And the next he stayed overnight with her. At Christmas he went to Philadelphia with her to visit her family. In February she told him she was pregnant. In April they were married by a judge in New York City. In July the twins were born.

"You think of the names," Claire said.

"I like Timothy," Harrison replied.

"Yes, that's quite nice. What about the other? Ralph?"

"Oh, no, not Ralph. Robert? Rory? Charles? Why not Charles? One of my favorite characters in fiction was called Charles."

"Charles Ryder, I bet," said Claire.

"That's right." He smiled at her.

"All right. Timothy and Charles. Timmy and Charlie. We'll have to face the nicknames eventually. Still okay? I think they're quite nice names. Tell me something, Harrison? Would you have married me if I hadn't been pregnant?"

"What a ridiculous question."

"What a nonanswer."

*   *   *

One night, when they were in bed, sleeping, the telephone rang. Claire, groping in the dark, picked it up.

"Hello? Hello?"

"I would like to speak to Harrison Burns please," said the voice on the other end.

Claire reached for the light switch and turned on the bedside lamp. It was two-fifteen in the morning.

"Could you call Mr. Burns back in the morning please," she said. "It's very late, and my husband is asleep."

"No, I must speak to him now," said the voice.

"Who is this speaking?"

"You won't know me."

"Then I can't wake up my husband."

"Your husband will know me."

"May I have your name?"

"Diego Suarez. He might remember me as Fruity."

Claire Burns had never heard of Diego Suarez, or Fruity Suarez, but there were many people in her husband's life whom she didn't know. "Fruity Suarez?" she repeated, incredulously.

Harrison, lying next to her, had been listening with his eyes closed, trying not to wake up, knowing that awakening would mean that he would not get back to sleep, but when he heard Claire repeat the name *Fruity Suarez,* his body jerked into full awareness.

"I'll take it," he said. "No, put him on hold, and I'll take it in the other room. I don't want to disturb you."

"No, Harrison, take it here. I'm already awake. Who is he?"

"Someone from school."

"Can't he call you in the morning? It's absurd for anyone to call at this hour."

He took the telephone from her without replying. "Hello?" Claire was struck by the hesitation in his voice.

"Hello, Harry," said Fruity.

"My word, what a surprise. It's been years," said Harrison.

"Seventeen. On March sixth, the anniversary of the day I was kicked out of Milford for conduct unbecoming, it will be eighteen."

"What can I do for you?"

"You've done well. I read you. I watch you."

140

"Surely this is not a fan's call."

"No, no it's not, Harry." There was a long pause.

"Are you calling from New York?"

"No."

"Where then?"

"Chicago. Did I ever tell you about a cousin of mine on my mother's side called Maud Firth?"

"I don't believe so."

"A charming young woman. A little wild, maybe, but charming."

"Yes?"

"This evening an unfortunate situation occurred in a hotel room in Chicago, and Maud's head was split open, requiring seventeen stitches."

"I don't see what this has to do with me, Fruity."

"It was Constant Bradley who caused Cousin Maud's head to require seventeen stitches."

"Dear God."

"They met at a polo match in Lake Forest. There was drinking. They went to a hotel room. There was a misunderstanding. Maud tried to leave. Constant knocked her down, and she hit her head."

Harrison, breathing heavily, did not reply.

"Are you there?" asked Fruity.

"Yes."

"Maud was afraid to tell her parents, so she came to me, her disreputable cousin, the family disgrace, who would be shocked at nothing, who just happened to be visiting the city."

"I still don't know what this has to do with me," said Harrison.

"I felt this was information that you should have. There was that murky business in Scarborough Hill all those years ago. What was her name? Winifred Utley?"

Harrison, aghast, did not reply.

"Are you surprised I know that? Country club gossip travels from club to club, you know, especially when it involves a handsome, rich polo player with political ambitions. I was merely wondering if there was a pattern of behavior being established here. You are, after all, on the side of law and order in everything you write. It is what people say about you."

"Is that all, Fruity?"

"No. I always knew he had a mean streak beneath all that charm and billion-dollar smile. I was the one he pissed on at Milford. I do mean pissed on, literally. Do you remember?"

"Yes."

"Do you have any idea how that made me feel?"

"Yes."

"Oh, I kept up a brave front. I've kept up a brave front all my life. I laughed with the rest of you. But I saw the look on his face. I saw those sapphire blue eyes turn mean."

"I'm sorry about your cousin."

When he hung up the telephone, he turned and looked at Claire. She looked back at him, questioningly. He picked up her hand and held it. "Claire," he said.

"What is it, Harrison?"

"I wonder if you would do me an enormous favor."

"What is it?"

"Don't ask me to explain to you what that telephone call was all about."

Harrison Burns started each day by writing in his journal. The morning after the encounter with Luanne Utley at Borsalino's, he wrote:

In retrospect, I am appalled at my duplicity with Luanne Utley last night. But was it really duplicitous? I have long since removed Winifred Utley from the forefront of my mind, removed her so completely it is as if what I saw sixteen years ago in a wooded grove in Scarborough Hill had happened to someone other than me. The memory of it rests within me in a dormant state. I have long ceased to dwell on what happened. I have not forgotten it, but I have packed it away, like something in a trunk in an attic. I do not want to deal with what the meeting with Mrs. Utley could awaken in me. Life goes on. Years get filled up. Other things happen.

And yet, I know, I know, I know I have a scene to play in life with Luanne Utley. She looked at me so deeply, almost staring inside me, as she told me about the reward, the fifty thousand dollars. There was no anger, no hate in her look. If anything, there was compassion. Her pale sad pretty face and the deep sorrow expressed in all her features moved me more than I can say. If Gerald had not provided for me, would I have remained

*silent all this time? Would I have told what I know? I don't know,
but I delight that I have returned every one of Sims Lord's
monthly checks since I started to earn my own living.*

He ended his entry. He put away his book. He began to go about the
business of the day: Esme Bland.

7

IT WAS when Harrison Burns was researching the life of Esme Bland, the madwoman incarcerated in a mental institution in Maine for shooting a young man who charged for his favors, that he met Rupert du Pithon. People in Esme Bland's circle were reluctant to talk about her. She was, as Blanche Islington said, "one of us," and the understanding was that people like them didn't talk about one of their own, no matter what she had done. "Poor Esme," they would say, "in and out of institutions for years," and then clam up and say no more. Blanche would add only, trying to be helpful, because she liked Harrison Burns, "You must talk to Rupert du Pithon. He knew Esme. He could tell you a thing or two. He knows everything about everybody." The subtle undertone was that Rupert du Pithon, for all his grandiosity, was not quite one of them, not born into it as they were, and would be more likely to talk about the unfortunate Esme, whom he knew, as he had known Esme's late father, the distinguished Esmond Bland, who was known far and wide as the friend of presidents and other important people.

The name *Rupert du Pithon* was not unknown to Harrison Burns. For years it had appeared in society columns with such frequency that it retained a place somewhere in the storage compartment of his brain, but he knew nothing specific about him.

"What does he do?" Harrison asked, trying to familiarize himself with the name.

"Do? He does nothing," cried Blanche Islington. "Never has. That's his whole charm. Or countercharm, depending on how he strikes you. Oh, he's marvelous at *placement*, of course. He can seat a dinner party better than anyone I've ever known. He knows everything about precedence, that sort of thing. Adele Harcourt used to rely greatly on him when she entertained the mighty. Did the bishop or the governor go on her right—that sort of thing. He always knew. His greatest life accomplishment was a dancing party he gave for Lil Altemus. We are not talking about a serious person."

"But why would he talk to me when none of you will?"

"It's a good time to get to him. He's somewhat out of fashion. He's not asked out the way he used to be. He rubbed several of the right people the wrong way. And once you get him started, he can't stop talking. He's one of those—talk, talk, talk. I would suggest taking him out to a fashionable restaurant. He likes to be seen, especially now that he's not much in circulation."

In parting, Blanche Islington added one more bit of information about Rupert du Pithon. "Oh, never share a confidence with him. It will come back to haunt you."

"Thank you."

"Oh, and one other thing. He wears a little wig." She held up her hands to her head, as if she were trying on a smart hat. "Sort of perched, like this. Pretend you don't notice. He thinks no one does."

Rupert du Pithon, or Rupie, as his intimates called him, became famous for knowing famous people. "You must call Rupie if you are in New York," people in his set once said. "He knows everyone." But of late his position had changed. He was no longer sought after by fashionable society. He had quarreled with important people. He had overestimated his social importance. His gossiping had become indiscreet, and his loud criticism of the wedding dress of Sally Steers's daughter, spoken as she was coming down the aisle of St. James's, had infuriated all of Sally's friends. "Paillettes? Her mother must be mad," he had said. It was, they all felt, the last straw.

The tables of his overcrowded apartment were overflowing with silver-framed photographs of film stars, nobles, and the well-born who had achieved social fame or disgrace. "That's Diana Cooper," he would say. "She was heavenly." Or, "That's Lady Kenmare. You know her story, don't you?" There were those who claimed the photographs were mostly of dead people who couldn't deny that they hadn't known him as well as he claimed they had. For years he was seated well in the best restaurants, although restaurant owners found him a difficult client; he often sent back his food, sometimes more than once, with loud complaints to the chef about the boeuf, or the soufflé, or the mousse. In waiters' circles, he was renowned as a notoriously cheap tipper. The recent change in his social and financial circumstances had disobliged the same restaurateurs from seating him well, and rather than suffer the shame of public demotion, such as getting a table on the wrong side of the room, he no longer presented himself at their establishments. "I never go there anymore," he would say. "Don't you think it's slipped?"

The number of his appearances at the best parties had also diminished. His popularity, if it ever was that, was in abeyance, and he now read about parties to which he was no longer invited. That he agonized and despaired over his exclusion was a secret he shared with no one. "I'm so sick of going to parties," he would now say, shaking his head. "The same people night after night. I simply declined. I said I wouldn't go."

His name and quotes on matters of taste and manners no longer appeared in fashionable magazines, as they had for years. "Oh, I never entertain on Saturday night. Everyone's in the country," he had said in one of his interviews, but the same editors now no longer sought his opinions. "He is stale, finished, out of date, no longer invited," said Dolly De Longpre, the doyenne of society columnists, and her dictum prevailed.

However, as Harrison Burns knew, people on the skids often had scores to settle. People on the skids often knew where the body was buried. Harrison was surprised that such a grand fellow as Rupert du Pithon answered his own telephone. He expected a butler. Or a maid. Or, at the very least, an answering service to monitor the calls. But the voice was unmistakably that of Rupert du Pithon. He had by then heard it imitated by several people, high, nasal, and bogusly aristocratic. Harrison identified himself. He said he was writing an article. He said he would like to meet Mr. du Pithon.

"Oh, you'd like to meet me?" asked Rupert, chuckling. "I'd like to meet me, too, if I didn't know me. But, unfortunately, there's not enough time in life to meet everybody. Or, maybe, fortunately."

Harrison had had experience with reluctant interviewees. He knew instantly when the reluctance was an affectation. He knew not to press. He understood the power of withdrawal. "Well, fine, thank you very much, Mr. du Pithon. I'm sorry if I've taken up your time."

"What did you say your name was?" asked Rupert quickly. He missed reading his name in the papers and magazines.

"Harrison Burns."

"Harrison Burns. Harrison Burns. Is it a name that I am supposed to recognize?"

"No, no, of course not."

"Wait a moment. Let me turn down Maria Callas on the stereo. Now I can hear better. Are you still there? There are so many people writing these days, it's hard to keep track of them all. So many magazines. So many books. One can't keep up. I always skip the first third of every biography. I'm not really interested in reading about people before they become famous or rich. I don't much care about humble beginnings. Don't you think I'm right? I never want to read another word about any of the Mitfords, thank you very much. Or Sylvia Plath, spare me, please. And I'm sick, sick, sick to *death* of Vita Sackville-West and that nasty business with Violet Trefusis."

"Good-bye, Mr. du Pithon," said Harrison.

"Oh, yes, of course. I know who you are," said Rupert. "Didn't you write *Candles at Lunch*?"

"No. That was Basil Plant."

"Oh, Basil Plant, yes. He used to be everywhere—you couldn't go to a party where you wouldn't see Basil—before he was dropped, with a giant thud, as he damn well should have been. It was so bad what he wrote. So naughty. He caused Ann Grenville's suicide, you know. Oh, yes he did, just as surely as if he'd pushed those pills right down her throat. Ann may have killed Billy, but she didn't fuck all those jockeys, like Basil said she did, believe you me. And what he wrote about poor Annabelle Mosley's husband! Annabelle never forgave him, you know, and they'd been such close friends, glued at the hip for years. Basil was desperate to see her before she died—she was riddled with cancer —to beg her forgiveness for what he'd written, but she wouldn't see him. Divine woman, Annabelle. But unforgiving."

Harrison knew he had a talker on his hands. "Basil Plant's dead," he said.

"Oh, yes, I know. Drink. Drugs. They all go like that, don't they?" said Rupert. "You know, the last time I saw Basil was at a brothel in Bangkok. I really shouldn't be telling you this. I don't even know you. Don't even know what you look like. Well, anyway, I had been thinking at last, finally, I could be myself, do all the things I've always wanted to without a care in the world of meeting anyone I knew, and then I heard someone through the mist, calling out, 'Yoo-hoo, fancy seeing you here,' and there was Basil Plant. Can you imagine? I was *furious*. Simply furious. If you knew the position I was in at the moment, a different Oriental at each orifice. It was the most embarrassing moment. This is all off the record, of course.''

Harrison didn't reply.

"Don't tell me what you wrote. I'll think of it myself.''

"Good-bye, Mr. du Pithon.''

"Friday!'' said Rupert, jumping in before Harrison Burns could hang up. He spoke very quickly, all his words running together. "Perhaps you should come Friday. The phone won't bother us. Everyone will be on his way to the country. Have a cup of tea. My Chinese lady who cleans for me comes Friday. Doesn't speak a word of English. I call her Cleanie Cleanie. About four? Four-thirty?''

Harrison Burns had failed to mention, not by accident, that the topic of conversation on Friday at four-thirty was to be Esme Bland, not Rupert du Pithon.

The telephone call from Harrison Burns interested Rupert du Pithon greatly. Excited him even. He was sure something would come of it. He was sure it would open new doors for him. Seeing his name in a magazine would remind old friends that he was still there. Yes, of course, he would be happy to see him. He knew exactly who Harrison Burns was, just as he knew what the titles of his books were. All about law and order, that sort of thing. But, he would have explained to anybody, if there had been anybody to explain it to, that it didn't do to let them think you were eager. The only people with whom he had daily contact were his Chinese maid, Cleanie Cleanie, who couldn't speak English, and Eloise Brazen, the real-estate woman, in whose hands he had placed the sale of his apartment, and Czarina, his Norwich terrier, to whom he told everything.

The very thought of having to sell his apartment, where he had lived for so many years, was almost too much for him to bear, but his money had run out. There was none left. Nothing. What had seemed like so much thirty years ago, when his mother, Sybil du Pithon, died, had dwindled to near nothingness. Mr. Mendenhall at the bank, boring, boring, boring Mr. Mendenhall, had called and written and begged him to take stock of his situation, but he had ignored Mr. Mendenhall, had made jokes about Mr. Mendenhall, had even imitated Mr. Mendenhall. He had not paid the maintenance on his apartment for nine months, and the board of directors of the building, many of whom he had snubbed over the years, had informed him that the services of the building would no longer be available to him. He would have to take his own trash down in the service elevator to the basement, as the staff of the building would no longer perform that service for him. He cringed in shame at the thought of himself carrying trash bags secretly, late at night, when everyone was asleep, down the service elevator. The elevator hallway outside his front door would no longer be cleaned by the staff. The lightbulbs would no longer be replaced in the outer hall. If the plumbing went awry, he would have to make his own arrangements. On and on. He was desperate to sell and fearful of selling. The market was down. He had no place to move to. He owed money everywhere. He was frozen with fear.

Then Eloise Brazen entered his life. She was, he was told, highly regarded in the real-estate world. She had once been, years before, the mistress of Gerald Bradley, and never stopped talking about it. "He was a pretty good fuck for an old guy," she had said to Rupert on the first day they met. Bradley had set her up in business. He had given her a mink coat from Revillon Frères that, even now, years later, had a rather distinguished look to it. "The only distinguished thing about her," said Rupert.

He loathed Eloise Brazen from the moment he met her. "Quite the most appalling person ever," he said about her to Cleanie Cleanie, who couldn't understand, but who didn't like her either. He hated the way she didn't seem to know who he was. He hated the way she walked through his apartment, without even bothering to take off her mink coat, peering at this, peering at that, flushing toilets, turning on switches, running water, opening windows, negative about everything. "This doesn't work, that doesn't work," she kept saying. And Czarina loathed her and barked ferociously at her whenever she came to the apartment to show it to a prospective buyer.

"Get away from me, get away from me," Eloise screamed at Czarina the first time she went to the apartment, and the dog barked and barked at her. She kicked at it. "I hate dogs."

"Don't you dare touch my sweet little doggie," screamed Rupert back at her. He leaned over and picked up Czarina. "Now, look, you've upset her. She's very high-strung. She has a pedigree of inconceivable grandeur. Can't you tell that, just looking at her? Don't you think she's elegant?" He covered Czarina's face with kisses. "Yes, you are. Yes, you are. *Elegant* is the only word, my little darling."

"The happiest day of my life was when my dog ran away," said Eloise. "What were you thinking of asking for this?" she asked.

"I thought two and a half million, something in that area," he replied grandly.

"Oh, honey, no way," she sang out. "Get real."

He looked at her. He couldn't bear her intimacy. He loathed being called honey.

She understood. She took off her mink coat, dropped it on a chair. Eloise said, "We're in a depressed market, Rupie. All that two million, five million, nine million, was in the last decade. Times have changed. Ronnie and Nancy are gone, gone, gone. Good-bye, Ronnie. Now, let me tell you how it's going to be. We'll ask a million, and we'll take eight hundred thousand."

"Eight hundred thousand! Oh, no. It has to be worth more than that," cried Rupert.

"No, it's not. I don't want to hurt your feelings or anything, but if this was a house rather than an apartment, it'd be a teardown. Let's be practical here. The place is run-down. You're smart to have those pink lightbulbs and pink lamp shades. It covers up all the cracks and peeling paint. The kind of person who would pass the board in this building would have to tear out the bathrooms, tear out the kitchen. It's going to cost a million dollars to put this place in shape."

She wandered over to a table filled with silver-framed photographs. "Is that Rosalind Russell?" she asked.

"Yes," he replied. His voice was almost a whisper after the news of the true value of his apartment. He was trying to figure out how much he owed, how much it would cost to move, how he could make ends meet on so little money.

"You knew Rosalind Russell? My God!" exclaimed Eloise.

"Oh, I adored Roz," he said, softening a bit. He liked to talk about his famous friends.

"She was my mother's favorite," she said. "Who's that?" She picked up a picture and held it before him.

" 'Who's that?' " he said, mimicking her voice, which he told Cleanie Cleanie was too common for words. "You don't know who that is? That's the Duchess of Windsor, for God's sake."

"Oh." She replaced the picture. "Was she the one who took the king off the throne, or something like that?"

"Dear God," he said. "She'll be written about in history books for the next five hundred years."

"Oh. And Marlene Dietrich! You knew her, too?"

"Oh, I adored Marlene. She used to come here and sing at some of my Sunday-night suppers. Alice Grenville, Elsa Maxwell, Billy Baldwin, Pauline Mendelson, when she was in town—they all came. Marlene always brought her girlfriend of the moment."

"Marlene Dietrich was a dyke? I never knew that," cried Eloise, thrilled with the inside news.

"She was not a dyke, for God's sake, woman. She was everything." His voice was steely. "It is so ghastly when you people reduce everyone's life to just *that*. She was a star, that's who she was, a star, a great star, who happened, incidentally, to have had a girlfriend from time to time, along with a great many boyfriends."

"Go on, go on, Rupie," replied Eloise, oblivious to his tone. "I want to hear everything. Who's this one? Look at that jewelry!"

"Oh, that's Sunny. Poor Sunny. Still in a coma."

"What's it like not to matter anymore?" asked Eloise. She asked it out of curiosity, not cruelty. "I mean, after being where it all was happening for so long, and now just sitting here all day long, with the phone never ringing."

He turned away from her. He did not want her to see how deeply she had hurt him. As he turned, she saw the wetness in his eyes.

"I didn't say anything wrong, did I?" she asked.

"You were born wrong, darling," replied Rupert.

They came to a working relationship. But the apartment did not sell. People came to look and left. There was this wrong with it. There was that wrong with it. Eloise always relayed back their remarks.

On the Friday afternoon that Harrison Burns was due to meet with Rupert du Pithon, Eloise Brazen arrived. She threw her mink coat on a chair in the hallway and walked into the apartment.

"Hi, Rupie," she called out. Czarina began to bark at her. "Shut up, you little piece of shit."

"Who is that?" Rupert called back, although he knew perfectly well who it was.

"It's Marlene Dietrich's girlfriend, who the hell do you think it is?" said Eloise.

"Out, out, out," cried Rupert. "You can't show the apartment today. I'm being interviewed for a national magazine, and I can't have people wandering through the apartment."

"Listen, Rupie, I've lined up Mr. Rock and Roll himself. He's a very important man. He needs a *pied-à-terre*—do you like my French? —in New York and he doesn't care what it costs. You do not put off Mr. Sol Hertzog and think he's going to come again some other time. These guys don't grow on trees.''

"No, no, impossible today. If you had called and said you had a client I would have told you, but, no, you just show up, as brash as brash can be. You have no feeling for other people, Miss Brazen. I don't think it would look right in the story to say the apartment is for sale and have Mr. Hertzog wandering around complaining about the bathroom fixtures. It might look like I'm on my uppers.''

"You are on your uppers, Rupie," said Eloise. "The elevator man said you haven't paid your maintenance in nine months. They're dying for you to get out of this building, in case you don't know it.''

"I do wish you'd stop calling me Rupie. You don't know me well enough.'' He looked at himself in the mirror and noticed that his little toupee was awry. "Christ, I look like Georgia O'Keeffe," he said, patting color into his face with his soft white hands with their protruding lavender veins. "Suppose he brings a photographer. I have to pull myself together. Go now, call me tomorrow, and we'll set up another appointment for Mr. Hertzog. I don't think I look eighty-four, do you?''

"No, no, Rupert. Eighty-three, maybe. Not eighty-four.''

"Tomorrow.''

"There just may not be another tomorrow," said Eloise. "I'm mad, Rupert, goddamn mad.''

In the hallway she picked up her mink coat. As she was about to ring for the elevator, the elevator door opened and Harrison Burns stepped into the hallway.

"You're not Sol Hertzog, I hope," said Eloise.

"No.''

"You don't look like a Sol Hertzog. You must be the reporter here to interview Rupie.''

"I'm here to see Mr. du Pithon.''

"I'm expecting this guy from Hollywood to see the apartment, and now Rupert won't let me show it because you're coming to interview him.''

"Is Mr. du Pithon here?''

"Oh, yes. He's preening and primping for you.''

"Is that the reporter? Is that Mr. Harrison? I mean Mr. Burns?'' called out the high nasal voice of Rupert du Pithon.

"Oh, he's finished making his toilet," said Eloise. "Yes, Rupie. Mr. Burns is here, waiting to see you."

"I thought you'd gone," he called back.

"I'm on my way out." She picked up her mink coat off a chair in the hall and handed it to Harrison. "I always like a gentleman to help me on with my coat," she said.

Harrison held up the mink coat. Inside he noticed a Revillon Frères label and the intertwining initials *EB*.

"What did you say your name was?" he asked.

"Eloise Brazen."

He looked at her, as his mind went back many years to a late-night telephone call Constant made to his father.

The room reverberated with Rupert du Pithon's shrieks of laughter. "Wait there. Wait there," he said to Harrison, covering the mouthpiece and indicating a chair for him to sit. "I'm on the telephone. Lil Altemus." He whispered the last two words, expecting Harrison to be impressed with the grand name. Then he returned to his call. "Are you there, Lil? Sorry. Someone came by. I'm being interviewed. I didn't even think to ask what for. Where was I? Oh, yes. Eloise. And *then* she said, 'People of our class,' and I said, 'Just a minute, Eloise, your class or mine?' Don't you love it? Don't you love it?" Again there was a shriek of laughter. "No, no, I can't tomorrow, Lil. I'm out all day. I'm lunching out. I'm cocktailing out. I'm dining out. Maybe Thursday. I'll call tomorrow, first thing. Big hug." He turned to Harrison. "Don't mind the doggie. That's Czarina."

Harrison looked at the dog. He nodded.

Rupert du Pithon sat grandly amid red lacquer cabinets and porcelain tureens, on a Queen Anne chair. The face that he had seen in the mirror a half hour before—pale, lined, haggard—bore little resemblance to the face that greeted his guest. "I have been reading Baron de Charlus," he said, holding up a book. "He is my favorite character in all fiction. What a sad end, don't you think?"

Harrison nodded.

"Hello, I'm Rupert du Pithon. Do, please, sit. I once went to a costume ball in Venice as Baron de Charlus. I was a sensation. Well, I suppose, actually, it was Annabelle Mosley who was really the sensation. She went as the Duchesse de Guermantes. She wore all her emeralds. Marvelous night. There's nothing like that these days. Oh, no.

That's all gone." He held up the third volume of *À la Recherche du Temps Perdu*. "You've read it, of course."

"Yes."

"In French?"

"No. English."

"Oh, I think you miss so much if you don't read it in French. The nuances. The subtleties. Don't you think?"

"I suppose," said Harrison. "I don't really know."

"You met Ms. Brazen on the way in, I see. She calls Proust Prowst."

Harrison did not pursue the conversation. "I wanted to ask you about Esme Bland."

"Esme Bland? Whatever for?"

"I am trying to locate Miss Bland. I have been told that you knew her."

"Yes, I know Esme. Or knew her. She's in the bins. Mad as a hatter."

"Tell me about her."

"Esme was hopeless. She had every advantage and took advantage of none of them. She had no idea how to do the flowers. No idea how to seat a table. She cared nothing about clothes. Cardigans, cardigans, cardigans."

"Perhaps other things interested her. Living in society is not everyone's goal," said Harrison.

"She was a terrible disappointment to her father," said Rupert. "Everything she did was wrong. She took a villa in Florence, but it was on the wrong side of the Arno. The Pitti side. And she never married. Loved the wrong man, that sort of thing."

"Did you know her father?" asked Harrison.

"Esmond? Oh, yes."

"Would you tell me about him?"

Rupert seemed confused. "You want to know about Esmond Bland?"

"Yes."

"Rarefied. Rode to hounds. Had a house in Middleburg. Divine house. Georgian, red brick, divine—you would have thought you were in England. Had some very good Stubbs horse pictures. A Munnings or two, I believe. He loved his Jack Russells. I suppose he was as close to an American aristocrat as there is. Why?"

"Tell me more."

"He was a friend to many presidents. Jackie *adored* him, always had him around. He spent lots of time in the Oval Office with Jack. Nelson liked him when he was vice president. Ronnie liked him, too. He was a modern-day Bernard Baruch, I suppose. Behind the scenes. Never really in public life, in a public sort of way, I mean. He refused several ambassadorships. I happen to know he was offered both London and Paris at different times. I always felt he didn't want to go through the confirmation hearings for one reason or another. He used to come here to my Sunday nights. Lots of money. A great gentleman, really. I went to his funeral at St. Thomas's. Quite extraordinary. It was a distinguished life. But why this great interest in Esmond and poor Esme? Their place in my life is treasured, but not of paramount importance, if you see what I mean."

Harrison nodded but persevered. "Could you possibly explain to me why I have this inner feeling that all was not tranquil in Esmond Bland's distinguished life, that perhaps there were secrets of a shabby nature, that perhaps Esme Bland is the keeper of his flame," said Harrison.

"I haven't a clue what you are talking about, Mr. Burns," said Rupert hastily.

"Have you heard of a man called Dwane Lonergan?"

"Dwane Lonergan was the man Esme killed."

"Did you know him?"

There was a long pause. "No," he answered finally.

"Why did you hesitate?"

"One knew about him, Dwane Lonergan. He was quite well known in a certain circle of, uh, rich men. But, you know, listening to you talk, I might be interested in letting you write my book," said Rupert du Pithon, looking at Harrison in a manner that suggested he was offering him something that would enhance his life. "I've never talked to anyone, really talked to anyone, in my whole life. I've told little bits to a lot of people, but never everything to one person."

"What book?"

"My life. It's utterly fascinating. Everyone will tell you that. I've known everybody in the Western world. All the royalty. All the politicians. All the film stars. You must have heard some of the stories about me."

Harrison, bewildered, nodded.

"About the duchess? Surely you heard that story?"

Harrison had not heard. "What duchess?" he asked.

"What duchess? What duchess indeed! *Wallis.* Windsor. In South-ampton? Black tie on Sunday night. Can you imagine? That lesbian who plays cards all the time, what's her name? She gave the party. Dead now. She was so fat the undertaker had to put her in the casket sideways. Anyway, I said I wouldn't go. I said only waiters and bandleaders wore black tie on Sunday night. And they changed the whole dinner at the last minute. Such a commotion it caused! It was frightfully funny, really. Wallis *adored* it. I have so many stories like that. I've been looking for the right person to put it all together for me. And now here you are at last, the perfect person, sitting right here in my apartment. Heaven sent, that's what I call it. I'm prepared to be very generous. I'd even consider a fifty-fifty split."

"I think that's not really for me, Mr. du Pithon," said Harrison.

Rupert du Pithon was undeterred, or perhaps didn't hear. "We could figure out a work schedule. I could tell you my stories a few hours each week, perhaps Friday afternoons, when everyone we know is leaving for the country and the telephone stops ringing. And then you could bring me pages that I could correct. Oh, it would be divine. Imagine! A book. Everyone's always said to me, 'Rupie, when are you going to write your book?' And now here you appear out of nowhere. Esme Bland, indeed. I'm a more interesting story than Esme."

Harrison shook his head and put up his hand. "No. No. I can't write your book for you, Mr. du Pithon. I have my own books to write. I have no time. Besides, your sort of life is not within my area of expertise."

"You mean you have come here just to talk to me about Esme Bland?" There was a tone of despair in his voice.

"Yes."

"That's all?"

"Yes."

"You see, I thought when you telephoned that it was me you wanted to see, to talk about me, to do an article or book about me."

"I'm sorry if I have misled you."

"How incredibly stupid of me."

"I wondered if you would prevail upon her to see me," said Harrison. "She has not replied to my letters."

"No, no, she will see no one, and certainly not someone from the press."

"You see, I think she has been wronged. I think there are mitigating circumstances. She knows things she has never told. I believe she is a woman with a secret. I am interested in people who carry secrets to the grave with them. I would be fair to her."

For a moment Harrison thought that Rupert du Pithon might cry. "I need a drink," he said weakly. "This has been quite a shock for me. I was expecting something quite different. Would you make it, please? I think Cleanie Cleanie has left out the ice and things."

Harrison walked to the drink table. "What would you like? There's white wine."

"No. I want a big girl's drink. A martini. Can you make a martini? If you can't do it properly, just give me gin on the rocks with a twist. I hate a bad martini. Did she leave lemons? She doesn't speak a word of English."

"There are lemons. And I can make a martini."

"I thought you had that look."

Harrison, in no hurry, went about the business of preparation and handed him the drink. Rupert took a sip.

"My dear, it's perfect. Simply perfect. So few people know how to do it, you know. They shake. They don't stir. They pour it over rocks. No, no, no. I watched you. You stirred. You iced the glass. You served it straight up and in a stemmed glass. Wherever did you learn?"

"When I was a schoolboy, a rich man in Connecticut taught me when I was visiting one of his sons."

"Who would that be?"

"Gerald Bradley."

"Good heavens. You are full of surprises. That ghastly woman you met in my hall, Eloise Brazen, was once one of his mistresses. Years ago it was. Not that that's such an honor, mind you, being the mistress of that man. She never stops talking about it, whenever anything about him, or one of his children, appears in the papers. She's consumed with curiosity about the handsome son, Constant. Do you know what she said to me once about Constant Bradley? She said, 'I'd love to go to bed with him. He wouldn't even have to buy me dinner.' That's the type she is. I always felt Eloise had something on Gerald Bradley. I don't know what. Do you know he's the only man who is allowed to smoke a cigar in the Four Seasons?"

"No, I didn't know."

"That's the sort of information I'm full of. And it's of use to absolutely nobody." He shook his head sadly.

"I had heard that you were a social gadfly."

"That is my reputation, yes."

"You seem deeper."

"I am deeper, but, you see, I have wasted my opportunities. I have been idle. There were things I could have done. I could have written, I'm sure. My eye was perfect. I missed nothing. I could turn a phrase better than anyone."

"But why didn't you?"

On his face was a look of profound weariness that had nothing to do with being tired. He stared straight up at the ceiling. Harrison was aware of a moisture that appeared in his eyes, as if he were fighting tears. He shook his head, and the aged papery skin of his loose chin shook a little. "It is a terrible thing to come to the conclusion that your life has been as unimportant as mine has been. What is it you wanted me to do, Mr. Burns?"

"To intercede with Esme Bland. To ask her to see me."

"She is in the Cranston Institute in Maine. It's where they send all the rich nuts."

"Yes."

"Nuns tend them."

"Yes."

"And you would like her to see you?"

"Yes."

"And you think a call or letter from me might do it?"

"Yes."

"Her father was a great friend of mine."

"Yes."

"Will you do me a favor in return?"

"Depends."

"My death would cause grief to no one," said Rupert. "But ending it is difficult to do, being a semi-invalid as I am. I think about it, but where do you get the pills? I haven't the courage to jump. Oh, I've looked. Late at night I've leaned out the kitchen window at the back of the building. I'd never do it where I would land on Park Avenue, I just can't bring myself to do that. Even in the alley. So messy, and I really wouldn't know what to wear. Bessie Talley wore just a raincoat when she jumped out of Five Fifty Park. Fitzy Montague wore his pajamas when he jumped out of Seven Forty, and the trousers flew off on the way down, and there he was, naked from the waist down when they found him, with a big red boil on his ass. I couldn't stand that. And it would be awful, too, if my hairpiece flew off—you probably didn't notice that I wear a toupee—and they made jokes about me.

You wouldn't get something for me, would you? A pill that would do it, or a lot of pills?"

"No."

"If you didn't want to hand them to me, you'd only have to leave them on a table, and I'd find them. Would you do that?"

"I wouldn't. I couldn't. I'm sorry," said Harrison.

"Are you Catholic? Is that it?"

"Lapsed."

"I would so appreciate it."

"No. I won't do that."

"I suppose Catholics are like that, even lapsed Catholics. They say it's always in you, your guilt. You never get rid of it totally. Then there's something else I want."

"What is that?"

"I am a great reader of obituaries. That page is the first I turn to each morning in the *Times*. Some I have even cut out and saved over the years. Magda Lupescu's, for instance. Alice Grenville's. And Cecil Beaton's. Their obituaries were works of art. So often recently, I have begun to wonder about my own, how it will read. I couldn't bear to have a bad obituary. I have led a life that very few people would understand. It could, in the wrong hands, make me look ridiculous. 'He went to more lunch parties and fashion shows than any man of his generation.' Or, 'He was especially gifted at *placement*.' Do they mention that you knew famous people? I don't think so. Have I told you that I was once, as a very young man, introduced to Hitler by poor mad Unity Mitford? Most people don't know that about me. 'He was a collector of people.' That is the sort of thing I would like said about me. 'He attended the legendary Beistegui Ball in Venice as Proust's Baron de Charlus in a costume, entirely in black, designed by Balenciaga.' I rather like the sound of that, don't you? It was reported once in a newspaper that I had the smallest waist in the United States Army during World War II, but I suppose you ought to leave that out. That would sound silly in print, don't you think? Would you write my obituary for me? Would you do that? I don't want to look like a fool after I'm gone. I don't want to be laughed at. If you write it, it will be left here in an envelope for Mr. Mendenhall from the bank to deliver to the *Times*, after my death. If you will do that for me, Mr. Burns, I will get Esme Bland to see you. She owes me one. I did her a great favor once. Perhaps she'll tell you that. Whether she tells you her secret, however, that is up to you. You will be kind to Esme, won't you? And to me?"

8

HARRISON took a plane to Bangor, Maine, where he rented a car and then drove the sixty miles to the town of Cranston. It was snowing. He checked into the Bee and Thistle Inn where he had reserved a room. There were Christmas wreaths on all the doors and Christmas lights in all the windows. Then he telephoned the Cranston Institute to verify his appointment that afternoon with Esme Bland which had been set up at the request of Rupert du Pithon. All was in order.

Esme Bland entered the visitors' room of the Cranston Institute in a friendly but hesitant manner. She was slim, shy, and sixty-six. She was expensively but primly dressed in a matching cashmere pullover and cardigan, with a tweed skirt and single strand of pearls, an upper-class-country-lady attire that Harrison correctly figured she had dressed in for most of her adult life. In her smartly coiffed, once-blond gray hair were two gold barrettes. She possessed the sort of aristocratic good looks that may have been called pretty in her youth, but never beautiful. She looked at her guest, appraised him, offered him her hand, then withdrew it, and offered it again, with a little smile at her own awkwardness.

"Mr. Burns?" she asked.

"Yes."

"I am Esme Bland."

"Yes, Miss Bland. It's kind of you to see me," said Harrison.

"It's difficult to resist Rupie," she replied. Her voice, governess-trained, matched her refined looks. "He's very persuasive. How is the old thing?"

"Frail. Not in the best of health. In financial distress, I gather. Talks of suicide, but I think it's all talk. He's still too interested in everything not to want to see what might happen."

160

"Oh, that's Rupie. Silly man, I suppose, but kind in his own snob-
bish way. I'm trying to think how old he must be. Eighty-three, or
eighty-four, I suppose. He was of an age with my father. God knows
what those two must have gotten up to together. Naughty, naughty,
naughty is all I can say." She smiled affectionately.

From outside the room came the screams of a crying woman.
"Thief!" she shouted. "Thief, thief!"

Esme rolled her eyes. "Oh, dear," she said. "Not again."

Into the room ran a nun dressed in the habit of a Sacred Heart
Madam. "You stole my rosary beads," she screamed at Esme.

Esme, unperturbed, replied, "No, I didn't steal your rosary beads,
Mother Vincent."

"Yes, you did, you did," the nun screamed, her voice bordering on
hysteria, tears streaming down her face. "They were sterling silver.
They were blessed by the Holy Father in Rome."

Esme Bland simply ignored the presence of the nun. "Go on, Mr.
Burns. Rupie said you had questions for me," she said.

"Thief!" screamed the nun again, her face now very close to
Esme's.

Esme turned to face her accuser. "Why would I want your rosary
beads? I am an Episcopalian, as you know perfectly well, Agnes, and
we do not use rosary beads," she said. Her voice took on a mildly
exasperated tone, as if she had had this conversation before.

A sister appeared, dressed in nurse's white. "Come, come, Agnes,"
she said. "Esme didn't take your rosary beads. No, no, we've found
them in the back of the drawer in your dresser, where you hid them
and forgot." She put her arm around the nun's ample waist and started
to lead her from the room.

"You found them?" asked the nun, her hysteria ceasing. "You
found my rosary beads?"

"Yes. In the back of your drawer."

"Oh, goody goody. Oh, thank you, Saint Anthony, for answering
my prayers. When you lose something and pray to Saint Anthony, he
will find it for you," said the nun. Her lips moved in a grateful prayer
of thanks.

"Yes, I know, Agnes. Now, come along. Esme has a visitor and has
visiting-room privileges for an hour," said the nurse.

"Oh, Sister Cagney," said Esme.

"Yes, Esme."

"Would you close the door behind you, please."

"Of course, Esme."

"Thank you." Esme, hands folded in front of her, waited patiently until the door was closed before she spoke. "I do wish she wouldn't call me Esme," said Esme, "but, of course, that is part of institutional life. It's all first names here." She smiled. "Now, where were we?"

"We were still talking about Rupert du Pithon. May I ask something?"

"Yes?"

"Who was the nun?"

"Oh, she's not a nun. She just dresses like a nun. She wanted to be a nun, apparently."

"She was dressed in the habit of the Sacred Heart order," said Harrison.

"How observant of you to have noticed that. But, of course, that's part of your business, isn't it, noticing details? She thinks she's the headmistress of a Sacred Heart convent. She calls herself Mother Vincent."

"Mother Vincent?"

"Yes. She says forty rosaries a day."

"Oh."

"Secrets," said Esme, suddenly.

"What?"

"Rupie said you were interested in secrets. Secrets that people carry within them to the grave."

"Good Lord," said Harrison. "I didn't know he was so specific."

"Why are you so interested in secrets?" asked Esme.

"I don't know that I really am."

"But you are. It is what you write about, Rupie says. And I know why secrets interest you."

"Why?"

"Because you are carrying a secret yourself. Am I right? Do, please, be honest with me. Or there is no point in all this. Am I right? Are you?"

Harrison stared at the woman. "Yes," he answered finally.

"There, you see? That wasn't so hard, was it?"

"No."

"It was about my father's death, was it not, that you wanted me to talk?" she asked.

"Well, yes, but primarily the death of Dwane Lonergan," said Harrison.

"Oh, Dwane Lonergan," she repeated, shuddering at the mention of his name. She crossed her arms in front of her, as if she were cold. "They are, how shall I put it, intertwined, in a way."

She rose from her seat and walked over to the window. Outside, it was snowing. She watched the snow for a while and then turned her chair toward the window and sat down again, this time with her back to Harrison. "Do you have your tape recorder on?" she asked.

"Yes."

"Good, I'm only going to say this once."

Slowly, she began to talk.

"It is a terrible thing to see your father dead, especially if you loved him the way I loved my father. It is a worse thing to see your father dead, naked, with an open jar of Vaseline on the bedside table and broken amyl nitrite ampoules all over the bed. Do you know what amyl nitrite ampoules are?"

"For the heart, I believe," answered Harrison.

"Yes, but for sexual pleasure, too, apparently," she said. "They transport you to mindlessness, so that there are no limits to one's, uh, activities, or so Mr. Dwane Lonergan informed me at a later time, shortly before I shot him, in fact."

She paused before she continued. "I didn't know what to do. I dreaded the thought of scandal. So I called Rupert du Pithon. I couldn't think of anyone else who might even begin to understand the sordid circumstance, and he had been a friend of my father's, sort of. I asked him what to do. He said, 'Wipe the Vaseline off his penis.' I said, 'I can't do that.' He said, 'You must. It's a giveaway. Someone at the funeral home is bound to notice, and those people report everything to the police or the papers. Just do it. Don't look.' It's the sort of thing I never would have thought of on my own. I suppose Rupie, the old gossip, told you all this."

"He didn't, no," said Harrison.

"Really? That speaks well for him, doesn't it?"

"Yes."

"It is the most unpleasant task to have to wipe Vaseline off your father's penis and out of your father's rectum, so the doctor and the undertaker will not know that the distinguished Esmond Bland, who dined frequently at the White House, died in bed with a five-hundred-dollar male prostitute who robbed him in death of his cuff links, wallet, cash, credit cards, and Rolex watch before he disappeared into the night, leaving the corpse behind, unattended. Does that answer your question, Mr. Burns?''

Harrison, stunned, nodded his head, and she, faced away from him, did not see his nod but continued, assuming his response.

"In many ways my father's death was a blessing. Not the manner of his death, but the act of dying. He was becoming indiscreet in his behavior. He dined in public with Dwane Lonergan, at places like Clarence's, where he was bound to run into people he knew. My father was in his seventies. Mr. Lonergan was at most twenty-five or -six or -seven, with a ring in his ear and a ponytail, and wore leather jackets and T-shirts. There was no way he could be passed off for a grandson. It was apparent just looking at him what he was. Trash. Lil Altemus saw them together at Clarence's. She said they arrived on Mr. Lonergan's motorcycle and were wearing helmets. I didn't know which way to look, I was so embarrassed when she told me. Forgive me for digressing.

"I changed the stained sheets—they were disgusting—with his body still in the bed, because I could not move him. My father was a big man, six feet three, a hundred and eighty-six pounds, in peak physical condition for a man his age. I put pajamas on him. Did you ever try to dress a dead person, Mr. Burns? It is very difficult. Then I aired out the room. The combined scents of amyl nitrite and sperm are very telling and most unpleasant. Then I called Dr. Parker. Silas Parker. Columbia-Presbyterian Hospital. Dr. Parker has been our family doctor for years and years. I can only assume he knew the family secrets, but I did not ask him. He signed the death certificate. Heart attack, he said. And, of course, it was, in a way. Father was wonderfully insured, and I was the beneficiary, and the insurance company paid off immediately. But I am getting ahead of my story.

"I have always been unstable, Mr. Burns. In and out of the Cranston Institute for years. Surely Rupie told you that? You don't have to answer. Years ago, when I was very young, back in the fifties, I was madly in love with a young man on Long Island called Billy Grenville. He was four or five years older than I. I went to Green Vale with one of his sisters, Felicity. Oh, how I loved him. I literally ached with love. I always thought we would marry. His sisters thought so. His mother, Alice Grenville, thought so. Even Billy thought so. But he met a chorus girl and married her instead. She was pretty, common, of course, frightfully common, but pretty. Billy's sisters hated her. Wrong side of the tracks, they all said. Married him for his money, they all said. I was devastated, completely devastated. I don't think anything ever hurt me so much, but I hid my hurt, of course. After all, it was a small community there on Long Island in those days. We all knew each other. We all saw each other. We all played tennis together. We all played golf together. We all belonged to Piping Rock. I even pretended to like Ann. That was her name. Several years into the marriage, it started going bad. She was no good, a tramp, really. She began sleeping around. Secretly, Billy started seeing me again. I was ecstatic. He said he wanted to divorce her. He asked me to marry him after the divorce. Then his wife shot and killed him. She pretended she thought Billy was a prowler, but she knew what she was doing. Prowlers aren't nude. Billy was. You must have read about that. They've written a book about it. They even made a miniseries about it. The thing is, they cut me out. They didn't use my character. That in a nutshell is the story of my life. Being cut out. It is why, at the age of sixty-six, I remain a maiden lady who has had a lifelong fixation on her father. After Billy's death, I had my first major breakdown. There had been a few little ones before. That's when I came here to the Cranston Institute the first time. But back to my father. Back to Dwane Lonergan. That is what interests you, I know.

"My father had quite an extraordinary funeral, almost royal in the trappings, French horns playing, that sort of thing. Glorious music. A chorus of fifty choirboys in red cassocks and starched white surplices. Oh, how marvelous they looked. So young. So scrubbed. I'm sure you read about it. Perhaps you were even there. Everyone else was. The world came. There weren't enough seats at St. Thomas's on Fifth Avenue for all the people, and that's a very large church. They had to pipe the eulogies to the crowds outside. The vice president was there in the front pew, across the aisle from me, representing President and Mrs. Reagan, and all sorts of dignitaries—the governor, the mayor, et cetera, et cetera, plus friends from everywhere and, of course, the curious, who came to look at the famous. We needed a person of noble stature to speak, and Dr. Kissinger agreed. His eulogy was magnificent. My father was on the board of the Met, so Jessye Norman sang. She was too glorious for words. Such a voice. The Episcopal bishop officiated. For a half hour, even I, who knew everything, who knew how false it all was, who knew the casket was empty, was caught up in the pageantry.

"Then the most extraordinary thing happened. Jessye Norman was singing Gounod's 'Ave Maria,' and the five-hundred-dollar male prostitute entered my pew and sat beside me. I can't think how he got past the ushers, most of whom I knew. He had a little ring in his ear. I hate that look, don't you? And a little ponytail. I hate that look, too. He began talking to me. He was extremely angry. He had been through my father's wallet, the wallet he stole, and discovered among his papers that my father was HIV positive. You do know what that means, don't you? He said that my father had not told him he was HIV positive and that his life was at risk. He said he would walk up on the altar and announce it from the pulpit if I did not agree then and there to pay him ten million dollars. He was talking loudly enough so the pallbearers and the people in the pews behind were staring. If you could have seen the look on his face. He was excited by the prospect of stepping up on that beautiful altar, amidst all those beautiful lilies so skillfully arranged by Robert Isabell, to address all those famous people. My heart almost stopped. I looked at him, aghast. He was breathing heavily. His looks were, curiously, sexual. I must confess to you, in an aside, that he was beautiful at that moment, simply beautiful, in a cheap way, of course. He began to rise, and I grabbed his hand and pulled him down. Of course, I agreed to pay him what he asked. The service went on. He did not move from my pew. I was his hostage.

"There was no burial. You see, knowing what I knew, I had had my father cremated immediately after his death, three days before his funeral, so there could be no autopsy. You see, I knew that he was HIV positive, and I didn't want there to be any problem about the insurance. After the funeral, there was a reception at the Butterfield Club, twelve blocks up Fifth Avenue. I stood at the top of those beautiful stairs and shook hands with hundreds and hundreds of people, who told me over and over and over again what a wonderful man my father was. Then I was driven back to Long Island. I gave the butler and the cook and the chauffeur the night off. They said, all of them, 'Oh, no, Miss Esme, we'll stay with you tonight,' and I said, 'No, no, I'm fine. Really I am.' Later, after dark, as arranged in the front pew during Jessye Norman's 'Ave Maria,' I met Mr. Lonergan. He came to my house. I didn't have ten million dollars to pay him, then or ever. Even if I had, I wouldn't have paid him. You can't pay those people. It never ends. He said to me, 'I've been fucking your father since I was seventeen.' Imagine saying such a thing to me. He said to me, and I quote, exactly, as I have never forgotten the look on his face or the tone of his voice, 'I have yet to meet the person, male or female, I couldn't get it up for if the price was right.' I have never been one to engage in cheap talk, but I think he was trying to come on to me, to continue his role of sexual service in the family. You know the rest of the story. Everyone does. I shot him dead.''

"Right between the eyes, I heard,'' said Harrison.

"Well, actually, I've always been a good shot. I was skeet-shooting champion at Piping Rock for six years,'' she said. "I had no fear about what would happen to me. I knew what they would say. 'She's been in and out of institutions all her life. She's mad as a hatter.' And they did. That's exactly what they said. And here I am, back in the institution. For life. But, of course, that is one of the many advantages of money. I feel lucky to be here and not in that ghastly place in Bedford Hills with poor Mrs. Harris. I went to Madeira, but years before Mrs. Harris became headmistress. Well, now I've told you the secret I was carrying with me to the grave. Do you have any questions?''

"I am stunned,'' said Harrison. "Why have you told me all this?''

"Why not? What difference does it make now?''

"What can I do for you in return?''

"There's a mother in Arizona. Perhaps with your sleuthing abilities, you could track her down.''

"Whose mother?''

"Dwane Lonergan's. She claimed his body and took it back.''

"What would you do if I did locate her?''

"Leave her some money, I suppose. You see, I have cancer. I've lost both breasts. It's metastasized. That means spread all through me. As one of the doctors said about me during the last operation, from behind his blue mask, thinking I was out, which I wasn't, 'She's riddled.' Yes, I am. I'm riddled. This is a wig I'm wearing. I bet you didn't know it, did you? Kenneth cut it for me, shaped it for me. Didn't he do a marvelous job? No one can tell. I have three of them. What I'm trying to tell you is, I haven't long to live. It will be a nice ending to your story, won't it? I suppose my father's the villain of the piece, isn't he? Poor Daddy. And now, if you've finished with me, Mr. Burns, I think I'd better go and rest. I really feel quite exhausted. All these revelations tire one. What is it about you that makes people talk? You don't say much. You didn't ask me many questions. Perhaps it's because you look a bit like a defrocked priest. Good-bye, Mr. Burns.''

"Good-bye, Miss Bland.''

At the door, she stopped and turned back to him. "About your secret. Tell it, whatever it is. Don't keep it inside. It eats away at you in there, just as if it were cancer. You have no idea how lighthearted I feel all of a sudden. Merry Christmas, Mr. Burns.''

That evening Harrison sat in the crowded bar of the Bee and Thistle Inn, reading over notes he had made from his afternoon with Esme Bland. Christmas lights lent a festive atmosphere to the room. From the next table, he heard a conversation between a man and woman.

"Look out the window. It's turned into a blizzard," said the woman.

"I've been watching," said the man.

"Pretty girl, there."

"Which one?"

"In the black Chanel suit."

"Who is she?"

"That's Gerald Bradley's youngest daughter."

"How do you know that's who it is?"

"I've seen her picture in the papers."

Harrison turned and looked. Had it not been for his neighbors at the next table, he might have walked past her, but it was Kitt, unmistakably Kitt, grown up, adult, elegantly dressed, and alone. He did not leap from his seat and rush over to her. Instead, he sat in his place and watched her for several minutes, adjusting his memory of the lively teenage girl he had last seen on the day he graduated from Milford with this fashionable woman so deep in some private reverie. In the intervening years, he had thought of her often, always with affection, and even wondered how she would turn out. It struck him that she had grown to look more like Constant.

She stared out the window at the snow piling up against the windowpane, unaware that she was being talked about at one table and stared at from another. Her foot, shod in a slingback shoe, tapped time to the beat of music coming from a trio playing in the lobby. On the table in front of her were a glass of wine, a pile of society and fashion magazines, and a quilted black bag with a gold chain. She was waiting for no one.

He rose and walked to her table. Standing behind her, he said, "It was at the Milford graduation in 1973, and you yelled out, 'Yay, Harrison,' and everyone laughed, and I got a much bigger round of applause than I ever would have gotten if you hadn't done that.''

She turned. A look of total surprise lit up her face. "I don't believe this," she said.

"Hello, Kitt."

"Hello, Harrison." She emitted a little shriek of pleasure.

"I'm not sure I would have recognized you."

"I would have recognized you," she said. "Am I glad to see you after all these years! I was just experiencing such a melancholy feeling, watching the snowstorm all alone. Kisses on both cheeks are in order. And a hug. Sit down. Sit down. I want to know everything. I guess everyone calls you Harrison now, not Harry, isn't that right? I read that somewhere about you."

"I answer to both. I must say, Kitt, you're looking very smart. There were no indications in your braces-on-the-teeth youth that you were going to turn out so well," said Harrison.

"We've followed in Ma's footsteps, if you can believe it, after teasing her about her clothes all those years. We're dressed by the couture, Maureen and Mary Pat and me. Of course, we did all live in Paris for three years when Pa was the ambassador, and Mary Pat lives there now since she married Philippe."

"And you live where?" asked Harrison.

"About," she replied. "Here, there."

"What happened to the house in Scarborough Hill?"

"Still there. Sis Malloy lives there. She's the keeper of the Bradley flame, a sort of spinster Mrs. Danvers, keeping everything up until the family returns, which they never will."

"How is Sis Malloy?"

"Same as ever. On the day of Mary Pat's wedding to the count, when she was all done up in her white satin and rose-point lace, looking too divine for words, Sis said, 'Don't ever forget your grandfather was a butcher.' "

Harrison laughed. "That's Sis, all right."

"The thing is, about Sis, she's right. We have all forgotten, and we shouldn't."

A woman approached their table. "Excuse me," she said. Harrison and Kitt turned to look at her.

"Is it you? Is it really you, Mr. Burns? I thought it was you. Look what I'm reading. One of your books. It's only the paperback, I'm afraid, not the hardback, but I'd be so appreciative if you'd sign it," said the woman. She looked at Kitt. "Please forgive me for interrupting, but it just seemed too strange. Maine, the snow, the inn, the book, and there he is."

"Yes, of course, I'd be delighted to sign," said Harrison.

"I know I'm being a nuisance."

"Not at all. Tell me your name." All the time he was thinking that he wanted to get back to his conversation with Kitt.

"Liza Lake."

"Is that L-I-Z-A or L-I-S-A?"

"Actually, it's L-E-E-Z-A."

"I'm glad I asked. I wouldn't have arrived at that. There you are." He handed her back her book.

"Thank you. I'm so glad Max Goesler is behind bars," she said, in parting. "It's where he belongs."

"You were charm itself," said Kitt, when she was gone. "Does that happen to you often?"

"No."

"It must make you feel good, doesn't it?"

"Yes."

"Constant reads every word you write. We all do." She looked at him. "I suppose I should say, 'What are you doing here?' "

"At the Bee and Thistle Inn in Cranston, Maine?"

"Yes."

"I could ask you the same question," he said.

"Oh, just a little vacation to get away from things. This is a lovely inn, don't you think? Marvelous walks, ample tennis courts, the air, the food, the rest, that sort of thing."

"No, no, no, don't say that, Kitt. We're in a near blizzard outside. I can't think you're taking walks or playing tennis. Let's not get off to a wrong start. I saw her today."

"Who?"

"Your sister, Agnes, in the Cranston Institute. The Bradley your family never mentions. You must be here visiting her."

Kitt made no reply.

Harrison sat down beside her. "Dressed in the habit of a Sacred Heart nun? Thinks she's Mother Vincent at the convent? Says forty rosaries a day? Claims her silver rosary beads blessed by the Pope were stolen? Am I ringing any bells?"

Kitt took a sip of her wine. "I have her habits made by a theatrical costumer in Boston, in case that was your next question. That's my little secret. Ma doesn't know. What the hell difference does it make if it makes her happy? Poor thing. She talks of the Pope's visit to Scarborough Hill as if it were yesterday rather than twenty-one years ago. It can't be much of a life in there, you know, fighting with a woman called Esme in the next room every day of her life."

She smiled at him. There were tears in her eyes. "Poor Agnes. Before they realized she was retarded, the older boys, Jerry and Des and Sandro, used to make such fun of her, and play such terrible jokes on her, and the pathetic thing was she just adored them in return. She looks like Pa, don't you think? Same chin. Sounds like Pa, too."

"Yes, I suppose she does," said Harrison.

"I come up every year at this time and spend a few days, and if I'm in the country, I come on her birthday as well. She loves presents. She looks at my hands first before she looks at my face to see what I've brought her. She loves unwrapping them and saving the paper and the ribbons. She claps her hands. I bring her prayer books and rosary beads and scapular medals and things. If this hadn't happened to her, I'm sure she would have become a nun. All the indications were there, but Ma and Pa simply wouldn't face it. They thought such a thing couldn't happen to us. Sort of typical Bradley thinking, don't you think?" She sighed, shook her head, and changed the subject. "You haven't answered me, you know. What are you doing here in Cranston, Maine, in a snowstorm a week before Christmas?"

"I was visiting Esme Bland," he said.

"Esme? On a story?"

"Yes."

"She killed someone, didn't she?"

"Yes."

"I suppose I'll be reading about it."

"Yes."

"The dining room closes in ten minutes. You wouldn't like to take me to dinner, would you?" she asked.

During dinner the electricity went out. Waiters and waitresses scurried to light candles on all the tables.

"Power failure," said the waitress as she lit a candle. "It's a bad storm."

"Sort of fun," said Kitt. "Don't you think? I saw a movie once about people who were stranded in an inn during a blizzard."

"Isn't there a generator in the inn?" Harrison asked the waitress.

"There is. It's in one of the outbuildings, but the door is locked and no one can find the key. They're looking, though."

"Oh, Harrison, I can't tell you how nice this is," said Kitt. "It's quite festive. We should probably finish the wine, don't you think? It's a pity to let it go to waste."

"I'll have another coffee," said Harrison.

"Hi, Mr. Burns. Would you like to join our table? It's Leeza, in case you can't see in this light. From before? With your book? There's a group of us. We thought we'd sit out the storm together in the bar."

"Oh, Leeza." He looked over at Kitt and understood her eyes. "Perhaps later, Leeza. We have some things to discuss," said Harrison.

Kitt smiled at him. "I love seeing you, Harrison," she said.

"There's bridge. There's backgammon. There's dancing. All by candlelight. Do any of the above appeal to you?" he asked.

"Not one. There's too much about you I want to know and too much about me I want to tell. Did you know I had a terrific crush on you when I was fourteen and fifteen?"

"No."

"Of course you didn't. And Maureen said, 'Don't fall in love with a scholarship student. That's not what Ma and Pa have in mind for us.' "

Harrison smiled and shook his head. "What a family you're from. I never liked Maureen much, as long as we're being so candid. And Jerry. I couldn't abide him, either. Once I saw Maureen talk down to a great architect, the one who built the Bradley Library at Milford, and I never forgot it. What's her life like? How has she fared?"

"Married to Freddy, quite happily. He handles the business affairs for the family, so the boys can be free for public service. Maureen turns out children in a fury, one after another, year after year, wanting to outpoint the parents, I suppose. She always thought she was far more intelligent than the boys, and she was, I suppose, but Pa was never one for wanting the ladies of the family to excel. Run the house, do the charities, have children, raise them to be good Catholics, that's the most we had to aspire to."

"Women these days do not have to do their father's bidding," said Harrison. "In fact, I don't know any who do."

"Well, there is the prospect of all that money sometime in the future. None of us wanted to monkey with that," replied Kitt.

"Do I detect the tiniest element of defeat?"

"I thought I kept that well hidden beneath this Chanel suit, this

172

organdy gardenia, and all these goddamn gold chains. I thought they gave me a look of superiority. Or does the writer's eye penetrate the costume?"

"I think Leeza and her group think we're rude," said Harrison.

"Yes, yes, we'll go over there in a minute. You mustn't disappoint your fans," said Kitt, but she displayed no intention of going. She poured the last of the wine into her glass. "When you first went away, I missed you. I was sad you didn't say good-bye to me. I always thought you liked me. What happened? What went wrong? How could you vanish like you did? Without a word. None of us understood. Ma wrote you a letter, and you didn't answer. Maureen and Freddy said they saw you in Rome, and you pretended you didn't know them."

"Oh, things happened," said Harrison. He shrugged.

"I'm sure. And I'm sure from that shrug you're not going to tell me what. Now, seeing you, I think I must have missed you all the time, although I didn't think about it after a while." She giggled. "I'm a little tight."

He smiled at her. "You've become much more than stylish, you know. You're lovely. You're really lovely, Kitt," he said.

"If you could feel the exquisite feeling going through me," she replied. "I've always wanted to be called lovely. Sometimes I'm called handsome, but never lovely. I was sure you were going to say I'd grown to look like Constant. That's what everyone says." She smiled at him. "We heard you were engaged."

"More. Married."

"Oh." She elongated the single syllable, bringing disappointment into her tone. "I didn't take you for the marrying kind."

"Apparently I'm not. We're separated at the moment."

"Do you miss her?"

"Sometimes, yes. I miss the boys."

"Boys?"

"I have twins. Age two."

"Oh, my, you *are* married. Who is she? Who was she? That's what Ma always asks."

"She was Claire Rafferty."

"Claire Rafferty! She was a bridesmaid in Maureen's wedding."

"Yes."

"You married an older woman."

173

"Five or six years, yes."

"Seven."

"Six."

"Was that the problem? Age?"

"No."

"She was a rude lady. She left before the reception. She dumped her bridesmaid's dress in a wastebasket. It cost seven hundred dollars. Ma was *furious*. She said she never heard of such bad behavior. No one could understand it. Ma said if she ever saw her again, she'd give her a piece of her mind. And now she's Mrs. Harrison Burns. I can't wait to tell this to Ma."

Harrison nodded.

"What do you have to say to *that* bit of information?" asked Kitt.

"You don't want to hear what I have to say to that."

"Oh, yes I do."

"On the night before the wedding, after the bridal dinner at the club, when everyone had gone to bed, your father came into the room where Claire was sleeping, the room that used to be Agnes's room, and tried to fuck her."

Kitt gasped. Her hand covered her mouth.

"Fortunately for Claire, your father came before he got it in her. Do you still think she's a rude lady? Can you blame her for not staying for the reception?"

"Oh, dear," said Kitt. She put her head in her hands. "No wonder none of my friends or Mary Pat's friends ever wanted to stay overnight. Their parents wouldn't let them. The word was out on our house. You'd better order me another drink on that one, if you don't mind. I might have a big girl's drink now. A brandy, perhaps. I always thought something like that must have happened. I thought maybe it was one of my brothers. The men in my family, they all fuck too much. I married another one, just like that."

"Really?"

"Oh, yes. Every man, or at least most men, have their outside activities, or so my brothers tell me, but it shouldn't cross over into the house and the family. Poor Ma. What she closes her eyes to. And it's all hush-hush in front of the help. 'You know how maids talk.' That's what Ma always says. That seems to be the big thing she worries about. Ma would die if she thought Bridey and the rest of them knew, but they probably do. Help always know everything, don't you think?"

"I don't know. We never had much help," said Harrison. "There was always rich-girl talk from you. I remember that."

Kitt laughed. "You're so prickly, Harrison. It's the scholarship boy in you coming out," she said.

Harrison laughed.

"You've changed, Harry. You're different somehow. You're not at all like that shy, quiet, blushing boy Constant brought home with him when he was kicked out of Milford. We used to think you were in love with Constant."

"I probably was, to a degree. But that was then."

"I remember you as always wanting not to be noticed, almost frightened of attention. Now you seem somber, maybe even a little grim. Have terrible things happened to you? Oh, I remember now. They caught those frightful boys who killed your parents. Is that it?"

"You've changed too, you know. I'm trying to think how old you must be," he replied.

"Avoid answering by asking another question, that old trick. I'm thirty."

"Thirty. My God. I see your name in Dolly De Longpre's column from time to time. Somewhere I saw pictures of you at a house party in Turkey, and I read about your marriage in *Town and Country*," said Harrison.

"Well, don't bother to send a wedding present."

Harrison laughed again. "Not going well?"

"Great wedding, lousy marriage. My sister the countess was the matron of honor. That added no end of glamour to the proceedings. She almost got more space in the papers than I did," said Kitt. "My father didn't want me to marry him. My father said, 'Can I tell you something about Cheever Chadwick, Kitt? He's never going to amount to a row of pins. That income is going to deball him. He doesn't have enough money for philanthropy, but he's got more than enough not to have to test himself. You mark my words, he's going to flit from one thing to another.' Whatever you say about my father, and I know a lot of people have a lot to say about him, mostly bad, but when it comes to money, he always knew what he was talking about."

"Why did you marry him then?"

"It's hard being a Catholic girl and hoping to make a good marriage.

And in our family, with my mother, you just had to make a good marriage. Maureen did all right with Freddy Tierney. And Mary Pat got the count. Everybody loves Philippe. Then I met Cheever in Aspen one year, at a winter wedding. It was my fourteenth stint as a bridesmaid and his tenth as best man. At first it seemed like a dream. Oh, I suppose I wanted to stick it to those girls back home who used to snub me at the club. I made the best marriage of the whole lot of them, Weegie Somerset or Belinda Beckwith, or any of those girls, except that I wasn't a bit happy with Cheever. His family hated the idea of him marrying a Catholic, which was part of the reason I was so determined. And, to boot, we made him convert, not that it meant a damn thing to him. We didn't get the papal blessing, like Maureen and the others did. Even Cardinal couldn't swing that one. Ma minded horribly about that."

Harrison said nothing.

"Maybe I always knew it wasn't going to last. Maybe that's why I didn't write thank-you notes for my wedding presents. I suppose I'll be the first divorcée in the Bradley family," said Kitt. "Shall we talk about our flop marriages? Do you want details?"

He laughed. "No. Not tonight. Tomorrow."

"Of course, you're right. Tomorrow. After Mass. There's an eight-thirty and a ten in the village."

"I don't go to Mass anymore."

"Naughty, naughty. Hell's fires for you." She reached for her bag. "It's two o'clock. I'm going to bed. You better join Leeza and her friends. How about breakfast?"

"They've closed the airport in Bangor, and the roads on the way to the airport are closed, too. We seem to be in a raging blizzard. The lines are down. The fax is out. We're trapped," said Harrison.

"It would be quite nice to be snowed in, wouldn't it? Marooned in Maine. Roads blocked. Sounds heavenly, doesn't it? This almost calls for champagne. Did you phone Claire?"

"Yes. Are you going to phone Cheever?"

"No. He's in Las Vegas with a hand model."

"It's like that, is it?"

They stared at each other.

"Were you thinking of kissing me?" she asked.

"Yes. How did you know that?"

176

"About time. I've been waiting for twenty-four hours. I began to think you were one of those who didn't kiss on the first date. Well, do it, for God's sake."

He moved toward her on the sofa and took her in his arms. They kissed each other, looked at each other, and kissed each other again. Their hands moved over each other's backs and shoulders.

"You're not thinking of Constant, are you?" Kitt whispered.

"Oh, no," he said. "I was thinking of you."

"Good. I'm mad about your tongue. I like a good strong tongue. Do you think I'm terribly forward?" she asked.

"Yes, but I like forward. I need a hand held out. I'm not good as the instigator," he answered.

Again they kissed. Their embrace became more passionate.

"What is it you want?" she asked.

"I'd like very much to see you undressed."

"I think that could be arranged. Quite easily," said Kitt.

"Your room or mine?"

"Mine, of course. How would it look for me to be sneaking around the halls of the Bee and Thistle after midnight? Gerald Bradley's daughter. Think of the talk. The door will be open. By open I mean closed, but unlocked. You will be able to walk right in."

That night Harrison became Kitt's lover. They did not emerge from Kitt's room for most of the next day.

"Ma, I won't make your party tonight. I'm snowed in up here. Worst storm in years. Roads closed. Lines down. I'm talking on a cellular phone. You won't believe whose cellular phone it is. You won't believe who I am sitting here with. Harrison. Harrison Burns. Constant's old friend from Milford. Do you remember?" There was a pause as she listened to her mother. Then she looked at Harrison, covered the receiver, and said, "She said you dropped out of our lives. She said you forgot all about us." Her attention went back to her mother. "Well, he's fine. Serious looking. Scowl line between the eyes. Staring at a word processor all day, I suppose. Oh, Ma, a lady asked for his autograph, and he signed it like he was used to it." She listened to her mother again and then said, "She said she reads your books. She wants to know what you're doing here. He's visiting someone, Ma. No, he's not writing about the place for a magazine, at least I don't think so. No, Ma. I won't tell him about Agnes. I promise. Oh, she's

177

pretty much the same. She fights with Esme in the next room. Over rosary beads mostly. You'd better get Cardinal to order some more, by the way. Blessed, and all that." When she hung up, she looked over at Harrison. He was looking back at her.

"Come here," she said.

"I find it odd that you ask no questions about Constant. Don't you have any curiosity about your former best friend?"

"How is he?"

"In Congress. You must know that. The youngest congressman there. He's going to run for governor. Pa thinks there's more visibility as a governor than there is in Congress if you want to make a run for the White House. Pa wants him to speak at the next convention."

"Ah."

"Something went off between you two, didn't it?"

"Boarding school friendships aren't necessarily meant to last forever."

"There are the occasional character flaws, I know. But you have to admit he's utterly charming, and he's done marvelous things in Congress."

Harrison said nothing.

"Now, Charlotte, his wife. That's another story. Oh, she's all right, I suppose. She thinks she's sweller than we are, which she is. She's a Weegie Somerset type, but, fortunately for everyone concerned, Cardinal located a Catholic grandmother in Charlotte's past, on her mother's side, got her baptized fast, and wham, bam, an instant Catholic, and a perfect political wife."

Still Harrison said nothing.

"She thinks we're too loud when we get together, but she hangs in there. She likes the money. She tried to leave Constant once, and Pa gave her a million dollars to stay. Then the next year she tried to leave him again, and Pa gave her another million. I don't know how many times she can pull that one off."

Harrison, reluctant to be a participant in the conversation, said, "Why does she want to leave him so often?"

"She claims he hit her, and you know perfectly well that's ridiculous. Constant wouldn't harm a flea."

* * *

"My father would like to see you," said Kitt.

"Gerald? See me? Why?"

"I don't know why. He called this morning. Ma told him we'd met. He seemed very pleased that I had discovered you again, if that is what I have done. Pa admires success, you know. He likes the way you write. He said, 'He's on the side of law and order. I like that.' "

"Your father actually said that?"

"Yes."

"Good heavens."

"He wants to take you to lunch at the Four Seasons."

"Oh, I don't think so."

"Please, for me, do it. Please, Harrison."

"No. I don't want to."

"There's something he wants to ask you."

"What?"

"I don't know. At least you'll get a good lunch. And you'll see everyone. My father is the only man allowed to smoke cigars in the Four Seasons."

"Yes, I know that."

"But how could you know that?"

"A man named Rupert du Pithon told me. He said it was the sort of information he was full of, that was of interest to no one."

"Will you see him?"

"When I get back. I'm going to Arizona right after Christmas."

"Pa doesn't like to be put off, you know."

"I said I'd see him when I got back from Arizona."

"Oh, what a stern look on your face. What's in Arizona?"

"The mother of Dwane Lonergan."

"Should I know who Dwane Lonergan is?"

"The prostitute Esme Bland killed."

"You fell asleep with your glasses on," said Kitt. Her face was radiant with tenderness. "I was watching you."

"How'd I look?"

"There are dark places inside you, Harrison."

"What do you mean?"

"Someday you should videotape yourself sleeping. Watch yourself thrash. Listen to yourself cry out. If I didn't know better, I'd think you were the killer of your parents. Oh, that's a horrible thing to say, Harry. I'm sorry. I went too far, as usual.''

"Forget it.''

"What happened to those boys?''

"Twenty years.''

"I feel envied, but unworthy. Seeing you, realizing what you've done, makes me see how purposeless my life is. What am I really? Just a rich man's daughter. I've made a lousy marriage. I haven't had a child. My life is all about having lunch, going to Kenneth to have my hair done, going out to the kind of party that gets written up in Dolly De Longpre's column, and sipping too much white wine. This is not how I ever imagined it was going to be for me. I thought I would do great things, but I haven't done anything really, except learn to speak French, fluently, and with a perfect accent, or so Philippe tells me, but that's not such a big deal, is it? Look at you, Harrison. Once they found the key that opened the door to turn on the generator, you were back in your room typing away on your laptop the story of Esme Bland and the prostitute she killed. What was that guy's name?''

"You haven't let them break your spirit, have you, Kitt?'' asked Harrison.

"By them, do you mean Cheever?''

"No, by them I mean your family.''

"The roads are open. The airport in Bangor is open,'' said Harrison. "I guess it's time to put the show on the road.''

"I'd like to stay here forever,'' said Kitt. "Let's stay through Christmas, Harrison. Just the two of us at the Bee and Thistle.''

"I can't.''

"Why?''

"I have two little boys to spend Christmas with.''

"And Claire, I suppose?''

"Yes. And Claire.''

"I can't bear to end this,'' said Kitt.

"Who said it's going to end? We just have to go back. The storm's over. Real life again.''

"Harry, I think I'm beginning to love you,'' said Kitt.

"No, let's not fall in love, Kitt.''

"No?"

"No. It's too complicated."

"Yes, yes, you're right, of course, no love. Lots of lovely lust. No love. It's already too complicated."

"Yes."

"But it's not going to end, is it? Tell me it's not going to end, Harrison. Please, please, please."

9

HARRISON took a plane to Phoenix, where he transferred to a plane for Tucson. The heat was scorching and the sunlight blinding. At the Tucson airport, he rented a car to drive the sixty miles south to the town of Nogales on the border of Mexico. On the outskirts of Nogales, he stopped and took out the directions Maxine Lonergan had given him over the telephone. "I'm on the American side, remember," she said. "Don't cross the border. You get on the Patagonia Highway at the Seven-Eleven store, just before you hit town. Stay on it for about six miles. You'll come to a dirt road called Vista del Cielo. Hang a left there for a couple of miles. On the right-hand side you'll see a mailbox with RFD and a picture of a red cow on it. Turn in there. That's me."

At the mailbox with the picture of the red cow he turned in, as directed. He had imagined a small adobe or a trailer home, but there was no house in sight. He drove on the dirt road for a couple of miles. At times his vision was impaired by the dust his car raised. On each side was barren desert land with an occasional cactus. He thought he had misunderstood her directions. Then he came to two stone pillars and a closed gate. On each side of the pillars there was a high brick wall that seemed to surround the area of the house beyond. Confused, he pulled up to the gate before he noticed a bell and a speaker on a freestanding post. He pushed the bell. He could see that a closed-circuit television camera directed at him was activated by the bell. A man's voice said, "*Sí?*"

"I think perhaps I've made a mistake," said Harrison into the speaker. "I'm looking for a Mrs. Maxine Lonergan. I thought she said to turn in at the post box with the red cow, but perhaps I misunderstood her. I wonder if you could direct me."

"Your name?"

"My name? Harrison Burns."

The gates opened. Harrison drove in. Inside was a green lawn with

182

gardens, and ahead, at the end of a gravel drive, was a long, low ranch house of handsome design and graceful lines with a red tile roof. He parked his rented car in the circular courtyard in front of the house. Almost immediately the door opened. A tall thin handsome young man dressed in cowboy clothes and wearing a gun in a holster stepped outside.

"Mr. Harrison?" he said.

"Burns, it is. Harrison is the first name," Harrison said.

"Right. Come in."

Harrison walked past him. Inside, the house was air-conditioned cool. There was a big central hall. To the right, through a set of double doors, was a large living room. Beyond it, through another set of double doors, was a smaller room. From the hall Harrison could see a giant television screen. A sound system was playing the songs of Dom Belcanto, the late Las Vegas and Hollywood singer who was widely believed to have had gangland connections.

"She's puttin' on her face," said the man with the gun. "She don't like nobody to see her until she's put on her face."

"I see," said Harrison. "Does she work here?"

"Who?"

"Maxine Lonergan."

"Work here? Are you kiddin'? This is her house."

"This is Mrs. Lonergan's house?" asked Harrison, unable to disguise the surprise in the tone of his voice.

"*Miss* Lonergan, not missus. Yeah, this is her house. What'd you think?"

Harrison nodded away his doubts. "Why do you have a gun?" he asked.

"I'm her bodyguard."

"Oh." He nodded his head. "Is it loaded?"

"Of course, it's loaded."

"Oh. Looks like it's a beautiful house."

"Yeah, it's beautiful. And safe. It's like a fortress, this house. The windows are all bulletproof. I could fire this gun right at that window, and it wouldn't do nothing but shatter the glass. See this button here? You push this button and zap, just like that, steel doors drop out from under the eaves, and you're encased. Completely encased. She's got buttons like that in every room."

Harrison nodded. "Who are you protecting yourself from?" he asked.

The question was ignored. "But," said the man, "as Maxine always says, if they're going to get you, they're going to get you, no matter what kind of security you got. Right?"

"Yes, I suppose so," agreed Harrison. "You don't think when you're driving up that dirt road that you're going to find anything like this." With a broad, two-handed gesture, Harrison indicated the impressive house in which he was standing.

"That's the whole fuckin' point, man," said the man, as if he were talking to an idiot.

"Yes, of course, I see."

"She says to tell you wait in the bar."

"I would like to use the men's room."

"That way. Down that hall. Turn left. Maxine always says, 'Turn left at the Renoir,' but that's her joke, not mine, so laugh when she says it, if you should happen to ask her to go to the bathroom again."

Harrison walked down the hall. There on the wall was a Renoir-looking painting. He peered at it. He touched it. He looked at the signature. He turned left and entered the bathroom. On the wall were two urinals, as in a public bathroom. He took out a pen and notebook and made a few notes.

" *'Fly me to the moon,'* " came a second voice from the hallway, singing along with Dom Belcanto's voice on the sound system. "I hope Pony took care of you," Maxine Lonergan said, as she came up behind Harrison, who was sitting on a tall stool in her bar. "No drink? Pony didn't offer you a drink?"

She had a cigarette smoker's voice. He saw her in the mirror behind the bar before he turned and looked at her, hopping off the barstool as they shook hands.

"Miss Lonergan, I'm Harrison Burns," he said.

"What do they call you? Harry?"

"Sometimes, yes. I prefer Harrison."

"Then Harrison it shall be," she said, smiling at him. "It's a nice name. Your mother's maiden name, I bet?"

"Yes, it was."

She was a tall, beautifully built woman of forty-five. Her face, chiseled regularly by a doctor in Brazil to retain its youth, was expertly made-up, as if she were about to go on stage. Her hair, blond, iridescent blond, had just been done in an elaborate manner. She was dressed in off-white cashmere slacks and an off-white silk blouse opened down several buttons. She wore no brassiere. Around her neck and on her wrists, fingers, and ears were a great many diamonds. "The daytime stuff," she said later, waving her hands in front of him, when he remarked on them. She walked behind the bar, snapping her fingers in time to the Dom Belcanto song on the sound system. There was about her a sense of friendliness and good humor.

"There better be ice out here, or somebody's going to lose her job. And there's not. Concepcion," she called out, rolling her eyes. "Concept-tione. *¿Donde està el hielo?* That's Spanish for where's the fucking ice," she explained to Harrison.

A Mexican maid rushed into the room with a Lucite ice bucket.

"*Gracias, Concepcion,*" said Maxine, taking the bucket. "And bring us some munchies. Or your guacamole dip."

"*Sí, señora.*"

"What will you have?" she asked Harrison. "You name it, we got it. This is what is known as a well-stocked bar."

"Just Perrier," he said.

She made a face at his choice. "I might have a little champagne myself. You sure you don't want to join me? The best money can buy," she said, waving a bottle of Dom Perignon in front of him.

"No, thanks."

She closed her eyes for a minute as she listened to the music, singing along with Dom Belcanto's voice. "Was he the greatest, or was he the greatest?" she asked. She didn't expect an answer. With eyes cast heavenward, she shouted out, "Oh, Belcanto, wherever you are, I love you, Belcanto."

"Are you a singer?"

She laughed. "No."

"An actress?"

"No."

"What?"

"I'm an ex–party girl who did well," she said. "Now I raise cattle. Santa Gertrudis cattle, to be exact. It's a crossbreed. Developed at the King Ranch in Texas about forty years ago. They're red, like the picture on the mailbox."

"Your place looks huge," said Harrison.

"Not really. Couple a thousand acres. Take the Obregon Ranch further down the Patagonia Highway. Now, that's huge."

Harrison nodded.

185

"I take it you were a friend of my son's?" she said.

"No, I actually never met your son. I've just heard about him," said Harrison. "I'm writing a piece on a possible insurance fraud on the death certificate of a man named Esmond Bland, and your son's name figured in my investigation."

She nodded. "I get letters all the time from men who loved him. Rich guys. Prince somebody, what'shisname? Flew him to Rabat, in Morocco. A couple of Hollywood studio heads. On and on. You're not one of those guys?"

"No."

"Oh. I got that screwed up, I guess. Dwane had something. There's no two ways about it. There's this myth building up about Dwane. Like James Dean."

"I have seen Esme Bland."

"She still in the nuthouse?"

"Yes. In Maine. The Cranston Institute. She is ill."

"I'll say she's ill. She's loony. She shot my kid. Right between the eyes."

"I meant that she is terminally ill. She has cancer. She wants to leave you some money in her will. I don't think she has any idea you live in this manner."

"You can tell Miss Bland that Miss Lonergan don't need her money, thank you very much." She began to sing. "*Miss Otis regrets, she's unable to lunch today, madam.* Tell her to leave it to AIDS."

"I must admit that I am confused myself by this sense of opulence about you, Miss Lonergan," said Harrison.

"Try Maxine, Harrison."

"You're an unlikely candidate for home-on-the-range, Maxine," he said.

"I'm a lady in retirement."

"I probably shouldn't say this, but I was expecting a trailer, or a mobile home."

She laughed. "I wasn't exactly born to the purple. I worked damn hard for my money. One hair from a pussy can pull a freight train, as Dwane used to say. You must know that. Dom Belcanto left me a bundle when he cooled. His wife, Pepper, wanted to contest my inheritance. It's called the fifth-wife syndrome. Gimme, gimme, gimme. I fixed her. I said, sure, honey, sue, go ahead, and I'll show you and the FBI and the president of the United States a few pictures of Dom and Sal and some of the boys, taken in Vegas and Havana and Hollywood, and right here at the ranch, where they came when they wanted to be really private for their confabs, if you get my point. Pepper shut up pretty quick after that. She moves in high society now. She didn't want that to come out. After all, I serviced Dom for a good ten years, and that wasn't always easy, especially when he was drunk and belligerent. And then, of course, there was Sal. Sal was the real love of my life." Her eyes misted over. She pulled a flowered Kleenex from a Lucite holder on the bar and turned and faced herself in the mirror as she dealt with her tear before it could roll onto her makeup. "Took me an hour and a half to put on this face," she said, looking at him through the mirror. "Can't fuck it up so soon. Sal really took care of me. He bought me the ranch, the pictures, everything."

"Sal?"

"Salvatore Cabrini. You heard about Lansky. You heard about Giancana. You heard about Trafficante. You heard about Roselli. Who you didn't hear about was Sal Cabrini. No relation to Mother Cabrini, by the way. Not even distant cousins. Silence. That was Sal's power. He kept a low profile. And he kept me. He would have married me. He wanted to. But he had this sick wife. Angela. Sick for years. And he wouldn't divorce her. We kept thinking Angela was going to die, but she never did. She's still alive. Lives in Miami. I liked that about Sal. He had honor. Then he got killed in a plane crash, flying to Miami for Angela's birthday. Well, those are the breaks. Anyway, you know something? I'm better as a solo act. Listen, would you like to see my pictures?"

"Sure."

"I love Monet, Van Gogh, and all that stuff," she said. "Some of them may be hot, for all I know. Sal started giving me pictures, and I always thought it was best not to ask questions. He didn't know shit about art. He just knew what they were worth."

Harrison laughed. "I saw the Renoir," he said.

"Oh, you went to the john already? Nuts. I always say, 'Turn left at the Renoir,' when guys ask me where the john is. Gets a laugh every time."

"Yes. Pony showed me."

"Sal had the urinals put in. You know, on the wall like that? Dwane used to love to stand at those urinals when he was a kid."

"Why was your son a prostitute?" asked Harrison.

"Dwane? He liked it. He enjoyed it. It was the money, the trips, the gifts, that made him erotic. It was an exciting life. He was just another version of me. If he'd lived, he'd have settled down after thirty, thirty-five, gotten out of the business. We make very good wives, us ex-hookers.

"I had this casket flown in from L.A. Eight thousand bucks. All brass. Gorgeous. I'll say this for Dwane. He was a beautiful corpse. I had him laid out in there at the end of the living room. Right in front of the big picture window. You could see the purple mountains beyond. It was a beautiful sight. The service was private. Just Pony and me, and Concepcion, and some of the cowboys, and the people who work on the ranch. Angela Cabrini sent flowers. I thought that was nice."

Harrison stared at her.

"Are you staring at my tits or my diamonds?" she asked.

"Actually, your diamonds," replied Harrison.

"Smart boy. The current boyfriend is the jealous type."

"Oh. Tell me about him."

"He has a very flat stomach, like yours."

"That wasn't what I meant."

Maxine laughed. "I know that. I just thought I'd toss it in. Dom Belcanto had a gut on him out to here, and I just didn't want you to think I was confined to men with that kind of figure. Actually, you already met the guy."

"Pony, with the gun in the holster?"

"Listen, he's honest. He works. He's not after my money. He's faithful. He's a pretty good fuck, three or four times a week, usually in the morning when he wakes up horny, which is not my favorite time, but so what? He uses Scope. You can't have everything. You want a refill on your water?"

"No."

"Here's a picture of Sal and Dom taken here at the ranch years ago. That kid next to Sal is Dwane when he was about thirteen or so. Cute, wasn't he? He left home when he was about sixteen and went out on his own." She gazed at the picture fondly. "All my fellas," she said.

Harrison stared at the photograph. "Who's that guy standing in the background behind Sal?" he asked.

"He used to work for Sal years ago, in slot machines in Atlantic City. Johnny Fuselli. He left Sal to go with that billionaire Gerald Bradley as a sort of right-hand man, i.e., pimp," said Maxine. "He was all right, Johnny, but he wasn't a player, not in the league with Sal and Lansky and those other guys. Strictly second echelon. Third, even."

"Small world," said Harrison. "I used to know him, sort of."

"Tell me this, Harrison. How would a guy like you ever meet up with a guy like Johnny Fuselli?"

"One of the Bradley kids was a friend of mine in school. I used to spend time with that family. That's where I saw Fuselli."

"Do you know what Sal thought about Gerald Bradley? Not much. That's what he thought. 'Don't be deceived by appearances,' Sal said to me once, after I saw Gerald in Vegas. Horny guy. He put the make on me and then sent me a fur coat. Sal said, 'He puts on airs and sends his kids to fancy schools and gets them into posh clubs and mixes with the high and mighty, but I know the real truth about the guy. He's a crook, same as me.' Sal hated his guts. Sal said he was a double-crosser."

"Amazing."

"Sal met with Gerald a lot in the early days, but he never wanted any of his sons to be in on those meetings. Even Jerry, the crippled one. He didn't want the association to rub off on his sons," said Maxine.

Harrison nodded.

"Are you aware there's a Bradley living here in Nogales?" asked Maxine.

"What? Some kind of cousin?"

"Not at all. Of the blood."

"How could that be?"

"Desi, he's called. Actually, Desmond Junior, I suppose."

"Really? How old?"

"Twenty. Twenty-one. That sort of age."

"I remember now. Des married a maid in the family house in Scarborough Hill, Connecticut. That was before I knew them, but I heard about it. What a to-do there was about that. Cardinal Sullivan got the marriage annulled. Mary? Was that her name?"

"No, Rosleen."

"That's right, Rosleen. They paid her off. They sent her away. Does she still call herself Bradley?"

"I guess so. I just call her Rosleen. She's the dental technician for Dr. Sabiston in Nogales. She cleans my teeth."

"Do you think you could arrange for me to see her while I'm here? Or to meet up with Desi?"

*   *   *

"How are the boys?" asked Harrison.

"Fine," said Claire.

"Tell them I miss them."

"They miss you, too."

"I bought them some cowboy hats."

"They love presents. Oh, yes, they'll love them."

Claire was not one to long for the impossible, to yearn for lost love. They sat together in Borsalino's, toying with Northern Italian food, making conversation. They had to talk about something. He did not tell her about meeting Rosleen Bradley and young Desi in Nogales, which she would have enjoyed hearing about, because it might accidentally overlap somehow into his reluctant reentry into the Bradley circle, with his imminent luncheon engagement with Gerald Bradley, whom she hated, or his love affair with Kitt, which he could not bring himself to discuss, for fear of hurting her.

"What do you want to do about the dining room table and the sideboard?" Claire asked.

"What about them?"

"They were your grandmother's, weren't they? That's what your aunt Gert said when we got married. Do you want them sent in to your apartment?"

"Oh, no," he said quickly. "Leave everything. Don't disrupt the house. I certainly don't need a dining table and sideboard. I don't think I've eaten home once since I moved there."

He tried to tell her about Esme Bland and Dwane Lonergan and Maxine, but she was indifferent to the complexities of their story.

"I think you get so involved in the lives of the people you write about so you can avoid dealing with your own," she said.

"That's not so," he said, although he knew it to be so. Claire had always seen right through him.

"It wasn't ever really good, was it?" she asked. He knew she was talking about their marriage.

"I don't think that's true," he replied.

"You're like a roommate, with privileges. You're not like a husband, or what I thought a husband was going to be like. What is the matter with you? There is a part of your life that is shut off. Sometimes I feel you have a terrible secret."

He sat in silence.

"Say something, for God's sake," said Claire.

"At the Cranston Institute, Esme Bland said that to me. She said I had a secret."

Leaving, he tried to kiss her, a kiss of affection, but she turned her head away.

"Love to the boys," he said.

"Yes."

"Don't forget the cowboy hats."

10

"WELL, Harrison, we meet again. Who would have thought?" said Gerald Bradley. He was already ensconced in his favorite booth in the Grill Room of the Four Seasons restaurant in New York when Harrison Burns was brought up to his table. Seated to his right was his son Jerry. In front of each was a martini in a stemmed glass. The crutches that Jerry now used were by his side. For a moment Harrison and Gerald stared at each other, assimilating the changes of sixteen years.

"Hello, Mr. Bradley," said Harrison.

"It's like old times," said Gerald expansively. "It's nice to have you back with us."

Harrison, momentarily bewildered by the words "like old times," merely nodded.

"You remember Jerry, of course."

Harrison and Jerry looked at each other but did not say anything.

"Sit down. Sit down, Harrison. What will you have to drink?" He clapped his hands and hailed the managers. "Julian, Alex, someone, come, come, come. This is Mr. Burns, a wonderful young writer and a great friend of my son Constant. They were in school together. He'd like to order a drink."

"Just Perrier, please," said Harrison, speaking directly to the captain.

"Wise choice, I suppose. You must still have things to write today," said Gerald. "But a shame to miss a good martini, I always say."

"Yes, I remember," said Harrison. "I was recently complimented on a martini I made. I gave you full credit as my teacher."

Gerald chuckled. "I always like recognition," he said. He watched Harrison as he looked about the room.

"You've been here before, of course."

"Once, but I was not seated in this room."

192

"This is the room to be seated in," said Jerry. "This is where you see everyone."

Harrison ignored Jerry.

"There's Dr. Kissinger over there," said Gerald.

"Yes."

"There's Felix Rohatyn. You know who he is?"

"Yes."

"There's S. I. Newhouse. Of course, you know him."

"Yes."

"In the corner there, Philip Johnson, with the owllike spectacles."

"Yes."

"I don't seem to be impressing you, Harrison."

"They're probably telling whoever they're with, 'There's Gerald Bradley. You know who he is, of course? He's the only man allowed to smoke a cigar in the Four Seasons.' "

Gerald chuckled again, as he lit a cigar.

"So you know that, do you?" he asked.

"It is a widely heralded piece of trivia," replied Harrison.

"You've seen my daughter, I understand?" said Gerald.

"I've seen two of your daughters," replied Harrison.

"I was speaking of Kitt," said Gerald. There was a slight sharpness of tone to his voice.

"Yes, I saw Kitt. It was quite a surprise."

"Did you find her changed?"

"Of course I did. I hadn't seen her in sixteen years. I'm not altogether sure I would have recognized her right off, but I heard someone else say, 'That's Gerald Bradley's youngest.' She was still wearing a retainer on her teeth and her hair was long, halfway down her back, the last time I saw her. What I saw in Maine was a thirty-year-old woman, extremely lovely, handsomely dressed, and terribly alone."

"And how did she seem to you?"

"As I just said, terribly alone."

"I didn't want her to marry Cheever Chadwick."

"She told me that."

"Cheever Chadwick's an asshole," said Jerry.

"Yes, yes, an asshole," agreed Gerald. "I rather think Cheever's got that word cornered. May I ask you what you were doing at the Cranston Institute?"

"It was a work-related visit," replied Harrison.

"Are you writing about it?"

193

"About the institute, you mean? No, not specifically."

"What then?"

"A person who has lived at the Cranston Institute for a great many years figures in an article that I am writing, having to do with a murder."

"Would that person be Esme Bland?" asked Gerald.

Harrison sipped his Perrier and did not reply. "Perhaps we should order," he said. "I have a great deal of work to do this afternoon. I'm on what we call in my trade a deadline."

"Yes, of course. We always order the swordfish, Jerry and I," said Gerald. "Grilled, no butter, splendid for the waistline. Not that you have to worry about your waistline, I see."

"I've become a swimmer," said Harrison, patting his slim stomach. "The swordfish is fine with me, too."

As Jerry waved for the captain and gave the orders, Gerald continued talking to Harrison. "I went to Esmond Bland's funeral. As you know, he was the father of Esme. I met him several times at the White House during my ambassadorship, and he dined with us in Paris once or twice. My God, what a funeral that was. Five, six years ago, it must have been. People had to stand outside on Fifth Avenue. There was no more room in St. Thomas's. He was a very popular fellow, Esmond Bland. A snob, but popular. Kissinger over there spoke, and Esme had this big black woman from the opera who sang. I forget her name. I often wonder about my own funeral. I wonder if anyone would come."

"It is interesting to me how many people worry about that," said Harrison. "I mean, what difference does it make? You're dead."

"You'd fill St. Patrick's Cathedral, Pa," said Jerry. "There'd be an overflow."

"I wonder," said Gerald, musing for a moment on the subject.

There was a moment's silence. Harrison looked at the Bradleys. "I think we should come to the point of this lunch," he said. "Kitt said there was something you wanted to discuss."

"You've quite changed, Harrison," said Gerald, who was not about to be rushed. "Not so wimpy as you used to be. I suppose early recognition has done that for you, given you that confidence. As I was being shaved this morning, I found myself reflecting about you and Constant, Harrison. Marvelous, when you think of it, the way both of you have done so well. I'm sure you've followed his career in Congress."

"Yes. Somewhat."

"How old are you now, Harrison?"

"Five years older than Kitt, the same age as Constant, but that's not the point of the lunch, is it?" said Harrison. He waved away the smoke from Gerald's cigar.

"Oh, does the cigar bother you while you're eating? Waiter? Would you take this away? Thank you. Yes, let's get down to brass tacks. I have a business proposition to make. How are you fixed for money?"

"What a peculiar question. Suppose I asked you that," said Harrison.

Gerald laughed. "I would answer, 'I'm fixed very well. Just read the *Forbes* list.' Seriously, I know you take nothing from the trust fund Sims Lord set up for you," he said.

"I do quite well on my own," replied Harrison. "Why this interest in my finances?"

"Yes, I know you do. We take a great interest in you, from afar, don't we, Jerry?"

Jerry nodded in agreement.

"I happen to know exactly what you make, as a matter of fact. I was impressed," said Gerald.

"How would you know that?" asked Harrison.

"I make it my business to learn things like that when I have a proposition to make."

"Johnny Fuselli up to his old tricks, stealing I.R.S. forms, I suppose," said Harrison.

Gerald chuckled. "I'll ignore that. I rather admire your feistiness. It comes through in your work."

They sat in silence for several moments.

"Well, I'm waiting," said Harrison.

"Would you like to make some real money?" asked Gerald.

"What is real money?"

"Oh, a house in the country. A Jaguar car. Tickets on the Concorde. A portfolio with Salomon Brothers. Any or all of the above. Whatever you want it to be. How would you describe that?"

"Provocative. What does one have to do to make real money?"

"Do what you already do so well. Write."

"Write what?"

"A book for my son."

"Which son?"

"Constant, of course."

"Write a book in Constant's name, you mean?"

"Yes."

"I would write the book and Constant would get credit for it as the author?"

"Yes."

"That cannot even be called a lateral move in a career. That is what is known as a backward step," said Harrison. "Why in the world do you think I would be interested in doing that?"

"For a great deal of money," answered Gerald.

"I earn enough money."

"Hear me out. Hear me out, Harrison. Constant is running for governor. A book would be a marvelous thing. It would give him a credibility. There is always that slightly playboy image to him. People say he drives too fast, he drinks too much, he chases girls. Actually, he has given up the polo, rarely drinks, and is married to Charlotte and has the children and so forth, but the image lingers."

"What sort of book are you thinking of?"

"A memoir. A family memoir. An American saga. Back to the grandfathers coming to this country from Ireland and working their way up. Bog Meadow. The Bradley butcher shop. The Malloy plumbing shop. My parents struggling to send me to good schools. Grace's parents struggling to send Grace to the Sacred Heart Convent. Our meeting. Our great love. Our marriage. Our children. Our tragedies."

"Your tragedies?"

"With so many in the family, you know, people like us have more tragedies than most to cope with. The miscarriages, for instance. Grace's little saints, she calls them, who look down on us. And Agnes. Agnes in the institution. I am aware you saw Agnes. We have done everything to protect her privacy over the years, but perhaps it's better to let that story come out. Jerry thought so. Not that she wears nun's clothes, I don't mean that. I understand you saw her in the Sacred Heart habit. I meant her affliction. There are so many families having to deal with the same tragedy, mental illness, it would be helpful, even inspirational, to discuss it with compassion. And coming from Constant, in his words—your words, but his words, if you know what I mean—it would give great importance to this fine young man to be the one to relate Agnes's tragedy for the first time."

Harrison put down his fork and pushed the swordfish away from him.

"Something wrong with the fish?" asked Gerald.

"No."

"And Kevin. Kevin, whom we rarely discuss, came after Jerry and before Des. Kevin died in Vietnam. We didn't want him to go. We could have gotten him out of going. Everyone else was getting out of going. But he signed up. He wanted to fight for his country. I have been able to locate a member of his crew. He would be able to provide you with the details of the flight."

Harrison stared at Gerald as he talked.

"Oh, God," said Gerald suddenly, spotting someone.

"What, Pa?"

"There's Johnny Fuselli coming up the steps. Head him off, Jerry. I asked him to wait downstairs, but you know Johnny. He always oversteps. Take him over to the bar and have him sit there and wait. I don't want him to come into this dining room. Tell him I'll be another half hour or so. And then come back here." Gerald waited until Jerry had lumbered to his feet, picked up his crutches, and was on his way before he turned back to Harrison. "Where were we?"

"You had located a member of Kevin's crew to discuss his death in Vietnam," answered Harrison.

"Right." He lit another cigar. "It's an amazing story. Never told before. And, of course, there's Jerry's terrible accident. I didn't want to discuss it in front of him. This fine young man, crippled for life. Look at him over there, talking to Fuselli. My heart aches for Jerry. And Desmond, the doctor, who took a bullet out of a poor kid's heart and saved his life, a black kid from Bog Meadow. Sandro, first in Congress, standing up for the rights of the poor and the homeless, and now in his third term in the United States Senate. Maureen and Freddy and their growing brood. Seven already, another on the way. The ambassadorship in Paris. Endless stories there. Mary Pat's wedding to Count Philippe de Trafford. And Constant's own marriage to Charlotte Stafford. It is a story of family and love. It is a story of the American dream. With pictures. There's hundreds of pictures to choose from. Thousands even. Grace has been marvelous about keeping scrapbooks over the years. The research will be relatively simple for you. What do you say? You're the perfect person, Harrison. You know us. You've lived with us."

"No way, Mr. Bradley. That may be a good idea for Constant, but it's not a good idea for me. I don't ghost-write," said Harrison quickly, wanting to terminate the encounter.

Gerald reached out a hand and put it on Harrison's wrist. "What I am about to tell you is extremely confidential. Can you keep a secret?"

"What an odd question for you to ask of me," said Harrison.

Gerald ignored his answer. "It is almost certain now that Constant is going to address the Democratic convention in New York in two years' time," said Gerald. "We are angling for prime time. We are hoping that he will make the nominating speech for the vice president. The national exposure for him will be staggering. There are those who say of Constant that he's just a rich man's kid who's a bit of a playboy, but this will give people a chance to see what he's really all about. Now what do you think of that, Mr. Harrison Burns?"

"I am thinking of the strings that had to be pulled to bring that one off. I am thinking of all the markers that must have been called in," said Harrison.

Gerald was dissatisfied with Harrison's answer. "You're a very curious person, Harrison," he said.

Jerry returned to the table and sat down.

"I'm off," said Harrison.

"No, no, no, you cannot dismiss it like that," said Gerald. "You have to give it some thought."

"No, I don't, Mr. Bradley."

"My father is offering you a golden opportunity," said Jerry.

Harrison turned to Jerry and pointed his finger at him. "I am here to talk to your father, at his request. I am not here to talk to you. I don't care what you have to say about anything. I am not interested in your opinions, or observations, or comments. If you are going to sit here, sit in silence, or I am going to get up and walk out."

"Well, haven't we changed with our success," said Jerry. "After all my father has done for you."

"Do you want your father's money back, Jerry? I'll be happy to write you out a check," said Harrison. "But let's make sure first we understand each other. That was no act of charity on your father's part, as he would be the first one to tell you. It had nothing to do with the greater good. That was a deal, a business deal, a proposition. He paid for my education. I gave him my vow of silence. Your father, as was always the case with him in business, got the better end of the deal."

"This is outrageous," said Jerry.

"Calm down, Jerry. Let me do the talking," said Gerald. He turned to Harrison. "Why? Just explain to me why. This is a role you have played before, and splendidly. It was the essay you wrote for Constant that was responsible for getting him back into Milford after that ludicrous episode with the dirty pictures."

"I think the library you gave to the school may have had a little more to do with it than my essay, Mr. Bradley," said Harrison. He moved himself to the end of the booth, preparing to leave. "Let me explain it to you this way. It is not what I do. It is like asking a landscape painter to paint your portrait. There are specialists in that field. What you are asking me to do is not my specialty."

"What is your specialty?"

"Crime. That is what interests me. That is what I do well."

"You mean, *The Case of the Missing Mummy? The Case of the Stolen Urn?*" There was a slight degree of mockery in the tone of Gerald's voice.

"No, that is not what I mean, Mr. Bradley."

"Tell me then. Explain it to me. I am interested in you. I want to know."

"I am fascinated by police work. I like to cover trials. I am specifically interested in people who get away with things. People who go free. Crime without consequence is a privilege of the very rich."

There was a long silence at the table. Gerald flicked the long ash of his cigar into an ashtray and then stubbed out the cigar.

"Would you do me one favor before you say no?" asked Gerald, detaining him.

"I have said no," replied Harrison.

"I would like you to meet with Constant. Just once, to discuss it. You used to be such friends."

"I don't think it's a good idea, Mr. Bradley."

"He would like so much to see you again, Harrison. He talks of you often."

Harrison ran down the stairs of the restaurant, wanting to be gone. Standing at the bottom of the stairs leaning against the wall was a tall man in his mid-thirties, possibly foreign, elegantly dressed in English-looking clothes and smoking a cigarette in a black holder.

"Hello, I've been waiting for you," said the man. His top coat was draped over his shoulders. He spoke in an affected mid-Atlantic voice.

"For me?" asked Harrison.

"You don't recognize me, do you? It's Fruity. Fruity Suarez."

"Good heavens," said Harrison. "How in the world did you know I was here?"

"I was sitting upstairs at the bar and got into a chat with a rather good-looking, in a cheap sort of way, Mafia figure. Mr. Fuselli, Johnny Fuselli, he said his name was. He said he was waiting for Gerald Bradley to finish lunch, and somehow or other your name came up, and he said it was you who was having lunch with Gerald Bradley. Imagine. Well, I thought, perhaps I should say hello after all these years. I hope you and your wife—Claire, isn't that her name?—are not still angry over that two-o'clock-in-the-morning telephone call about poor Maud Firth? Maud's all right, by the way. Got a handsome settlement. That's one thing I'll say in Gerald Bradley's favor. He does pay off for his precious Constant's, uh—how shall I put it?—problem."

"This is a surprise. I'm in a bit of a hurry, Fruity," said Harrison.

"Not so much of a hurry that you can't have a quick drink with an old friend after all these years. Not that we were actually friends. Acquaintances, I suppose, would be a better word," said Fruity.

"All right, if it's quick. Shall we go back up to the bar?" said Harrison.

"Oh, no, no, no. I decided I wasn't comfortable up there. All those people who run the country and all those billionaires lunching in the same place at the same time made me feel quite uneasy. One terrorist bomb up there, and imagine the state of the city and the country. And, besides, I got Mr. Fuselli's telephone number. You never know when someone like that, with his sort of connections, might come in handy. No, there's a little place around the corner here at Fifty-third and Second called Miss Garbo's. Do you know it? It has a sister bar of the same name in Los Angeles."

"What sort of bar?" asked Harrison.

"Oh, don't worry," he said, in a mock scolding voice. "You'll be perfectly safe. The afternoon crowd are just drinkers. Nothing untoward, I promise you. After midnight is when the untoward action starts."

On the street Fruity walked very fast, oblivious to people who turned to stare at his exotic presence. The sleeves of his top coat waved around him. He never stopped talking, all the time holding the cigarette holder clenched between his teeth. Inside, the bar was dark. The bartender greeted him warmly.

"Look who's back in town. You again, Fruity," he said.

"Hello, Clint," replied Fruity. "I bring you regards from Zane in Los Angeles." He turned to Harrison. "Do you prefer to stand at the bar or sit at a table?"

"Table, I suppose," answered Harrison, looking around him.

"Don't worry. Don't worry. You're not going to run into a soul you know. Did you ever hear of someone called Dwane Lonergan?"

"As a matter of fact, I have," said Harrison.

"This is where he got started, in this bar. He became a legend, you know. A legend in certain circles, I mean. A great many rich men of my persuasion knew Dwane. He was always being flown coast to coast, sometimes on private planes by those rich Hollywood studio types. You know the group. Sometimes he was flown to Europe. The royal prince even had a go at Dwane, or so they say. He was famous. Oh, how he loved all the attention, and all the money. Like certain film stars, there are those who are meant to die young. Perhaps Esme Bland did him a favor without knowing it, shooting him like she did. People like Dwane Lonergan are not meant ever to reach forty."

Harrison reached in his pocket and took out a pen and notebook and jotted down something.

"What in the world are you writing?" asked Fruity.

"Oh, sorry. I'm always making notes like that. I think if you don't write down thoughts the moment they occur to you, you can never remember them in quite the same way later," said Harrison.

"You sound like you're addressing the Santa Barbara Writers Conference."

Harrison laughed. "Sorry, Fruity. I'm all yours. Actually, I don't feel right calling you Fruity. Diego, isn't that your real name?"

"Oh, you can call me Fruity. It's how you knew me. Learning a new name for someone is always difficult. Besides, I've become rather fond of it, in fact."

"What have you been up to all these years, Fruity?"

"Oh, failing in a very expensive way. My career, or careers, I guess I should say, have been inconspicuous. A little of this, a little of that. Interior designer. Restaurateur. A garden furniture shop. A little stint in Hollywood. A few other things that are slipping my mind, but you must have gotten the picture by now. Thank God for my trust fund. I make the sign of the cross every time I see an advertisement for Firth Sewing Machines. Mother was a Firth. Now you, Harrison, would have been the last person in that miserable class in that miserable school we both attended that I would have picked for glory."

"Hardly glory, my friend."

"Oh, yes. Your books get published. Your name is in *Newsweek*. You are spoken about. That, to me, is glory. I read you. I read about you. I even brag I once knew you. I've always been a bit of a star fucker, as you may remember."

Harrison laughed. "Yes, I remember your story of those two lesbian movie stars. Who were they? I've forgotten."

Fruity shook his head at Harrison's inquiry and proceeded with his own thoughts. "I liked your book about the financier, Mr. Renthal. I like the prison part the best. Prison is where he belongs, you kept saying, without actually saying it. The sound of that cell door closing behind him, nuts and bolts settling into place. Oh, my dear. It sent a chill right through me. And Max Goesler, who raped that child. Oh, how you described him—those smarmy eyes, those wet palms. I could smell his stinking armpits from your description." Fruity gestured dramatically with his cigarette holder.

"But I sense something in you, Harrison. Something you haven't arrived at yet, but will, I hope, some underlying thing I feel in your writing."

"What is that?" asked Harrison warily.

"*Rage*. Blind rage. I sense always there is something more to come out of you. These books of yours are fine and moral, high-minded, on the side of justice. But there is more. It is almost as if you are skirting the main subject of your life, the cause of this quiet rage, this inferno inside of you, and I don't associate it with your parents' frightful deaths. Does any of this make any sense to you, Harry?"

Harrison turned his face away from Fruity.

"Why are you so silent? Why are you looking away from me? Isn't there something you can reply? I can't be that far off base. I am, after all, sensitive. That's what they said about me when they kicked me out of Milford. My God, Harry. You're not crying, are you? You are. And no handkerchief. You should always carry a handkerchief. Two, even. One for show and one for blow, my father, the ambassador, used to say. Here. Use this. Charvet. Paris. You can keep it. Nice color, don't you think? Go ahead, cry. No one's looking. Get it out of your system. I think it's marvelous to cry. The nice thing about a dump like Miss Garbo's is, no one gives a shit. Imagine crying in the Four Seasons Grill Room with Dr. Kissinger looking on, although he did watch Nixon cry, didn't he? Now, Gerald Bradley, that's a different story.

202

He would say things like, 'Get a hold of yourself, Harrison.' Are you feeling better?''

"Yes. I'm sorry." He wiped his eyes with Fruity's handkerchief and handed it back to him.

"Don't be sorry. I'm afraid I hit a nerve. Did I?"

"Perhaps. Let's talk about something else."

"Tell me about your wife, Harry. I woke her up. She wasn't a bit pleased with me that night."

"She is taller than me. She is older than me. And she has left me."

"Dear, dear, dear. Is the third part of that answer crushing for you?"

"I haven't arrived yet at the feeling it is. It is a fairly recent situation. I miss my little boys."

"There is a rumor going round about you," said Fruity.

"What could that be?"

"That you are involved again."

"Oh?"

"No need for names."

"No. Where did you hear such a story?"

"My new best friend, Mr. Fuselli. Would you like some unsolicited advice? Stay away from them, all of them. They will destroy you. What is there about that family that you find so irresistible, Harry?"

"I must run," said Harrison, looking at his watch. "I'm on a deadline."

"Yes, of course you must."

Harrison made for the door and walked out onto the street. Outside, he thought for a moment, turned, and reentered the bar. He walked over to Fruity.

"Did you forget something?" asked Fruity.

"Yes. I forgot to say thank you."

"For making you cry?"

"I suppose."

"Oh, my God, Harrison, why haven't we tried *that* before?" gasped Kitt.

"I'm still out of breath," said Harrison.

"Well, I should think so after what you just did."

Harrison laughed. "It takes two to tango."

"I love these afternoon trysts in your apartment, Harrison. I like getting here ahead of you, letting myself in, changing the sheets, getting undressed, being ready, waiting, anticipating, longing to have you come back from wherever you are so that I can help you tear off your clothes, going mad if you're ten minutes late. Love in the afternoon. It's divine. It's wonderful. It's erotic.''

"They're on to us, Kitt," he said. "We're being talked about."

"Who?" asked Kitt.

"A man called Fruity Suarez heard it at the bar of the Four Seasons from Johnny Fuselli, while Johnny was waiting for your father to finish having lunch with me."

"Does it worry you?"

"It worries me about Claire, yes. I don't want to hurt Claire. Doesn't it worry you?"

"About Cheever? Good God, no. Cheever doesn't mean anything to me," said Kitt. "About my brothers, no. About my parents, yes. What's all right for the boys is not all right for the girls in my family. Ma still believes the Blessed Virgin cries when I whistle. Imagine if she knew what we just did. Who's Fruity Suarez?"

"He was in our class at Milford. He once spread the rumor that I was transfixed with Constant."

"Quite a gossip, old Fruity." She sat up and put on Harrison's dressing gown. She walked over to a mirror and began combing her hair with Harrison's brush.

"I like to watch you brush your hair," said Harrison. He could not remove his eyes from her face, her neck, her bare arms, her shoulders.

She smiled at him in the mirror, pleased by his look. "What are you thinking?"

"I want to kiss you there."

"Where?"

"Your neck. Your throat."

"This is nice, Harrison. I like your leisurely pace. Cheever was always so quick."

"Where did the flowers come from?" he asked.

"Me. It's so monklike here. Only basics. I wanted to dress it up a bit," said Kitt.

"There's a photograph of the twins."

"But not in a frame. Just thumbtacked."

"There's books."

"Yes, lots of books, but no bookcase."

"I guess it's only temporary, until I know where my life's going."

"I'm not complaining, you know. I'm getting rather fond of the monk look. We've always lived in decorated rooms, where the fringe on the pillows matches the color of the walls. Ma likes her rooms decorated."

"I remember."

"I love you, Harrison."

"Don't."

"Oh, yes, let me. If I get hurt, I get hurt. So what?"

"Oh, Kitt."

"The lunch went well, I hear," said Kitt.

"That's what you heard?" asked Harrison, surprised.

"That's what Pa said. Didn't it?"

"Inconclusive, I felt. Your father is not one to take no for an answer, and I said no."

"He said you really hate Jerry."

"That part of the account is accurate."

"Pa said to tell you he'll send the helicopter to fly you to Southampton over the weekend. You've never seen that house. It's divine. Everyone will be there, the whole family. Like a reunion."

Harrison groaned inaudibly.

"You could try to show a little enthusiasm, Harrison. A lot of people would die happy to get there."

"What's your life like out there?" asked Harrison.

"We're popular with movie stars, and politicians, and English lords and ladies when they want a free place to stay during their American visit, but the nice people never seem to like us wherever we move, no matter how big our houses are or how available we make our tennis courts to them," said Kitt.

"I would have thought that would have passed by now," said Harrison.

"Oh, no," replied Kitt. "I don't know why, but we've never really been accepted anywhere. It upsets Ma, you know. She'd love to be on all those committees and boards, not just the Catholic ones. Pa always says we're enough unto ourselves, the family, but that's only a front. They mind. They really do. But they'd never say it. You will go, Harrison? Please?"

"Will you be in the helicopter with me?"

"No. I don't want Ma to suspect anything. I'll drive out with her and some of Maureen's kids. There's something else, Harrison."

"And that is?"

"There must be no you-know-what under Ma's roof. Not even looks across the room."

"I wasn't planning on exposing myself," he said.

She laughed. "You can expose yourself now, if you want. I'll even help with the zipper."

"A call came in while I was here waiting for you," said Kitt.

"Did you answer it?" asked Harrison.

"Of course not. But I listened to the machine. Someone called Eloise Brazen. She called to tell you that Rupert du Pithon died this morning. She went in to show the apartment to a rock and roll man from Hollywood, and Rupert was dead in bed."

"Ah, poor Rupert," said Harrison.

"I met Rupie a few times. In Southampton. In Beverly Hills. Wherever there was a party, there he was, talking about *placement*. Silly man."

"Perhaps. I liked him. I wrote his obituary for him. He's the guy who got me in to see Esme Bland."

"I ran into a relation of yours last week," said Harrison.

"Let me guess. Fatty Malloy."

"No."

"Then it must have been Sis Malloy."

"No."

"I don't think we have any other relatives. It must have been an impostor. Who?"

"Rosleen Bradley."

"Rosleen Bradley? I don't know a Rosleen Bradley."

"Yes, you do. She was a maid in your mother's house in Scarborough Hill."

"Oh, *Rosleen*. Who opened the doors, who passed the peas, as Mother used to say. Oh, yes, who married Desmond for ten minutes, didn't she? I'd almost forgotten about Rosleen. She wasn't with us long, you know. Don't tell me she calls herself Bradley, for God's sake? The nerve! Miss Whatever-her-name-is, Ma always called her. Even Bridey thought she was impertinent, and Bridey was related to her. Cardinal had the marriage annulled immediately."

"She lives in Arizona."

"That doesn't make her a relation, Harrison. I just said the marriage was annulled. She's nothing to us."

"She has a son by Desmond. That makes him your nephew."

"You can't be serious!"

"He's twenty. Rosleen calls him Desi."

"Desi? You mean, like Desi Arnaz?" she asked.

"He was the valedictorian of his class in the local high school. He's a freshman at Arizona State. He's going to be a journalist."

"I don't believe it. Probably a trick to get money. People know who we are. They know there is money. They think of our money as a bottomless pit," said Kitt. "All these people living off the fat of the land on our money."

"I would hardly call it the fat of the land," said Harrison. "Rosleen is a dental technician. She gets a couple of thousand a month from Sims Lord. That's all. She got the job to support the boy."

"I don't believe it," she said again.

"I saw him. He's Des's kid, all right. Same dimpled chin. All those big white Bradley teeth. A head that will never go bald. Believe me, this is a Bradley."

"I don't think it would be a good idea to bring that up this weekend," said Kitt.

"I hadn't planned to."

II

THE BRADLEY house in Southampton, palatial and Florentine in design, had been built in the 1920s by a railroad baron whose wastrel and impoverished descendants were forced to sell it for a pittance in the 1950s to a girls' school that subsequently went out of business in the 1980s. There had been talk of pulling it down. It was not a practical house by the standards of the day. The halls were as large as rooms and the corridors as wide as galleries. There were fourteen bedrooms, a ballroom, a garage for twelve cars, a guesthouse, a gardener's cottage, and three small houses on the property. The tall windows on the first floor looked out on a formal garden of clipped boxwood hedges, all-white flowers, and weather-beaten statues of the baroque period.

It was here that Gerald Bradley moved his family each year from spring through fall. Sally Steers, who took over as president of Cora Mandell's decorating firm after Cora's death, had been called in to put the Bradley house in order. Peach and green were the colors decided upon for the downstairs reception rooms. "Not green green, more celadon green. Keep it bright. Keep it airy," dictated Sally, as she marched through the house, notepad and gold pencil in hand, talking very fast. "There's plenty of room for dancing in the front hall, if it's dancing you want. Turn the ballroom into a projection room. You can run pictures and everyone will want to come. I'll have some marvelous sofas made up, ten feet long, rows of them, covered in, oh, I'll find you something wonderful, maybe in coral. And sisal on the floor. Divine, don't you think? Now here, on the loggia, do all your entertaining. It will be marvelous for lunches, marvelous for dinners. Six, twelve, or thirty-six, it won't matter. There's a bamboo auction coming up at Christie's. I've seen the catalog. Heavenly. I'll find you some wonderful things there. And lots and lots of wicker, and some wonderful wrought-iron tables on all the terraces. Billowy curtains, very sheer, on all the windows, will blow in the breeze when the French doors are open. It'll be divine, formal but very informal, if you know what I mean. Perfect for summer.'' Grace agreed to everything. Sally Steers, at almost sixty, had become formidable, taking on all the mannerisms of the late great Cora.

The single greatest decorating problem for Sally Steers was to find a location for the large color photograph of His Holiness the Pope that used to hang over the fireplace in the library of the house in Scarborough Hill. Grace insisted on a prominent place. ''He came to tea with us, you know,'' said Grace. She never tired of repeating the story. ''He held Kitt on his lap.'' But Sally didn't want to hear the story again. ''You can't, can't, *can't* hang it in the loggia. Please, Grace. Not the drawing room, either,'' moaned Sally. But Grace was adamant. Finally, reluctantly, the front hall was decided upon by Sally. It was hung over a console table that held a large platter of dark glasses.

As always with the Bradleys, there were difficulties with the clubs. As always, Gerald's business dealings were badly looked upon by certain members of the old guard. The one club he could get in, the new one, he didn't want to be in, not wanting to be grouped together in people's minds with the sort of members they took. Rather than risk the embarrassment and gossip of being blackballed, Gerald was advised by his lawyer, Sims Lord, who belonged to all the clubs, except the new one, to withdraw his application.

''No, no, it has nothing to do with your Catholicism,'' said Sims, patiently. ''You're acting as if the world of ethnic limits in which you grew up is still in place, Gerald. It isn't. Oh, I don't mean it doesn't exist. I mean it's moved on to other persuasions than yours that are now scratching at the doors. Where you went wrong is that you've apparently had some bad business dealings with Webster Pryde, and Webster is vehement in his dislike of you, and Webster's father and grandfather, all Prydes, were members of the club before Webster, so whatever Webster doesn't want, the club doesn't want either.''

Gerald knew when not to press. ''What about golf then?'' he asked.

''Guest arrangements can be made. I'll take care of that,'' said Sims.

''It's important that the boys play golf. And Kitt and Maureen, too,'' said Gerald.

''It will take a certain amount of planning each weekend, Gerald, but it can be worked out. You'll be guests of this member one week and guests of that member another, and so on and so on. You'll have to leave that up to me to handle in my own way. Here are the names of a few people you should start asking to your movie screenings. They all hate to wait in line outside the theater in the village."

The helicopter landed at the East Hampton airport. Harrison carried his canvas tote and hanger bag into the terminal and looked about. Constant was not there to meet him. Nor was Charlie, the Bradleys' chauffeur. Then a man approached him.

"Harrison, is that you? The old man sent me to meet you. I don't know if you'll remember me or not. I'm Johnny Fuselli."

"Oh, hello, yes, I remember. Where's Charlie? Kitt said Charlie would pick me up," said Harrison.

"Charlie's getting old. The old man gives him two days a week off now. If you want to know the truth, he gets nervous with Charlie driving in this Friday-afternoon traffic. The old man says all the wrong sort of people are coming out to the Hamptons these days, and the roads are blocked solid from Friday to Sunday nights. Day-trippers, he calls them. And then there's these condo people. You got bags?"

"Just these. I'll carry them. I always thought rich people's helicopters landed on the lawns of their estates," said Harrison.

"Neighbors complained. The Prydes. They kept calling the police. Grace complained, too. She said it ruined her hydrangeas. Pulled 'em right up by the roots. Old Gerald didn't give a shit about the neighbors, but he stopped doing it for Grace's sake. They've been married almost fifty years now, Gerald and Grace."

"Yes, they're an example," said Harrison.

"They're all getting old in that house. Bridey's pushing seventy and still cooking three big ones a day. Now she's got all these grandkids to feed, too. And she always remembers how every single one of them likes their eggs. And Maureen's got some real brats, let me tell you. I probably shouldn't have said that."

"I'm not a talker," said Harrison. They got into a Mercedes station wagon. "Nice car."

"Charlie keeps the cars great. He polishes, he tunes up, he gasses, he checks the air in the tires," said Johnny. "It's about a half hour's drive to Southampton. Depending on the traffic."

Harrison nodded. "Are you still such a swimmer?"

Fuselli grinned and turned to Harrison. "Hey, how'd you remember that?"

210

"I used to watch you through the field glasses that summer in Watch Hill. It seemed like you were swimming forever."

"I can't get over that, that you remember, famous guy like you."

"I like to swim," said Harrison.

"Yeah? I hear you write books now."

"Yes."

"What do you write about?"

"Criminals. Criminals who get away with things, mostly."

Johnny looked at Harrison. They drove on in silence for a mile.

"Yeah, I still swim," he said, finally. "Good for the gut. Chicks like a flat stomach. Have you noticed that?"

"Such a fact has recently been pointed out to me. By a woman in Arizona called Maxine Lonergan."

"Maxine Lonergan! Now, there's a name from the past," said Johnny. On his face appeared a benign smile, the sort of smile that materializes on a man's face when he hears the name of a woman with whom he once engaged in a pleasurable dalliance and from whom he has long parted, without rancor. "Where the hell did you meet Maxine Lonergan?"

"She lives on a ranch outside Nogales. A couple of thousand acres. Raises Santa Gertrudis cattle. She's done all right for herself," said Harrison.

"My God. Maxine Lonergan." Johnny nodded his head at the memory. "I wonder whose balls she's licking these days. Let me tell you something, Harry. Maxine Lonergan was one of the all-time-great cocksuckers. On a scale of one to ten, she was about a thirty-six."

"I think she would be touched that you remember her so fondly," said Harrison.

"Maxine Lonergan, my God," he said. "Just between us, strictly off the record, as you guys say, I fixed up Gerald with Maxine one time in Atlantic City. Old Gerald likes his nooky, you know, and he had a taste for fellatio. You know what that means, don't you?"

"Yes, I do."

"Oh, of course you do, you being a writer and all. You'd be surprised how many guys don't know."

"Really."

"Well, Gerald thought he died and went to heaven after an hour with Maxine. He sent her a mink coat from some French place in New York City, I forgot the name. He used to say to me, 'Hey, Johnny, get me that Maxine girl,' but by then she was with the big man, and if you knew what was good for you, you didn't fuck around with Sal Cabrini's girl. Right?''

"Apparently."

"If memory serves, the son was a fagola," said Johnny. "Right?"

"Memory serves."

"I never once took a leak at Maxine's house that the kid didn't follow me into the john, stand at the next urinal, and sneak a peek at my equipment."

"He's dead."

"AIDS?"

"No, a gunshot between the eyes."

"No shit!"

"I'm waiting for you to say he died like a man," said Harrison.

"Right. That's right. You know, Harry, it's nice having a real conversation with you like this. I've been with this family for, lemme see, almost twenty years now, and Grace has never spoken to me, not once. You're not like what I thought you'd be. I remember you when you and Constant were in that fancy boarding school, and then you turn out to be this big success. You never can tell, can you?"

"That's right, Johnny. You never can tell."

If Constant Bradley and Harrison Burns no longer saw each other, they continued over the years to remain aware of each other. Constant missed his friend. In his own way, he grieved for him; there had been no contact between the two for sixteen years. In the intervening time, Constant had become the focus of much attention. Except for a minor incident or two, his years at Yale had been everything and more than his father could ever have hoped. He was one of those undergraduates whom people talked about. His nickname on campus was Magnifico. When girls came to New Haven for football weekends, they always said to their dates, "Point out Constant Bradley to me." On weekends he spent less and less time in Scarborough Hill, preferring to visit friends in New York and Long Island. "All doors are open to him," Gerald bragged proudly. His name and photograph appeared frequently in newspapers. During summers, he spent part of each vacation working in Washington in the office of his brother Sandro, who had gone from the House of Representatives to become a senator. Constant loved the Hill, as he called it. After his six-week stint with

Sandro, he took off for a trip to Europe each year, a combination of playtime on the Riviera, where he mingled in the set that surrounded the princesses of Monaco, and more serious weeks studying the coming collapse of the communist regimes in the Balkans, as arranged for him by representatives of his father's various business activities. After graduation, he received a great deal of notoriety as a polo player, a pastime he abandoned, on the advice of his family, when, at the age of twenty-six, he ran for and won a seat in the House of Representatives. His marriage to Charlotte Stafford, from an old Baltimore family, was held at the Cathedral of Mary Our Queen in Baltimore with a reception following at the Stafford farm in Glyndon, Maryland. Class. That's what everyone said about Charlotte Stafford. She had class.

Through a peculiar twist of fate, Constant's wedding to Charlotte and Harrison's wedding to Claire Rafferty took place on the same day, although in different states, a fact noticed by no one at the time except Harrison. The society wedding of Constant and Charlotte received a papal blessing and a great deal of publicity, while the Philadelphia wedding of Harrison and Claire was a small and private affair, unreported in the press.

All was not always well in the Constant Bradley marriage. There were breakups from time to time, and expensive reconciliations. Gerald, who saw in Charlotte the perfect qualities for a political wife for his favorite son, came to the rescue over and over.

"What happened? What's gone off?" he would ask Constant.

"We've just gotten sick of each other, I suppose," Constant would say.

"That's not a good enough reason."

"When you can't get it up anymore, it's time to move on, Pa."

"Grow up, kid. Grow up. You need Charlotte. And don't you ever forget it."

When Harrison entered the marble-floored hallway of the Bradley house in Southampton, he expected to be greeted by Constant, but it was a young Irish maid in a pink afternoon uniform and white apron who opened the door and took his bag. He looked around at the elegance of the hall and of the rooms opening off it. Only the large color photograph of the Pope looked familiar to him.

"The family's all out playin' golf," she said. She spoke with a lilt in her voice. "They'll be back sometime after four. Bridey particularly wanted to say hello to you. Do you want to go into the kitchen before I take you up to your room?''

"Yes, of course," said Harrison. "Which way?"

"There, through the dinin' room. It's her rest time between lunch and dinner, but she's waitin' there for you."

"Bridey," said Harrison, when he entered the kitchen. She was sitting on a comfortable chair in a small alcove off the kitchen, reading. "No, no, don't stand up. I'll come over there. You look wonderful, Bridey."

"Oh, no, I'm gettin' old. Be seventy in August. Let me look at you, Harrison. You didn't grow too tall. You're awful serious looking, but you was always a nice boy, Harrison. Always nice manners. Always came in the kitchen and said 'Thank you, Bridey' before you went back to school. Not many of them did, you know, the ones who came to visit. And once, after I did your laundry, you gave me a tip, two dollars, and I knew all the time you was in that fancy school on a scholarship and didn't have two dollars to give away, so I stuck the money back in your pants pocket that night."

Harrison laughed. "So that's where that two dollars came from? I've got to give you a big kiss on that one, Bridey."

"Do you still like your eggs poached in the morning? Five minutes?"

"No, Bridey. I'm strictly Grape-Nuts Flakes with strawberries and skim milk these days."

"Shame on you. You need a good breakfast to start the day."

"Everybody's out, I guess," said Harrison.

"They'll be back soon enough. Golf, golf, golf, that's the big thing now. They all play golf. Even Missus, if you can believe it. And her not so young, either. Look what I'm readin', Harrison. I hold it like this, with your picture on the outside, and I say to the girls at Mass on Sunday, 'I happen to know the author.' ''

"Oh, Bridey."

"Terrible man, that Max Goesler. Imagine doing such things to a little girl. Good for you for exposin' all these awful people. And I'm glad they caught those two who killed your parents. The looks of them in the paper at the time. On drugs, the paper said. There's the car. They're coming back. I'm happy to see you, Harrison."

"Hello, Harrison," said Gerald. "I'm sorry there was no one here to greet you. I had hoped to be back. I was out playing golf with Des and

Sandro at the Maidstone Club in East Hampton, and the traffic was terrible getting back here. The worst-looking people you ever saw, in the worst-looking cars. These people are ruining the Hamptons. The condominium people, and the day-trippers who come to look at the big houses. Grace and the girls are at a committee meeting for the Southampton Hospital dance this summer. I hope you'll be able to come back and sit with us that night. We've taken four tables."

"I haven't seen Constant," said Harrison in reply.

"He'll be along. Just between us, he's had a little fight with his wife. Nothing serious, but he got delayed. You know how women are, Harrison. I know Constant has a bit of a wandering eye, and sometimes these little misunderstandings occur."

"You have not set a particularly good example, Mr. Bradley," said Harrison.

"What do you mean by that, Harrison?"

"You have left a coast-to-coast trail of mink coats from Revillon Frères."

Caught, Gerald smiled. "I suppose you could say I'm a man with a healthy appetite for pussy," he said.

"An appetite your son has inherited."

"All my sons, I am proud to say. It is an important part of a man's life, Harrison. Let's face it. Constant is a young man who is mad about women," said Gerald.

"I've never been convinced of that," said Harrison.

"Oh, yes. He likes the way they walk, talk, smile. He finds women intoxicating. He once told me he couldn't imagine a greater pleasure in life than being with the woman he loved. Now, that's a beautiful thought."

Harrison paused. "Then why does he hit them?" he asked.

Gerald, taken aback, paused. His nostrils flared slightly. He leaned away from Harrison and looked at him with disapproval, but the softness of the words that followed belied the anger he held in check. "Don't you think he's suffered enough from that old allegation?" he asked.

"I'm not sure *allegation* is the correct word, Mr. Bradley."

"What's the matter? You don't like women, Harrison? What happened? Your marriage didn't work? Who did you marry?"

"Claire Rafferty."

The look on Gerald's face suggested that the name had a familiar ring to it.

215

"Who?" he asked.

"She was a bridesmaid in Maureen's wedding. You tried to fuck her in the guestroom of your house in Scarborough Hill the night before the wedding."

Gerald, momentarily nonplussed, stared at Harrison. He spoke in a hearty voice as if he were the good-natured brunt of a practical joke. "No, no, no, there is some mistake here. You shouldn't make jokes like that, Harrison. Now, hold on. Hold on. I think I hear a car on the gravel." He walked over to one of the long French windows, pulled aside a fluttering curtain, and looked out. "Yes, yes, yes. There he is. That's Constant's Testarossa. Isn't it a beauty?"

"Some car," said Harrison, walking out the front door.

"Not bad, huh?" answered Constant.

"Some house," said Harrison.

"Not bad, huh?"

"Urns in niches. Very West Egg."

"Very what?"

"Gatsby. It looks like Jay Gatsby's house."

"Oh, my God, you're not still on Gatsby, are you?"

The two old friends looked at each other. Constant was lean, startlingly good-looking, aware that he had become the focus of much attention, but there was also a complacency on his face, a slight boredom, even. Harrison wondered if his arranged life had not come all too easily for him. Constant opened his arms and walked toward Harrison and hugged him.

"Still got all your hair," he said.

"You, too."

"That's a given with the men in my family," said Constant, laughing. "There's no such thing as a bald Bradley. I've missed you, you son of a bitch. You just went off and dumped me."

"That's not exactly how it happened, Constant," replied Harrison. "Or words to that effect."

With a dismissive gesture, Constant brushed off further exploration of that line of conversation. "Let me see. You're married, I know. Two children. Twins. Boys. And successful. On the road to fame, I hear. Oh, I keep track of you. Let me look at you. You look great. How do you stay so thin?"

"I swim every day."

"Swim? You didn't even make the team at Milford."

"I probably still wouldn't. My swimming has nothing to do with speed or form. I'm more interested in distance than style. I swim every day at my club, but in the summers, or when I'm in Florida or California, I swim in the ocean. I set goals for myself. It's the one time of day I'm not haunted. Don't ask me what haunts me."

"Well, there's a pretty big ocean right out there for you to try out."

"It might still be a little cold."

"Johnny Fuselli uses a wet suit."

"Maybe I'll try."

"Well, I'm waiting," said Constant.

"For what?"

"My compliment. How do I look after all these years?"

"I see your picture in the paper all the time, so I'm not surprised you're still the best-looking man I ever saw."

"People say you used to love me."

"A poor boy's crush on a rich boy. No more than that. That was long ago. Over and out. A moment in time."

"You're different," said Constant.

"Oh, I hope so," replied Harrison.

They sat in Harrison's room and caught up. In times past, in Scarborough Hill, they had either shared a room when the house was particularly crowded, or had rooms side by side with a connecting bath, Harrison's room being the room he always thought of as Agnes's room, as that was what Grace had called it the first time he had visited that house. There, in Southampton, there was no room remembered as having once been Agnes's, and Constant no longer was in the next room.

"Pa's impressed with you. I can see that. They've given you the best guestroom in the house," said Constant.

"It's pretty swell. I've never slept in a bed with a tufted headboard and a canopy before," said Harrison.

"Sally Steers did it up."

"Not Sally Steers? You can't be serious. This is where I came in."

They burst out laughing.

"Strictly on the up-and-up these days. All business. Sally's almost sixty now, and a little hefty. Too many creampuffs. Pa likes 'em younger, and slimmer," said Constant.

"Where's your room?" asked Harrison.

"Charlotte and I have one of the cottages. Des and Lee have another. Maureen and Freddy have the biggest cottage, with all those kids. Sandro has a couple of rooms at the end of the hall for when he comes."

"Des is married then?"

"Oh, yes. For years."

"Children?"

"Two girls." Constant stood and looked out the window toward the sea. "You're going to launch me, I hear. Write my book for me."

"I told your father no. I can't write that book for you, Constant," said Harrison. "It's not what I do. Besides, I wouldn't much enjoy watching you on the TV chat shows taking credit for a book I'd written."

"You've got to give me a better reason than that," laughed Constant.

"I told your father this, but he insisted that I come anyway to talk it over. You know how your father is when he wants something."

"But it would be like old times, Harry," said Constant. "Do you remember the Christmas speech at Bog Meadow? What a hit you made me that afternoon. The old biddies couldn't get enough of me. Oh, and the paper for Shugrue, to get me back into Milford after the putz kicked me out. That was a wow. And my graduation speech."

"It was the delivery," said Harrison.

"What did you say?"

"Nothing. I was just remembering something Kitt once said in Watch Hill. You're really going to go through with this, are you? The run for governor?"

"Yes, of course. Pa thinks you get more exposure as governor than as a congressman."

"What is this necessity you have to live center stage? Explain that to me. There are less public ways of getting through life."

"Pa says I'm a born politician."

"Do you really want it, Constant? Or are you living out your father's fantasy of having a son in the White House?"

"Yes, I want it."

"You know what it will be like, don't you? That whole business will come up again. What happened back there in Scarborough Hill. There's people back there—"

"You know, I never had a friend again like you. At Yale, I was a big deal. My nickname was Magnifico, did you know that? I was popular as hell. Of course, there were a few people who disliked me too, although I never much minded what people thought about me. But I never had a real friend to say everything to. Do you remember how we used to talk for hours on end?"

"Yes."

"Hey, how's Aunt Gert? I forgot to ask you about Aunt Gert."

"Poor Aunt Gert. She's in a home. St. Mary's Home. Gaga."

"No more Maryknoll Fathers?"

"No. The amazing thing is that she's afraid to die. She's lived a life of utter goodness, and she's afraid to let go. She used to say to me, 'Bradleys, Bradleys, Bradleys. That's all I ever hear. You are bewitched by those people, Harrison.' "

"Were you? Bewitched, I mean?"

"You are different, all of you. I've never known anyone like you."

"I don't see what's so different about us," said Constant. He sounded irritated, as if he had heard this before.

"None of you will ever have to earn a living. None of your children ever will, either. Nor, very probably, their children. Your father has made enough to guarantee that for all of you. Each child or grandchild gets a million bucks at birth that he can't touch until he is twenty-one, by which time, in a good economy and wisely invested, as it surely will be, it will be worth a minimum of six million for the kid to start out life with. What do you mean, you don't see what's so different about you?"

"You sound jealous," said Constant.

"Oh, what a misreading of me you have made," said Harrison. "I'm not a believer in trust funds, especially for young men. I think you will never really realize your potential because of it. You take too many shortcuts. Too much is done for you."

Constant was stung. "My father believes in us serving our country by entering public life, especially the boys, and he has provided for us so we can do exactly that," he said hotly.

Sitting among the fashionable set at one of Grace Bradley's beautifully arranged luncheon tables in the loggia, Harrison felt detached from much of the conversation, which was mostly society gossip about parties he hadn't been at and people he didn't know.

219

"I'm off to India, guru hopping, with my new beau, who's much too young for me, but divine, so good-looking," said someone named Baba, who was seated next to him. She meditated daily, she said. She claimed to have levitated at an ashram in India. Grace had whispered to him before lunch that she was from the pharmaceutical family of the same last name.

"This lamb is divine, isn't it? So pink. It's very important to have a butcher who cuts beautifully, don't you think?" asked someone named Lulu on his other side. Kitt and Constant, who never mentioned to anyone that their grandfather had been a butcher, looked at each other across the table and tried not to laugh.

"I arrange all my own flowers," said Grace. "I wouldn't dream of letting anyone else do them."

"Everything looks so pretty, Grace," said a man called Count Stamirsky, who ate a great deal and spoke very little, saying only, on five separate occasions, that Grace Bradley was a great lady, thereby earning his meal that day and others to come.

The guests talked of plays and films and fashion and auctions. A man named Sonny, who wasn't English but spoke with an English accent, said he had left a bid at Sotheby's on a collection of Chinese porcelain that once belonged to Fitzy Montague, who jumped out the window of 740 Park Avenue.

"Poor Fitzy. His pajamas flew off on the way down. I bet you didn't know that," said Sonny.

"I did, too. He had a boil on his ass, I heard," said an English peeress named Honour, who held a dog in her lap.

"Bingo told me kind of a cute AIDS joke last night at the Fraziers'," said Lulu.

"We already heard it," said Baba.

They talked of servants and summer houses and parties and dances and a wedding in Pisa that everyone was flying over for. Grace said she had known seven First Ladies, five of them on a first-name basis. They talked of a couple everyone knew and no one liked.

"His wife is screwing the carpenter who built their new redwood deck," said Lulu.

"Serves him right," said a woman named Thelma, which she pronounced Telma. "He's awful."

"*Shhh.* Don't let Grace hear you. She's very opposed to adultery," whispered Sonny.

Bridey was called in and everyone applauded her for her fig mousse.

220

"Yummy," cried Thelma, who tried to lead a standing ovation. There was a great deal of laughter and a great deal of wine. "That's enough, Kitt. No more wine for you," said Grace.

"You were bored with those people, weren't you?" asked Kitt.

"The smart set," said Harrison.

"You hated it, I know. But you didn't even try to enter in."

"What's the point, really? I'll never see any of them again."

"Yes, you will. They'll be at the movie tonight. Ma always invites them. I've decided Ma's a secret social climber," said Kitt. "Last year she said she didn't want us to call her Ma anymore. She wanted us to say Mummy, but none of us could break the habit. All we could do was laugh when we tried to say it."

Harrison laughed.

"Then she wanted us to say *Mère*, the French way, from our years at the embassy, and that really sent us all into hysterics every time we said it, even Mary Pat, who speaks French all the time, so it was back to Ma."

Harrison laughed again. "I'm going swimming," he said.

"Too cold."

"I borrowed a wet suit from Johnny Fuselli."

"*Brrrr*," said Kitt, pretending to shiver.

Gerald encouraged his wife's efforts to move in society, although he had no interest in the sort of people she met. He rarely attended her lunch parties or her charity benefits, and he often chuckled with Jerry about the sort of men who came to lunch. "A bunch of losers," he said.

"Nice obituary in the *Times* for Rupert du Pithon," said Grace. "I always thought he was rather a fool myself, but I didn't know he'd done those brave things in World War II. Won a medal. Imagine. *Rupert*. Of all people. Of course, Sally Steers *hated* him. Do you remember the rude remark he made about little Sally's wedding dress when she was coming down the aisle at St. James's? Actually, in his own way, Rupert was right, I suppose. All that white satin billowing around little Sally when everyone in the church knew she was three months pregnant. I'd die, I'd simply die, if any of my girls did anything like that. Where are you going, Kitt?"

*   *   *

"How far did you swim?" asked Constant.

"Not so far. Maybe three miles. I'll go farther tomorrow," said Harrison. "Maybe four or five. In France once, I swam up to ten."

"I'm impressed. How long did it take you today?"

"A couple of hours."

"How far out do you go?"

"About two hundred yards. Past the waves. You want to avoid the kelp. Then I always turn in a northerly direction. You only breathe out of one side of your mouth so you can judge the distance from the shore and make sure you're going in a straight line. You keep a standard pace. Your speed doesn't change."

"I repeat, I'm impressed. Even though I was brought up on the water every summer, I have this fear of deep water," said Constant. "It's so big, the thing you're in, and you're so small."

"That's what I like," said Harrison. "This vast watery space under me, floating in an unknown zone."

"Is that when you stop being haunted? That's what you said to me: it's the only time of day you're not haunted."

Harrison continued as if he had not heard.

"It depends on the water temperature, of course. It's all in the breathing. The breathing will change your whole life. After about half an hour a sense of euphoria comes."

"Tell me about it."

"What?"

"The feeling."

"Oh, hell, I can't describe it to you, Constant. You feel like you can walk into heavy traffic and cars won't hit you. Listen, enough of that, where's the famous Charlotte? I want to meet her."

"Famous Charlotte and I are not speaking."

"That's quite a morsel for an about-to-be gubernatorial candidate."

"We'll work it out. We always do. I wish you could see the way she returned my clothes to me. One hundred and fifty Turnbull and Asser ties just jammed into a grocery bag, like snakes. My suits hung backwards on hangers. Morty Sills suits, can you believe it? Two thousand per. I couldn't believe it."

"You thought she should have packed everything in tissue paper?" asked Harrison.

222

"I'm not sure how I should react to what you just said," said Constant.

"You left her for another woman. Right?"

"Only temporarily."

"You temporarily left her for another woman. You asked her to return your clothes. Don't you think she might have a right to be a little angry and shove them in a bag?"

"Are you so happily married?"

"No, I'm not. But I went back to get my own clothes."

"What's the new maid's name, Bridey?" asked Grace.

"Debbie, madam," said Bridey.

"That's what I thought she said. No, Bridey, I don't want a maid named Debbie. It just doesn't sound right to me. Debbie. It's too, well, I don't know what it is, but it's not right for a maid's name. Ask her to change it, will you? Mary's fine, or Catherine, or Margaret—that sort of name."

"I already spoke to her about it. She says she don't want to change it, madam," said Bridey.

"Well, if she 'don't' want to change it, tell her she 'don't' have to work here in my house, thank you very much," said Grace.

"Yes, madam."

"Didn't we used to have a Colleen with us? Years ago? Back in Scarborough Hill?"

"Yes, madam."

"She couldn't tell left from right, do you remember? I'd say, 'Serve from the left, remove from the right,' over and over and over again, and she never got it straight, do you remember? She said she had to write in the air first in order to tell. I wonder whatever happened to her. Let's call Debbie Colleen, Bridey. Now, Bridey's such a nice name. Why aren't girls called Bridey anymore?"

"I don't know, madam."

Charlotte arrived. She drove straight to her cottage on the other side of the twelve-car garage without stopping in the main house first to say hello to Grace and Gerald, which was the habit of the house. Everyone stopped talking for a minute when they saw her green Jaguar drive by the windows, much too fast.

223

"My children are outside playing on the grounds, Constant," said Maureen indignantly. "You might try telling your wife there is a speed limit of fifteen miles per hour when driving on the estate."

"Oh, shove it, Maureen," said Constant.

"Ma, did you hear what he said?" asked Maureen.

"The children are over by the fountain, Maureen," said Grace. "I can see them from where I'm sitting. They're nowhere near the driveway."

"It's the principle of the thing, Ma." Maureen got up and went to the window and looked out. "Winthrop! Choate! Where's Nanny? I don't want you playing in the fountain unless Nanny's there. How many times do I have to tell you that?" She turned to Freddy Tierney and said, "I'm going to fire that nanny. Right now. Leaving those children alone like that."

"She had terrible morning sickness this morning," explained Freddy after Maureen left the room.

Kitt said, "Maybe she'll have triplets this time, and then she'll have more kids than you and Pa, Ma, and she'll be champion at last."

"Don't talk nonsense, Kitt," said Grace. "I want all this bickering to stop before Father Bill arrives. Let me see your needlepoint, Kitt. Oh, lovely, darling. Lovely colors."

"The green's pretty, don't you think?"

"It's not green. It's celadon."

"Don't you think you ought to go over to the cottage and see Charlotte, Constant?" asked Gerald.

"Sure, Pa. I just wanted to show Harrison my polo trophies in the library first."

"*Now*, Constant," said Gerald.

"Yes, Pa."

"Who's Father Bill?" Harrison asked Kitt.

"Ma's latest favorite priest."

"I can't help but notice that you haven't been near me for quite some time. Don't misunderstand me, Constant, I'm not yearning for your touch. But I like to have things laid out on the table. Are you involved with someone else? Or are we entering into a new phase of our marriage?"

"Oh, come on, Charlotte."

"When I say someone else, I mean someone other than the someone

elses you see daily—the quickies. Someone on a serious basis is what
I'm trying to say," said Charlotte.

"No, no, of course not," said Constant.

" 'No, no, of course not,' " she repeated, imitating him. "You'd lie
when the truth would sound better, Constant. It was just a show, this
marriage, wasn't it? Just one long ten-year show. I had the class, and
your father had the brass. I can see just what it's going to be like, as
clear as if I were a psychic. Me in an Adolfo suit, looking lovingly up
at you through speech after speech, and only you will know that I
won't be listening to a single word you're saying."

"No, you're wrong, Charlotte. It wasn't a show."

"A show," she repeated. "That's all it ever was."

"No. I loved you."

"Oh, puhleeze."

"Come on, Charlotte," he said. "Pa's going to run out of money if
you keep leaving me like this. Come on, honey. I find you very attractive when you're angry. Your cheeks all pink like that. Your pits a
little sweaty. A little musky odor coming from you. Oh, my, lookit
here. Look what's almost, but not quite, hard. Look what needs your
helping hand."

It amazed her that she could be so physically attracted to a person
she despised so much both before and after the act of love. No matter
how strong was her intention each time to resist him, he had only to
unbutton his shirt to reveal his chest, or unzip his fly and place his
hand inside, running it along the length of his penis, for her to fall on
her knees and beg him to take off everything, everything, quickly,
placing her face in his most intimate parts, and beg for him to take her
in any way he wanted her, it mattered not how.

Afterwards, he said to her, "After your bath, come over to the big
house. I want you to meet my friend Harrison."

"Oh, yes, Harrison. The old family friend. He's the one who's going to write the book that you are going to say you wrote, so all the
voters in the state will know you're just a regular guy. That Harrison?"

"You can be a real bitch, Charlotte."

"They don't call me rich and heartless for nothing, Constant."

"I'm Harrison."

"Oh, yes, the old school friend," said Charlotte, when at last she met Harrison standing by the fountain. They looked at each other, each sizing the other up.

"What happens when you meet up with all those people you write about afterwards?" she asked, not waiting for the usual preliminaries of a new acquaintanceship.

"They're usually in prison," Harrison answered.

"Mrs. Goesler isn't. Mrs. Renthal isn't. The girls they left behind, I mean."

"We don't travel much in the same circles."

"No, I suppose not. I felt sorry for Ruby Renthal. Care to walk for a bit?" she asked. "You can't swim all the time."

"Sure."

"I was prepared to dislike you," she said.

"I was prepared to dislike you, too," Harrison replied.

She smiled at him.

"You've probably heard terrible things about me, from Kitt and Constant. And Maureen. And that ghastly Jerry. I just hate Jerry, don't you?"

Harrison smiled. "He was never my favorite in this family," he said.

"Don't you think it's odd that you're the only real friend my husband ever had?" asked Charlotte. "He talks about you all the time. When he heard you were coming this weekend, he was beside himself."

"That was years ago," said Harrison.

"That's the story of his life. He's rich, beautiful, dazzling, witty, charming. People line up to look at him. They want to be close to him. He's wonderful on the campaign trail. New people in a new town every day. That's when he's at his best. He says exactly the right thing to each one. Perfect, personal, charm personified. But what I've found over the years is that no one stays around long. Even you. Eventually they begin to discover that the very qualities to which they were first attracted only mask his inadequacies. Everyone knows it except his father."

It was not a conversation that Harrison wished to pursue. He shifted the subject. "What's it like being in the family?"

"Strange. Difficult. I was an only child. I'm from one of those old Baltimore families that had run out of steam, not to mention money. I never knew from one year to the next if Daddy was going to be able to scrape up the money to send me back to Foxcroft. The year I came

226

out, there was no money for a dance, so I came out at a tea. If I hadn't been pretty and popular, it would have been a joke. Then I met Constant. I had a Catholic grandmother, so I qualified. He was the best-looking thing I ever saw, and so rich. Daddy was ecstatic, of course, even though he couldn't stand Gerald. Micks. He called them all micks. I said, 'If you know what's good for you, Daddy, you'll lose that word from your vocabulary forever.'

"But with the Bradleys, you marry into the whole family, this big vast army of people, with no privacy. Every weekend together. Twenty or more people sitting down to every meal. Those spoiled brats of Maureen's, screaming all through dinner. And now with Grace getting so social, she has the worst kind of hangers-on coming to lunch every day. Of course, I never thought Grace was as blind to what goes on in this family as everyone thinks. I actually kind of like old Gerald, in his rough-and-tough way, but every time he snaps his fingers, all his children jump, and they're now all in their thirties and forties. I see you're maintaining a diplomatic silence."

"I hadn't seen any of them for years until yesterday," said Harrison.

"I've never really been a member of the family. I was married to Constant for two years before I even heard there was a sister called Agnes in a madhouse somewhere, or that Des was once married to a maid."

"They tend to hush up those things."

"What is there about you, Harrison? I feel like I've been to confession."

Harrison laughed.

"Actually, I quite like being a Catholic. I adore confession. Oh, wait until you see us go to Mass on Sunday. They line up to look at us. I like that, too. And I can do a better job than Nancy Reagan of looking up at Constant whenever he makes a speech, no matter how many times I've heard it before. Of course, I'm not listening, but no one knows that. I bet she wasn't, either."

Harrison laughed. "I don't think you're as bad as you make yourself out to be."

"You're not really going to write this asinine book for Constant, are you?"

"No."

"I didn't think so."

*   *   *

"We've got things to talk about, Harrison," said Constant. "Mass is at eight-thirty and ten in the village. Bridey and the maids go to the eight-thirty usually, and we all go to the ten. Then the family breakfast. After that we can spend the day together. Walk on the beach, talk, figure it out about the book. It would be great working together."

"You go. I'll wait for you here."

"No church?"

"No church," replied Harrison. "I have ceased to be a practicing Catholic."

"Since when?"

"Since I could no longer receive Communion."

"Why can't you receive Communion?"

"Because I witnessed a murder and did nothing about it. It's not the sort of thing you can tell in confession and expect to get absolution from the priest. Apparently you don't have the same qualms," said Harrison.

"Jesuschrist, Harrison." Constant looked toward the closed door, as if Harrison had uttered words of unspeakable vulgarity in front of his mother. Any reference to that long-ago night in Scarborough Hill was brushed aside as if it had not been heard. It was a thing never discussed. "My father felt—" Constant stopped before he completed his sentence, and turned away.

"Oh, of course. I understand. Your father felt it wouldn't look right for a son in politics not to attend Mass and receive Communion. Did your Cardinal Sullivan give you some special dispensation, or do you just confess the fuck and booze sins and overlook the murder sin?"

"What's gotten into you all of a sudden, Harrison?"

"It's not all of a sudden."

"I've had enough of this. I have no memory of what you are talking about."

"Yes, you do, Constant. It's like a big black cloud hovering over the two of us. The unmentioned subject. The thing we pretend never happened. The thing we blocked from our minds that we carry with us year after year. Dare I even say the words? Winifred Utley."

Constant, breathing heavily, stared at Harrison and shook his head and waved his hands in front of him, as if he were warding off a curse.

"I should never have come here," said Harrison. "My life was going along fine, in its own sick, neurotic way which I have grown to find normal. I had put all this in the back of my brain somewhere. Then your big-deal father began to interfere. 'Write a book for my son. It'll

228

be good for him.' Puffing away on his big fucking cigar. I didn't want to come. I didn't want to spend the weekend here. But as always, with you people, I revert back to the awestruck scholarship boy and end up doing what you want to do, not what I want to do. You and I should never see each other again, Constant. *Never*."

"You are becoming hysterical," said Constant.

"Yes, I am, aren't I? And I am not ashamed of my hysteria. I don't seem to possess your composure. Where does this reserve of yours come from? I am eaten inside by what I know, and I am not responsible, while you, who are responsible, act as if what happened is some inconvenience in your life, like being kicked out of school for reading a dirty magazine. Ever since I saw you again, that night is all I can think of."

"After all, it wasn't deliberate," said Constant.

"Oh? What was it then?"

"You are tiresome, Harry. It's over, forgotten. Why do you linger with it?"

Constant rose and walked slowly toward Harrison. He reached out to him and pulled him to his feet and shook him, all the time breathing heavily and staring into his eyes. Then he kissed Harrison fully on the lips and put his arms around him, enveloping him into his own body.

Harrison, impassive, neither resisted nor acquiesced. "No, Constant, that's not going to do it," he said.

"I've got a hard-on," said Constant.

"I don't," said Harrison.

"Do you want to see it?"

"No, I don't."

"There was a time."

"Yeah, there was a time, but that was long ago, and we were very young."

"I remember when we used to jerk off at school looking at *Playboy*, you always used to look at me, not the beaver shots," said Constant.

Harrison remained impassive. "Over. Out," he said, pulling back from Constant. "You've always talked a great deal about erections. Have you noticed that about yourself? I wonder if, perhaps, you have trouble getting one, or maintaining one. I wonder if that is not the cause of the rage that made you do what you did. What did you do that night? Stand there in the path and wait for her to go from the Wadsworth house to the Utley house?"

Constant, enraged, roughly pushed Harrison away from him.

229

"We've done a lot for you in this family," he said. The tone of his voice was unpleasant.

"Listen, you son of a bitch, you haven't done as much for me as I've done for you," said Harrison, matching Constant's tone. "You killed a woman, and I kept my mouth shut for you. I hate you for having involved me in that terrible act. What the hell more do you want out of me?"

Constant, momentarily frightened, looked at him. "You could have said no that night, you know," he said. "I didn't force you to lift her up. You came along willingly enough."

"Next thing you'll have it worked out that it was I who raised the baseball bat and crushed in her head. Get real, Constant. The schoolboy crush is over. I know who you are. I know all about you. No more games between us. Tell me about Maud somebody or other."

"Maud?"

"Yes, Maud. The one in the hotel room in Chicago, who cracked her head on a bedside table, who had seventeen stitches. Surely, you must remember Maud."

"Maud Firth, you mean."

"Yes, Maud Firth."

He dismissed Maud with a gesture. "She was drunk. She fell. That was all. However did you hear about Maud Firth?"

"She was a cousin, or some relation, of Fruity Suarez. Fruity told me."

"Who's Fruity Suarez?"

"The one you pissed on at Milford."

"Oh, her. Fruity. Didn't she get kicked out for kissing somebody's dick? Or trying to? How is old Fruity? Still pursuing bachelors, I assume. Is this who we're listening to these days? Is this our source of information? Fruity-fucking-Suarez?"

"That's nice talk. *She. Her.* That'll go over big with the gay vote when you run for governor," said Harrison.

"How is Fruity involved?"

"He called me out of the blue at two in the morning a few years ago. Woke up my wife. Maud went to him after you left her there in the hotel room. She was afraid to go to her parents. Your version of the events of that night differs somewhat from Fruity's."

"I hear you're fucking my sister," said Constant.

"What a Bradley way to put it."

"My father says you seem to have an affinity for his children."

"Tell your father Eloise Brazen said he was a pretty good fuck for an old guy."

"Who's Eloise Brazen?"

"You have no memory for names, Constant. A bad trait for a politician. Eloise Brazen was the one you called looking for your father on the night you killed Winifred Utley."

"Lower your fucking voice, Harry. We're in my mother's home. Not everyone understands your kind of humor."

"Humor, huh? Is that what it is?"

"You see, I don't remember anything about that night. Not one single thing."

"Don't remember?"

"Nothing."

"Oh, I see. The old blackout cop-out. Is that it? You were drunk. And don't remember. So therefore not responsible."

"If it ever came to that, yes."

"I could blow a hole in that story a mile wide," said Harrison.

"But you won't," said Constant.

"How do you know?"

"I just know."

"You're right, Constant. I won't," said Harrison.

"Is this true?" asked Constant.

"Is what true?" asked Kitt.

"You and Harrison? Are you sleeping together?"

"You're not getting moral with me, are you, Constant?"

The two youngest, Kitt and Constant had once been each other's favorite in the family. Young, they shared secrets. They discussed their older siblings endlessly. Kitt, of all the others, had understood Constant's moods. She knew that somewhere he felt inadequate to the great expectations his father had for him. "It should have been Jerry," he once confessed to her. "Not me."

"What about Cheever?" Constant asked.

"What about him?"

"You're still married to him."

"Your marriage doesn't seem to have curbed your wayward habits. Surely, you of all people are not going to discuss the sanctity of marriage with me?"

"It's different."

"It's not, Constant. That's Pa's thinking. It's all right for the men, but not the ladies. You're never going to win an election with that line of thinking. I might not even vote for you."

They were walking on the beach. Far off, they could see Harrison swimming. Both watched.

"Are you curious about him? Is that it? Are you curious what it's like, Constant? It's marvelous. Does that answer your question?"

"That is not what I meant."

"I think it is."

"He has disrupted our house by coming here," said Constant.

"He didn't want to come here. Pa insisted. I insisted. You wanted him to come. He didn't want to," said Kitt.

"I think he could be a little nuts, Kitt. Be careful of him."

"What is there I don't understand about the two of you?" asked Kitt.

Grace Bradley sat alone in the rose-shaded drawing room of her house, saying her rosary. The scent of wilting peonies filled the room.

"Not seeing the movie, Mrs. Bradley?" asked Harrison from the hallway, as he passed by.

"Certainly not, not after what Father Bill told me about that movie. That Madonna woman is a disgrace. The Vatican asked Catholics to boycott her concerts in Italy. Did you know that? I don't like having films like hers shown in my house," said Grace.

"Your friends in the projection room seem to be enjoying it," said Harrison. "Sonny and Baba and Thelma."

"She pronounces it Telma. Is Constant there?"

"I didn't see him. Charlotte's there."

"Come in and talk to me, Harrison. You haven't said a word to me all weekend. I remember the nice talks we used to have in Scarborough Hill."

"Yes, I remember, Mrs. Bradley."

"You could call me Grace, you know, after all these years. Sit there. That bergère chair is awfully comfortable, I find. Just move the pillow if it's in your way. Pretty, isn't it? Kitt did the needlepoint, and Sally Steers got the fringe in Paris."

Harrison moved the pillow and sat down by Grace.

"Isn't it nice that Kitt ran into you in Maine like that? And here you are back in the family. Don't you think that some things are meant to be? Oh, I do. I believe that. You saw Agnes?''

"Yes.''

"How did you find her?''

"As I had never seen her before, I had no basis for comparison.''

"Poor Agnes. She always wanted to be a nun, from the time she was a little girl. Always had a vocation. I was just saying my rosary for her. I say one for her every night before bed. I sit in here, after the guests leave. No one ever comes in,'' she said, smiling at him and holding up her silver beads.

"Do you miss the house in Scarborough Hill?'' he asked.

"I do, yes. I loved that house. We built it, you know. We tore down old Governor Scarborough's house that had been standing on that site for years and years and built our house. Oh, what a to-do there was about that. All the old guard of Scarborough Hill were up in arms over it. Louise Somerset, our neighbor, didn't speak to me for years. She was born a Scarborough. They were happy years there. All the children growing up. These other houses we've lived in, like this house, and the house in California, and the apartment in New York, they're beautiful houses, but they were other people's dreams, not mine.''

"Sis Malloy lives there, I hear,'' said Harrison.

"Yes, Sis. She's such a dear. Someday we'll go back, I'm sure. You didn't bring your wife with you.''

"No.''

"Does she work?''

"She is an editor in a publishing house.''

"I don't suppose you need a nanny for your children, do you? Maureen just fired an awfully good one. A cousin of Bridey's.''

"We have an au pair. A Swiss girl.''

"Odd about Maureen. She can't keep help. Do you know how many years Bridey has been with me? And Charlie? I've lost count actually, but since the children were small. It's very important to know how to treat help. Don't you think?''

"I guess. It's not a thing I've ever had to deal with,'' said Harrison.

Inevitably, Grace brought the conversation around to Catholicism. "Did you marry a Catholic?''

"Yes.''

"Your children were baptized?''

"Yes.''

233

"I notice you didn't go to Mass today."

"Yes."

"I disapprove of that under my roof."

"I'm thirty-five years old, Mrs. Bradley. With all due respect for your opinion, I feel that is my own business."

Grace, taken aback by Harrison's answer, retreated. She was used to having people say "Yes, Ma" or "Yes, Mrs. Bradley" when she made her dictates about their religious practices. Harrison was no longer the compliant boy she remembered, as agreeable to all the Bradley suggestions as Sis and Fatty Malloy. "Yes, of course," she said finally. "Perhaps you'll go back to it one day. Wait until you have the first big tragedy in your life. It often happens that way. Does your wife go to Mass?"

"My wife and I are separated, but I don't think she does."

There was a silence. At that moment Kitt walked into the room. "Harrison married Claire Rafferty, Ma," she said. "Do you remember? She was a bridesmaid in Maureen's wedding."

"Oh?" said Grace. "Really?" A look of displeasure crossed her face. "Well, it's late. Past my bedtime, at least. Good night, everyone."

"Good night, Ma," said Kitt.

"Good night, Mrs. Bradley," said Harrison.

"Ask that new parlor maid to take out the peonies, will you, Kitt? I think her name is Colleen. The peonies are wilting, tell her."

"Yes, Ma."

"I can still see that beautiful, beautiful bridesmaid's dress jammed into the wastebasket," said Grace to no one in particular as she walked up the stairs. "It cost seven hundred dollars, which was still quite a lot of money back in 1973."

Kitt watched her mother until she had reached the top of the stairs and walked down the hallway to her room. "You should probably have gone to Mass, you know, Harrison. Since it means so much to her. What difference does it make, really? It's just an hour out of your life."

Harrison said nothing.

Kitt continued. "If for no other reason than the family show we put on. People wait outside the church to look at Constant and Charlotte and their kids. They look like the American dream family as they march up that aisle to take their seats. Whatever happens between them in private, you would never know a thing was wrong when you see them together in public. They both know how to play it. She's as good at it as he is. Pa just beams with pride when everyone stares at Constant. No wonder he wants Constant to be president."

Still Harrison said nothing.

"I can't call the new maid at this hour," she said. She took the vase of white peonies from the top of the piano and carried it into the front hall where she placed it on the console table beneath the photograph of the Pope. When she returned to the drawing room, it was in darkness. "Harrison?" she said.

"Over here. I turned off the lights." He spoke in a low voice.

"Oh, my darling," she whispered, walking toward his voice. They kissed in the darkness. Their arms wrapped around each other's bodies. He reached inside her dress. "Yes, yes," she whispered.

"No bra?" he whispered back.

"Just in case an opportunity arose."

"It has arisen."

"Two whole days without touching you. I thought I would go mad," she said. They kissed again, their passion growing, their hearts pounding. He reached to the bottom of her dress and pulled it up, placing his hand between her legs, gently grasping her, and massaging it back and forth as they continued to kiss, their tongues pressing together.

"Oh, my God," she whispered. She reached down and unzipped the fly of his trousers. She put her hand inside his trousers until she got a firm hold on his erect penis and pulled it out.

"Oh, baby," whispered Harrison. "Oh, Kitt."

Kitt dropped to her knees and took Harrison's penis in her mouth. They became lost in their pleasure.

From the main hallway came the sound of strident high heels on the marble floor. "Ma? Ma? Why are all the lights out?" It was Maureen. "Ma? Nanny stole two of my best cashmere sweaters when she went back to New York today after I fired her. Ma?" She pushed the wall switch, and the room was flooded with rosy light from all the lamps. There, at the far end of the room, in front of the fireplace, stood and knelt Harrison and Kitt. Maureen gasped. Both of her hands flew to her mouth in horror. The very idea of what she was witnessing appalled her, made her shudder and turn crimson. Then she made the sign of the cross. "Dear God! Holy Mother of God! In all my life, I have never, never, *never* seen anything so disgusting. In my mother's house. How could you? Cover your breasts, Kitt. How could you sink so low?"

Kitt rose and readjusted her dress, pulling her skirt down and straightening the top around her breasts. Harrison leaned down and pulled up his boxer shorts, which had fallen to his ankles, and then leaned down again and pulled up his trousers. He buttoned them at the waist and then zipped up his fly.

Maureen, breathing heavily, watched them with disgust.

"You'd better go upstairs, Harrison," said Kitt, quietly. "I'll handle this."

"Are you sure?" asked Harrison.

"Oh, yes."

"Will you be all right?" asked Harrison.

"Oh, yes. Good night."

"Good night."

"I love you, Harrison."

When Harrison left the room, he did not look in Maureen's direction. She followed him out with her eyes, hatred showing in her face. Both sisters watched him ascend the stairs.

"Does it interest you at all that earlier today the new parlor maid, Debbie or Colleen or whatever her name is, saw him kissing your brother?" asked Maureen.

"Don't talk nonsense," said Kitt.

"I think your behavior is deplorable," said Maureen, turning toward her sister. "Animals behave better than that. *Animals.* Do you want to kill your mother? Because that's what would happen. She would die if she knew this. Involved with that user, Harrison Burns. He got everything he could out of this family, dumped us, and then he came back, grubbing for more out of us."

"As usual, Maureen, you have everything wrong," replied Kitt. "I hope you are not under the impression that he is a big fan of yours."

"I am completely indifferent as to what his feelings are for me. He's a married man, as you are a married woman, in the eyes of God. And married to that horrible Claire Rafferty to boot. That's the only part of this vile episode that's giving me any pleasure. Do you know what she did at my wedding?"

"Oh, please, Maureen. Don't start in again on her seven-hundred-dollar bridesmaid's dress. Just don't. We've all heard the story. Over and over again."

"It was one of the rudest things I have ever heard of in my life," said Maureen.

"I happen to be in an awkward position with Claire and the last person in the world who should be coming to her defense, as I am currently fucking her husband, as well as sucking her husband, as you just clearly saw, but she had every right to trash her bridesmaid's dress. If what happened to her happened to me, I would have shoved the dress down the toilet, not just jammed it in a wastebasket."

"What do you mean what happened to her?" asked Maureen.

"Guess. *Guess,* Maureen. The same thing that happened to Mary Elizabeth Moylan when she came to visit Mary Pat at the embassy in Paris. And the same thing that happened to Puff Rooney when she came home with me from Sacred Heart. The reason none of our friends wanted to spend the night in our house. Or why their parents wouldn't let them."

"I don't know what you're talking about," said Maureen.

"Oh, yes, you do, Maureen. Yes, you do. It's one of the dozen or so things we pretend we don't know anything about in our family. Like that Johnny Fuselli is a gangster. Like the existence of the girl with the paralyzed back who was in the car with Jerry. Like what happened to Winifred Utley."

"Shut up," screamed Maureen. With all her strength, she slapped Kitt across her face.

Kitt, reeling from the blow, was thrown backward into the room. She fell against the chair in which Grace had been sitting. Tears filled her eyes. Slowly she got to her feet. "Oh, go have another baby, Maureen," she said wearily, and walked out of the room. She started up the stairs. Then she turned back and walked out onto the loggia. There, at the far end of the room, the bar table was still set up from the luncheon party that day. She picked up a bottle of vodka, removed the cap, and drank from it, gulp after gulp.

"Maybe this wasn't such a good idea," said Gerald.

"What, Pa?" asked Jerry.

"Having Harrison out here."

"I told you to stay away from that guy, Pa."

"He said some odd things to me. He said some odd things to Constant, too. He kept bringing up that old matter. Constant's very upset," said Gerald.

It had been the belief of Gerald and Jerry and Des and Sandro that time would diminish the memories of that long-ago Easter occurrence in Scarborough Hill. "People forget," Gerald often said. They even believed that time would diminish the grief of Luanne Utley, the mother. Surely, she had dealt with it by now and gone on with her own life, Gerald reasoned.

"Constant thinks he's a little crazy," said Gerald.

"This guy's a walking time bomb, Pa."

12

SEVERAL HOURS after midnight the telephone rang in the Bradley house in Southampton. The telephone in Gerald and Grace's room had been turned off before they retired. Grace, who went to early Mass in the village every morning, did not like her rest to be disturbed once she closed the door of her bedroom. Kitt, who swallowed nearly half a bottle of vodka after her fight with Maureen, had passed out on her bed and did not hear the telephone. Maureen had returned to her cottage on the property. The telephone in Jerry's room, which was at the farthest end of the house, was a private line of his own, disconnected from the main telephone of the residence. Harrison, whose room was at the top of the stairs, was awakened by the constant ringing but felt that it was not his place to answer a telephone in a house where he was an increasingly unwelcome guest. Finally, after twelve rings, there was silence.

But the silence did not last. In a few minutes, Harrison was disturbed again by the sound of crying in the downstairs hallway. He rose from his bed, grabbed a terry cloth robe from the bathroom door, and opened the door of his room. There, coming up the stairs, was Bridey. She was dressed in a full-length robe and slippers. Her hair was covered by a nightcap. She was weeping.

"Bridey, what in the world is the matter?" asked Harrison.

"It's the police on the phone, Harrison. There's been an accident."

"Who?"

"It's Constant. He hit a telephone pole on the Montauk Highway. They've taken him to the Southampton Hospital."

"I'll get dressed. You'd better wake up Mr. and Mrs. Bradley, Bridey."

"Oh, I hate havin' to be the one to tell them. She's had nothin' but a lifetime of sorrow, the poor woman."

"Is it serious?"

She looked in both directions to see if anyone was listening, and then whispered in Harrison's ear, "He was drinkin'. At a bar in Sag Harbor."

Within minutes, every light in the huge house seemed to have been turned on. Maureen had been telephoned in her cottage, and ran up to the main house to be with her mother. Kitt had been awakened. Jerry was on the telephone with Johnny Fuselli, with Gerald barking orders into his ear. Des and Sandro took off for the hospital before the others. Bridey made coffee in the kitchen. Harrison, watching, noticed that Charlotte was not present. He walked outside and over to her cottage. He rang the bell and knocked on the door at the same time.

"Who is it?" he heard a voice say behind the door.

"It's Harrison, Charlotte. Open up."

The door opened. Charlotte, in a nightgown, stood inside, peering out.

"There's been an accident," said Harrison.

"Constant, I suppose," she said.

"Yes."

"Is he dead?"

"No. He's been taken to Southampton Hospital."

"I'll get dressed," she said.

By four in the morning, most of the family had gathered in the corridor of the Southampton Hospital. Only Grace remained at home, with Bridey. It was her plan to come after the eight o'clock Mass. Harrison, standing apart, watched. Gerald and Jerry and Des were in consultation with a bearded Indian doctor in a pale blue turban at the end of a corridor outside the intensive care unit. Maureen, without makeup, sat on an orange Naugahyde sofa with Charlotte, saying a rosary with her silver beads. Kitt, hung over, stared out a window into the black night outside. Freddy Tierney was sent out to an all-night diner to bring coffee back for the family. "And call the main house," Maureen shouted after him. "Tell Bridey to tell the new maid to go over and stay with the children in the cottage until we get back. What a swell time for Nanny to walk out on us."

*   *   *

"It's a concussion," said Des to the family.

"How bad?" asked Kitt.

"He's still out. They've taken a lot of stitches in his head and face. Dr. Puthli, in the blue turban, seems to think he'll be all right."

"What was the liquor content in his blood?" asked Harrison.

Everyone turned to him in amazement at his question.

"I hold you responsible for this," said Jerry, pointing his finger at Harrison. His face was contorted with rage.

"Me?" asked Harrison. "You hold me responsible?"

"It was you who upset him. He hadn't had a drink in months. You were the one who got him all riled up."

"You know something, Jerry? If you weren't a cripple, I'd kick the shit out of you," said Harrison. "How dare you say that to me?"

Jerry, stunned, was momentarily speechless.

"That is an outrageous thing to say to my son," said Gerald. His voice was harsh. His face and eyes expressed coldness and hostility.

"I demand you apologize to my brother," said Maureen, bristling.

"I will repeat it before I apologize for having said it," said Harrison to Maureen. "The idea of holding me to blame for your brother's drunk-driving accident is the guilty plea of an enabler, which is what all of you are."

"What are you doing here anyway?" asked Maureen. "You're not one of us. This is for the family."

"Of course, you're right," said Harrison. "I'll go back."

"He can stay," said Kitt. "I want him here."

"You'd better get Sims Lord down here," said Gerald wearily, to Jerry. "We need to prepare a statement in case the papers get hold of the story. Where's Fuselli?"

"He's still at the police station," said Jerry. He had given orders to Johnny Fuselli, who knew everything and could do anything and was known in various police stations and courtrooms as the dispenser of funds when records needed to be expunged. "Better let him be. He knows how to handle these things."

Harrison wandered down a corridor until he found a soft drink machine. Standing at the machine with her back to him was Charlotte, pulling wildly at the levers.

"I can't get this damn thing to work," she said. "You do it, will you? I stuck the dollar in there, like it says, but nothing came out."

241

"You've got George Washington facing the wrong way," said Harrison. "What do you want?"

"Diet Coke. Oh, I don't care. Just push any one. I had to get away from that family. I probably shouldn't even be talking to you. Now you're the enemy, apparently. I love what you said about them being enablers. Didn't I tell you about Jerry?" She looked down the long hospital corridor to where Jerry and Maureen were talking quietly. "Two shits that pass in the night," she said.

"What happens now?" asked Harrison.

"Now the Bradley machine goes into operation. Johnny Fuselli. Sims Lord. A publicist from New York. And Jerry in charge," said Charlotte. "I don't know what Jerry does with himself between family crises."

"What happens when the machine goes into operation?"

"I'll be photographed rushing into this hospital with concern and love on my face, carrying some white peonies cut from Grace's garden —they think of all those things—and some brownies that Bridey just baked all covered in Saran Wrap. A perfect little statement will have been written for me to give to any reporter who asks what my husband was doing out in a car with another woman going eighty miles an hour on the Montauk Highway at two o'clock in the morning."

"I didn't know he was with another woman," said Harrison.

"They haven't told me that yet either, but I've played this scene before, Harrison, and there's always another woman in the car in this family," said Charlotte. "That's probably why Johnny Fuselli's at the police station, to get her name removed from the records and pay her off."

"Have you seen Constant?"

"Yes."

"And?"

"Maybe a few facial scars will do him good. Give him a little character. He's too good-looking."

"Will you be all right?" asked Harrison.

"Oh, sure. You get used to these things. You mustn't think for a moment this was a first. The only reason I haven't turned into a secret drinker is that there's already one drunk in the family," said Charlotte.

Harrison turned back down the corridor.

"Oh, Harrison?" called out Charlotte.

"Yes?"

242

"It was nice of you to come and get me. None of them would have remembered."

"As drunk-driving accidents go, it was not a serious accident," said Johnny Fuselli. "There were no deaths. The main destruction was to the Testarossa. Of course, Constant is banged up pretty good, but the girl's not too bad. I got her transferred to a hospital in Garden City."

"Who is she?" asked Gerald.

"Nobody really, Pa. A townie he picked up at the bar," said Jerry.

"Name of Wanda Symanski, some name like that. Polish, I think," said Johnny Fuselli.

"Symanski, good God," said Gerald, about the name, in much the contemptuous manner that Leverett Somerset once used when he pronounced Irish names that caused him distress.

"She's nobody," repeated Jerry.

"I'm not so sure about that," said Gerald. "Society girls don't go public. Townies do. Especially when they get a sniff there's money. You better find out everything there is to find out about her, Johnny. Marriages, divorces, abortions, any kind of police record. Go to the bar. Talk to the bartender."

"Hey, hey, Gerald. I know what to do. I know who to talk to. That's what you pay me for."

Kitt and Harrison stood looking out the hospital window.

"It's getting light," said Harrison.

"There's something I want to ask you," said Kitt.

"What?"

"Did you kiss Constant yesterday?"

Harrison looked at her and smiled. "No," he said.

"Maureen said the new maid said you did."

"Good old Maureen."

"Did you?"

"Constant kissed me."

"It's not true!"

"It's true."

"Why would he do that?"

"He wants me to write his book, I suppose."

"Are you going to?"

"No. I told everyone that before I came. I can't wait to leave, Kitt. I do not want to get sucked back into this family. I haven't enjoyed this weekend a bit, except for that blissful moment when Maureen switched on the lights and caught us with my dick in your mouth."

Kitt smiled. "You should have heard her tantrum." She took Harrison's hand. "What did you say to Constant that's got Pa and Jerry so upset?" she asked.

"I told him he shouldn't run. I told him all that business from Scarborough Hill could be dragged up again."

"Oh, that old allegation. Don't you think he's suffered enough from that?" said Kitt. Her voice was surprisingly testy.

"That's exactly what your father said," said Harrison, looking at her. "You all say the same things. Do you rehearse?"

"Why don't you drop it? Please. Constant was meant to lead. He was born for it."

"Then Constant should fashion his behavior to his ambitions."

"You're a prig, Harrison. So self-righteous."

"Can I ask you something, Kitt? If it was you who was killed that night and not the new girl in town no one really knew very well, do you think your father and your brothers would have put up with such a half-ass police investigation as that one was? If they couldn't have gotten the satisfaction they wanted from the police, they would have gotten Johnny Fuselli and some of his cronies to take care of the suspect Mafia-style," said Harrison.

"I don't want to hear this conversation, Harrison. I don't want to hear it! That was all so long ago. Especially now, here, in the hospital. We don't even know if Constant is going to make it."

"I'm going to leave, Kitt. I'm going to go back to New York."

"When will I see you?"

"I don't know."

"Don't say that, Harrison. Say Tuesday afternoon. Or Wednesday noon. Or Thursday morning. Or Friday midnight. Anytime. Anyplace. Give me a date. I'll be there. Please, Harrison. Please. I love you, Harrison."

They were interrupted by Des. "My father wants to see you, Harrison," he said.

"Where is he?" asked Harrison.

"In with Constant," said Des.

"With or without Jerry?"

"Without."

When Harrison left, Des said, "Pa said for you and Maureen to go home, Kitt. Constant's going to be okay."

"How are you?" Harrison asked Constant.

Constant, bandaged heavily, nodded. His handsome face appeared swollen and heavy beneath the bandages, his eyes bloodshot.

"I'm sorry about this," said Harrison.

Constant nodded again.

"I believe we should have a little chat, Harrison," said Gerald. He was sitting in a chair at the foot of the bed.

"Is Constant all right?" asked Harrison.

"Banged up a bit. But all right," said Gerald. "Sims Lord has been here. I would like you to have a talk with him. I told him you would be at the house at eight. After breakfast, he would like to talk to you."

"I've decided to return to New York, Mr. Bradley. I'm just going over to your house to pick up my bag, and I'm going right into the city."

"No, I'm sorry. You're going to talk to Sims Lord first. I insist. Do you understand?"

Harrison looked at Gerald. Then he looked at Constant. Each stared back at him.

"Is this the machine at work? The Bradley machine again?" asked Harrison.

Gerald ignored his question. "Sims will be waiting for you in the projection room. No one will disturb you there."

"I don't take orders, Mr. Bradley," said Harrison. "Constant here, the gubernatorial candidate–to-be, when he recovers from his drunk-driving accident, he takes orders. Des, the famed heart surgeon, takes orders. Sandro, the senator, takes orders. And Jerry, your deputy, your secretary-companion, takes orders. Johnny Fuselli takes orders. We all remember about the garbage bag, with the baseball bat and the clothes, do we not? But I do not take orders. I am not a member of your family, nor, thank God, am I in its employ."

"Yes, yes, of course," said Gerald, immediately conciliatory. "I understand that. Let me say that I would be most appreciative if you would meet with Sims."

"I would like to be told what it is Sims Lord wants to talk to me about in the projection room at eight o'clock in the morning before I decide whether I will see him or not."

Gerald looked at Harrison for a long time before he spoke. "You have alluded on more than one occasion this weekend to the sad event that occurred in Scarborough Hill years ago."

"Apparently I do not possess the facility to forget that you people all have," said Harrison.

Gerald ignored him.

"Would you all be so forgiving if it were Mary Pat or Kitt who got whacked over the head twelve times that night?"

Constant turned his head away. Gerald continued to ignore Harrison's words.

"It is important for you to know from a legal point of view what your own complicity is in that long-ago event," said Gerald.

"Oh, I see. I have already told your son that I would not go to the police," said Harrison. "Did I not, Constant?"

Constant did not reply.

"Still, I would like him to tell you," said Gerald.

"I know what it is. I am, I suppose, an accomplice. I carried a body. I lied to the detectives. I kept my mouth shut," said Harrison. "But what about you, Mr. Bradley?"

"What about me?"

"What about your complicity in the case?"

"Mine?" There was surprise in his voice.

"You bribed me to keep me silent."

"I never bribed you."

"What do you call it then? You paid for my silence. Which of the two of us is going to look worse? A seventeen-year-old orphaned scholarship student who allowed his education to be paid for? Or a multimillionaire father who paid for it to protect his son?"

"Lies, lies, lies. Yes, I paid for your education, but it had nothing whatever to do with a bribe. People of great wealth have always helped the less fortunate. My reputation for truth is well known," said Gerald.

"I beg to disagree with you, Mr. Bradley, about your reputation for truth. The first time I ever met you was in a limousine driven by Charlie after Constant was kicked out of Milford for having pornographic pictures of women eating each other's pussies. We drove in silence most of the way across Connecticut from Milford to Scarbor-

246

ough Hill. I sat in the jump seat. I might not have been there for all the attention you paid me.''

"Where is this long story going?'' asked Gerald.

"I'm getting to the punch line. When we reached Scarborough Hill, you said to your then sixteen-year-old son, and I quote, 'You're not like your brothers. You'll always get caught. You could have lied, you damn fool, you could, should, have lied, said those pictures weren't yours.' ''

"Like Jews who can spot anti-Semites, I can spot a Bradley hater, and you're one. I said no such thing, ever.''

"Yes, you did, didn't he, Constant? So don't talk to me about truth, Mr. Bradley. Tell Sims Lord I'll see him.''

"Did you enjoy the Madonna movie last night, Sims?'' asked Harrison, pointing to the screen of the projection room that had once been a ballroom. They sat looking at each other sideways on chairs that looked forward to the screen. Neither seemed anxious to begin the conversation.

"I did, yes. Did you?'' asked Sims Lord.

"I didn't stay for it,'' replied Harrison. "All those socialites nattering away drove me out, those friends of Grace's. Baba and Sonny and Thelma and the rest.''

"Hmmm.'' He was having difficulty starting.

"I am aware that I am an accessory,'' said Harrison, helping him. "Shall we start there?''

"That is the correct word, yes,'' said Sims. "My criminal law mavens tell me that you could be charged with a variety of offenses, some of them serious, Harrison. Of course, I addressed my questions to them in veiled terms. What if? I asked. What if? No names. Suppose there had been such and such a crime, I said. Suppose there had been an accessory. That sort of thing. Nothing that could possibly be connected to an actuality. It is a common thing to do in the practice of law. Let me read from my notes here.'' Sims reached in his pocket and took out his glasses. He put them on and reached into his inside pocket and took out a piece of paper. "Let me see here. Yes, yes, here it is. 'Hindering a prosecution, being an accessory after the fact, conspiracy to obstruct justice,' '' said Sims. "Of course, the specific laws vary from jurisdiction to jurisdiction.''

"Yes, yes, I am aware of those charges. But you forgot one. You forgot receiving a bribe. You forgot that I could be charged with that too, Sims," said Harrison.

"Bribe?" asked Sims Lord.

"Yes, Sims, bribe. You remember bribe. Writing out checks? For travel? For a year in Europe? For a higher institution of learning? That sort of bribe."

"I don't understand," said Sims.

"Oh, yes, you understand, Sims. You sent me the checks."

"Helping out a poor boy on a scholarship by paying for his education is not a bribe," said Sims Lord.

"When it pays for the poor boy's silence, it is," said Harrison.

Sims, angry, folded his paper and put it back into his inside pocket. He removed his reading glasses. He rose quietly and began to leave. At the entrance to the projection room, he turned back to Harrison, who had not moved from his theater seat.

"Have you given any thought to Grace Bradley in this? Are you not aware that she is a wonderful woman? I myself am not a Catholic, but it is my understanding that she is soon to be made a papal countess by the Holy Father in Rome for her outstanding work in Catholic charities. Do you have any idea what this will do to her? Have you no thought for that?"

"What is it you are saying to me, Sims? Because Constant has a nice mother, his crime should be overlooked? I want to make sure I understand. The problem with Constant is that his trespasses have been forgiven him over and over, all his life. And all of you know it. It's not enough that his mother is a nice woman."

"This is a tough guy," said Sims Lord, reporting back.

"Harrison Burns a tough guy? That's a laugh," said Jerry, laughing disagreeably. "We all used to think he was a little light in the loafers, if you want to know the truth."

"I don't mean tough, like tough in the boxing ring, Jerry. I mean a tougher kind of tough, like integrity tough."

"Did you read him what the charges would be against him?" asked Gerald.

"I did. He already knew."

"And?"

"I don't think he cares. I think he's prepared to take the conse-

248

quences. I think he wants to clear his life of this. I think having him here to the house with the entire family might have been a terrible mistake. I think it might have reawakened his sleeping demons. That is what he called them, his demons. That is why he swims. He said it is the only time he feels at peace."

"Fuck his demons. What's the bottom line, Sims?" asked Jerry.

"I think this man is becoming increasingly a loose cannon in your lives."

"Fatty Malloy sent me a newspaper clipping, Pa," said Jerry. "I didn't want to bring it up in front of Sims until I had talked to you."

"About what?" asked Gerald.

"From the Scarborough Hill paper."

"About what?"

"It says, 'Police see progress in Utley case, but won't offer details.' "

"I thought that story was over and out seventeen years ago."

"It says since Mrs. Utley offered her fifty-thousand-dollar reward for information leading to an arrest, several things have come to light," said Jerry.

"Bullshit," said Gerald. "That's a totally bullshit item, meant to scare. That's all. Nobody knows anything, except us and Harrison."

They looked at each other at the mention of Harrison's name.

"That's what I mean," said Jerry.

"Where is he?" asked Gerald.

"He's swimming."

"He's always swimming."

"What are we going to do, Pa?" asked Jerry.

Gerald rose and walked to the window and looked out at the sea. "You handle it, Jerry. Do whatever you have to do. I don't want to know. I don't want to be told. Understand? I don't want to know anything."

Jerry and Johnny Fuselli sat in the front seat of Constant's red Ferrari Testarossa. The windshield was shattered from the accident. The grille and the left fender were badly damaged.

"Do you like this car?" asked Jerry.

"Oh, man, it's my dream car," said Johnny Fuselli. "How he could have fucked it up like this is beyond me. If I had a car like this, a Testarossa—I even like the sound of the name—I would be kissin' its ass, morning, noon, and night."

"It's yours," said Jerry.

"You're kiddin' me."

"No. It's yours. Pa said to give it to you. We'll pay for all the repairs. There's a guy in Southampton who repairs—"

"Have you asked Constant about this?" asked Johnny.

"He'd like you to have it, too," said Jerry.

"Have you asked him? I mean, I don't want to get my heart set on it, and then when he gets out of the hospital, he decides he wants it back, and then I got to give it up, after I fell in love with it."

"Pa's ordered him a new one."

"Oh," said Johnny. He thought for a moment. "What's the catch?"

"There's something I want you to do," said Jerry.

"I figured that."

"I'll drive back to the city with you," said Kitt.

"I guess I'm not getting the helicopter treatment on the way home," said Harrison.

"There's plenty of cars," she said. "I have to play bridge at Sonny and Thelma's. I promised Ma. We'll go after that. All right? About six?"

"I don't want any marks on him," said Jerry. "It's a drowning, no more."

"The guy's a great swimmer," said Johnny Fuselli. "He can swim for hours. He can swim for miles. I watched him with the binoculars yesterday."

"He's a great swimmer who drowns," said Jerry, quietly. "You wear a wet suit. You wear a mask. You swim out behind him. Wait until he's past the beach club. Wait until he's past the public beach. He won't see you. He's looking ahead of him. You go underwater. You swim under him. You grab his arm. Or his leg. And you pull him under. And hold him under."

"And he's supposed to think it's a shark? Come on, Jerry."

"It doesn't matter what he thinks," said Jerry. "The guy's a danger, to you as well as us, you know."

"Hey, listen, Jerry, this is not exactly in my line of work," said Johnny. "I mean, let's be totally practical here. For a secondhand Testarossa that's just been wrapped around a telephone pole on the Montauk Highway, it's not what you call an even deal."

"Plus fifty thousand dollars," said Jerry.

"That's what I told the girl who was in the car with Constant she'd get," said Johnny. "Plus her hospital bills."

"Sixty thousand," said Jerry.

"Pa, I want everyone out of the house this afternoon," said Jerry. "I've made arrangements through Sims for you and Des and Sandro to play golf at the National. Be there at two. Don't get home before five. Or later."

"The National, huh?" said Gerald, impressed. "Wait till Webster Pryde sees us at the National. I wish Constant weren't in the hospital. Then I'd have the whole crowd there."

"Have Sims buy you some drinks when you finish."

"What's this all about, Jerry?"

"Just do it, Pa. I don't want anyone in the house this afternoon, except Bridey and the maids," said Jerry. "Maureen and Freddy are going over to Quogue to visit some girl she was at Sacred Heart with."

"Where's your mother going to be?"

"Ma and Charlotte and Kitt are going to play bridge at Sonny and Thelma's."

"And you?"

"I'm going to see the Madonna movie in the village."

"You saw the Madonna movie in your own house last night."

"I'm seeing it again. I don't want anyone in this house except the maids this afternoon."

Each day of his visit, Harrison swam a greater distance in the cold water. He entered the water on the beach at the end of the road where the Bradley house stood. He swam out two hundred yards offshore until he was well beyond the waves and kelp. Then he turned and swam in a northerly direction. He concentrated on a goal. The first day he swam three miles. The second day he swam four miles. That day he turned in a northerly direction, planning to swim five miles. From the shore he was only a small head in the water. Then he was nearly out of sight. Even with strong binoculars, he was difficult to pick up in the rolling sea. He was never in a hurry. His pace was steady. His stroke was unvarying. His feet were in perfect accord with his strokes. His speed never changed. After a half hour, the process of swimming became automatic to him. He did it without focusing on what he was doing. He concentrated all his energy into the center of his forehead. Oh, yes, oh, yes, he thought as a total calm came over him. He felt peace. He felt nirvana. He felt supreme.

Suddenly, from below, from beneath the surface, Harrison's right foot was grabbed from behind in a viselike grip. He snapped from his reverie, and chills of fear passed through his body. Trying to swim forward, he felt himself being pulled from behind. In an instant, Johnny Fuselli locked the foot beneath his arm and with both his hands grasped Harrison's leg above the knee as hard as he could and pulled him down beneath the surface. He released one hand from the leg and grabbed Harrison's hair and held his head under the water. Harrison kicked furiously with his left foot. His heel connected with Fuselli's face, and the water became clouded with blood. Fuselli let go of Harrison's body.

On the surface, gasping for breath, both men vomited water from their lungs. Exhausted, they lay on their backs trying to regain their breath.

"I didn't take you for a killer, Johnny," said Harrison. "A remover of records, yes. A buyer-off of witnesses. A dumper of garbage bags, filled with evidence, but not a killer."

"You would have been my first," said Johnny.

"Look what I've spared you," said Harrison. "There better not be any sharks around, or we're both going to be goners, with all this blood."

"You broke my nose," said Johnny. He was having difficulty breathing. He put his hand to his heart. "You got some kick for a drowning man."

"Who put you up to this? Gerald or Jerry?"

"Be careful of Jerry. He's the one who's out to get you."

"You fucked up your assignment, didn't you?"

"My heart was never in it," said Johnny.

"Jerry's going to be one freaked-out Bradley when he sees me walk in that house."

"I think I'm having a heart attack," said Johnny, sick and exhausted, his arms flailing, he choked and coughed.

"Johnny, I can't drag you in. I would if I could, but I can't. That fight tired me out. I don't even know if I'm going to make it myself."

"I'm too old for this line of work. I was going to be forty-six tomorrow. Once, I thought I was going to make the Olympic team."

"Sorry I broke your nose."

"Harrison, listen to me. You're a nice guy."

"Johnny, there's something I've got to know. You're the only one who can tell me. And I've got to know, John. Please."

"What?"

"The garbage bag."

"Huh?"

"The garbage bag that was in the trunk of Bridey's car on the day Winifred Utley was murdered."

"I don't know."

"Johnny, you drove her car, a Pontiac, and dumped the bag, the bag with the baseball bat and the bloody clothes that Constant wore when he killed Winifred Utley. Where did you dump the bag? Tell me, tell me. Please, Johnny. These guys, your great friends, the Bradleys, they were turning you into a murderer, Johnny. And if you'd been caught, you would have taken the rap, not them. Where did you dump the garbage bag, Johnny? Don't go under, Johnny. Tell me. It could be your salvation. Don't go under. Don't, Johnny."

13

IT WAS six o'clock. Charlotte, carrying white peonies from Grace's garden, had gone to the Southampton Hospital to visit Constant. "Oh, he's so much better, really," she replied to a reporter's query. "The accident wasn't a bit serious. A few scratches, a few stitches. More of an inconvenience, really. He's so anxious to get on with the campaign in Connecticut. Yes, aren't these lovely peonies. They're from my mother-in-law's garden."

"When will we be able to see him?" asked the reporter.

"Soon, I think. He should be getting out in a day or so. It wasn't a bit serious."

Since Constant's accident on the Montauk Highway, Charlotte had been dutiful in her hospital visits to her husband. She arrived each day, gifts in hand, and spoke charmingly to one persistent reporter who waited each day for news, always engaging her in conversation. She did not know that the reporter was named Gus Bailey. She did not know that Gus Bailey had once firmly believed that a cover-up had taken place in the investigation of the murder of Winifred Utley years back in Scarborough Hill. She did not know that because of his persistence Gus Bailey had lost his job at the Scarborough Hill *Times,* which had mysteriously been bought and closed down. She did not know that Gus Bailey had moved away and resided for sixteen years in Los Angeles. She did not know that her husband had once been questioned during the investigation of the murder of Winifred Utley. She did not even know that there had been such a person as Winifred Utley.

The fact that Constant had been drunk and that he had had in the car with him a woman named Wanda Symanski, who had been transferred to a hospital in Garden City, had not appeared in the newspapers. Inside, in Constant's room, Charlotte sat each time for fifteen minutes before returning to her car. In those fifteen minutes, she rarely spoke

254

to her husband unless there was a nurse or doctor in the room. Instead, she watched the news on television or read a magazine until the appropriate time for a hospital visit was over.

The rest of the family had returned from their various afternoon pursuits. Drinks were being passed in the loggia.

"Any calls, Bridey?" asked Jerry, when he returned from the movies.

"No, sir," said Bridey.

"Any callers?" he asked.

"No. Were you expecting someone?"

"No, no. Just curious."

"Did you see Harrison, Bridey?" asked Kitt.

"No, Miss Kitt. I haven't seen him since he went out to go swimming at about two," said Bridey.

"Surely, he should be back by now," said Kitt. She glanced at her watch.

"Jerry, you didn't go to see that disgusting movie again? I don't believe it," said Maureen. "Freddy and I walked out on it last night."

"Father Bill said that the Vatican asked Catholics not to see her concerts in Italy," said Grace.

"That only sold more tickets, Ma," said Jerry. "How was the golf, Pa?"

"The senator was the big winner today," said Gerald, making an expansive gesture toward Sandro. He and his son were playing backgammon. "I wish you could have seen our friend from next door, Mr. Webster Pryde. He was in a foursome playing just behind us. Then, on the fourth hole, some charming lady recognized Sandro and insisted on getting his autograph. And then she wanted him to meet her husband, and we had to wait until his golf cart caught up with us, and all the time Webster was waiting to play. He was furious. It did my heart good."

"I guess I'm in the wrong business," said Des. "No one asks doctors for their autographs. You have to be a movie star or a senator, I guess."

"If you'd listened to your old man way back when, you'd have them lined up getting your autograph," said Gerald. "I wanted all my boys to be in politics."

"Oh, Pa, don't start that again," said Des.

255

"I don't understand why Harrison isn't back," said Kitt. "It's not possible to swim this long. You can't swim for four hours."

"Maybe he went to visit Constant in the hospital," said Grace. "Isn't he supposed to write a book or something? Wasn't that the whole point of having him here? Didn't someone tell me that?"

"Yes, that's probably where he is, at the hospital," said Jerry. "Charlotte can bring him back."

"I must admit," said Grace, "that I am very disappointed that Harrison has given up his religion. I was really quite shocked last night when he told me that. And he's separated from his wife, and there's two little children. Can you imagine? It probably has something to do with that business with his family, his parents being murdered, and all that, and no brothers and sisters. He never had a proper family life. Except for us, I suppose. Did you know he married Claire Rafferty? Did you know that, Maureen?"

"Yes, Ma, I knew," said Maureen.

"The thing about marriage is, you just work it out," said Grace. "You just don't run off and separate every time you have a little spat."

"I've never been such a fan of Harrison's as you have, Ma," said Maureen. "I think he's a user. I think he's used all of us in this family to get ahead. Beware of scholarship students who get too friendly is what I always say. Jerry and I have been on to Harrison for years, haven't we, Jerry?"

"I never liked the guy," said Jerry.

"You see?" said Maureen.

"You are hateful, Maureen," said Kitt, in a low voice. "You are really hateful."

A doorbell rang.

"That's probably Harrison," said Grace. "Wouldn't you think he'd just walk in and not ring the doorbell? Now, you must stop talking about him, Maureen. And you too, Jerry. I've always had a soft spot for Harrison, and I know one day he'll come back to the Church. They always do."

Bridey walked into the room. "It's a taxi. Did someone order a taxi?" she asked. "He said he was told to come here to this address."

Murmurs of no went through the room. "There's some mistake, Bridey," said Grace. "Why in the world would someone need a taxi in this house with all those cars out there? Unless it's one of the maids. Is one of the maids going into the city, Bridey?"

"No, ma'am," said Bridey. "Not that I know of. I'm sure I would have been told. Not since Maureen fired Nanny the day before yesterday. She ordered a taxi."

Down the stairs walked Harrison carrying his two bags. "I ordered the taxi, Bridey," he said. "I'm catching the seven-oh-two train into the city."

"I didn't know you were in the house, Harrison," said Bridey. "When did you come back?"

"Oh, a while ago. There was no one around, so I went right upstairs."

Jerry, stunned, looked at Harrison and then over at his father.

"Harrison," said Kitt, "we've all been worried about you. I was about to call out the Coast Guard. I just finished saying no one could swim for four hours."

"Could you give these bags to the driver, Bridey," said Harrison as he walked into the room and over to Grace. "Thank you very much, Mrs. Bradley," he said. He ignored Gerald Bradley. He ignored Maureen. He walked over to Kitt. "Good-bye, Kitt," he said.

"I don't understand, Harrison," said Kitt. "I'll drive you back to the city. There's no reason for you to take the train."

"No, thank you, Kitt. I'm going to go on the train." He walked out of the room to the hall.

Kitt followed him. "Harrison, what's happened? Something's wrong. I can tell."

"Ask him," said Harrison, pointing to Jerry. He walked out the front door.

"What is it, Jerry?" asked Kitt.

"I don't know what he's talking about," said Jerry. Jerry, ashen, followed Harrison outside.

Harrison opened the door of the cab. "The railroad station," he said to the driver as he got in. He rolled down the window and looked out at Jerry. Gerald and Kitt were behind him. "Do you remember when we used to be shocked by murder, before it became an everyday thing, Jerry?"

Jerry stared at Harrison.

"Your friend Johnny Fuselli ought to wash up in Shinnecock Bay by tomorrow morning, Jerry. I believe that was the direction of the tide. That is, if he hasn't been eaten by sharks. I thought for a moment he was a shark. He came from behind and below me. He grabbed my leg.

He pulled me under. He held his hand on my head to keep me from surfacing, but my rage to live exceeded his strength. I kicked him pretty hard and broke his nose. He was bleeding badly."

Jerry, speechless, listened openmouthed to what was told him, scarcely able to believe his ears.

"Then, after we talked, he had a heart attack in the water," said Harrison. "All that swimming at his age. That was quite an assignment you gave him, Jerry. You sent him on a mission his heart wasn't in. Even people like Johnny have their limits. We had a very nice talk there in the water, in the last minutes of his life. I would like to have brought him in, but I wasn't sure I was going to make it in myself, I was so tired out from the struggle. He said he understood. Nice fellow, Johnny."

"What are you talking about?" asked Kitt, moving to the door of the taxi. "What are you saying, Harrison?"

"Go into the house, Kitt," said Gerald.

"No, I won't go into the house," she replied.

"Go into the house. Now," screamed Gerald.

Kitt, shocked, looked at her father. He had never spoken to her in such a fashion before. The sound of his harsh voice speaking so loudly brought several maids to the windows of the house. Then Kitt turned to Harrison, trying to understand what had been said. She turned and walked back to the house, where she stood in the hall and looked back.

"Oh, for your records, Jerry, when you confess this to Father Bill next Saturday, so you can receive Communion on Sunday, Johnny drowned bravely," said Harrison. " 'Say hi to Maxine' were his final words before he went under. We had a mutual friend, Johnny and I, in Arizona, called Maxine Lonergan. I believe your father knew her, too. Didn't you, Mr. Bradley? She was celebrated for her oral expertise."

"Did he say that Fuselli drowned?" Gerald asked Jerry, ignoring Harrison.

"Yes," replied Jerry.

Gerald, gray faced, suddenly looked old and sickly. "Good God," he said. Years before, Gerald Bradley had hired the brash Johnny Fuselli away from Salvatore Cabrini when he was in charge of the slot-machine operations in Atlantic City. It was the habit of Grace Bradley never to acknowledge Johnny Fuselli's presence and to instruct her daughters to do the same, but over the years Gerald Bradley had developed an affection for Johnny, although he had failed ever to tell him so.

"Is your father suggesting I should have allowed myself to be drowned so that Fuselli could carry out your orders successfully?" Harrison asked Jerry, ignoring Gerald, in the manner and voice that Gerald had just ignored him.

Jerry nervously looked toward the taxi driver to see if he had heard.

"Third World. Don't worry," said Harrison, indicating the driver with a movement of his head.

"I wish you had never come here," cried Jerry.

"Your father shouldn't have insisted when I declined his offer," replied Harrison.

"I mean, in the first place—back in Scarborough Hill!"

"So do I. Finally, Jerry, you and I agree on something."

"Get out. Stay out. We don't ever want to see you again. I am speaking for my sister, Kitt, as well. Stay away from her. Right, Pa?"

Gerald Bradley, watching the exchange, suddenly toppled over and fell onto the gravel driveway. "Pa!" screamed Jerry.

Kitt ran to the porch, down the flower-bordered path, and onto the driveway where her father was lying. "Pa! *Pa!*" she cried. The sound of her troubled voice carried. Charlie heard it in the chauffeur's quarters above the garage. From elsewhere in the house, maids came running, as did the maids and gardener from the Webster Pryde house next door.

Gerald lay on the ground muttering something, but his tongue had become useless. His stern and forbidding expression had altered to one of fright and submission. His eyebrows twitched. His eyes, fearful, looked timidly and uneasily at the people looking down on him. He saw them exchanging glances. Then his eyes closed. Charlie, the chauffeur, crossed himself in the Catholic manner with an automatic movement of his right hand, knelt on the ground, and with downcast eyes bowed his head in prayer.

"Get up, get *up!*" snapped Jerry. "Don't let him see you like that, Charlie, for God's sake."

Gerald, hearing, slowly opened his eyes. Seeing his children, he moved his lips to speak but only a choked sound came out, its meaning unintelligible. Again his eyelids drooped.

"I'll get Ma," said Kitt, quickly.

"No," said Jerry. "We'll carry him inside. Charlie, come here and help. Will you help, too?" he asked the Prydes' gardener, who was standing watching the family drama. "Please, take a leg, will you?" he

259

said to one of the maids. Gerald moaned piteously, and there was difficulty raising him.

"I read somewhere you're not supposed to move them until the ambulance comes," said the Prydes' gardener.

"Just lift him!" snapped Jerry. "I know what I'm doing."

"It said you could get sued if something goes wrong," insisted the gardener.

All this Harrison watched from the interior of the taxi. Kitt looked over at him beseechingly.

"You gonna miss train," said the driver.

Harrison reached into his pocket and took out a ten-dollar bill. "Here," he said to the driver. "I'm getting out. Get my bags out." He walked over to where Gerald was lying on the ground and took the leg that the Prydes' gardener was reluctant to lift.

Slowly, they lifted Gerald by his shoulders and legs and carried him inside. Grace, standing at the doorway with Bridey, watched as her husband was carried past her.

Gerald looked at Grace imploringly and tried but failed to hold out his hand for her to take.

"Call Father Bill at the parish house," Grace said calmly to Bridey. "Tell him to come quickly." Bridey turned and ran toward the kitchen. "Bridey," Grace called out after her.

"Yes, ma'am?"

Grace spoke in a loud whisper. "Tell him the last rites."

"He's wet his pants," said Jerry, as they lifted him toward a long sofa.

"Don't put him there, for heaven's sake," said Grace. "That's just come back from the upholsterers. Put him there on the cane seat. Get some paper towels, Kitt. Don't you think perhaps an ambulance, Jerry?"

"Yes, yes, an ambulance is coming, Ma," said Jerry.

"Your mother doesn't appear to be grieving too much," said Harrison, as they waited for the ambulance.

"Oh, but she is, in her own way," replied Kitt, shaking her head almost imperceptibly, as a slight scowl appeared, clouding the clearness of her forehead. He had seen that look before, on Constant's face. It appeared whenever there was what was perceived to be a criticism of anyone in the family.

260

When the ambulance arrived, the family watched as the attendants expertly placed Gerald on the stretcher.

"Try to get him the room next to Constant's," said Grace. "Bridey, call Cardinal."

"Wait for me," whispered Kitt to Harrison. "Don't leave until I get back." She went in the ambulance to the hospital with her father.

When she returned to the house two hours later, she raced in the front door and asked Bridey where Harrison was.

"He's in the loggia, Miss Kitt," she said.

"Oh, thank God, Harrison. I was afraid you would have gone," Kitt said when she saw him. "It took forever at the hospital."

"Things are bad, apparently?" asked Harrison.

"Yes. Terrible. There's doctors coming from everywhere. I should go back, but I wanted to see you."

"I'm going to go now, Kitt," said Harrison, putting down the newspaper he had been reading. "I just waited to say good-bye."

"You were kind to carry Pa," she said. "After what happened. You must tell me this: did I hear correctly about Fuselli?"

"That he drowned?"

"No, that he pulled you under."

"Let Jerry tell you."

"Oh, Harrison, I'm sorry."

"I am too, Kitt. It's over. You know that. It has to be," said Harrison.

"I know. I knew. I knew from the day you got back from lunch with Pa at the Four Seasons that it was a matter of time. There was a look in your face I hadn't seen before. It was a mistake. I should never have told them I'd found you in Maine. I should have kept you all for myself. Your afternoon mistress. I would have settled for that, you know. I could have gone on for years and years, Harrison."

"Oh, Kitt. You're worth much more than that."

"Will you go back to Claire?" she asked.

"I think maybe I'm one of those people who was born to be a solo act," said Harrison.

"I don't believe that for a minute. You were a continual surprise to me," she said. She opened her bag and took out a handkerchief and touched the corner of her eye. "Don't worry, I'm not going to cry. I promise you that."

"I know."

"Let me ask you something, Harrison. Think back, years ago. Breakfast in Scarborough Hill. What we didn't know then, sitting around that table, was that Winifred Utley was dead. At least some of us didn't know. But you were so silent that morning. You knew something, didn't you? I could tell. You didn't say a word all through breakfast."

"I never had much to say in those days, if you remember."

"You laughed at my jokes, as if I were the funniest person alive. I was always so touched by that. But you knew something that morning, didn't you?"

"Yes."

"You have to understand something about us, Harrison. About being a Bradley, I mean. I'd lie under oath on the stand if I had to."

"You don't really mean that, Kitt."

"Yes, I'm ashamed to say it, but yes. I hope I won't ever be asked to, but in our family you do what you're told."

Outside, a horn honked.

"That's Charlie," said Harrison. "He said he'd drive me."

"Listen, Harrison. It was great," she said.

"It was great," he repeated. He took her hand.

"I know I wasn't supposed to fall in love. That was part of the arrangement. But I did."

"Maybe it's better to have a lot for a short time."

"You mean, it's better to have loved and lost than never to have loved at all. That old crap? I suppose I can come around to believe that in time, but not now. I ache. I'm going to ache worse. Until this minute, I never believed there was such a thing as a broken heart."

"What will you do, Kitt? What will happen?"

"Oh, I'll be very predictable. Nothing out of the ordinary. Probably I'll drink too much. People will say, 'That's Gerald Bradley's youngest daughter they're carrying out of the party.' "

"I can't bear to think of you like that."

"Oh, darling, you wouldn't be to blame. It's what you might have saved me from. It's not what you led me to."

Alone in her room, Grace sat upright on a peach damask bergère chair, rosary beads in hand, in preparation for receiving the impending news of her husband's death. Thoughts of black veils bordered in black grosgrain ribbon filled her mind. There was an ample selection of black dresses in readiness in her closets; each year in Paris she ordered one or more, "just in case," which, abetted by pearls and brooches, did double duty for cocktail parties and theater evenings. Thoughts that had never entered her mind, thoughts of a new life, free from her errant and faithless husband, filled Grace's head. Widowhood will become me, she allowed herself to think. She had seen so many wives who, like herself, had lived in their husband's shadow and then emerged in widowhood to full self-realization. She knew that was the way it would be with her. She saw herself as a great benefactress, much beloved, surrounded by her famous and successful children, dispensing her great wealth to the needy and hopeless, and becoming, in time, a papal countess, honored by the Holy Father in Rome for her philanthropic works. It was her most ardent secret wish to be known as Countess Bradley.

Then, horrified, she grasped her silver rosary beads to her breast and prayed that she not be tantalized by such thoughts, as if they were temptations from the devil. She asked for strength to be able to handle the tribulations that lay ahead for her and her family. She had long since ceased loving her husband, a revelation that she had only alluded to once in her life. That one time was to Cardinal, in one of their long afternoon chats over tea in Scarborough Hill, after she realized that Sally Steers was her husband's mistress and had slept in her bed while she was away in Paris for her fittings, a disclosure she had managed to extract from the ever-faithful but reluctant Bridey. That bed, its mattresses, pillows, blankets, blanket cover, sham, sheets, and pillowcases, had been removed from her room and burned. She could look away from Gerald's ruthlessness in business, but she could not forgive in her heart that he had strayed from his marital vows.

Alas, she was to be denied her widowhood. Gerald did not die that day. He simply became paralyzed and lost the power to speak.

14

FROM AFAR, the Malloys, Fatty and Sis, kept up on the doings of their affluent cousins. "One day they'll be back," Sis Malloy always said. Once a week, usually on Thursday nights, they dined together in the maids' dining room of the Bradley house in Scarborough Hill, which had not been lived in by the Bradley family for years, although it was visited from time to time by one or another of the members of the family when they had business in the city. Their visits were short, hardly longer than a day and night in residence, and then they were off again to the house in California, or the apartment in New York, or the house in Southampton. Sis, at the insistence of her aunt Grace Bradley, the sister of her late father, Vinny Malloy, had become its chatelaine. Although it was Grace who first used the word *chatelaine*, in an expansive moment to describe Sis's position, she actually meant housekeeper, and Sis understood. She never overstepped the bounds of her position. She slept in the room that had always been referred to as Agnes's room, not in one of the frillier rooms that had belonged to Maureen, or Mary Pat, or Kitt. She entered the living and dining rooms only to see that everything was in place after the weekly dusting and vacuuming by the single maid who now ran the house. Sis fervently believed, and Fatty agreed, that one day the great house in Scarborough Hill would be alive with activity again.

Sis had grown up plain. It was a given that she would never marry. Most nights she sat in the library, read the Scarborough Hill paper, and watched television. Occasionally she entertained girlfriends from her Bog Meadow childhood or from her parochial high school days and treated them to tours of the grand house where she now lived, although her role was that of guide, even in front of her friends, never of proprietor. "That is the chair where His Holiness the Pope sat when he came to visit the family. He blessed them all and gave Constant his white biretta off his head. That's it, there, under the Lucite covering. Con-

264

stant was the dearest little boy you ever saw. Like an angel." Her
friends, who had become teachers or nurses or secretaries in the great
insurance companies of the city, always exclaimed in wonderment
over the Pope's visit, no matter how many times they heard the story.
They complimented Sis on her clothes. And she was always quick to
answer that the smart suit or dress she was wearing had been Kitt's or
Maureen's, sent to her by Aunt Grace, as she shyly showed her friends
the Paris labels.

The single evening dress in her closet, which she wore every year to
the Sodality of Mary dance at the St. Martin of Tours parish hall, was
her bridesmaid's dress from Maureen's wedding sixteen years before.
Once rose colored, it had long since been dyed black for practicality.
Being a bridesmaid for Maureen had been one of the great experiences
of her life, and her girlfriends often got her to recall the events of that
memorable day. "There she was, Cora Mandell, the fanciest decorator
in New York City, already an old lady, pinning up this French fabric
to the inside of the tent, and, *boom,* she fell off the top of the ladder,
twenty feet down, and she broke both her legs."

"No, Sis!" exclaimed her friends in horror, clapping their palms
together.

"As God is my witness," said Sis, raising her right hand. "Thank
heaven for my cousin Des. He was chief of staff at St. Monica's then.
He set both legs for the old woman, and the wedding went right on,
and no one knew anything about it. They have a way in the family of
keeping things silent and going about their business as if nothing is
wrong."

Sis had no inkling of any of the family scenes that had preceded her
role of bridesmaid.

"Oh, Ma, please don't make me have Sis Malloy as a bridesmaid,"
Maureen had pleaded. "None of my friends know her, and she won't
fit in."

But Grace was firm. "She's your first cousin. She's your same age.
And she's going to be a bridesmaid whether you like it or not. Whatever would I say to your uncle Vinny if you didn't have her?"

"Please, Ma," begged Maureen. "Please, please, please. She'll talk
about Bog Meadow and priests and nuns and the butcher shop, and I
won't know where to look."

"If you'd only had three or four bridesmaids, it would have been
fine not to have her, but you're the one who insisted on ten, Maureen.
Besides, she sent you a lovely silver tray."

"Silver-plated," snapped Maureen.

"Even so, it was very nice of her," replied Grace.

Sis, who got hives when she was nervous, was covered with red blotches on her face, neck, and arms, and her bouquet of white orchids shook perceptibly in her hands as she walked down the aisle, paired with Claire Rafferty, but no one noticed her discomfort; she was not one of the ones stared at that day.

Fatty, like his sister, had never married. He continued to live in the old Malloy house on Front Street in Bog Meadow. His early dreams of being a fireman had been thwarted by his uncle, Gerald Bradley, who did not want a relation of his in a blue uniform when his sons rose to the heights that he expected them to attain. Gerald offered to pay Fatty's tuition to Holy Cross, or Villanova, or Loyola, or St. John's, but Fatty, who had never been much of a student, wanted to get down to work and on with life. For a while he sold shoes at Kofsky's Shoe Store in Bog Meadow. Then he spent several years as a salesman at Ted and Joe's Hardware, also in Bog Meadow. Then he became assistant manager of Riley's Market near the Malloy family home, where during peak hours he often doubled up his duties packing grocery bags at the checkout counter, a task at which he was considered an expert. "Fatty'll show you how to pack a plastic bag right," the manager often said to new employees, and Fatty always beamed with pleasure at the compliment. He enjoyed it when the other employees pointed him out to customers as a nephew of Gerald Bradley, or a cousin of Senator Sandro Bradley, or Dr. Desmond Bradley, or Congressman Constant Bradley, or even the Countess de Trafford of Paris, whichever one of them happened to be in the news at the time. On Saturday nights, after his friend Corky got off work at The Country Club in Scarborough Hill, where he had risen from bartender in the men's locker room to the post of maître d' in the dining room and assistant banquet manager, the two often got together to knock back a few beers and talk over old times. Fatty and Corky had been friends since they were classmates at Our Lady of Sorrows High. There was just one subject that Fatty and Corky never discussed. Corky had his suspicions about what had happened that night years ago in Scarborough Hill, and he had told Captain Riordan what he thought at the time. He also told Fatty, and Fatty told Sis. "If you know what's good for you, stay out of that one," Sis had said to her brother at the time. His Saturday nights with Corky and his Thursday nights with his sister were the nights of the week that Fatty most looked forward to.

"Poor Kitt," said Sis, giving her brother her weekly news report. Sis kept in close touch with Bridey, at whichever of the residences the family happened to be in, through weekly Sunday afternoon telephone calls. "She has fallen in love with that writer who used to be so quiet when he stayed here in the old days. They called him Harry then, but now it's Harrison."

"Kitt's in love with him?" asked Fatty, between mouthfuls of roast beef and mashed potatoes. "What about what'shisname she married? Who skied all the time?"

"Cheever Chadwick," replied Sis. "They've separated, or at least they're living apart. You know Bridey. She goes only just so far with a story, and then she stops. With her, the sun rises and sets with Aunt Grace."

"Is Kitt getting a divorce? I can't believe it. A divorce in the Bradley family." Fatty whistled in wonderment.

"Certainly not until after the election," said Sis. "They couldn't afford that kind of publicity. I said at the time, and I still say, she should never have married a non-Catholic, and I know for a fact that Aunt Grace concurs with my feelings on the subject."

"I remember that guy Harrison. He wrote the speech for Constant that Christmas in Bog Meadow, when we handed out the turkeys and the oranges to the poor people. Remember?"

"That's him."

"I thought he dropped out of sight. Where'd she meet him?"

"At the Cranston Institute in Maine. Where Agnes is. No, no, Fatty, no thirds. Save some room for dessert. I've got a beautiful treat for you, a peach cobbler with whipped cream."

"I always got room for dessert, Sis."

"How's your friend Corky?"

Father Bill, at the request of Grace Bradley, performed extreme unction, the last rites for the dying, anointing Gerald with consecrated oil in a brief ceremony at the Southampton Hospital. But death was not yet at hand. Only paralysis. And a long recovery period. Doctors expert in stroke therapy were flown in from Chicago and Los Angeles, or helicoptered in from New York.

*   *   *

Grace went to the hospital to visit her husband and her son. She had managed to have them put in rooms next to each other.

"You've heard about your father, Constant?" she asked.

"Yes, Ma," replied Constant.

"One minute he was walking on the grass. The next he was lying on the ground. You never can tell about life. That's why it's so important to stay in a state of grace. How are you feeling, Constant?"

"I'm all right, Ma. Just banged up."

She looked about the room. "Are those white peonies from my garden?" she asked.

"Yes. Charlotte brought them."

"It's been a wonderful year for peonies," she said. "You should have the nurse change the water."

"Yes, Ma."

"Were you drunk when your car hit the pole?"

"No, Ma. I'd had a few drinks, that's all."

"There wasn't enough liquor at home? You had to go out to a bar on the Montauk Highway?"

"I was antsy, Ma."

"Were you with a woman?"

"No, Ma. Why would you ask that?"

"I remember that night with Jerry, when his car crashed."

Jerry and Sims Lord came into the room. They prepared a statement for the press announcing that Gerald Bradley, the multimillionaire financier, had suffered a minor stroke at his home in Southampton, New York, and was resting comfortably at the Southampton Hospital. His son, Constant Bradley, the gubernatorial candidate for Connecticut, was in the same hospital recovering from a minor automobile accident a day earlier on the Montauk Highway.

"A stroke, Mrs. Bradley, is a blood clot in an artery of the brain," said Dr. Sidney Dickey, from New York. "We call it an intracranial thrombosis. What we have done is perform an arteriogram, which means that we have injected radiopaque dye into the main artery of the neck and photographed its flow through the vessels of the brain by high-speed X ray. Do you understand?"

"Yes, Doctor," said Grace, nodding.

"We have found to our regret that it is inoperable."

"Yes, Doctor."

"But you must not be discouraged. A partial recovery is not only possible, it is almost certain."

"Yes, Doctor."

"Recovery, however, is a long, slow process," said Dr. Ernest Bogner from Chicago. "I feel, though, in time, your husband will be able to dress himself, at least partially, and brush his teeth. In time, perhaps, he might even be able to talk a little, at least to be able to make himself understood, so that he can ask for what he wants. You must understand his brain is working perfectly. There is no damage there. He is alert. He understands everything. But he is unable to express himself. He makes sounds, not words. He will be angry that you do not understand him. He will be irritable much of the time. All around him must learn to be patient."

"Thank you, Doctor," said Grace.

"I have given your son the names of some physical therapists who are expert in the field. I would suggest that after a few weeks he begin a daily program of physical therapy."

"Yes, Doctor," said Grace.

"I am, of course, always at your service. I will fly here on a moment's notice."

"You are very kind, Doctor."

"My colleague, Dr. Foreman, is located in Manhattan, at Columbia-Presbyterian, and happens to have a summer place nearby in Quogue. He has twice been to the hospital this week with me. He is aware of the case."

"Thank you, Doctor. Would you care to stay for lunch? My cook has made a marvelous cheese soufflé."

"We will need to install an elevator, Ma," said Jerry, several days later.

"Fine," said Grace. "Have it installed."

"So that the wheelchair can move from the second floor to the first," said Jerry.

"Install it, I said," said Grace.

"We will have to have a whirlpool bath put in," said Jerry.

"You handle that, Jerry," said Grace.

"There will be other therapeutic devices necessary also," said Jerry.

"Jerry, I know nothing about those things. You must take care of it. There's no need to check with me on every detail. Simply do what has to be done," said Grace.

"Yes, Ma."

"When your father comes home from the hospital, he should be put in the guestroom at the top of the stairs," said Grace later in the day to Jerry.

"Not in your room, Ma? Do you think that's wise?" asked Jerry. "That's where he's used to being."

"No, not in my room. Make whatever arrangements need to be made about hospital beds and whatever else he needs being put in there. It's a lovely bright airy room, and so pretty, with those nice colors that Sally Steers suggested."

"Yes, Ma. Now, about the nurses."

"No, no," said Grace. "There's nothing more depressing than nurses in a house. Those white uniforms cast a pall, and nurses gossip so. Oh, do they gossip. It was Fitzy Montague's nurse who told everyone he had a boil on his buttocks after he jumped out the window of Seven Forty Park and his pajama bottoms flew off. Imagine her telling that. And they don't want to eat with the maids, and we certainly don't want them to eat with us, or we'd have to censor every word coming out of our mouths, and I can't, I simply can't, ask Bridey to do a third sitting. Bridey's almost seventy."

"So what do we do, Ma?" asked Jerry.

"Get the Malloys out here. Fatty can carry your father to the bathroom and put him in the wheelchair or put him in the car or the therapeutic bath or whatever it is. He can watch the physical therapist and in time do some of the therapy himself. It's just moving legs back and forth, after all. They did that with my father. And Sis can tend to him, push the wheelchair, read to him, all that sort of thing. I always used to think Sis wanted to be a nurse."

"Fatty's got a job, Ma."

"Where?"

"Riley's Market in Bog Meadow."

"Doing what?"

"Checkout."

"Checkout? You mean putting the groceries in the plastic bags?"

"And toting it up."

"I always knew Fatty was never going to amount to much. We

offered to send him to Holy Cross, Gerald and I, or Villanova, or
Loyola, or St. John's, along with Bridey's nephews—pay his way, the
whole thing—but no, he wanted to go right to work. Certainly his
aspirations were conventional, weren't they? Toting up at the checkout
counter. Imagine. There's a career for you, all right." She held back
her head and laughed. "Sis was always the one with possibilities."

"Ma, Pa needs nurses. Real nurses," said Jerry.

"Later, if he gets worse. We'll talk about it when I get back from
Paris. But we don't want pretty young ones, remember that. Not with
Constant in and out of the house, we don't."

"Yes, Ma. You're going to Paris? Now?"

"Yes, for my clothes. I always go at this time."

"Yes, Ma."

"Oh, Jerry. Perhaps Father Bill should come and hear your father's
confession. Just in case, you know. Constant, too. I notice he didn't
receive Communion at Mass last Sunday. Cardinal's coming for the
weekend to see your father and to see Constant. Everyone should be
in a state of grace. Where's Kitt? I'd like to see Kitt."

"In her room. She hasn't come out of her room for two days."

"Get her, will you?"

"She's a bit tipsy," said Jerry.

"Kitt tipsy? No, not my Kitt," said Grace.

"Actually, she's not a bit tipsy at all. She's drunk. She's shitfaced,"
said Jerry.

"Oh, I hate that word, Jerry," said Grace.

Kitt rose from her chaise and replied through the closed door, "Go
away." Since Harrison had left, she could not eat or sleep. She had
grown visibly thinner. She missed her lover. Although she did not
understand exactly what had happened, she knew there was no possibility of the resurrection of their romance. There was a bitter feeling
toward Harrison in their household.

"Ma wants to see you, *now*," called Jerry through the door.

"I can't."

"You better get down there."

Ten minutes later, Kitt appeared. "You wanted to see me, Ma?"
asked Kitt.

"You're not looking well, Kitt," said Grace. "You should do something about your hair. Call Kenneth. Get an appointment. Do your nails. Get a massage. Make a day of it. All this staying in the house all the time is not good for you."

"Yes, Ma."

"Would you like to come to Paris with me? Stay at the Ritz? See Mary Pat? Get some new clothes? It might be just the thing."

"No, thanks, Ma."

"Jerry said you were drinking. You're not drinking, are you, Kitt?"

"Yes, Ma."

"Well, stop it right now. Cardinal's coming for the weekend, to see your father and to see Constant. Perhaps you should go to confession," said Grace. "How long has it been since your last confession?"

"Bless me, Cardinal, for I have sinned. It's been two weeks since my last confession," said Kitt, in a singsong voice.

"Stop being sacrilegious, Kitt. Stop."

"Since my last confession, I have committed adultery nine times—no, ten."

"Stop being so vulgar, Kitt," snapped Grace.

"I repeat, ten times. Including once, downstairs in the living room after you went up to bed. That was the one I forgot."

"You should have your mouth washed out with soap. I am sorry that Harrison ever came into our lives again. After all we did for him in this family."

"Don't blame Harrison, Ma. I was the aggressor. I was the one who started it. I begged for it."

"I will not listen to this filthy talk," said Grace, covering her ears with her hands.

"Then help me. Help me."

"There's always Mass. The rosary. Our Lady. Prayer."

"Oh, for God's sake, Ma."

"The old lady don't seem to be taking it too hard," said Debbie, the new parlor maid, who was now called Colleen, in the kitchen.

"And just what do you mean by that, miss?" asked Bridey, bristling indignantly.

"She's got a husband who's going to be a cripple for life, drooling all over himself, not able to talk, and she's going off to Paris to buy new clothes, like she don't have enough in those closets already?" said Colleen.

"Don't you ever let me hear you call her 'the old lady' again. Her name is Mrs. Bradley, and don't you ever forget it. The woman is a saint on this earth, and one more word like that out of you and you're back on Aer Lingus to Roscommon, where you come from."

"And Kitt? Where's Kitt?" asked Grace. "It's time to leave for Mass."

"She's drunk, madam," replied Bridey.

"Well, sober her up. Slap her face several times, very hard. Make her drink several cups of black coffee. Make her use Listerine. I don't want Cardinal to smell liquor on her breath when she receives Communion."

"I can't slap Miss Kitt, madam," said Bridey.

"Yes, you can, if I ask you to. The girl can't miss Mass. It will be a mortal sin on her soul, and you want no part of that, Bridey."

"Yes, madam."

"Where's my lace mantilla, Bridey?"

"Right there in your top drawer with all your mantillas."

"No, no. Those are the black ones. I want the white one the Duchess of Alba gave me last year in Madrid."

"How did you find the two patients, Cardinal?" asked the reporter, when Cardinal Sullivan left the Southampton Hospital accompanied by Grace, Maureen, and Kitt Bradley.

"They are both, father and son, making remarkable recoveries," said Cardinal Sullivan, smiling. "Constant, I believe, is due to go home tomorrow or the next day, and Gerald in about a week or ten days' time. What a joy it will be when the whole family is reunited again. You know, people think of Gerald Bradley as a man completely interested in the accumulation of money. But that is not so. I have known Gerald for almost forty years. Isn't it close to forty years, Grace?"

"Almost, Cardinal. Thirty-nine, actually," said Grace, smiling.

"Thirty-nine then. And I can tell you his greatest pleasure lies in the success of his children. He is the most family-oriented man I've ever had the pleasure of knowing."

"Can my photographer take a couple of pictures, Cardinal, of you and Mrs. Bradley and her daughters?"

273

* * *

That night Harrison went to see Claire and the boys in New York.

"Aren't you going to take them out?" asked Claire. "They've been looking forward to it all week. You told them on the telephone you'd take them to Serendipity."

"No. I thought I'd order in. I thought all of us could have dinner together," said Harrison.

"I have a book to edit," said Claire, dismissing his idea.

"Please, Claire. It's important."

"Are you all right? You're not ill or anything, are you?"

"No."

"What then?"

"There's something I have to tell you. After the boys go to bed."

"About you and Kitt Chadwick, you mean?" Claire was matter-of-fact in her question.

Harrison looked at her, wondering how she knew. "No," he replied.

"Tell me now, Harrison. I'm not one for waiting. I don't believe in setting dates for important conversations." She looked over at the boys. "They're perfectly happy watching television."

"It has nothing to do with Kitt," he said.

"What then?"

They talked for thirty minutes in low voices, heads together, leaning across a kitchen table to each other. He told her about Winifred Utley, about the night, about Constant, about himself. Claire, stunned, listened intently, but she was not one to show alarm. There were no tears from her. There were no cries of "What will this do to me and the children?"

"So that's where the money came from," she said, finally. "For the year in Europe and the four years at Brown."

"Yes. Hush money, I suppose you could call it."

"You will not come out of this unscathed, you know."

"Yes, I know."

"I'm hungry, Dad," said Timmy, coming over to where his parents were talking.

"I'm hungry," said Charlie, following his brother.

"Your father will take you out, boys. Get your coats," said Claire. She looked at Harrison. "I always knew there was something. I always said there was a secret in your life."

"Yes, you did."

"I thought it was further back, though."

"What do you mean, further back?"

"From an earlier period. I have always found it odd that you have never mentioned your parents to me, other than to say they were murdered. Never once have you talked to me about them. No reminiscences, no childhood memories. It's not as if they died when you were four, and your memory of them is dimmed by time. You were what? Sixteen? Seventeen? Do you ever think of them? Did you ever mourn for them? Do you ever go to their graves? You didn't come back from Europe for the trial of the men who killed them. I always thought that was strange. You have always seemed to me, somehow, incomplete."

He looked at his wife and nodded. "Yeah, you're right. I think the reason I hated Jerry Bradley so much, almost from the first night I met him, at dinner with the Bradley family in Scarborough Hill after Constant had been expelled, was that the mocking tone he used when speaking to me reminded me of the way my father had always spoken to me. My father berated me, mocked me, for being a sissy. I can say that word now, and even smile saying it, but it was for me the most painful word in the vocabulary when I was a child. It was more painful because he knew it was painful. He was a reasonable man in many ways, but I enraged him. I was not what he wanted for an only son. He beat me. He beat me with leather belts, or wooden hangers, and when the hangers broke, as they often did, he went back to the closet and got another and continued with the beating. My legs and ass were often red with welts. I realize now he was trying to beat what he thought of as my sin out of me. No, I never have been to his grave."

Claire looked at him. "Oh, Harrison," she said. For a moment, they stared at each other.

"Here, help me," said Charlie, handing Harrison his coat.

Harrison helped his son into the left arm and then into the right arm and then buttoned the coat. Claire, doing the same with Timmy's coat, watched Harrison.

"What are you going to do?" she asked.

He told her.

"Does Kitt know?"

"No."

"Does anyone know?"

"Only you."

"How curious I should be the one you tell."

"Oh, I don't think it's curious, Claire."

275

"It's called burning all your bridges, what you're going to do. You know that, don't you, Harrison?"

"Yes, I do."

"Aren't you afraid?"

"Afraid? Of what?"

"Of what they can do to you. They're pretty powerful."

"They've already tried to drown me."

Two days later, there was a small item in the *Times* saying that the body of an unidentified swimmer had washed up on the beach in Shinnecock Creek near Hampton Bays, New York. The six-foot-one-inch dark-haired white male was clad in a wet suit. He appeared to be in his early to mid-forties. As of that time, no one had come forward to claim the body.

"You wished to see me, Mr. Jerry?" asked Charlie, the chauffeur, coming into the loggia.

"Yes, Charlie."

"Are you going into the city? You want me to drive you?"

"No, Charlie."

"Do you want me to take things over to the hospital for Mr. B.?" asked Charlie.

"No, Charlie. Sit down. There, on the bamboo chair. It doesn't look comfortable, but it is. You know Sally Steers wouldn't let one of Ma's guests sit on an uncomfortable chair."

Charlie, suddenly nervous, smiled.

"How many years have you been with us now, Charlie?"

"Oh, let me see, twenty-five, twenty-six, like that, I don't remember exactly. You're not thinking of retiring me, are you, Mr. Jerry? I'm still fit, you know, as fit as I was when I came here to be with the family."

"No, no, of course not, Charlie. We wouldn't ever retire you. My father's going to need you more than ever when he comes home from the hospital. What I wanted to discuss was something of a different nature. A man has washed ashore in the Shinnecock Creek near Hampton Bays. A swimmer. His body has been taken to the medical examiner's office in Hauppauge and is now in the morgue there. Do you know Hauppauge, Charlie?"

"I'm not sure I do."

"It's thirty miles west of Southampton."

"Oh, right, yes, I know Hauppauge."

"I have reason to believe the body is that of Johnny Fuselli," said Jerry.

"Johnny! No!" said Charlie, shocked.

"I fear so. He went swimming a few days ago, and no one has seen him since. What I'd like you to do, Charlie, is claim the body, if it is indeed Johnny, have it sent to the local funeral home in Hauppauge, and make whatever arrangements have to be made for cremation."

"Shouldn't you be the one doing that, not me, Mr. Jerry?" asked Charlie. "I'm only the chauffeur here."

"Under normal circumstances, yes, Charlie, but with the publicity in the papers from Constant's automobile accident and my father's stroke, there seems to be enough attention on our family. We thought, my brothers and I, that you could do this and attract no attention."

"It could be pricey, you know, for the cremation and all."

"Yes, it could. I think you will find there is sufficient cash in this envelope to cover whatever expenses there are. Thank you, Charlie."

That night Harrison Burns stood at a pay phone at the corner of Park Avenue and Sixty-second Street on the Upper East Side of New York and dialed a number.

"Hello?"

"Mrs. Utley?"

"Yes? Who is it?"

"This is Harrison Burns."

"Oh, Harrison," she said. She spoke in a friendly tone. "How strange you should call right now. I've just been reading your article on Esme Bland and Dwane Lonergan. What a story."

"Yes."

"I adored that woman in Arizona who raises cattle."

"Maxine."

"Yes. This is a rare piece for you."

"Rare? How?"

"A crime without villains."

"That's right."

"Your anger was missing."

"Yes, I suppose it was. But it has returned. I would like to invite myself for a cup of tea, or a glass of water, or whatever you have to serve."

"Yes, of course. When?"

"I'm standing at a pay phone outside your building. I was thinking of right now."

When Harrison got off the elevator on her floor, Luanne Utley was standing in the entry hall, the apartment door opened behind her, waiting for him. For a moment they stared at each other. She understood this was not a social call.

"Come in, Harrison," she said.

PART THREE

1993

Harrison Burns

15

HOW CAN I describe to you the furor that the arrest of Constant Bradley caused? What was it? His congressional background? His gubernatorial aspirations? His famous family? His multimillionaire father? His glamour? His racy reputation? His extraordinary good looks? It's anyone's guess. All of them together, probably. Who can ever forget the photograph of him, with a marshal on each side, arriving at the police station in Scarborough Hill, Connecticut, to turn himself in? It is not true that he was handcuffed, as several papers claimed. He was not. It was a condition, arrived at beforehand, that if he came to the police station on his own no handcuffs would be put on him. He was fingerprinted. Bail was set at a million dollars and paid immediately. And he left, waving, smiling sadly but affably at the barrage of cameras outside the police station. On the advice of counsel, he made no statement, only a charming helpless gesture. Then he entered the family station wagon and was whisked away.

But, of course, you must remember all of that. It was the story of the night on all three networks and CNN. It was on the front page of every newspaper the next morning, even the *Times*. But, as most people know, the carrying-out of justice is a very slow process. As the weeks and months went on, the story became relegated to the sort of media known to some as tabloid and to others as trash. Several members of the Bradley family asked for police protection from the hordes of reporters, photographers, and cameramen who blocked their driveways, tied up their telephones, and provoked several ugly incidents. One photographer, on a cherry picker, managed to get close enough to a second-floor window of the Bradley house to get a picture of Gerald Bradley being fed his soup by Sis Malloy. The photograph of the pathetic and helpless man appeared in papers across the country, and cries of outrage were heard on all sides. Once more, the members of the media were referred to as vultures. Other principals in the case, like Luanne Utley and me, went into hiding, separately, refusing to be interviewed, declining to participate in the circus atmosphere, even though it was I who had caused that atmosphere.

I have always enjoyed writing about people. People have always talked to me, even people who were reluctant to be interviewed. Claire has said to me on more than one occasion that I became involved in their lives as a way of not dealing with my own. Perhaps. Now the shoe was on the other foot. With the decision I made to come forward and tell what I knew about Constant Bradley, a great deal of attention came my way. Photographs of me appeared in all the newspapers. I discovered very quickly, and the discovery was no surprise to me, that I did not enjoy being written about. Poor Claire. How she loathed it, especially when a picture of her and the twins appeared in the *National Enquirer*. She left New York and rented a house in a remote village in Connecticut, doing her editing at home. Much of what was written about me was unfavorable. There was a perception, circulated by the family, that I had done it for the reward money. The word *betrayer* was used to describe me.

There have been times, more often than I care to remember, when I have said to myself, What have I done? What have I brought about?" Have I ever doubted the wisdom of my late-night visit to the apartment of Luanne Utley in May of 1990 and the confessional hours that followed? Oh, yes. Often I have awakened in the middle of the night, soaked with sweat, heart beating madly, screaming, "What have I done?" If I had it to do over again, would I do what I did? I would like to say, "Oh, yes, yes, yes," but, in truth, I wonder.

Would not my life have been easier if I had followed my instincts and not gone to Southampton that fateful weekend, during which I might have ended up drowned instead of Johnny Fuselli? Oh, yes. But now, thinking back, I realize that the process was set in motion for me on the night in New York at Borsalino's restaurant when I encountered Mrs. Utley again after so many years. Thoughts long dormant began to awaken, even though I resisted the stirrings. Then, in Maine, at the Bee and Thistle Inn, the process accelerated when I ran into Kitt Bradley, Constant's image, and became her lover. I did not want to meet with Gerald Bradley at the Four Seasons restaurant in New York, but I allowed myself to be talked into doing something I did not want to do. That day, Fruity Suarez appeared, like an apparition, standing all in gray at the bottom of the steps, to warn me not to take the road I was about to take. He understood, in Miss Garbo's bar, that I was being sucked into a vortex. How often I have thought of his words: "Stay away from them. All of them. They will destroy you. What is there about that family that you find so irresistible, Harry?" I did not want to go to Southampton. Everything told me not to, but again I allowed myself to be talked into doing something I did not want to do. I did not want to see Constant again. I have never been able to totally erase from my mind the picture of that beautiful person using the tail of his white Brooks Brothers shirt to wipe Winifred Utley's blood and his fingerprints off the bat with which he had just killed her.

I have come to believe there is a plan for each life, and these encounters were part of the plan—beyond my ability to halt—to bring me to this day. You see, I knew, or I think I knew, even before Johnny Fuselli tried to drown me, that I was going to do what I have done. The weight on my soul was too great.

I saw Kitt one more time after our parting in Southampton. I could not, after what had happened between us, go through with what I was about to do without letting her know of my intentions. I couldn't do that to her. I had by then been to see Luanne Utley. I had also been to see Captain Riordan, now retired. From him I learned what the next steps would have to be. I left a message on her machine, saying it was important that I see her on a most urgent matter. She left a breezy message on mine: "Come to lunch Tuesday. Tuna fish." With Bridey always in her life, she had never learned to cook, but she often bragged about her tuna fish casserole, which she called her one culinary accomplishment.

Our meeting was brief. She lived in a small but stylish suite of rooms, with its own kitchen, in the Rhinelander Hotel. The Rhinelander was, is, an elegant place on the Upper East Side of New York where many fashionable women live between marriages. I had been there during our affair, but she had preferred coming to my Spartan apartment for our afternoon meetings. "It's more erotic," she had said more than once. She liked arriving before me and changing the sheets and putting the wine in the refrigerator and arranging flowers she bought at a Korean market on the corner. She hated my one vase. "Tacky," she said. She hated my two glasses. "Tackier," she said. She bought a new vase and two new glasses. Sometimes, when I unlocked the door of my apartment, she was already undressed, prepared for what she called the frolic to follow, wearing only my dressing gown. As long as I had known her, she could make me laugh. I missed her.

She answered the door that Tuesday, the tuna fish Tuesday, and then stepped back, watching me. She was wearing the glasses she sometimes wore when she read, but she pulled them off and held them in her hand as she smiled nervously, in the way that lovers do when they meet again after their first fight. I entered. I stood inside her door, looking at her looking at me. I believe, to my shame, that she thought the urgency of my call to her had had to do with sexual desire. A quickie, which she would have gone through with if that had been my intention. She had been to the hairdresser. She was dressed as if for lunch at "21." The suit, the pearls, the gold pin. Behind her, I could see that a table was set for two, with plates and glasses and silver and napkins and a bottle of wine. The bottle was open, and she had poured herself a glass, perhaps even two. From the kitchen, I could smell her tuna fish casserole.

"Hello," she said. Her voice was almost a whisper.

"Hello, Kitt."

"Oh, Harrison. I was so excited when I heard from you. I couldn't stop thinking that you were coming. I only stayed for two acts of the opera last night and left. I wanted everything to be perfect today. How do I look?"

"Kitt, I'm not going to stay. You must listen to me. You must let me talk. You must not interrupt me. Something terrible is going to happen, and I cannot bear that you find it out from someone other than me, as I am the one who is responsible. Constant is going to be arrested for the murder of Winifred Utley in 1973. No, no, don't disagree with me. I was there that night. I saw. I helped him carry her body from the place where he killed her to the place where she was found under the pine tree. Your father knew. All your brothers knew. Your mother didn't, of course. Nor any of your sisters. I could not live with this secret another moment. That is why Johnny Fuselli tried to drown me. I have gone to the police in Scarborough Hill and told everything I know. That's it. That's all I have to say. I am sorry to hurt you like this, and your mother. I loved you, Kitt. I want you to know that. But I had to do what I have done."

She stared at me, unbelieving. Her face looked as if I had struck her. Her mouth hung slack. Then, as if her chin were too heavy for her

face, her head fell forward to her chest. Her glasses dropped out of her
hand. As she turned to walk to a chair, she stepped on her glasses with
her high heel and broke a lens. Uncaring, she fell into the chair. Her
hands went to her face and covered it. Then I turned, opened the door,
and left her. Outside her door, in the hall of the Rhinelander Hotel, I
could hear a moan coming from her, like a lamentation for the dead. I
wanted to go back. I wanted to tell her I was sorry for having inflicted
pain on her. I didn't. I walked quickly to the elevator and pushed the
Down button.

It is not uncommon for crazies to confess to crimes they did not commit, or for people to pretend that they have knowledge of a crime that
they do not have. For that reason, the police always withhold some
information from the media, something vital, that only the killer could
know, or someone who has actually witnessed the killing. Look back
at those old newspapers from 1973. You will read that Winifred Utley
was wearing a pink party dress, that her white panties were on, and
that she had not been raped. What I knew was that her panties were
down by her ankles. I had seen that when I lifted her. I had seen her
pubic hair. It was the one bit of information I needed to establish my
credibility. They already knew my whereabouts that night. It was in
the files. What I suspected but did not actually know was that rape had
been the intention, but penetration had not taken place. I had a theory
about Constant, but I kept that to myself.

Captain Riordan came with me on that day. Although retired, he had
never been able to forget the case, about which he had always had
very strong suspicions. Through the years, he had checked in with
Luanne Utley several times a year and had established a warm relationship with her. Things had happened after I had gone to Europe that
I knew nothing about. Captain Riordan told me that a cardinal and
several priests had interceded for the family. He told me that the
cardinal had told Gerald in front of him that he should not let Constant
submit to certain tests that Riordan wanted. He said they would do
more harm than good, although what that meant no one knew, but no
one was about to question a cardinal, and the cardinal knew that.

The new police chief, Homer Dundee, had come to Scarborough
Hill after Captain Riordan's retirement. He resented Captain Riordan's
involvement. He said that he was quite capable of handling the case

himself. He said that he did not want any interference from Captain Riordan. Captain Riordan left. Thereafter I met him only in private, or with Luanne Utley.

Homer Dundee asked me if I knew why Winifred's chin, nose, and forehead were marked with cuts unrelated to the blows on her head from the bat. I said that I assumed the cuts were made by Constant when he tried to drag her by the hair across the path before he came to get me to help him lift her. Homer Dundee nodded.

"Are there any people who might be able to corroborate any of what you have told me?" he asked.

"There is a cook in the family called Bridey. I don't know her last name. She has been with the family since the children were small. She is devoted to Mrs. Bradley," I said.

"What about her?"

"She woke up that night, when Constant and I returned to the house and were getting out of our clothes in the kitchen. Her room was off the kitchen. She called out to us. It was two in the morning."

Homer Dundee wrote down her name. "Anyone else?"

"There was a maid called Colleen. It is a different Colleen from the Colleen who works for the family now."

"What about her?"

"The next day I overheard her tell Bridey that she had heard Constant and me talking outside the house in the night. Her room was on the top floor, and she said our voices traveled up there. Bridey told her to forget what she heard."

"Do you know her last name?"

"No."

"Anyone else?"

"There is a real-estate broker in New York called Eloise Brazen. She is listed in the book. She lives on Park Avenue. At the time she was having an affair with Gerald Bradley. Constant called his father at her apartment that night to tell him something terrible had happened and to come home at once. I know for a fact, from someone she knew who has since died, that she remembers the night."

"What happened to the bat?" he asked, suddenly. "The other part of the bat?"

I told him Constant placed the bat in a garbage bag. I told him about taking off our shirts and trousers and undershorts and shoes. I told him about Johnny Fuselli driving off with the bag in the back of Bridey's car. I told him what Johnny told me before he drowned.

*   *   *

Following my visit with Kitt, news of my intentions traveled fast. My wife was harassed by anonymous telephone calls. When I say my wife, I am still referring to Claire, from whom I am separated but not divorced. Initially the calls were relatively harmless. "You will not get into the club you have applied for," said the voice. She had in fact applied for membership in a small beach club in Black Point, where there were many children for our boys to play with. Or, "Your children will not get into the school in which you are trying to enter them." The school was no more than a playschool. The point of the calls was for her to use her influence on me to not go forward with the trial. Claire is a strong woman, not easily frightened. Once, she engaged her tor-mentor in conversation. She said later to me, "I think I know who that is." I, of course, thought it might be Jerry, or even Des. But Claire felt quite sure it was Freddy Tierney, the husband of Maureen Bradley, whom she had known years ago in Palm Beach, before he married into the Bradley family. Once she confronted him. "Is this you, Freddy Tierney? You asshole," she said. The caller hung up. The calls stopped. Freddy had apparently been indoctrinated into the Bradley machine, but flunked his first assignment. Like poor drowned Johnny Fuselli, his heart probably wasn't in it. Recently, the calls have started again, but with a different voice. They are hideously vulgar anonymous hate calls. Claire has stopped answering her telephone, letting the ma-chine pick up on the first ring and taking the call only if she recognizes the caller. Twice she has been fooled, but she taped those calls and turned the tapes over to the police. The calls have stopped.

Stories were circulated that Gerald was making a remarkable recovery. It was not true. He had aged greatly since his stroke. Visitors to the house, mostly priests and close family friends, who complimented him on his remarkable recovery, reported later that he had a tendency to fall asleep, that he was forgetful of recent happenings but remembered remote events with clarity, and that he cried frequently and was given to bouts of irritability. A paralysis had set in. The left side of his face was distorted, and he was unable to speak intelligibly. He made sounds that he thought made sense but made sense to no one else. When those closest to him failed to understand his orders and desires, he became enraged. Only Sis Malloy was able to interpret his sounds. "Make sure

Sis is in the room," a family member would say, warning the others of his possible wrath.

Although Grace rarely came face-to-face with Gerald, she tended to his needs through her daily contact with Sis Malloy and Miss Toomey, the head nurse.

Every day Sis read the newspapers to him, the *New York Times* and the *Wall Street Journal*. She had become expert in reading the stock-market quotations, and sometimes took telephone calls from Gerald's traders, passing on the information to him and calling back with his reply. His skills at making money had not left him. It was the happiest time of day for Gerald. She bought every tabloid paper and read him every detail of the scandal involving his son that was riveting the country.

"What is he saying, Sis? I cannot understand him," said Jerry impatiently.

"He said that Constant must not be handcuffed, under any circumstances," said Sis.

"Yes, of course," said Jerry. "He will turn himself in, and we will post bail immediately. The bail is set for a million."

In the meantime, Bradley family life went on as if there was not a dark cloud overhead. The public pose was to treat the charge of murder as no more than an inconvenience, a mad person's revenge which would soon be straightened out in a court of law, at which time they could go about the business of their lives again. It was a family trait never to mention their scandals or adversities. Agnes's madness, Jerry's crippling accident, Des's marriage to a maid, and Gerald's mistresses were things never mentioned. In the face of the terrible publicity, the Bradley public relations apparatus was constantly at work. Sandro gave a rousing and widely praised speech in the Senate, opposing a presidential nomination for an appointment to the Supreme Court. Maureen gave birth to twins, her eighth and ninth children. Grace's seventy-second birthday was celebrated with great fanfare, and a new white rose was named in her honor, the Grace Bradley rose. Constant was photographed wheeling his father to the garden. I knew Gerald was unwell, but I was unprepared for the sight of him. The man I had seen only eleven months earlier in Southampton had diminished in size. Slack-jawed, unheeding, he sat in his wheelchair, playing his part in the family playlet, watching Constant dig the hole to plant the rose bush. Earlier on that same Sunday, Maureen's fifth child, Eugenie, made her First Communion. The entire family attended, except for Gerald.

"It will be a wonderful look for Constant, holding little Eugenie's hand, with her in her veil and her lovely white dress that Ma bought her in Paris," said Maureen. "After all, he is her godfather."

"But he's not her godfather," said Freddy Tierney. "My brother Tom is."

"Oh, for God's sake, Freddy. Who the hell is going to know? And some godfather your brother is, by the way. He hasn't remembered Eugenie's birthday for the last three years."

Freddy, cowed, retreated. "He does have cancer, darling."

"Even so."

In private, tales of Kitt's drinking circulated. People who loved her said, "What a shame." Publicly, she traveled to Paris to visit her sister Mary Pat, the Countess de Trafford.

The book that Gerald had wanted me to write in Constant's name, the chronicle of a great American Catholic family, was written in short order, and anonymously, by a Mrs. Goldberg, who had written books for a former cabinet member's wife, a famous hairdresser's ex-wife, a former president's daughter, and a film star, all in their names. She wanted no glory and was content to remain discreetly in the background while Constant took bows as the author. She was paid, I was told by Claire, who always knew the publishing news, a half million dollars up front. Speed was of the essence in her assignment. If the book made the best-sellers list, she was to receive another quarter of a million dollars. Called simply *Family,* Constant Bradley's book proved to be amazingly popular. Denials were issued by the publisher of a rumor that Bradley representatives around the country purchased thousands of copies of the book from the key bookstores that reported their sales figures to the compilers of best-sellers lists. There was an elaborate publicity campaign, with television appearances on every chat show of consequence by Constant, as the author of the family memoir, and even, on occasion, by Grace, as the mother of the author. On television, Grace, who had always been in the background of the family, proved to be an immensely popular figure, beloved by the audiences.

"If you could see this son of mine and his wife Charlotte and his adorable little children go to Mass every Sunday, you would know what a family man he is. I have always said that the family that prays together stays together," said Grace on "The Oprah Winfrey Show."

"That's a very lovely sentiment, Mrs. Bradley," said Oprah, who led the studio audience in applauding Grace. Grace smiled and waved at the audience and at the camera.

Then Oprah became serious and turned to Constant.

"Congressman Bradley, you yourself at this moment are going through a personal crisis in being charged with the killing of a young girl nearly twenty years ago in Scarborough Hill, Connecticut."

"Of course, this is a false accusation, Oprah, which will shortly be proved in a court of law. There are certain limitations put on me at this moment as to what I can and cannot say. I'm sure you will understand that."

"Yes, yes, of course. I will not ask you anything specific about the case itself. What I am interested in is how do you account for what has happened, for the state of affairs in which you find yourself?"

"The whole thing's perfectly ridiculous," interjected Grace.

Constant spoke very seriously. "I believe there has been pressure in the community of Scarborough Hill, where, as you know, the Bradley family lived for many years, to solve this tragic crime that has been on the books there for nearly two decades due, probably, to inefficient police work at the time. The body of poor Winifred Utley, who, by the way, I had only met once or twice in my life, was indeed found close by the property of my parents' house. And, as I am probably the most visible, the most highly profiled, of all the people who saw Winifred Utley on the last night of her life, at a dance, who better for the new chief of police, who is apparently anxious to make a name for himself, to point his finger at than me?"

"He was in bed that night, Oprah," said Grace. "The mother of the girl called me at two in the morning, looking for Winifred, and I went into his room, and there he was, sleeping like a baby."

"Yes, Mrs. Bradley," said Oprah. She turned back to Constant. "The person who has brought the accusation against you, Mr. Burns, I believe, Harrison Burns, is, or was, rather, a great friend of yours, was he not?"

"That is what is so surprising. That is what none of us in our family understands," said Constant.

"We were so good to that boy," said Grace. "We took him in. He became practically a member of our family after his own parents were murdered.'' She whispered the last word and nodded her head at the same time, as if it were a significant factor.

"The Bradleys are fighting the case on TV, Your Honor. They have access to every talk show program. They are pretending to push Constant Bradley's book, but they are using the air time to fight their case and prejudge the legal process,'' said Bert Lupino, the prosecutor, in court two days later.

Judge Edda Consalvi pulled at her dyed black hair. She reached over and poured herself a glass of water from a thermos. "What is it you are asking, Mr. Lupino?''

"What I am requesting is a gag order put on all parties so that the case may not be won or lost by the media before the trial starts,'' said Bert Lupino.

"Request granted,'' said Judge Consalvi.

The district attorney said about Bert Lupino, "He is our star. We have great faith in Bert. Last year he was named prosecutor of the year. He has nearly a hundred percent track record for convictions.''

It was true, but the convictions were for drug and robbery cases. He had never handled a murder case. I did not feel altogether safe in his hands. There was a shrillness about him when he became excited. His father was a dentist, and he flossed his teeth incessantly during our private sessions.

"Please stop doing that,'' I said, finally. "Please, please, it's driving me crazy watching you do that.''

"Hey, hey, calm down, Harrison,'' he said.

From the day before Constant's arrest, a search was on for the best defense lawyer in the land. Gerald, through Sis Malloy, who was his interpreter, wanted the lawyer who had won an acquittal "for that guy who tried to kill his wife in Newport, the one who's in the coma.'' Constant had reservations. "I don't want a lawyer whose name is in the papers all the time, Pa,'' he said. Others in the same category were interviewed. It was Sims Lord who came up with the name of Valerie Sabbath.

"Valerie Sabbath will fight to the death for her clients,'' Sims Lord told the male members of the Bradley family. "She is best known for having saved nine people from death row.''

"Good heavens," said Sandro, who was always cautious, both at home and in the Senate. "Won't that make it appear that we think Constant is guilty if we have a lawyer with that sort of track record? Saving nine people from death row. It has a wrong kind of sound to it. Does anyone agree with me?"

"I think we should listen to what Sims has to say, Sandro," said Jerry.

"We all know Constant's innocent, Sandro," said Des, "but we're still facing a murder trial."

"Go on, Sims," said Constant.

"All that I'm saying is that when there is a murder rap, Valerie Sabbath is the best that money can buy. She is considered one of the most merciless cross-examiners in the legal business. She has a remarkable ability to degrade and confuse prosecution witnesses. Remarkable. I've sat in on some of her cases. I've watched firsthand. She loves to intimidate. She loves to humiliate. She thrives on it. She knows when she has you. She can twist and turn a witness's memory."

Jerry liked the sound of her. He passed on to his father the recommendation of Sims Lord. Gerald listened and nodded his head.

"She's not quite a lady, Pa," said Jerry. "She's a toughie."

Gerald nodded.

"We could never take her to the club for dinner. She's loud. She uses four-letter words. And she'd hate all those people as much as they'd hate her."

Gerald listened. He beckoned to Sis Malloy and mumbled something in her ear.

"What's he saying, Sis?" asked Jerry.

"He wants to know how much she's going to cost."

"A million."

Gerald mumbled again.

"He says, 'Hire her.' "

"The prosecution's going to try to establish a pattern of behavior, Pa. They've subpoenaed both Weegie Somerset and Maud Firth. Just keep your fingers crossed about Wanda Symanski. No one knows about her yet. Valerie says they don't have a chance. What Valerie actually said is, 'They don't have a fucking chance.' That's the way she talks, Pa."

Gerald chuckled.

"Valerie says they'll never be able to bring those girls to the stand," said Jerry. "She's an authority on patterns of behavior. Sims said she once had a case where a mother was on trial for killing her child. She was able to keep the jury from finding out that the same mother had killed another child seven years earlier by convincing the judge that one case had nothing to do with the other. What, Pa? What's he saying, Sis?"

"He said don't let that story about the mother with the two dead kids leak out to the papers."

"Have you been able to get any information on the judge?" asked Jerry.

"She lives with her mother, and her father wears a rug," said Eddie Bargetta. Eddie had taken Johnny Fuselli's place.

"Oh, Christ, how I miss Johnny Fuselli," said Jerry. "Look, I don't give a shit if her father wears a rug. I want to know about her. Is she married?"

"No."

"Ever been?"

"No."

"Where'd she go to high school, college, law school? That's the kind of thing I want to know."

"She was a scholarship girl, all the way through Sacred Heart Convent and college."

"Sacred Heart? Now, that's interesting, Eddie. That's very interesting."

The day of the arraignment was a warm, wet autumn day that alternated between a descending mist and a heavy, slanting rain. I had not come in my own car to the courthouse in Stamford. A member of the prosecutor's office had driven me in order to fill me in on new information before I got to the courthouse.

Valerie Sabbath sat at the defense table chatting amiably with Constant, their heads close together, smiling, laughing. Then she leaned forward and straightened his tie. In a photograph published the following day, they looked like guests at a lunch party rather than a defense attorney and a client at an arraignment for a murder trial. When Maureen, through Jerry, questioned the propriety of such frivolity in the courtroom, Valerie replied, looking directly at Maureen, whose question she knew it was, "If you don't show the jury that you love your client, that you believe in your client, the jury will never buy it that your client should go free."

"But there is no jury at an arraignment," insisted Maureen.

"There's going to be at the trial," said Valerie, who had taken an instant dislike to Maureen. "And, besides, I think Constant's adorable."

Several times Constant turned and smiled encouragement to members of his family. Then he was told to rise. He rose from his seat and stood in place at the defense table.

The judge, Edda Consalvi, spoke in a lugubrious, knell-like voice as she read the charge that had been brought against him. "You have been charged with the murder of Winifred Utley, lying in wait for her, bludgeoning her to death with multiple blows from a baseball bat, for which, if convicted, you could receive life in prison. How do you plead?"

There was silence in the courtroom, as the spectators and reporters waited for him to reply. The television camera was trained on his face. The only sounds that could be heard were the clicking of the shutter of the single still camera that Judge Consalvi allowed in her courtroom. Instead of replying from the defense table, as was the norm, Constant approached the bench, walking slowly. Once there, he leaned forward and looked Judge Consalvi straight in the eye.

"Not guilty, Your Honor," he said. Then he turned and walked back to his seat.

"That was a nice touch, walking up to the bench and looking at Consalvi like that. It looked sincere. Whose idea was that?" asked Sandro. "Jerry's?"

"No. Valerie Sabbath's."

At the end of the day, the deluge was at its most violent. The lawyer who had driven me had been called to the district attorney's office. Other members of the team had dispersed. I found myself without transportation. I called for a taxi. Because of the storm and the close of the business day, all the taxis were taken. The dispatcher told me to wait in front of the courthouse, and he would send the first available cab there. I stood without an umbrella and waited. From the underground garage came the Bradley station wagon, filled with lawyers and family members. Constant sat in the front seat, with Maureen between him and the driver. Behind, in the center seat, sat Jerry, with Valerie

Sabbath on one side and a member of her defense team on the other. At the same moment they all spotted me, standing, soaked, waiting for the taxi. Even in the pounding rain, I could hear the roar from inside the car. I had become the enemy of the family. The station wagon veered toward me, splashing the muddy water from a curbside puddle over me. I could hear the shouts of laughter as the car went on.

Five minutes later, when the cab had not arrived, I turned to go back inside the courthouse. A car pulled up. The driver honked his horn. I turned. The driver rolled down a window. "Need a ride?" he called out.

"Yes, yes," I called back. I ran and got into the front seat. "I'm soaked, I'm afraid. I'll get your car all wet."

"It don't matter," he said. "Where to?"

"The Hessian. It's a hotel on Wentworth Street."

"Yes, yes, I know."

"This is very kind of you. I made a terrible mistake today and let myself be driven. I won't do that again."

"No, you're right. You should always have your own wheels."

"Yes."

"You don't recognize me, do you?"

I turned. He was a stout man with a friendly Irish face. I didn't recognize him. I wondered if he had been a policeman on one of my many visits to the police station in Scarborough Hill.

"Fatty Malloy," he said. "When I knew you, they used to call you Harry."

"Oh, my God. Fatty. How are you? It's been years."

"What's that expression? A lotta water over the dam."

"Yes, you can say that again, a lotta water," I said. "It's a wonder you would pick me up. The family station wagon just splashed a reservoir over me."

"I saw. That was probably Constant saying, 'Get him.' They always like a good joke. You must remember that," he said, laughing. When Fatty laughed, his eyes disappeared into slits, and he looked, momentarily, Chinese.

I did not respond.

"Are you sorry you got into this?" he asked.

"You know, Fatty, I don't really think I should be discussing this with you. Anything I say, you could repeat back to them. We're on opposite sides here."

"Not necessarily."

"What does that mean?"

"The family dropped me like a smelly turd when I refused to quit my job at the market to be an orderly for Uncle Gerald after his stroke."

"Why did you do that?"

"I didn't want to carry Uncle Gerald back and forth to the toilet and have to wipe his ass for him, and that's what they had in mind for me to do. There's a lot of people who make a living doing that who could use the work."

"Good for you."

"I don't like it that they snap their fingers and expect you to change your life to accommodate them when they get themselves into trouble, especially when you haven't heard from any of them for years, except Aunt Grace, who sends a Christmas gift each year. The first thing Constant said to me when I went out to Southampton was, 'Hey, Fatty, show us how you pack the grocery bags,' and they all laughed, and then they say, when they think they may have hurt your feelings, 'Aw, we're only kidding you, Fatty. You know we love you.' My job at Riley's Market may not be a big deal in their eyes, but I like doing it, and I'm good at it."

"What about Sis?"

"Oh, Sis went. She'd do anything Aunt Grace wanted her to do. When it happened, you know, when Winifred Utley got killed way back in '73, Jerry tried to get me to take the fall, to say I was in the house that night, that I was drunk, that it was an accident. He had a scenario all worked out. He said I'd get just a couple of years for manslaughter, but that Sis and I'd be taken care of for life."

"Are you serious?"

"Yep."

"Would you testify to that?"

"No, I couldn't do that."

"Who knows this?"

"Nobody. Not even my sister. She worships all of them, especially Aunt Grace."

"Dear God," I said.

"Listen, Harry, if they could have pinned it on you, they would have, you know. I'm sure it was discussed," said Fatty. "But you were too smart, and they all knew it."

We pulled up to the hotel. "Come on in and have a drink with me," I said.

"No. Too risky. Besides, you better get some dry clothes on."

"You know, Fatty, I should have gone to the police back when it happened. I shouldn't have lied. It's haunted my life, knowing what I knew."

"Let up on yourself, Harry. Look at it this way. If you'd gone to the police, or even threatened to go, something might have happened to you. You were not a very noticeable character in those days. Who the hell would have missed you? You had no parents, no friends to speak of, except Constant. Only your aunt Gert. What's the matter?"

"A chill just went through me."

"You're soaked, that's why."

"Yes, that's why."

"They used to laugh at your aunt Gert, you know, when you weren't there, just as they used to laugh at Sis and me."

I couldn't bear to think that they had laughed at Aunt Gert. After I showered and changed, I drove over to St. Mary's Home in Ansonia, where she had been a patient for years. I hadn't been to see Aunt Gert in ages. The last time I had seen her, she hadn't recognized me.

"Visiting hours are over," said the nun on duty.

"Yes, I know, but can't you bend the rules just this once? I would like to see her. I have come a long way. Please. I am her nephew. I pay her bills here."

"Let me see if she's asleep," said the nun.

Finally I was let in. Aunt Gert looked tiny in her bed. Her face was very pale and her hair very white. She looked over at me, and I knew she recognized me. I leaned over and kissed her forehead. She reached out her hand, and I took it and sat on the edge of her bed. I didn't tell her that Claire and I were separated. I didn't tell her that I was involved in a murder trial. I didn't tell her that I had more or less abandoned my career, at least for the present time, because I could not concentrate on anything but what was happening in my life. I could, and did, talk about the twins. She loved hearing about Timmy and Charlie. I had brought her a picture of the boys, and her face lit up with joy. Then I stood up to leave.

"I wanted to say thank you, Aunt Gert, for taking care of me after they died," I said. She knew I meant my mother and father. With her, I always said they died, not that they were killed, or murdered. "I don't think I ever told you that before. I don't think I was ever grateful enough. I didn't understand how good you were to me. I didn't understand how important your advice was to me. Once you said to me, 'You are bewitched by those people, Harrison.' Do you remember that? I was. You were right. I didn't listen.''

She looked at me.

"I know you're getting tired. Before I go, I want to ask you something. Do you still pray so much? Do you? Pray for me."

I leaned over and kissed her cheek. I never realized that I had loved her. Her eyes followed me.

"Thank you, Aunt Gert. I love you."

16

I GREW FOND of Fatty Malloy. Occasionally we would meet, always in secret. He talked to Sis every day and kept me abreast of the doings in the family.

"Gerald has become very religious," he said. "Communion every day. Cardinal has sort of reconverted him back. Cardinal said to Sis, 'He has reembraced his Catholicism with fervor. It is a beautiful thing to see.' "

"Gerald religious?" I was incredulous.

"According to Sis, Cardinal says he's abandoned the sins of the flesh."

"I would think at age seventy-five, after a massive stroke, it was time to slow down in the flesh department."

Fatty roared with laughter.

"How's Kitt?" I asked.

"She's always falling down, covered with bruises, or breaking a toe, or something."

"Who is that girl?" asked Kitt. She was sitting in the car outside the courthouse with Maureen.

"Her name is Maud Firth, from Lake Forest. Winston Firth's daughter," said Maureen.

"Oh, yes, Maud Firth. I thought I recognized her."

"You know her?"

"I went to her coming-out. What's she doing here?"

"The same thing Weegie Somerset's doing. Testifying against Constant."

"Oh, dear," said Kitt. "I never heard about that."

*   *   *

On the day of the preliminary hearing to discuss the admissibility of the testimony of Weegie Somerset, who, married, was now known as Louise Belmont, and Maud Firth, the atmosphere in the courtroom was tense. The prosecution felt that the testimony of the women at the trial was vital for a conviction, as it showed a pattern of behavior on the part of Constant Bradley. Valerie Sabbath was equally determined to keep the two women from testifying in front of a jury.

"Let me go over this with you one more time, Constant and Jerry, so you absolutely understand what 'pattern of behavior' means in a court of law," said Valerie, speaking low to her client and his brother at the defense table. "At the risk of appearing a little crude, I'll give you an example. If you had pasted on a red mustache every time you fucked these women, and you only fucked them up the ass, and all the women were Chinese, that's a pattern of behavior. But just knocking them around a little bit doesn't necessarily constitute a pattern of behavior. Understand?"

The brothers looked at each other.

"Do you understand?" she repeated.

"Yes," said Constant.

"Weegie what'shername in the cabana, who later tells Captain Riordan you didn't hit her, and then almost twenty years later says you did, forget it," said Valerie. "I scared the shit out of that girl, with her little pageboy and her little gold barrettes, when I took her deposition. She'll cave in on the stand, you mark my words."

Constant didn't reply.

"Take Maud Firth. That's a little different. She had seventeen stitches. There are hospital records. But she took money, am I right? A settlement? And she was loaded when it happened, right? That won't look so good when I get her up there. There's a fruit cousin, called Fruity Suarez, if you can believe that name, whom she went to see that night. He wants to testify how beat up she was."

"Fruity Suarez got kicked out of Milford for kissing dicks," said Constant.

"Good to know," said Valerie, making a note. "You mark my words, Judge Consalvi will disallow the testimony of these ladies."

A smartly dressed woman walked down the corridor of the courthouse.

"You probably won't remember me, Harrison," she said. "I'm Louise Belmont. When we knew each other in Scarborough Hill, I was Weegie Somerset.''

"Of course, I remember you, Weegie," I said.

"I just hate today. I'm terrified," she said. "My husband's furious with me for agreeing to testify at this hearing. I think it's wonderful what you did, Harrison."

"The betrayer, I'm called. A snitch, a sleaze, you name it."

"I don't call you any of those things. My parents don't, either. There's a lot of people cheering for you."

"Why did you always say he didn't hit you that night in Watch Hill? I was out by the cabana that night. I saw. I heard. But you told Captain Riordan after Winifred was killed that it wasn't true. Why did you do that?"

"I loved him then. I ached with love for him. I'm sure if I had gone to the police then, Winifred might still be alive today. I felt responsible in a way, and now that I've got a little girl of my own, I had to come forward when Mr. Lupino called me in for a deposition."

Valerie Sabbath was chatting in a corner of the corridor with Charlotte Bradley. A woman quite unlike Weegie Somerset and Maud Firth walked by, her hair in a snood.

"Who's that?" asked Charlotte.

"Wanda Symanski," said Valerie.

"The one my husband picked up in the bar in Sag Harbor?"

"Yes."

"Is she testifying?"

"Not yet. She's made charges that are unprovable."

"She's not even waitress-pretty," said Charlotte.

A television news cameraman came precariously close to their faces with his camera. "Take that camera out of my face," Valerie yelled at the cameraman. Charlotte withdrew quickly, out of camera range, but Valerie was incensed at the intrusion. As the cameraman withdrew, he held the camera on her. She followed him down the length of the corridor, holding up her middle finger to the lens. "This what you want? This what you want?" she screamed in a taunting voice. By this time, the corridor was filled with reporters. "You people think you own the courthouse," she screamed at them. "I was having a private talk with Mrs. Constant Bradley, and he stuck his camera right in my face. You sleazoids will go to any length. You ought to be ashamed of yourselves."

"Oh, dear," said Maureen.

Maureen and Kitt and Charlotte sat unblinking and stony-faced as the prosecutor, Bert Lupino, gave graphic descriptions of the depositions of Weegie Somerset and Maud Firth. Their hands were folded in their laps. Through the years, they had heard whispers that there had been an altercation with Weegie, but they did not know about Maud Firth. They had never heard that she had been knocked down in a hotel room and had seventeen stitches taken in her head.

"I don't believe a word of that," said Maureen.

Neither Kitt nor Charlotte said anything.

Judge Consalvi said she would make her ruling on the admissibility of the women's testimony on the first day of the trial.

The more salacious newspapers and television shows reported the event with painful prominence.

"Oh, dear," said Maureen, watching the television news.

For the first time in years I had days with nothing to do. My time was taken up only with waiting for the trial to start. Each postponement requested by Valerie Sabbath and granted by Judge Edda Consalvi was agonizing. I lost interest in the sort of stories that used to fascinate me to write. I could no longer cover trials. I was in one. I went on leave from my career. I had no office to go to. I had no deadlines to keep. I stopped swimming. I read *War and Peace*. I read the six Palliser novels. I rented videos, six at a time, but rarely saw one all the way through. Other than Fatty Malloy, to whom I became devoted, I had no one to talk to who was not involved in the case. I missed Claire. I missed her intelligent conversation. I missed being married. I missed the day-to-day life of watching my sons grow up. I telephoned them each evening at six, eager to hear their tales of playschool and Halloween costumes and the class pageant. More and more I drove up to the country to see them, and take them out to McDonald's, but also to talk to Claire. I asked her to tell me about the book she was editing. She was totally involved with the work of an author she had discovered, and read me passages from her first novel. For those moments my turmoil abated. She never asked, "What's the latest?"—meaning about the case—for which I was grateful. But when I spoke, I would start sentences with "When the trial begins" or "When the trial is over." It was the moment in my life that I was waiting for and dreading. All things led to it and away from it. Claire understood without saying she understood. Once she said, "Are you keeping a journal? Are you keeping track of all this? You should, you know." When I left them, I often had nowhere to go. I began driving with no purpose in mind, looking at towns and villages and covered bridges and seasonal changes, things I had never spent time doing before.

One day, stopping to look at a sign, I realized that I was near the village where the Milford School was. I had never gone back there since I graduated in 1973. I rarely read the school magazine they sent me, even though I heard from time to time I was written up in it. I knew that Dr. Shugrue had retired and become headmaster emeritus. Once I had a letter from the new headmaster asking me if I would come and speak at the school, but I declined, saying that I was going to be on assignment in Europe, although that was not the truth. I drove through the village, which had become a small town. The local theater where Constant and I had sneaked to movies had become a cineplex. At the far end of Main Street, I turned to the right and drove up the hill. At the top of the hill was the entrance to Milford. THE MILFORD SCHOOL said the sign. What a strange feeling it was to look down on the school that sprawled below. I had forgotten how happy I had been there, until it happened.

Ahead of me, beautifully situated, was the Bradley Library. The last time I saw the building, on the day of my graduation, when Gerald Bradley took me inside and gave me the plane tickets for Europe that were to ensure my silence, it was in its final stages of completion. The handsome red-brick Georgian facade was still bare. Now ivy had grown up its walls, and lovely elm trees, transplanted fully grown, were in place around it. It appeared to have been there for a hundred years.

I went in. It was almost twilight. The lights were on. Ahead was a reading room. On a table were magazines and newspapers, neatly lined up. On a green leather chair, an old man in a tweed jacket and bow tie was sleeping. His horn-rimmed spectacles had slipped down his nose. A copy of the *New York Times* had fallen to the floor beside him, open to the page he had been reading. It was Dr. Shugrue. I wandered about, looking here, looking there at the lovely building. It was early evening, and there were no students about. When I looked back at the figure in the chair, I saw he was looking at me. He had righted his glasses.

"It's Harrison, isn't it?" he asked. "Harrison Burns?"

"It is, sir. I am flattered that you would recognize me after so many years, and so many students," I said.

"We have your two books here in the library. We're quite proud of you," he said.

"Thank you."

"Is Elias Renthal still in jail?"

"Prison, not jail."

"Prison, of course."

"Yes, he is."

"Good. And Max Goesler?"

"Yes, and for a long time to come."

"Nasty piece of work, wasn't he?"

In my years there as a student, the headmaster and I had never actually engaged in conversation. I was colorless then, not the type of student sought out by a headmaster. My one extended conversation with Dr. Shugrue occurred when I was sent to his office from study hall and he told me my parents had been murdered. I spent the night in the guestroom of his house, comforted by his kind wife, whom I knew must have thought it odd that I shed no tears.

"Sit down. Sit down," he said. "This is a lovely, quiet time here. The boys are in the dining room. That's why I come now. Of course, I should say the boys and *the girls* are in the dining room. Milford's coed now. It's something I have never gotten used to. I took it as the signal that it was time to retire."

He told me that he continued to live on the grounds of the school in a small Federal house that the trustees had given him for life. He enjoyed coming to the library each evening to read the *Times* and the latest magazines. He said he took no part in the running of the school, appearing officially only at fund-raising events and graduation ceremonies. He had kind words for his successor. It was an enjoyable conversation, but I felt that there was something he wanted to say to me, a reason he had for holding me. There was.

"You are involved in quite an event, Harrison," he said.

"You are aware, then? I wasn't sure," I replied.

He laughed. "How could one not be?"

There was a long silence. Neither of us knew whether to proceed or to withdraw from the topic.

"The library is lovely," I said finally. "When I graduated, it wasn't quite finished."

"Yes, it's a marvelous building. One thing about Gerald Bradley: once committed, he went all the way. There were no cut corners. If his name was going to be carved into the granite over the front door, it was going to be beautiful and built to last. It is considered the greatest accomplishment of my twenty-seven years here as headmaster. I was the envy of every headmaster of every boys' school in New England when it was built. Too bad about those two windows, isn't it? It's the one architectural flaw. Poor Mr. Kahn, the architect. Dead now. How he hated giving in on that." He lowered his voice. "It was Maureen Bradley who insisted."

"I remember. I was there that day. I heard the exchange. It was a foretelling of her life, in a curious way," I said.

"Her son is here. Gregory," said Dr. Shugrue. He beckoned me to lean forward to him and whispered, "A terribly spoiled boy."

I smiled.

"Have you remained Catholic, Harrison?" he asked.

"No."

"I guessed as much. So you haven't confessed your complicity?"

"Only to the law. Not to a priest."

"I admire what you have done, Harrison," he said. "Coming forward as you have."

"You do?" I replied, surprised. "So few seem to. *Betrayer* is the word I keep hearing."

"Oh, but I know you are telling the truth," he said.

"Tell me why," I said.

"Do you remember when Constant was expelled over those pornographic magazines?"

"I certainly do."

"Cardinal Sullivan was sent to see me by Gerald about Constant's reinstatement."

"Yes, I remember."

"A library was offered."

"Yes."

"I have to confess to you that I was bewitched by all that Bradley money. I knew that the credit would come to me for the building, that the public appearance would be that I was a brilliant fund-raiser. Still, I hesitated. It had nothing to do with the dirty magazines. Certainly I've coped with far worse than that over the years. Fruity Suarez, for instance. But that's another story. What I knew was that Constant Bradley, for all his charm and beauty, was a lightweight, a snob, and, worst of all, a lout.''

I was fascinated. I have learned over the years of interviewing people never to interject, or exclaim, or agree or disagree when a person begins to talk in earnest about a private matter, lest he think twice about his revelation and reroute his conversation. I am a person to whom information comes. People tell me things. They always have. Fatty Malloy, the most unlikely source, kept me abreast of the goings-on in the Bradley house once the family closed the house in Southampton, decided not to open the house in California, and moved back to Scarborough Hill. Dr. Shugrue continued.

"There was a maid here in those days. You would have no reason to remember her. She did housework for Mrs. Shugrue in the headmaster's house. She was a local girl from the village. Teresa Miller. Her father worked in the piano factory in Deep River. There was an incident." He looked at me. "You didn't know this?"

"No."

"I wondered. Your great friend Constant never told you?"

"No."

"He tried to seduce her, you see. Apparently, she was not unwilling. But, uh, how shall I put it? He failed. He could not perform. He became enraged, as if his failure were her fault. He struck her. He would have hit her more, but she screamed, and he ran. He had a totally different version of the story, of course, but I believed her. That was why I was so unreasonable about the pornographic pictures.''

We looked at each other.

"No one ever said this world was a fair place, Harrison. Even my wife, who was captivated by Constant's pretty face, said the girl had to go, not Constant. When that poor Utley child was killed so brutally a year later, and you and Constant came back from the Easter holiday, after attending her funeral, I stared at him, and stared and stared. He could not meet my eye. I saw the color rising in his face. I was tormented by what to do. A Captain Riordan from Scarborough Hill came here to ask about Constant, and about you, too, by the way. Character things. He knew that Constant had been expelled, and wanted to know the reason why.'' He stopped talking for a minute. He turned his face

306

away from me. "By that time, ground had been broken for this new library. The foundation was laid. The lovely red bricks, truckloads of them, arrived from Vermont on the very day of Captain Riordan's visit. I said, uh, nothing about Teresa Miller."

He rose from the green leather chair. He folded the *New York Times* neatly and replaced it on the library table, on top of the previous day's edition. He looked very old.

"I think Mrs. Shugrue will be getting worried about me. We usually have a glass of sherry about this time. Or a cocktail. Would you care to join us, Harrison?"

"I think not, Dr. Shugrue. I'm driving back to the city."

"Yes, I understand. I've never told that story before. I'm glad I did. Perhaps you should tell it to your prosecutor. Good-bye, Harrison."

"Good-bye, sir." We shook hands. "Please give my warmest regards to Mrs. Shugrue."

"I will. I will. She has always remembered the night you spent in the guestroom of our house. I would like to repeat that I admire you."

"Did you tell all that to Cardinal on the day Gerald sent him to see you?" I asked.

He paused. "Would you mind terribly if I didn't answer that?"

"What happened to Teresa Miller?" I asked.

"I don't know," he replied softly.

I walked to the door with him and opened it for him. We both walked out. It had grown cold, but neither of us remarked on the weather.

"Do they despise you?" he asked.

"Of course."

"Yes, I imagined as much. Are you frightened of them?"

For what seemed a long time, I didn't answer. Then I said simply, "Yes."

17

FROM THE
New York Times, **October 29, 1991:**

The Countess de Trafford, the former Mary Pat Bradley, daughter of the multimillionaire Gerald Bradley,
has arrived in New York from her home in Paris to
attend the trial of her brother, onetime Connecticut
gubernatorial candidate Constant Bradley, who is accused of murdering Winifred Utley in 1973. The countess was met by her sisters Maureen Bradley Tierney
and Kitt Bradley Chadwick.

"The whole thing is too absurd, too utterly absurd,"
said the countess, in a brief statement to reporters,
after her plane landed at Kennedy Airport this afternoon. "It is a travesty that such a trial could take
place. My brother is innocent, totally innocent. This
man who has accused him was once in love with him."

The sisters proceeded immediately in a family limousine to Scarborough Hill, Connecticut, the home of
the Bradley family. The trial will begin on Monday in
Stamford.

During the four weeks of the trial, the Bradley sisters and sisters-in-
law came to be known in the press as the Bradley Ladies. Arriving
each day in a serviceable car, all wearing dark glasses, they gave an
unprecedented display of solidarity, waving at the reporters, smiling at
the photographers, nodding in a friendly manner. Their attitude be-
spoke confidence in Constant's innocence. "That's Charlotte, Constant's wife," spectators would say as she raced past. "Isn't she
pretty?" Or, "That's the Countess from Paris. Mary Pat. Do you think

that's a Chanel suit she's wearing?'' Or, "Which one is that? Is that Kitt, or is that Maureen? I get those two mixed up.'' "Have you noticed, Maureen and the Countess are always guiding Kitt, one on each side of her? Is there something wrong with her? Kitt's not the crazy one, is she?''

Any one of the Bradley Ladies, except Kitt, was capable of stepping up in front of the bank of microphones and addressing the large crowd that waited outside the courthouse to stare at the famous family as they gracefully alighted from their car. Actually, it was a rental car that the Bradley Ladies were driven in. Maureen thought it looked better than for them to have one of their own more fashionable cars. "No limousines and no chauffeurs,'' she said, laying down the law. "It won't look right. It will be misinterpreted. People don't like it if you look too rich.''

Maureen had finally found the role she always craved. She became the organizer. She made the rules. "No mink coats, no matter how cold it gets,'' she said another time. Each night, with lists in hand, she designated which of the family would go to the courtroom for the next session, who would drive in which car, and who would sit where. "It's important for the jury to see that we are a family,'' she said over and over. It was she who gave them answers to say in the event that any of them was asked a question by a member of the media. It was she who located the priests who sat with the family in the courtroom each day. "Tomorrow it's Father Dennehy from St. Justin's in the morning session and Father Collins from Our Lady of Sorrows in the afternoon. Make sure they sit where the jury can see them,'' she said. "Behind Constant and to the right. That way they can see Father over Constant's shoulder.''

Behind the scenes, there was occasional disharmony. Sis Malloy told Fatty of family scenes, and Fatty passed them on to me. Kitt had developed a disturbing habit of disappearing from the courthouse, often to a bar on the corner, O'Malley's, so Maureen and Mary Pat kept her between them at all times, never letting her out of their sight. In private, Charlotte had ceased speaking to Constant or to any member of her husband's family, except Kitt, although she complied with her daily instructions as outlined each evening by Maureen and Jerry in a strategy session in the dining room of the house in Scarborough Hill.

Except for Constant, it was Charlotte that the crowds wanted to see most. She was the most frequently cheered and the most often photographed. Her popularity irritated Maureen. "Look this way, look this way, Charlotte," the photographers yelled at her, and she obliged. She no longer made a secret of her dislike of Maureen. She found her bossy and pushy and couldn't stand the way she always took the front seat of the car and the aisle seat of the courtroom, as if the best seats were hers by rights.

One morning, as they were preparing to leave the house to go to the courthouse, Charlotte grabbed the back of Maureen's Adolfo suit as she was getting into the front seat of the rented car and pulled her back.

"I am Constant's wife, Maureen, and you are only one of his sisters," she said, in no uncertain terms. "Or, at least, I am Constant's wife until this trial is over, when I intend to be on the first plane to Puerto Rico or the Dominican Republic or wherever it is these days that they have the quickest of quickie divorces. Until then, I am Mrs. Constant Bradley. It is my husband who is on trial for murder. I go first. I sit in the front seat of the car. I sit in the aisle seat in the courtroom. Do you understand?"

"Oh, a thousand pardons, madam," said Maureen sarcastically, at the same time bowing elaborately and abjectly as if to a queen.

"Besides, they're more interested in seeing me than you, Maureen. I'm prettier. Those litters of children of yours have taken their toll."

That day Maureen, still bristling from her setback with Charlotte, walked up to the bank of microphones the reporters set up to interview Valerie Sabbath and Bert Lupino each morning and evening, or Constant if he could be persuaded to speak, or any member of the family who would be willing to talk, and began to give a speech.

"Good morning," she said. "I'm Maureen Bradley Tierney. My whole family is here to support my brother Constant—*our* brother Constant, I should say. Oh, are the microphones on? And the television cameras? I said we are all here to support Constant, who has served so ably in the House of Representatives in Washington and who, until this, uh, this tragic circumstance, intended to run for the governorship of the state. And will again, when this is over, you can mark my words on that. My brother Senator Sandro Bradley is here from Washington, as is my brother Dr. Desmond Bradley, the chief of staff at St. Monica's Hospital. And my brother Gerald Junior, whom we in the family call Jerry. And my sisters Kitt and Mary Pat, the Countess de Trafford, who has come all the way from her home and family in Paris to be with her brother. This trial is a sad spectacle, as I'm sure you all know, the revenge of a jealous man who never had a family of his own, who took, took, took from our family—if you only *knew* what my mother has done for him—and then paid us back with this ugly smear.''

Valerie Sabbath, entering the courthouse with her staff and Jerry Bradley, stopped for a moment to listen to Maureen. ''Will you get your sister the fuck out of there, Jerry,'' she said, and walked on.

Maureen looked up and saw Jerry signaling to her. ''What? What, Jerry? Oh, I think my brother is giving me the speed-up signal,'' said Maureen. ''Thank you so much for letting me speak. I just want to say that we are a very close family, and I wish all of you the gift of loyal family relationships.''

On the way into the courtroom, Maureen swanned past Charlotte and smiled sweetly. ''Where's Father Lynch? Has anyone seen Father Lynch? He was going to sit with us today.''

Outside the courthouse, leaning against the family station wagon in a leisurely fashion, Constant appeared to be waiting for someone. His new Testarossa was nowhere in sight. It remained on blocks in the twelve-car garage of the house in Southampton, locked away from public view as too expensive a toy to be understood by the masses. Women crowded around to look at him or snap his picture with their Instamatic cameras. He was fully aware that he was attracting everyone's attention, that his presence was enough to astonish some people, mostly young women, but he was as much at ease as if he were leaning against the mantelpiece in his parents' drawing room.

''Are you worried, Constant?'' asked one young woman.

''Not for a minute. There is not a shred of truth to the absurd story, not a shred,'' said Constant. He smiled at the assembled group, dazzling them, and enjoying their bedazzlement. Each day, the crowd of women who cheered him when he entered and left the courtroom grew larger.

''Hello, Miss Maureen,'' said the woman standing in the corridor outside the courtroom.

''Hellohowareyou,'' replied Maureen, walking on without stopping. ''Who was that woman who just spoke to me? She looked familiar.''

''That was the first Colleen, years ago. Remember her? Ma could

311

never get her to serve the right way. She'd pass from the right, instead of the left. She couldn't get it straight no matter how many times Ma went over it with her," said Mary Pat.

"What's she doing here? Sightseeing?" asked Maureen.

"Jerry said she's an unfriendly witness. Jerry said she claims she heard Constant and Harrison talking outside her window that night. After all Ma did for her," said Mary Pat.

"I always say, don't get too friendly with the help. It has a way of backfiring. Haven't you noticed that? Be polite to them. That's what I tell my children. Always be polite, but don't go any further," said Maureen. "They take advantage every time."

On the first day of the trial, Judge Edda Consalvi disallowed, without comment, the testimony of Louise Somerset Belmont and Maud Firth. There were gasps in the courtroom. In the newsroom, where the press was assembled, there were moans. Reporters used to covering trials understood what that meant. If the prosecution could not establish a pattern of behavior on the defendant's part, it remained only for the defense to establish a reasonable doubt to guarantee an acquittal.

Valerie Sabbath was happy with the ruling. She preened at the defense table and patted Constant's hand affectionately. During the morning recess, she took Senator Sandro Bradley up to the bench to introduce him to Judge Consalvi. The judge, normally taciturn, rose in her seat and leaned forward to shake hands with the handsome senator. "What a great pleasure, Senator," she said.

"Please state your name," said the bailiff.

"Bridey Gafferty."

"Raise your right hand."

"It's raised. It's as far up as it goes. I've got a little rheumatism."

"Do you swear to tell the truth, the whole truth, and nothing but the truth?"

"I do."

"Is it Miss or Mrs. Gafferty?" asked Bert Lupino.

"Miss."

"Would you mind stating your age?"

"I would, yes," said Bridey.

There was laughter in the courtroom.

"All right. Will you tell us how you are employed, Miss Gafferty."

"I am the cook for Mr. and Mrs. Gerald Bradley."

"At which of the Bradley residences do you work?"

"I travel with the Bradleys. I work at the house in Scarborough Hill, the house in Southampton, the house in Beverly Hills, and sometimes, not always, at the apartment in New York."

"Will you tell us how long you have been employed in the Bradley home, Miss Gafferty?"

"Oh, bless me, let me see. How long has it been now? I came to the house right after Mr. Constant over there was born. He was still a wee one in his diapers."

"In years, Miss Gafferty," said Bert Lupino.

"Oh, thirty-five, thirty-six, something like that. It's not a thing I go addin' up every day, sir."

"You were employed at the Bradley mansion, then, on the night of April thirtieth, 1973?"

"I suppose I was, yes, sir. I don't remember the dates like that, but I suppose I was."

"On this floor plan of the Bradley mansion, will you point out to us where your room is?"

"Yes, sir. There's the kitchen, here. To the left of the kitchen, there's the maids' dinin' room, with the TV and the comfortable chairs for sittin' in the afternoons after the luncheon dishes are done and before it's time to start settin' up for the evening meal. Through the door there is the cook's room, sir, my room, as it's been for thirty years or more."

"When you are in your room, are you able to hear conversations in the maids' dining room?"

"Oh, yes. If the girls get too loud, I'm out there in a jiffy to shut them up. You never know if Missus is sleeping upstairs or somethin'. We don't want to disturb Missus, you know."

"When you are in your room, are you able to hear conversations in the kitchen?"

"Yes, sir."

"On the night of April thirtieth, 1973, or, to be more specific, in the early morning of May first, 1973, did you hear a conversation between two men in the kitchen?"

"I recall no such thing, no."

"A conversation between Mr. Constant, as you call Constant Bradley, and Mr. Harrison Burns, who was a guest of Constant Bradley at
the time?"

"No, I don't remember nothin' like that. Nothin' particular. The
kids in the house sometimes came down to the kitchen in the wee
hours to raid the fridge, after their parties, and leave a terrible mess
for me to clean up in the morning. Eggs out, half bottles of milk out—
like that."

"Did you not call out to ask who was there?"

"I don't recall, sir. I don't think so."

"At two in the morning? The boys were undressing. The boys were
putting their bloody clothes and shoes in a garbage bag from under the
sink."

"Objection," called out Valerie Sabbath. "Conjecture. Leading the
witness."

"Sustained."

"You did not call out to the boys to ask who was there?"

"No, I don't recall no such thing. Harrison was such a lovely boy in
those days. What a nice friendship those two boys had. He was a
scholarship boy, and they was all so good to him in the family."

"You did not say, 'Who's out there?' "

"I doubt it. I fall asleep once my head hits the pillow, and I don't
wake until six, when I get up to take Missus to early-morning Mass at
Saint Martin of Tours."

"No further questions," said Bert Lupino.

"I have no questions, Your Honor," said Valerie Sabbath.

"You may step down, Miss Gafferty," said Judge Consalvi.

"Thank you, Your Honor."

On that day Honour and Thelma and Count Stamirsky, Grace's friends
from Southampton, appeared in the courtroom.

"Wasn't Bridey sweet?" said Honour.

"*Ador*able," said Thelma. "And such a dream of a cook. I'll never
forget her fig mousse."

Smartly dressed, they looked on their day in court as an adventure,
something they would pass on to their friends at a dinner party in New
York later that evening. They waved at family members from their
spectator seats on the side, gave seemingly rapt attention to the witnesses of the day, and entertained the sisters with gossip during the

breaks. "She's such a hooker," said Thelma, talking about an un-named person known to them all. "All that he has to do is dangle another diamond bracelet in front of her and she looks the other way about the little boys." Shrieks of laughter could be heard coming from the room where the family sat. When the television news reporters descended on these new faces, they were happy to state their opinions on the case.

"The whole trial is simply *too* ridiculous," said Honour.

"It's a travesty of justice," said Thelma. When asked to identify themselves, Thelma quickly said, "Just say we're old family friends who've come here for the day to buck up the spirits of the Bradleys."

"Mr. Wadsworth, you were dancing with Winifred Utley at the junior club dance that night?"

"Yes."

"What was the age group of the dance?"

"Fourteen to sixteen."

"Was Mr. Constant Bradley at the dance?"

"No."

"Why?"

"I don't know why, but he was past the age of those at the dance."

"Yet he came in to the dance, although he was not at the dance?"

"Yes."

"Did Mr. Bradley dance with Winifred Utley?"

"Yes."

"Did Mr. Bradley say anything to Miss Utley that you remember from that evening?"

"Yes."

"Will you tell the court what Mr. Bradley said?"

"Objection," said Valerie Sabbath. "Hearsay."

"It is not hearsay, Your Honor. It was said in the presence of the witness," retorted Bert Lupino.

"Objection overruled," said Judge Consalvi.

"Will you tell the court what Mr. Bradley said?" Lupino repeated.

"He said, 'Do you mind dancing with a man with an erection?' "

"I have no further questions. Thank you, Mr. Wadsworth."

*　　*　　*

I passed Bridey in the garage under the courthouse. She was driving out in her old Pontiac, the one she used for grocery shopping. She lowered the window and looked both ways before speaking to me.

"I'm sorry, Harrison. You had to understand. I did what I had to do. God spare me."

"Of course, I understand, Bridey."

"I can't talk to you, you know."

"I know."

"I mean, ever."

"I know. It's okay, Bridey."

"I'll never forget that tip you gave me."

"I wish you hadn't given it back."

"Good-bye, now."

"Your car's getting old, Bridey. They ought to buy you a new one."

"It's good enough for the likes of me."

Being a witness, I was not allowed in the courtroom except when I was testifying, but I was in the courthouse each day, available for consultation, hidden away in the prosecutor's office, a floor below the courtroom, where a television monitor had been set up for me to watch the proceedings. Each morning I drove my car to an indoor parking lot two blocks from the courthouse. There I was met by an assistant from the prosecutor's office, who drove me to the underground garage beneath the courthouse in order to escape the phalanx of photographers, reporters, and media personalities who congregated around the public entrances to the building, always ready to pounce on anyone connected with the proceedings.

There are tedious days in every trial, even one that had caught the imagination of the country the way this one had. The testimony of expert witnesses, for instance, can be deadly dull, time-consuming, and confusing to the jury. The Bradley defense team had hired a dozen or more. One afternoon, during the testimony of an expert who had analyzed the dirt and wood particles on the back of Winifred Utley's pink party dress, I decided to leave early and go to visit Claire and my sons. At the end of the corridor, I pushed the Down button for the elevator. When the door opened, I walked inside. The door closed behind me before I noticed there was another person standing in the corner of the elevator. It was Kitt Bradley. For an instant we looked at each other. The elevator started down. Neither of us spoke. She went immediately to the buttons to stop the elevator so that she could get off. She pushed buttons wildly, one after the other. The elevator came to an abrupt stop, lurching a little, but the door did not open. Looking out the little window, I saw that we were between floors. I pushed on the buttons, but nothing happened. For what seemed a minute, we stood there without speaking or looking at each other.

"It's stuck," I said.

"Great," she replied.

Again we were silent.

"There must be an emergency button, isn't there?" she asked. "This cannot be an insoluble problem."

"I pushed it," I replied.

Again we stood in silence without speaking.

"Do you remember me? We used to sleep together," she said finally.

"Yes, I remember," I replied.

She opened a bag that hung from her shoulder on a gold chain and took out a package of cigarettes and a lighter. She put the cigarette in her mouth with one hand and lit the lighter with the other, but she had difficulty connecting the flame with the cigarette.

"Cheap lighter," she said.

"Or shaking hand," I replied, taking the lighter from her hand and holding it for her.

"Don't you start on me," she said, inhaling deeply.

"No, I won't. I didn't know you smoked."

"Something new," she said.

I pointed to a sign. "It says, 'No smoking in the elevator.' "

"What are you going to do? Turn me in? Like you turned—" She stopped. "That is a sentence I am not going to complete."

"Thank you."

"Oh, what have you done, Harrison," she cried out. "How could you do such a thing? How could you bring such a charge against a member of my family? Against your friend?"

"In my place, would you have done it differently?"

She didn't reply to my question. "I couldn't stand it in that court-room another minute," she said. She pushed the elevator button again. Nothing happened. She opened her bag and took out a pair of glasses and put them on to scrutinize the buttons. I noticed that one of the lenses was cracked.

"Isn't it confusing for you to see life out of a shattered lens?" I asked.

317

"I'm used to it."

"I remember the day you stepped on it. It was almost a year ago."

"So what?" she replied.

"How are you?" I asked.

"I'm a mess. Doesn't it show? My sisters say it does. My sisters have become my keepers. Haven't you noticed them? One is always on each side of me, trying to keep me from doing what I have just done, escaping from them." She took another deep drag on her cigarette.

"Where were you headed?" I asked.

"I was going out for a drink, if you want to know the truth. I've found an Irish bar called O'Malley's on the corner. Maureen thinks I'm in the ladies' room now."

"Wait until they find out where you are and who you've been stuck with," I said.

"I've been thinking that." She laughed. "I miss you," she said in a voice so low I could hardly hear it.

"I heard you hated me," I said.

"I do hate you, but I miss you, too. It wasn't long enough with us. It hadn't worn out yet."

"No, it hadn't."

"Do you think about it?" she asked.

"Yes."

"I hope you suffer a little."

"I do."

"Good," she said. "You have become, uh . . ."

"What?"

"More attractive, I suppose. Almost good-looking. I never thought of you as good-looking. You were too intense."

"What you see is relief. I've let go of a burden I've been carrying for almost twenty years. I'm not like your brother. I couldn't forget it. At least I couldn't forget it once I saw him again."

"What if he's acquitted?"

"I will still know that I have done the right thing. That's all that matters to me."

There was silence again. "Have you read the letters in the *Times*?" she asked.

"Yes."

"Ninety percent of them are pro-Constant. Well, eighty percent. They believe him. Doesn't that mean anything to you?"

"Yes, it does. It means he fooled them, that's all. But you know the truth. And so does your whole family. He killed Winifred."

"No, don't start. Please." She waved her hands in front of her face, not wanting to hear any more. "I can't. I can't hear it."

"No, I won't."

"I don't want to be in the courtroom on the day you take the stand and tell what happened," she said. "I couldn't even read through your deposition."

"Look, we're stuck in this elevator. It might be for a long time. We should talk about something else. How's your mother?"

"She's tuned out of the whole thing. She just talks about priests and nuns and dresses all the time. Mary Pat talks in French, like she's forgotten English. I stay loaded. Only Maureen seems to be thriving."

"There must be other things going on in the world than this trial," I said.

"Yes, yes, there must be. Esme Bland died. Did you know that?"

I was surprised. "No, I hadn't heard."

"Cancer."

"I knew she had cancer."

"Poor Agnes. She is bereft, inconsolable."

"Agnes is bereft over Esme?"

"Oh, yes. She says Esme was the best friend she ever had. They needed each other, you see. She left Agnes her wigs, those beautiful wigs Kenneth made her. Agnes wears them all the time now. She's stopped being Mother Vincent."

"Oh, Kitt," I said.

"Sometimes I think Agnes has it made," said Kitt. "Being ten, staying ten forever. It sounds like bliss to me."

She looked so unbearably sad. Forgetting my resolve, I started to move toward her, but the elevator jerked. We went back up. The door opened. Maureen and Mary Pat stood there along with several maintenance men, a security guard, and a crowd of people waiting for the elevator.

"Are you all right?" asked Maureen. She looked at me with fury in her eyes.

"The elevator got stuck," Kitt replied.

"You didn't speak to him, did you?" asked Maureen.

"No, I didn't," said Kitt, in a deep, weary voice. "Not a word."

319

*　　*　　*

Despite a passionate plea by Valerie Sabbath that Grace Bradley be allowed to attend the trial each day, her request was turned down by Judge Edda Consalvi. Like me, Grace was a witness, and therefore not allowed to sit in the courtroom until her time came to be on the stand. Valerie made no secret of her displeasure with the judge's ruling. Grace's good works for the poor of the city were well known, and Valerie felt that her daily dignified presence would offset the seamier aspects of the case in the eyes of the jury and the public. "More than any person I know, Grace Bradley understands the responsibilities of the rich for those less fortunate than themselves," she said on television in an irate voice after the judge's ruling. "It is ridiculous that this woman cannot be there with her son."

Grace, according to Fatty Malloy, who got all his information from Sis, could not bear Valerie Sabbath, despite that woman's kind depiction of her. "She's the most vulgar woman I've ever met," said Grace, shuddering. "I've never heard anyone use language like that. I had to cover my ears." The judge's ruling was a great relief to Grace. Unlike her daughters and sons, she did not want to attend the trial. She rarely watched it on television. She didn't read the newspaper accounts. She absented herself from the nightly strategy sessions held in the dining room after dinner. On evenings when lawyers were present, she took to having dinner on a tray in her room, often with Kitt. She was never without her rosary.

"What do you pray for, Ma?" asked Kitt.

"Oh, just the souls in purgatory, darling," Grace replied.

"I always think of purgatory as being like jail, with all the prisoners waiting for parole," said Kitt.

"Oh, no, no, darling. Mother Vincent would be ashamed of you if she heard you say that. Purgatory is a place for contemplation of what is ahead, for atonement for what is behind, for purification, for expiation. It is a preparation for the sight of God."

Suddenly, without warning, Grace started to cry.

"Ma, what is the matter?" said Kitt, concerned. "I've never seen you cry, ever. What happened?"

"I don't want to take the stand. I don't want to take the stand. I don't want to take the stand." Her sobbing became out of control.

"But Ma, they're only going to ask you about Mrs. Utley's call that night. What time she called, that sort of thing. And they're going to

ask you if Constant was in bed when you went to look for him. That's
all. There's nothing else they can ask you."

"I know," said Grace, blowing her nose.

"Constant was there in bed, wasn't he, Ma? You've always said he
was. He was there, wasn't he? Tell me, Ma, wasn't he?"

"On the night in question, Mrs. Bradley, did you receive a telephone
call?" asked Bert Lupino.

"Yes," replied Grace. She spoke in a whisper, barely audible in the
courtroom.

"You will have to speak up, Mrs. Bradley," said Judge Consalvi.
"It is important that both the jury and the court stenographer hear
your answers."

"Yes," replied Grace, speaking in a louder voice. She looked
straight ahead, not at the jury or at the lawyer questioning her.

"Can you remember approximately the time of that call, Mrs. Bradley?" asked Bert Lupino.

"It has been a great many years, you know. I believe it was two in
the morning, or thereabout."

"Will you tell the court who called you at two in the morning, Mrs.
Bradley."

"Mrs. Utley."

"Mrs. Utley, the mother of Winifred Utley?"

"I know of no other Mrs. Utley," said Grace.

"Will you tell the court the nature of Mrs. Utley's call, Mrs. Bradley."

"Mrs. Utley was looking for her daughter, Winifred. She had been
to a dance at the club and had not returned home."

"Was there anything else?"

"She said that my son Constant had danced with Winifred at the
club. She wanted to know if Winifred was at my house. I believe I told
her she was not. She asked me if I would check to see if my son was
at home."

"Did you do that?"

"Yes. I went into Constant's room."

"Who was in the room, Mrs. Bradley?"

"Harrison Burns was in one bed. Constant was in the other. They
were both asleep."

"You are sure that your son Constant was in the other bed?"

321

"Oh, yes. I remember it distinctly. It is not the sort of thing a mother forgets."

That night Grace Bradley did not come down to dinner. Nor did she receive any of her children who came to her room to congratulate her on her appearance on the stand. At eight o'clock the doorbell rang at the house in Scarborough Hill. Bridey, knowing in advance who it was, answered the door and escorted the young priest up the stairway to Grace's room.

"Who was that?" asked Jerry in the dining room.

"Father Ryan," replied Maureen. "He's Ma's new favorite priest."

Valerie Sabbath's cross-examination of me was withering, mocking, ruthless. She skirted perilously close to the allegation, propagated by Mary Pat, the Countess de Trafford, that I had once been in love with Constant, but the prosecutor called out, "May we approach the bench, Your Honor?" In a whispered session at the bench, out of earshot of jury and spectators, but recorded by the court reporter, Bert Lupino let it be known that if Valerie Sabbath proceeded with that line of questioning he would introduce into evidence my love affair with Kitt Chadwick, beginning at the Bee and Thistle Inn in Cranston, Maine, and ending in Grace Bradley's drawing room at the house in Southampton, when Kitt was discovered on her knees in front of me by Maureen. Bert said he would call Maureen to the stand for verification.

Valerie Sabbath asked for a recess. As it was late in the afternoon, Judge Consalvi decided to break for the day. The participants in Constant's defense then repaired to the Bradley house in Scarborough Hill to consult on the matter.

Jerry was called. Maureen was called. Des was called. Sandro was consulted by telephone in Washington.

"If this comes out in the newspapers, that Kitt had an affair with Harrison, it will kill Ma," said Maureen. "Kitt's still her baby, you know. And Ma's been acting very strange as it is."

"Besides, it'll blow the whole family image we've managed to build up here," said Jerry. "Nobody ever told me Kitt was giving him a blowjob right in Ma's house, for Christ's sake."

"How can we go into that with Father Bill sitting in the courtroom?" said Maureen. "He's come all the way from Southampton to give support to Ma."

The matter was dropped.

"Mr. Burns, were you a classmate of Constant Bradley at the Milford School?" asked Valerie Sabbath.

"Yes."

"Were not your parents murdered in your fifth-form year at Milford?"

"Yes."

"And they left no money. Is that correct?"

"They left very little money."

"Did not Constant Bradley's parents take you in?"

"They were kind to me."

"Were you not a frequent visitor at the Bradley estate in Scarborough Hill?"

"I was."

"Were you not given a room in the Bradley mansion that you used so often it became known as Harrison's room?"

"If that is so, I was unaware of it. I remember it always being called Agnes's room."

"Did Mr. Bradley pay your tuition for your sixth-form, or senior, year at Milford?"

"As part of a business deal, he did. I wrote a paper for Constant that helped get him reinstated—"

"Just answer the question yes or no. Did Mr. Bradley pay your tuition for your senior year at Milford?"

"Yes."

"Mr. Burns, after graduation from Milford, did you not enjoy a year of travel on the Continent, flying in business class and staying at first-rate hotels?"

"I studied in Europe for a year, yes," I said.

"You accepted this yearlong holiday?"

"I do not think of it as a holiday."

"This was a gift, was it not, from Mr. Gerald Bradley to you, an orphan with no money?"

"It was not a gift. It was a payment for a service rendered."

"You allowed yourself to be paid for, did you not?"

"I remained silent about what I knew."

"You became used to taking money from Gerald Bradley, didn't you? It is my understanding that your tuition at Brown University was paid by a trust set up for you by the Bradley family. Is that correct?"

"Yes."

"There was, was there not, a fifty-thousand-dollar reward for information leading to an arrest? A fifty-thousand-dollar reward offered by Mrs. Luanne Utley, the mother of Winifred Utley, whom you visited on the night of May ninth, 1990?"

"I think if you examine the facts, you will see that I did not take the reward money. It was donated to the National Victims Center, but not through me, through Mrs. Utley. I did not wish to come near that money," I said.

The reporters in the pressroom had taken a dislike to Bert Lupino. They found him dull in the courtroom. They preferred the theatrics of Valerie Sabbath. She always gave them something to write about.

"Lupino may not be the worst prosecutor I have ever seen in a courtroom, but he's close," said Gus Bailey, the troublesome reporter from the Scarborough Hill *Times,* who had followed the case from the day after the murder in 1973 and was once thought to have been silenced by Gerald Bradley. "I don't care if he was named prosecutor of the year last year. Valerie's making Harrison look like a chump, and Lupino's not coming to his aid."

"He has his list of questions to ask each witness written on a lined yellow pad. He never veers from it. While the witness is answering him, his attention is focused on his pad for his next question. There is no opportunity for spontaneity," said the reporter from the *Miami Herald.*

"Lupino has no sense of drama. He doesn't know how to build a story," said the reporter from the *Detroit Free Press.*

"If I were a believer in conspiracies, I would think that he is in the employ of the Bradleys," said the reporter from the *Hartford Courant.*

"If I were writing this as a novel, that's the way I would write it," said Gus Bailey. "But it's not a novel, and Bert Lupino is not in the employ of the Bradleys. I just think he's out of his element. I think he's intimidated by Valerie Sabbath. Did you hear her call him Shorty in the corridor this morning? I don't think you can put a person three years out of law school up against a million-dollar defense attorney and expect him to win. I never understand why district attorneys make the same mistake over and over again.''

"Tell Miss Sabbath to say the Bradley *house*, not the Bradley mansion, Jerry, when she talks about the night of the murder," said Maureen. " 'Mansion' has a bad sound to it. It makes us sound too rich. The jury won't like that. And tell her not to say 'the Bradley estate.' ''

"I am trying very hard, Jerry, to restrain myself and not say 'Fuck off' to your sister. Will you kindly tell her not to tell me what words not to use. When you hire me, for my measly million-dollar fee, you do things my way. If I prefer to say 'estate' and 'mansion,' *estate* and *mansion* are the words I am going to say. I am the one who has to talk straight talk to the jury, not your sister. The jury would refer to your house as a mansion, and your place in Scarborough Hill as an estate, and I am more interested in their reaction to my words than your sister's reaction to my words. Do we understand each other?"

"Yes, yes, of course, you're right, Valerie," said Jerry. "It's just that Maureen gets a little—"

"Oh, you don't have to tell me how Maureen gets," said Valerie.

"Well, excuse *me,*" said Maureen, when Jerry repeated what Valerie Sabbath had said.

In cases such as this, there is often the man off the highway to blame it all on. The vagrant, the transient, the drifter. Do you remember the prowler on the roof of the Grenvilles' house on the night Ann Grenville shot and killed her husband? They are conveniences of the rich. They are expendable people. Blame them. They are no one.

"Did you see Constant Bradley raise the bat and strike Winifred Utley?" asked Valerie Sabbath.

"No," I replied.

"You did not see him strike Miss Utley?"

"No. I did not realize immediately what had happened. I thought there had been an accident of some sort. I thought she might have fainted or had a heart attack or something. It was not until I touched her and felt the blood that I realized she had been struck."

"You did not see him strike Miss Utley?"

"No."

"It would have been possible, then, for a vagrant off Interstate Ninety-five to have killed Miss Utley, would it not?"

"I do not believe so."

"It would have been possible for Constant Bradley to have found Winifred Utley already struck down when he went to the path at the edge of the Bradley estate for his rendezvous with Miss Utley, would it not?"

"I do not believe so."

"I would like to read to you from your statements made to Captain Riordan at the time you were questioned at police headquarters in Scarborough Hill on May first, 1973." Valerie Sabbath turned around to the defense table and picked up a copy of a police report. She put on her glasses and placed the pages on a podium in front of her. "Captain Riordan: At any time after you went to bed did you get up from your bed and go outside? Harrison Burns: No, sir. Captain Riordan: Did Constant Bradley ever leave the room you were sharing that night to go outside after you returned from The Country Club? Harrison Burns: No, sir."

Valerie Sabbath removed her glasses and turned back to me on the stand. "Now you are telling the court, Mr. Burns, that you were awakened at two o'clock in the morning by Mrs. Grace Bradley, the mother of Constant Bradley, who asked you to go downstairs and look for her son, and while downstairs you heard a tap on the window and were asked to go outside by Constant Bradley. Will you explain the discrepancy in your two versions of the story?"

"That is what I had been instructed to say by Gerald Bradley and his son Jerry. I was rehearsed in the afternoon," I said.

"And you are telling the court that it was in your nature to do anything someone else told you to do. Is that correct, Mr. Burns?"

"I was sedated with Valium at the time," I said.

"Ah, you were sedated with Valium at the time? Your story gets better and better, Mr. Burns," said Valerie.

"Dr. Desmond Bradley came to my room late that afternoon and gave me Valium to calm me down before the police arrived. Later he gave me another Valium before dinner, which was when the police arrived at the house.''

The headline in the *New York Post* the following day said HE'S A LIAR. Dr. Desmond Bradley, brother of former gubernatorial candidate Constant Bradley, emphatically denied having given Valium to Harrison Burns before he was interviewed by police in connection with the murder of Winifred Utley in 1973. "This man would do anything, say anything," said Dr. Bradley. "I am shocked by his statement."

On the Friday of that week, the two oldest of Maureen's children, Gregory and Sarah, seventeen and sixteen years old, were in the courtroom. Gregory had been excused from Milford to attend the trial, and Sarah had been excused from the Sacred Heart Convent. Maureen felt that it was important to show the next generation of Bradleys to the jury, the courtroom, the crowds outside, and the media. It was expected that it would be a day of technical experts, not of any real dramatic importance, and the better-known members of the family had decided to stay at home. However, the father-in-law of the medical examiner who had performed the autopsy on Winifred Utley had died the night before, and the medical examiner had therefore telephoned in his regrets for not being able to keep his scheduled appearance, as he had to leave immediately for Pittsburgh. The soil expert who had examined the dirt stains on the back of Winifred's pink party dress was also unexpectedly indisposed, having suffered an attack of food poisoning after dining the evening before on sushi at a Japanese restaurant. And so Constant Bradley was suddenly and unexpectedly called to the stand. There was great excitement in the courtroom and pressroom. Reporters raced to the telephones.

"Your Honor, I would like to call Constant Bradley as a witness, but I want to make sure the state cannot open the door on cross-examination and enter evidence that the court has ruled as inadmissible," said Valerie Sabbath. She was referring to the testimony of Maud Firth and Weegie Somerset.

"Granted," said Judge Consalvi.

Gregory Tierney was dissatisfied with his seat. He wanted to be in a better spot to watch his uncle on the stand.

327

"I know you're disappointed with your seat, but don't take it out on me," said Sarah to her brother.

"We should be there in those seats," said Gregory, pointing to two seats in the front row of the spectator section. In those seats sat a young man with a woman who might have been his mother.

"Ask them if they'll change with you," said Sarah.

Gregory stood and walked over to where the couple was seated. "I wonder if you'd mind trading seats with us," said Gregory to them. He spoke in an overly gracious manner, sure the couple would rise.

"Yes, we would mind," answered the young man.

Rebuffed, Gregory returned to his seat and glared at the couple. The couple paid no attention to him. Then Gregory rose, passed the couple, and went to the rear of the courtroom, where he complained to the bailiff that the couple had the seats he felt he should have. "Would you please ask them to move," said Gregory.

"Hey, fella, it's first come, first served in Judge Consalvi's courtroom. There's no reserved seats here. If they got there first, the seats are theirs."

"But we are members of the Bradley family," said Gregory.

"It don't matter who yuz are in Judge Consalvi's courtroom," said the bailiff.

Undaunted, Gregory approached the couple again. "My sister and I would like to sit here while Constant Bradley is on the stand," he said.

"I'm sorry, we're not moving," said the woman.

"You don't understand. We're family," said Gregory.

"No, you don't understand. I'm family, too," said the young man.

"He is my uncle," insisted Gregory.

"He's my uncle, too," said the young man.

"How is he your uncle?"

"My mother was a maid in your grandmother's house. She married your uncle Des. You might like to tell your family that Rosleen Shea Bradley is here with her son, Desi."

"We're always meeting at soft-drink machines," said Charlotte. "I still haven't figured out which way George Washington is supposed to face."

"I'll do it," I said. I put the bill in for her. The can of soda dropped out. I took it, opened it, and handed it to her.

"How's Gerald?" I asked.

"Just managing to keep his head below water," she said.

I laughed, and she joined in, but I could see that she was near to tears.

"I haven't laughed in a year," she said. She looked up and down the corridor. "Tell me something, Harrison. I have to know. Did he do it?"

"Yes."

"They all say you are making this up."

"Do you think I am, Charlotte?"

She shook her head slowly. "Imagine if they find him guilty," she said. "Imagine if they put him in prison. I haven't a clue how I'll play that scene."

"Do you still love him?" I asked.

"I am attracted to him from time to time, but I don't love him. I haven't loved him for a long time. He is incapable of deep affection for another person."

When Constant entered the courtroom, there was a gasp from the audience even though they had seen him each day sitting at the defense table. He was dressed in a gray flannel suit, a blue shirt, and a red tie. He walked elegantly and eagerly to the witness box, as if it were the moment he had been waiting for, rather than dreading.

"How are you feeling, Mr. Bradley?" asked Valerie Sabbath.

"I am a little nervous, but I am also looking forward to this moment on the stand. I have lived with this terrible accusation for over a year now, and I relish and cherish the opportunity to free my name so that I may return to the business of my life," said Constant.

"Were you drinking that night, Mr. Bradley?" she asked.

"I had taken a few drinks, yes," he answered. He turned and spoke directly to the jury. "Earlier in the day, the family had been talking about our brother Kev. He was killed in Vietnam. We were remembering the last time we had been together as a family, before Kev went off to fight for his country. He didn't have to go, you know. He hadn't been drafted. He volunteered."

The jury watched Constant, mesmerized.

"What sort of day had it been?"

"It was a family day, and we talked about our sister Agnes. Agnes is a retarded person. She has today the mind of a ten-year-old. She has been for years at an institution in Cranston, Maine. But we think about

329

Agnes and love her and talk of her often. It was a day for reminiscences about Kev and Agnes, our missing members.''

A Mrs. Perez in the front row of the jury box wiped a tear away from her eye with a Kleenex. Watching Constant on a television set in the prosecutor's office, I wondered why Bert Lupino did not raise an objection.

"Afterwards, when the family dispersed, I offered to take my sisters Mary Pat and Kitt to The Country Club for dinner. I wanted to shake off the depression of the conversation about Kev and Agnes.''

"Was there anyone else with you?''

"Yes, Harrison Burns. He was a frequent guest in our house at that time. My father paid his tuition at our school.''

"You went to the club with your sisters and Mr. Burns?''

"Yes. I was underage, and the waitress, Ursula, whom we have known at the club for years, quite rightly would not serve me a drink, so I went into the bar in the men's locker room and bribed the bartender, Corky, to give me a few drinks. It was wrong, yes, and it compromised Corky, who could have lost his job, but I wanted to shake off the depression of the afternoon and make a cheerful evening for my sisters, who were returning to the Sacred Heart Convent the next day.''

"Did you ask Winifred Utley to dance?''

"No. Winifred Utley asked me to dance. I was leaving the club with my sisters when she came up to me and asked me.''

"Is it true that you said to Miss Utley, 'Do you mind dancing with a man with an erection?' '' asked Valerie Sabbath.

"I did, yes. It was meant to be funny. It was, in fact, funny at the time, in a teenage way, but I realize how appalling it sounds now, all these years later, in view of what happened to Winifred. I cringe every time I hear the line repeated in this courtroom, but yes, I did say it.''

"Did you ask Winifred to go home with you?''

"Yes. But she said she had come with Billy Wadsworth and that she would go home with him.''

"To the best of your knowledge, did Billy Wadsworth take Winifred home?''

"I believe Mr. Wadsworth, Billy's father, drove them home. I don't think Billy had a driver's license then. A group of people from the dance went to the Wadsworth house for Cokes.''

"Had you made an arrangement with Winifred to meet her after she left the Wadsworth house?"

"I did."

"Tell us what happened."

"When I got there, she was already dead. I saw her lying there."

"Why did you not tell that to the police?"

"I thought they wouldn't believe me. It is one of the sadnesses of my life that I did not."

Watching Constant on the television monitor in the prosecutor's office, I marveled at the facility with which he told his story. I believe now that Constant had the ability to forget. It wasn't that he was out-and-out lying so much as that he had convinced himself that what he was saying was the truth.

"Where is Father Murphy?" asked Maureen. "He is supposed to be here for the closing arguments."

"Father Murphy has declined to be present."

"I don't believe it. After all the money my mother gave to that parish."

"He has declined."

"What about Father Burke?"

"We have heard from Vincent Corcoran, or Corky, as he is called, who was, at the time of the murder, the bartender in the men's locker room at The Country Club, that Constant Bradley drank six vodka drinks in the space of half an hour," said Bert Lupino in his closing arguments. "What he drank when he went back to his house is a matter of conjecture. He was annoyed that Winifred Utley would not dump the young man she had gone to the dance with, Billy Wadsworth, to go home with him. He called Billy Wadsworth 'Pimple Face.' Constant Bradley knew that Winifred Utley would pass that way on that path at the rear of the Bradley estate to get from the Wadsworth house to her own house on Varden Lane. It was the path used by all the young people in the neighborhood. There he waited in the dark for her. He was, uh . . ." He paused, searching for a word to describe Constant's state at the time. "Lascivious," he said finally. "But Constant Bradley has a problem. Constant Bradley is a man who talked a great deal about erections, but Constant Bradley is a man who could not maintain an erection."

Constant, listening, remained impassive in expression, but there was a slight coloring of his face. Watching him, I knew his heart was beating fast inside him. I knew that for him it was the worst sort of revelation. I knew that he knew it was I who had told that to Bert Lupino.

"And with the loss of that erection came rage, the kind of rage that causes a man, a certain kind of man, that is, to strike a woman, as if the blame for his sexual inadequacy was hers, not his. It is the kind of rage that could cause a man, a certain kind of man, that is, to kill, to pick up a baseball bat that happened to be lying there near that path and strike the head of an innocent woman over and over again until she was dead. This is a man who could then calmly, in the presence of her dead body, use the shirttail of his Brooks Brothers shirt to wipe the fingerprints off the baseball bat with which he had killed her. I ask you, I beseech you, to find this man guilty of this terrible crime, which his family's wealth, power, and privilege have managed to keep hidden for almost twenty years."

It was Bert Lupino's finest hour.

"He'll get off," said Fatty Malloy. "It's not even his word against hers. It's only his word, and the Bradley machine. Don't tell me any Bradley is ever going to spend a night behind bars. It doesn't work that way in the American system."

"Then what will happen?" I asked.

"They'll get him out of the country. He'll show up in Taiwan or Brazil, doing good works for the poor. All will be forgiven. All will be forgotten."

"There are two Italians, two Poles—or Lithuanians, one or the other, I can never tell—and a Puerto Rican mother of six. A couple of Jews. A black lady. But it's the first group I'm interested in. They're probably Catholics. I assume they'll be going to Mass on Sunday at St. Monica's."

"Yes?" said Constant.

"I thought I'd try to find out what Mass they will be going to."

"Where is this leading, Jerry?" asked Constant.

"I thought you should go to the same Mass, with Charlotte and the children, and all receive Communion and, of course, take no notice of the jury, as if you have no idea they are there. You know, rosary beads, missals, the works. It's bound to make a favorable impression."

Constant laughed. "Charlotte will never agree to that."

"Yes, she will."

THE JURY is in its third day of deliberation. Early in the day, the jury foreman requested from Judge Edda Consalvi that the testimony of Bridey Gafferty, the Bradleys' cook, be read back to them, and in the afternoon the foreman asked to see the baseball bat, which had no fingerprints on it, and the autopsy pictures of Winifred Utley's bludgeoned body, the pictures that had caused so much distress to Winifred's mother, Luanne Utley, when they were presented as exhibits by the prosecutor. After both requests, there was much comment in the press corps and, as always in this case, much diversity of opinion. The air was charged with tension. Judge Consalvi had proved to be a martinet. The previous day she had ordered the bailiff to oust from her courtroom the reporter from *Newsweek* after he had grinned broadly and snickered when the court reporter reread Billy Wadsworth's statement that the defendant, Constant Bradley, after moving in on his date at the club dance, said to Winifred Utley, "Do you mind dancing with a man with an erection?"

During the three days the jury was out, Constant Bradley wandered up and down the crowded corridors of the courthouse, behaving like a genial host, elaborately friendly, moving from one group of reporters to another. He had an astonishing ability to remember reporters' names and to comment on what they had written about the case, often with wit. Great whoops of laughter were frequently heard in the vicinity where he was. "I really like the guy," you heard over and over again, even from those who suspected that he was guilty.

At twenty minutes before five on the third day of deliberation, the door of the jury room opened, and the foreman informed the bailiff that the jury had arrived at a verdict. The bailiff carried the word to Judge Edda Consalvi in her chambers, where she was waiting. Valerie Sabbath and Bert Lupino were informed in their offices in the building. Many of the principals and much of the media had dispersed to coffee-houses and bars in the neighborhood of the courthouse. Runners were sent to fetch them. Constant Bradley, his wife, Charlotte, and his sisters and brothers were waiting in the special room on the fourth floor that they had used throughout the trial. I was in the prosecutor's office. Forty-five minutes later, everyone who needed to be present was seated in the courtroom. Constant looked tense and withdrawn.

"Everyone rise," called out the bailiff.

Judge Consalvi entered and took her seat behind the bench.

"Would you bring in the jury, please," Judge Consalvi said to the bailiff.

They entered. By then, I knew all their names. It was impossible to read anything on their faces, although they looked like people who had a secret that they were not going to share. The minutes seemed like hours.

Judge Consalvi cleared her throat. She warned the court that there were to be no demonstrations, no cheers, no boos, no noise of any kind when the verdict was read. She warned the court that appropriate measures would be taken if there was any violation of her order. She then turned to the jury.

"Members of the jury, have you arrived at a verdict?"

The foreman rose. "We have, Your Honor."

The television set in Gerald Bradley's room had been on the whole day. At times, Gerald dozed off in his hospital-size electrically operated bed. He had waited for three days.

"Uncle Gerald!" cried Sis Malloy. There was joy in her voice. She picked up his hand, translucently white, and shook it gently to arouse him as she called into his ear. "Uncle Gerald. The verdict is in. Can you hear me, Uncle Gerald? The verdict. They have found Constant innocent! Your son, your beloved Constant, is innocent. Innocent. *Innocent!*" She almost shouted the words into Gerald's ear.

Gerald, awakening, listened. In the year of his illness, he had aged greatly. His sight was failing. His interest in living was waning.

Every telephone line in the house had started to ring. Below, in the main part of the house, screams of delight could be heard from the maids watching the television set in the servants' dining room. "We knew. We always knew," they could be heard screaming. "Yay, Constant!"

335

"Can you hear them down below, Uncle Gerald?" cried Sis. "It's the maids downstairs. They are rejoicing. Can you hear?"

A slight smile appeared at one corner of his mouth.

She looked out the window. "The reporters at the end of the drive are all jumping up and down, Uncle Gerald. Look, look, Uncle Gerald, at the television set. Let me hold you up. Constant is coming out of the courtroom. The people are cheering for him. Look, Uncle, he's going to speak. He's going to the microphones to speak to the people. Can you see? Can you hear?"

Gerald, watching, listening, held up by his niece, suddenly felt conscious of an aloofness from everything earthly. He felt a lightness of existence. He knew his moment was at hand. He knew he was about to pass on. He felt not the joy that Cardinal had told to expect at this moment but fear. He grasped Sis Malloy's hand. He looked in her eyes. He told her things. He knew that he had not been good. He had cheated men. He had mixed with bad people. He had been responsible for Johnny Fuselli's death. His wife had barely spoken to him for years. His children were imperfect and unhappy. And now, his youngest son, his favorite child, had been found innocent of a murder he had committed.

Despite Judge Consalvi's admonitions, despite her commands for propriety in her courtroom, despite the efforts of the bailiffs, jubilation reigned. There were shouts of joy and applause and stamping of feet and Indian war whoops, in the manner of the behavior at Bradley weddings. "Sit down, sit down, Mrs. Tierney," Judge Consalvi screamed at Maureen. "Sit down, Father Burke!" Valerie Sabbath ignored the judge and embraced Constant and began a little dance around the defense table. "Sit down," screamed Judge Consalvi. "You are still in my courtroom! I will hold you in contempt!" But they all ignored her. The trial was over. They didn't need her anymore. They would never see her again. She was history.

Outside, in the corridor, Constant and I passed each other. I was alone. He was surrounded. For an instant, our eyes connected. For that same instant, his triumphant smile diminished. I felt I saw a flash of fear. Mine was a face he never wanted to look upon again. Then he was swept along in his victory march.

I waited, pressed against a wall, until all the revelers had crowded into the elevators, and the corridor was quiet again. In a phone booth, I called Claire.

"It's over," I said.

"I know."

"How are the boys?"

"Fine. They watched you on television after the verdict. They ran up to the screen and kept saying, 'Daddy, Daddy.' "

"They didn't understand what it was all about, did they?"

"No."

"Someday they will."

"I suppose. Are you all right, Harrison?"

"I think so."

"I thought you looked remarkably well, considering. I wanted to tell you something."

"Yes?"

"I'm proud of you, of what you did."

"I wondered if I could drive up tonight."

I had to go back to the prosecutor's office to speak to Bert Lupino. He was devastated, I knew, poor fellow. Despite his stirring closing argument, he had been publicly scorned each day in the press and on television, his legal performance mocked by the sort of lawyers hired by networks and news services to comment on the case. He was decent. He was good. He was also too young, too fresh out of law school. He was simply outmatched by the ferocious Valerie Sabbath.

As I walked along to his office, the door to the ladies' room opened cautiously, as if the person inside was checking the activity in the corridor before emerging. Out came Luanne Utley. She had been a quiet and dignified presence during the trial, avoiding publicity as much as the Bradleys craved it. I could see that she had been crying, and probably hiding. She looked defeated and wan. The trial had aged her. We stopped. We looked at each other. We did not embrace. She shook her head slightly. I understood she didn't want to discuss the verdict. There would be times in the future to do that. She simply touched my cheek with her hand and said, "Thank you, Harrison. I'll never forget."

"Do you need help getting out of here?" I asked.

"Oh, I do. I do. I can't be besieged by those people with their cameras and their questions," she said.

"I know a way through the garage in the basement," I said. "If you'll just wait here three minutes while I say good-bye to Bert Lupino, I'll get you out. They'll be parked outside your apartment when you get back to New York, you know."

"Leverett and Louise Somerset have asked me to stay with them for a few days until it quiets down," she replied.

Although it was brisk and cold outside, Constant declined to wear the coat held out to him by Desmond. He always knew how he looked best. The wind blew his hair. He walked briskly to the bank of microphones. Behind him, his wife, his sisters, his brothers, and his lawyers stood. Valerie Sabbath was beaming. All were smiling. All were waving. There was joy on every face. The scene had the appearance of a political victory rather than of an acquittal for murder. Constant stood for a moment, forty television cameras trained on him. Then he raised his left arm and waved. A great cheer went up from the crowd outside the courthouse. When he raised his hands again to hush the crowd so that he could speak, they responded to his instruction.

"There is an old saying of Saint Thomas Aquinas, quoted to me by my father from the time I was a child, that truth will always find its way. Always. And we always knew, my family and I, that truth would prevail. We never doubted, for even an instant, that the magnificence and fairness of the American judicial system would arrive at the verdict that was so obvious today. I have enough memories in my heart to last a lifetime. We have always been a very close family, and I wish now to thank my family: my wife, Charlotte, my mother, Grace Bradley, my father, Gerald Bradley, and my children, little Charlotte and Constant Junior, who, fortunately, are too young to understand this travesty that we have witnessed and been subjected to for the past six weeks, but their young lives have been horribly disrupted by it. And also, I would like to thank my brothers and sisters: Jerry, Des, Senator Sandro Bradley, Maureen Bradley Tierney, Mary Pat de Trafford, who has left her family behind in Paris to be here with me these past six weeks, and Kitt Bradley Chadwick, as well as my nieces and nephews. They are my family, my wonderful family, who have been for the whole of my life the most important element. And, of course, my most special thanks to Valerie Sabbath. Come up here, Valerie. I'm sure it's you that these people want to talk to, not me. Thank you very much, everyone." He waved again.

Cheers went up from the crowd.

338

"Class, the guy's got class!" screamed a supporter.

"What are your plans?" shouted a reporter.

"My immediate plans are to go to my family's home in Scarborough Hill and embrace my father. This ordeal has taken its toll on my father's health."

"And after that? Any political plans?" shouted the reporter.

"Yes, but I am not prepared to discuss them at this moment. As you know, my plans to run for governor of this great state that I am privileged to call my home state were thwarted by this unfair charge that was brought against me, but I have acquired a new strength during this ordeal that I have never possessed before, and soon I will be back in the arena, ready to announce my plans. Now you must excuse me. I have to be off to see my father."

"You've got our votes, Constant," screamed a female voice, followed by more cheers.

As Constant left the bank of microphones, guided by his brothers and lawyers, a woman in a mink coat rushed up to him, grabbed him by the lapel of his jacket, and began to engage him in earnest conversation. Constant listened for a moment and then laughed. In her hand was a piece of paper which she handed him.

"Mr. Bradley, do you have any words for Mrs. Utley?" shouted one reporter. It was Gus Bailey.

Constant paused in his exit, turned away from the woman, and returned to the microphones. "Mrs. Utley has from me what she has always had, my profound sympathy for her great and tragic loss. I so regret for her that she has had to go through this terrible ordeal. Thank you, and good-bye."

In victory, the rented cars were forgotten. The family limousine waited at the curb, with a beaming Charlie, tears in his eyes, holding the door open.

"Congratulations, Mr. Constant," he said.

Constant hugged the old chauffeur. "Thank you, Charlie. Now, Charlie, burn rubber, man. I want to see my father."

"Where'd you get that Saint Thomas Aquinas quote?" asked Jerry. "It worked great. I never heard that one."

"I just made it up," said Constant.

"Who was that woman who grabbed hold of you?" asked Des as they raced to Scarborough Hill.

339

"I couldn't believe it. She said she wanted to go to bed with me," answered Constant.

There were roars of laughter in the car. "Whatever she said, she made you laugh," said Des.

"She did. She said I wouldn't even have to buy her dinner. She slipped me her telephone number."

As the crowded cars returning from the courtroom turned into the long driveway of the Bradley house in Scarborough Hill, horns began to honk. Maids appeared at the windows. *Beep. Beep-beep-beep. Beep-beep.* Shouts of laughter could be heard. The front door opened. The family, lawyers, priests, and secretaries rushed in. Maids were hugged. War whoops were raised. The sound of the family racing up the winding stairway in a thundering herd, the way they had raced down those stairs as children on Christmas morning, could be heard throughout the house, accompanied by cheers and cries of "Get out the champagne, Bridey! A celebration is in order!" The sounds of racing feet and shouting voices increased as they ran down the long hallway to Gerald's bedroom.

"Pa, your son is free!" screamed Jerry, pushing Constant into the room ahead of him, followed by Des and Sandro and Maureen and Mary Pat and Kitt. The family, crowding against one another, squeezed into the room. "Pa, *Pa,* have you heard?"

But Gerald was dead. They had only to look to know. Sis had already closed his eyes.

"Oh, my God," said Jerry.

"Is he . . . ?" asked Mary Pat.

"Yes," replied Sis.

"When did he die?" asked Maureen.

"Just," replied Sis. "Not five minutes ago. He knew. He knew of Constant's innocence. I told him. The television was on. I heard the verdict. I told him. He watched your speech, Constant. I turned up the volume as loud as it would go. He looked me straight in the eye. He understood. There were tears in his eyes. Look, the rosary beads are in his hands. He was thanking God, and then he began to go into convulsions. His whole body shook, almost violently. He didn't want to let go. I think he didn't want to let go until you got here, Constant."

Sis did not tell them that he had screamed out in his last moment, a scream that was heard throughout the house.

They stood, staring at the corpse of their father. Constant put his hand to his mouth in shock. Slowly, the brothers and sisters made their way to the bed, surrounding it.

"Oh, Pa," said Maureen, starting to cry. "I want to tell you how much I love you."

"Yes, Pa," said Jerry. "Thank you for everything you always did for us." He kissed his father's forehead.

"Yes, thank you, Pa," said Constant.

"Oh, Pa," said Mary Pat, kneeling by the bed. "I love you, Pa."

Des and Sandro began talking aloud to their father. "Without you, we would be nothing, Pa," said Sandro.

Kitt and Constant moved to the foot of the bed and looked at Gerald.

Maureen began to pray aloud. "Our Father, who art in heaven, hallowed be Thy name." The others joined in. "Thy kingdom come, Thy will be done, on earth, as it is in heaven—"

"Wait a minute. Hold on. Where's Ma?" asked Maureen. "She has to be here. We can't do this without Ma."

"She's in her room, I suppose," said Sis.

"Does she know? Does she know Pa's dead?" asked Jerry. "Didn't anybody tell her?"

"Yes, she knows," said Sis. "I went to her room right after it happened."

"I'll go get her," said Kitt quietly. She left the room. The family stood in silence until Kitt returned moments later with Grace. They all turned to the door to look at their mother. She was perfectly composed, already dressed in black. In her hands was a rosary.

Grace walked over to the bed. Jerry and Maureen separated to make room for her. Jerry drew up a chair for her to sit on, but she declined his offer with a shake of her head. For a long moment she looked down at her husband. "Put this rosary in your father's hands, Jerry," she said.

"He already has a rosary, Ma. He has Sis's rosary," said Jerry.

Grace nodded. "What priests are downstairs, Maureen?" she asked.

"Father Burke, Father Bill, from Southampton, Father Cahill, and Monsignor Flynn," said Maureen. "Father Burke and Father Bill were at the courthouse. Father Cahill and Monsignor Flynn were here at the house when we returned."

"Ask them to come up," said Grace. "I think we should say a rosary here by the bedside. And your children, Maureen. Aren't some of them here? Gregory and Sarah? The whole family should be here. Oh, and Bridey. Get Bridey.''

"Well, there goes the victory party," said Colleen, the maid, who used to be called Debbie, when word reached the kitchen that Gerald Bradley was dead upstairs. She had been looking forward to the celebration. "We got enough hams and beefs and au gratin potatoes here to feed an army, not to mention three kinds of salad and chocolate profiteroles. Poor Bridey, all that cookin' for nothin'.''

"Don't worry, Colleen, it won't go to waste. There'll be the wake, and everyone gathering here after the funeral," said Rose, another maid.

"Where's Bridey?" asked Colleen.

"She's up in the room with Missus," said Rose. "They're saying a rosary. We got all those priests to feed tonight as well, remember.''

"Did you hear him scream out like that before he went?" asked Colleen.

"*Shhhh,*" said Rose. "Don't let Bridey hear you.''

"It sounded like he must have saw hell," said Colleen.

"*Shhhh.*"

"Well, darling, I'm so happy for you," said Grace to Constant when he came to her room later. "Kiss me, darling. What a relief that this terrible trial is over. I don't know if I could have stood it another day. We knew always how it would end, didn't we, but hasn't it been a drain on all of us? The other night at the club, on Thursday, Mrs. Somerset walked right past me without speaking. Can you imagine? After all these years of living next door? Well, I certainly hope she was watching her television set tonight. I thought your speech was lovely, darling. I was so glad to hear you quote Saint Thomas Aquinas.''

"I'm sorry about Pa, Ma," said Constant.

"Thank you, darling. My feeling is that he died a very happy man, Constant. Sis was holding him up to the television set, so he knew. He heard your speech. You spoke so beautifully about your father. You're quite a public speaker; we've always said that about you. It's a glorious way to die, when you stop to think of it. He was in a state of grace. He received Communion this morning, so at least we know he's gone

342

straight to heaven, and he went out watching a great victory for his
most beloved son.''

"Yes, Ma," said Constant.

"Now, where's Bridey? Where's my precious Bridey?'' asked
Grace.

"Right here, madam,'' said Bridey. Her eyes were red from weeping.

"That's sweet, Bridey. He was so fond of you. Do you know how
long Bridey's been with me, Constant? Just about all of your life, that's
how long. She's family. Get out all my black dresses, Bridey, and
we'll start making decisions. There'll probably be two days of calling.
Whether they'll have Gerald laid out here in the house or in the funeral
home, that will be up to you boys to decide. For myself, I think it's
depressing in the house, don't you? After my father died, I couldn't go
into the living room for almost two years. I kept seeing the casket at
the far end of the room by the piano. In those days we had open
caskets. That's when I moved the Holy Father's picture from the living
room into the library. And all those people from Bog Meadow will be
coming to pay their respects, wandering through the house. You know
how they worship this family. Oh, and the terrible flowers they always
send. Gladiolas, don't you hate them? Orange and pink, the worst
colors. And stock. I can't *stand* the smell of stock, can you? Most of
them have never seen a house like this, you know. That's what they're
coming for. A tour. God knows what will be missing. We'll have the
maids take away all the little things on the tables. I think you should
tell your brothers the funeral home, Constant, rather than the house.
Ahern's does a wonderful job. I went to Monsignor Hannon's wake
there last week. There's a lovely big room. So that will be two black
dresses for the calling days, Bridey. And another for the funeral. I
think the one with the gold-link chain at the waist for the funeral. Cut
off the gardenia at the neck. And I'm going to want a double thickness
of black veils. I want to talk to Mrs. Saltzman at Bergdorf's. Remind
me to call her in the morning. I want black grosgrain ribbons at the
bottom of all the veils. They hang so much better with the weight of
the borders, and they don't blow if there's a wind. Let's get to it,
Bridey. There's work to be done.''

Gerald Bradley's obituaries were long and respectful, but his funeral
was private. Only family, and a few others. Sis and Fatty Malloy were

there, and Sims Lord, and all the secretaries, and all the nurses, and all the servants from all the houses. There were unkind people who said the funeral was private because so few people would have come. Some of the same unkind people even said they were glad he was dead. It wouldn't have done at all for any member of that family to have a sparsely attended funeral. If it wasn't to be a mobbed cathedral, then it was to be private. That was the decision made by Jerry, who set about making many decisions within hours of his father's death. Grace, the widow, was informed after the decision was made. She didn't mind. She had never liked crowds. She only wanted to make sure that the flowers on the altar were all white, that the Mass would be a high requiem, and that Cardinal and a great many priests were going to be there.

That there was not an outpouring of congratulations over Constant's victory from the inhabitants and townspeople of Scarborough Hill was attributed by the family to respect on their part for the concurrent sadness of Gerald's death. "It's so typically Yankee, isn't it?" said Des, laughing.

His father's death had deprived Constant of the celebration that he felt his triumphant vindication merited, and on the eve of Mary Pat's return to Paris, he decided on the spur of the moment to host an evening for the family that had stood so staunchly behind him. It was a Thursday night, known in Scarborough Hill as cook's night out, and he suggested to his brothers and sisters and their wives and husbands that they dine together *en famille,* as Mary Pat called it, at The Country Club before dispersing to their own lives and families. All accepted except Charlotte, who, having played her part to perfection throughout the trial, left that day for Maryland to visit her father.

Constant fully expected that the appearance of the large and glamorous family together for the first time in years at the club would be the occasion for congratulations and even applause from a membership that had held them at arm's length for so long. They grouped together at the entrance to the dining room, waiting for Corky, now the maître d' of the room, to come and lead them to their large table. When he did, Constant, in a spirit of good sportsmanship, extended his hand in friendship to the former bartender in the men's locker room who had testified against him during the trial as to the amount of liquor he had drunk at the club on the night of the murder. "No hard feelings,"

Constant said, smiling in the friendly manner of a victor. The exchange caused the presence of the family to become noticed, and slowly silence descended on the crowded room. Corky performed his seating duties and menu passing with formality but without a greeting or a response to Constant's gesture. The Somersets, the Frenches, the Prindevilles, the Wadsworths, and the Thralls, among others, lowered their eyes as the family passed. Only old Bishop Fiddle, now retired from his Episcopal duties at the American Church in Paris, his mouth full of vanilla ice cream, spoke out to his wife in the loud voice of the hard-of-hearing. "Extraordinary, those people coming here, don't you think?"

AFTERWORD

THE VERDICT was a grievous disappointment to some, like Luanne Utley, a cause for delirium to others, like the Bradleys, but a surprise to no one. I have, I suppose, legally lost, but I feel almost delirious. And certainly victorious. I have never been one who automatically equates an acquittal with innocence.

From the moment of the first day of the trial, when Judge Edda Consalvi disallowed, without comment, the testimony of Weegie Somerset Belmont and Maud Firth, who had been assaulted by Constant Bradley in fits of rage, the die was cast. Even if Wanda Symanski had come forward, as she was tempted to do but didn't dare, having taken compensation, or Teresa Miller, who chose not to when I located her in Deep River, it would not have mattered. Only reasonable doubt had to be shown, and it was. Valerie Sabbath earned her million, and her fame increased. She appeared on all the morning news shows and all the afternoon chat shows and was widely praised when she said she prayed nightly for poor Winifred Utley.

The charges against me were dismissed. They could hardly send me to jail for my participation in Winifred Utley's death when Constant, who killed her, had been acquitted. There was enough doubt in enough people's minds so that if the charges against me had not been dismissed, an uproar would have occurred, with Gus Bailey leading the fray. The Bradleys, to give them their due, must have been happy at that turn of events. Another trial, with me at the center, would only have perpetuated the unwanted attention on them, and they might not have been so lucky the second time around.

It was impossible not to think that Gerald's death, coming when it did, was some form of comment on the fruits of victory. Certainly it muted all the celebratory aspects of the victory.

It was crushing, of course, for Luanne Utley, who wanted only to settle the unfinished business of her daughter's life. She has returned

to New York. She is making a new life for herself. One night I took
her to dinner at Borsalino's. It was only at the end of the evening,
when I returned her to her apartment at Sixty-second and Park, that
we both realized we had not mentioned the trial once. She said she
thought that was progress.

From the day he returned home from the Southampton Hospital, Constant had been intending to go away someplace, so as not to be near
Charlotte. Since his accident on the Montauk Highway and the discovery that Wanda Symanski had been in the car with him, their personal
relationship had become acrimonious. But Johnny Fuselli's death, and
the family's certainty of my intentions, had thwarted Constant's plans.
   Charlotte stuck by Constant all through the trial as the most loyal of
wives. She even went through with a television appearance with Constant on ''20/20,'' after his acquittal, in which she introduced her children, little Charlotte and Constant Junior, to Barbara Walters, her
interviewer, and played the role of wife in a happy American family
that had come through a distressing ordeal. After the trial, she waited
nearly a year before she slipped off quietly to the Dominican Republic
and divorced Constant. She returned to Baltimore with her two children. When Henry Valentine Jessup, Jr., receives his divorce from
Margo Jessup in June, he and Charlotte Bradley plan to marry, although those plans have not, as of this time, been made public. They
have bought a farm in Frederick, Maryland. Visitation rights preclude
little Charlotte and Constant Junior from visiting their father in Scarborough Hill.

Rosleen Shea Bradley returned to Nogales, Arizona. She has resumed
her position as dental technician in the office of Dr. Hector Sabiston.
Her son, Desi Bradley, has returned to Arizona State, where he is
majoring in journalism. Other than Maureen's son, Gregory, no member of the Bradley family saw Desi, although he and his mother were
visited at their hotel by Sims Lord. A handsome financial settlement
was offered Desi, which he declined.

Six months ago, in February, Kitt Bradley Chadwick burned to death
in her bed in her apartment at the Rhinelander Hotel in New York.

According to the newspaper accounts, the cause of the blaze was a dropped cigarette. At the request of her family, the alcoholic content of her body was not made public. The funeral Mass was at St. Thomas More Church in New York. I slipped into the choir loft, unobserved, to watch and say good-bye to dear Kitt. They were all there, including Cheever Chadwick, the estranged husband whom she had never divorced. The Mass was low. There were no eulogies. There was no music. Only the unexpected appearance of a hysterical, grief-stricken woman, who threw herself on the casket during Communion, upsetting the spray of white orchids, marred the tranquillity of the service. It was Agnes Bradley, wearing Esme Bland's gray wig, who escaped from the Cranston Institute in Maine to attend the service for the only member of the family who had consistently visited her and brought her presents over the years. Kitt once told me she told things to Agnes she told to no other person in the world. "She is the only person I feel safe discussing my family with," she said. Grace, Countess Bradley, recognized Agnes at once, but the others didn't, not having seen her for years and years. She was returned to the Cranston Institute in Maine the following day.

Later, I met Claire for lunch at Borsalino's. She wanted to hear about Kitt's funeral. Claire and I have gone back together. The boys are overjoyed. As are we. We talk now. She reads everything I write. "Put yourself into this more," she says. Or, "Distance yourself here. You're too involved." We are having another child in August. We are hoping for a girl this time, although we refuse to let the doctor tell us what he knows it is going to be.

At the 1992 Democratic Convention at Madison Square Garden in New York, Constant Bradley did not make the vice-presidential nominating speech for Senator Albert Gore, as had been his father's fervent wish and for which his father had pulled strings and called in markers. Nor did he make the seconding speech. He was at the convention, however, on the floor of the Garden, often glimpsed in intense political conversations with important figures in the party. He was interviewed often by television newspersons, several of whom he had come to know during his trial. Each time he let it be known that he was going to run for his old seat in Congress. "I am sensitive to the fact that the electorate's perception of me personally has become an issue," he said. Before he could finish, however, his interviewer spotted Mrs. Harriman in the crowd and shifted his camera over to her.

Grace Bradley was granted her most ardent wish: she was made a papal countess by Pope John Paul II for her philanthropic work. She does not use her title in the United States, but she does register as Countess Bradley at the Ritz Hotel in Paris when she goes abroad twice a year to order her clothes. She still belongs to The Country Club. She dines there every Thursday night, her cook's night off, accompanied now by Sis Malloy, who has become Grace's companion. "Get my shawl, Sis. It's chilly in the dining room tonight. Ask Corky to turn up the heat." Corky does quite a good imitation of her. Sometimes a granddaughter accompanies them, a daughter of Maureen or Des. Grace goes early and is out before most of the members arrive. No one speaks to her. She has not heard from her Southampton friends Honour and Baba and Sonny and Count Stamirsky since Constant's trial. She still goes to Mass at seven every morning, driven by Bridey, who has surrendered her kitchen duties to a younger relation. "I never sit in the same pew with Missus," said Bridey to Fatty Malloy recently. "She don't like that. I always sit in the back of the church, and she's way up in front where the priest can see her."

"I don't see any of them from one year to the next," said Mrs. Leverett Somerset. "Someone could have a dinner dance for two hundred, and they wouldn't be there."

Hurricane Carmela blew out the windows on each side of the main doors of the Bradley Library at the Milford School in Connecticut, severing the arm of Gregory Bradley Tierney, the grandson of the late Gerald Bradley, who donated the library in 1973. The arm has been sewed back on, but it will be a year before doctors can tell whether the operation was successful. An associate at the Boston office of Louis I. Kahn, the late architect who designed the building, issued a statement today saying that the windows were not part of the original plan for the library, but had been added later at the insistence of the patron's daughter.

In the hurricane, the porte cochere of The Country Club in Scarborough Hill was ripped off. Grace Bradley was not asked, as her late husband had once been, to undertake the rebuilding of the porte cochere, which was not covered by insurance. Nor would she have contributed if she had been asked.

In August, two boys were fishing off a rowboat in Whalebone Cove in Hadlyme, Connecticut. It was the season for carp. One boy had a bite on his line. Or thought he had a bite. He needed assistance from his friend to pull in his catch, but it was not the giant carp he thought it would be. Instead, it was a brown garbage bag, years old. Inside, they found part of a baseball bat. There was a shirt with a label from Brooks Brothers, old and worn after years in the water, darkly stained on the shirttail. There was a pair of loafers from Lobb in London, and another pair from Kofsky's. The boys took their find to the Country Store in Hadlyme.

"What do you suppose it is?" asked one.

Paul, the proprietor, remembered that several years earlier two divers sent by the police in Scarborough Hill had spent several days in Whalebone Cove looking for a brown garbage bag. Somewhere, in some drawer, he had their card.

I was struck by the memory of Johnny Fuselli, blood pouring out of his broken nose, his eyes accepting the fate that was befalling him. "Tell me, Johnny," I screamed at him. "Where? Where did you dump the garbage bag? It will be your salvation, Johnny. Tell me! It will be your salvation!" His head was going underwater; only his lips showed. "Whalebone Cove," he said. I told it to Luanne Utley. I told it to Captain Riordan. I told it to the new chief of police in Scarborough Hill. They found the name on a map, a tiny little cove off the Connecticut River, but the searches came to naught.

Salvation at last. Purgatory behind him, I know now that Johnny Fuselli has ascended into the Kingdom of Heaven.